Thief

Ratcatchers, Book 2

by

Matthew Colville

Dedication

Melody Anne Colville
"I got the horse right here!"

Special Thanks

Once again, the inestimable Tim Denee supplied the amazing cover, the interior design and layout!

Beta Readers

In every instance these volunteers provided critical feedback that led to significant edits. The book within would be very different without them.

Aaron Contreras, Roland Cooke, Denise Harwood, Kurt Klockau, Raymond Lukes, Zane Lyon, Tamerlane Mohammad, Arthur Monteath-Carr, John Petersen, Shao Qu Zi, Jaime Sue, Manny Vega

THIEF

The Players

In this city of Celkirk, in this nation of Corwell, blessed by Cavall and his greatest saint, Llewellyn.

The Hammer & Tongs
HEDEN – The Arrogate. A quasi-official agent of the church. Owner of the Hammer & Tongs

VANORA – A trull. Sentenced to death for demonic possession. Saved by Heden.

BALLISANTIRAX – a cat.

The Church
CONMONOC – Bishop and Hierarch of the Church of St. Llewellyn, the Valiant.

GWIDDON – His attaché. The man sent to spy on the king for the bishop.

THE ABBOT – A secretkeeper

The Special Watch
THE CASTELLAN – Master of the citadel. Enemy of organized crime. Also known as the ragman.

AIDEN – A newly minted special watchman.

FANDRICK & RAYK – Veterans of the special watch.

The City Watch
DOMNAL – A captain of the watch in one of the city's wards.

TEAGAN – A watchman under Domnal's command. Formerly a ratcatcher.

The Thieves

The count – Master of the Guild of Blackened Silk.

Garth – His fixer.

Brick – Master of the Cold Hearth.

Aimsley Pinwhistle – His fixer.

Calvus – The Hearth's alchemist

The Truncheon – Master of the Darkened Moon. Also known as the Midnight Man.

Roderick Tam – An alchemist.

The Rose Petal

Miss Elowen – Owner and proprietor.

Bann – A demi-urq and Miss Elowen's muscle.

Martlyn – A trull.

Caerys – A trull.

Special Guests

Hapax Legomenon – Occultus quaesitor for the Lens, a wizard's order

Zaar – A blacksmith and former ratcatcher.

Richard – King of Corwell.

Prologue

The last green holly berry bled out its color, turning a pale milky-white.

Bishop Conmonoc looked at the seven white berries, twirled the sprig in his hand. He tossed it onto the massive oak desk.

"I want you to leak word of this to the king," he said.

Gwiddon took a deep breath, brought himself back to reality.

"Easily done," he said, trying to read the bishop's face. "What am I leaking word to him about?"

The bishop sat quietly staring in the direction of a bookcase for what seemed to Gwiddon an unnatural length of time. He felt he could see the gears whirring in the old man's head. Finally, the bishop turned to him and took a deep breath.

"Tell him the north is no longer secure. Tell him to prepare for invasion."

Gwiddon nodded. "I can do that," he said. "I can point his men in the right direction, they'll find out about the Green, learn about their duty, what happened to them. Convincing him an invasion is coming might be harder."

"But well within the scope of your talents," the bishop said, nodding deferentially to his attaché.

"It'll be easier once we know more," Gwiddon said. "Once Heden returns to the city. He'll need to be debriefed." He looked at the centuries-old sprig of holly, once immortal, now dead. "There's too much we don't know about...."

"You will not wait, you will leak this information immediately. Already one town has been destroyed by forces rampaging out from the Wode, without benefit of the protection of the Green. More will fall. The king must do something."

"Already one...," Gwiddon said. "You know this?"

"I do."

"Llewellyn told you this?" Gwiddon asked. He wasn't sure why he was asking, something didn't feel right. The bishop's information covered strange territory and omitted much.

"He did," the bishop said.

"Your Grace," Gwiddon began, "Did Llewellyn tell you what happened to Heden?"

The bishop sniffed. "He did not think it important, neither do I. I understand he is your friend…."

Gwiddon took a measured breath, smoothed the front of his silk shirt, dared to interrupt. "He is an agent of the church, your grace. He was reluctant to go and I convinced him. At your request. He may now be dead, and I manipulated him into going."

"It is your job is to manipulate people. And if he is dead, he died redeeming himself," the old man nodded at the holly berries.

Gwiddon was briefly overwhelmed with anger. "I wasn't aware, your grace," he recovered magnificently. He wished someone was here to watch his performance. Someone besides the bishop. "That Heden was in any need of redemption."

"Don't you see?" the bishop said. He appeared genuinely surprised that Gwiddon didn't find this all obvious. "Heden is," he paused and nodded a concession to Gwiddon, "perhaps indirectly, responsible for the collapse of our power."

Gwiddon looked around the bishop's private office, situated in the heart of the massive granite cathedral of St. Llewellyn. The largest building in all Vasloria. "When you say, 'collapse…'"

"You lead a charmed existence," the bishop said sadly, but not without affection. "In your capacity as my royal attaché, you enjoy the privilege of ignoring how far we've fallen since Aendrim."

"You're talking about the deathless."

"I'm talking about our growing irrelevance in a world without them. The world Heden delivered us into. I intend to restore our standing."

Gwiddon nodded. He understood. The church's two great briefs were protecting Corwell from deathless and fiends. Fiends, more powerful, but far more rare. The church performed many mundane functions across the lives of the followers of Cavall and his saints, but these functions did not require a massive granite cathedral. Or a bishop.

"I will do as you ask," Gwidd said. "The king will learn of the fall of the Green and I will plant the idea that the wode and its denizens are a threat."

The bishop was pleased.

"It might speed matters along if I knew what reaction we want King Richard to have to this news."

"Well, ideally, he'll send the Hart into the north to investigate," the bishop said. "But I'll be satisfied if he comes to the inevitable conclusion that the church's martial brief should be expanded to protect the people."

"That last, I think is reasonable. But he will not send the Hart," Gwiddon said.

The bishop frowned. "He will want first-hand knowledge of what happened in the Wode, who better to send?"

"The Hart are the king's only way of exerting power in the city," Gwiddon explained.

"What of the castellan?"

"The castellan does not work for the king."

"He was appointed by the king!" the bishop said, his ignorance of local, temporal affairs showing.

"Appointed for life. Before this castellan, that meant three years typically. This one's been running the city for nine. Best to think of it like this; the king governs Corwell. The castellan runs the city."

"Interesting choice of words," the bishop said, with a deferent nod to Gwiddon's knowledge. "In any case, I will hold out hope Richard will deploy the Hart. It's not critical either way."

"Why the interest in the Hart? What do we gain?"

The bishop waved a wizened hand. "A tactical advantage," he said. "Nothing more. Only one piece on the great board."

"A game of shere," Gwiddon said. "That's all this is. You maneuvered your piece, now you expect Richard to do the same."

The bishop smiled, mistaking Gwiddon's criticism for admiration. "He *will* do the same, and he *will* choose the Hart, and this *is* a game of shere, and I intend to win!" the bishop said with some little glee. Exactly as though he was playing a game.

He noticed Gwiddon's apprehension. "I must say, I expected you to see this more clearly. You are my first confidant in this plan. I thought you would appreciate it."

It was clever, Gwiddon admitted, and it would probably work. He couldn't tell the bishop his real reason for being concerned, but could not directly lie.

"I'm concerned about my friend," Gwiddon explained. This was true.

"As I recall," the bishop said with humor, holding up a wizened, bony figure, "*you* said we should not be concerned for Heden. We should be concerned for the Green Order."

"I was," Gwiddon said. He looked at the holly.

"But they're dead."

CHAPTER ONE

In was easy. Getting out….

He reckoned three days. The ragman liked prisoners to stew for a while, wind themselves up before pressing them. Any longer than that and Alret would spill what he knew.

That meant a lot of talking, drinking, trading favors. He didn't think of it as a three day job, he thought of it as three months. The time he'd have to pay on the back end for all the favors he'd owe.

He needed to know shift times, that was easy. A few drinks. He needed to know where Alret was kept, but getting that information direct meant blackmail and he didn't have that kind of time. So some educated guesswork.

First he needed a plan of the citadel. Probably Brick had one, but he couldn't use it or ask for it, or Brick would know what he was doing and that defeated the entire purpose of the Fixer. If he was caught, the ragman would string him up, but it ended there. If Brick could in any way be connected with this, it meant the whole guild going down.

A plan of the citadel wasn't hard; it just required some lateral thinking. The place needed repairs, like any other. There were seven masons could be trusted with the job, so he burgled them all. That only took a few hours. Plans of the citadel wouldn't be labeled, which actually made them easier to find. He'd have to return them later, but later he'd have plenty of time.

The composite sketch he was able to build from the burgled plans wasn't complete, it wasn't a perfect system and not all unlabeled jobs were secret repairs for the castellan's secret jail, but it was good enough.

The place was huge, much larger below than above, and some of the rooms were oddly shaped. Probably their geometries affected whoever was held inside. That kind of thinking gave him a headache.

Alret wasn't that kind of threat, which meant a cell in the first three levels, the mundane prisoners.

Now he just needed a catalog of who had been admitted, released, and when and this was by far the most arduous part of the job. But he was in his element. It meant talking to criminals, men who'd been inside. Most had no way of knowing exactly where they'd been held, but each had a piece of the puzzle.

After three days horse trading, he had a pretty accurate map of the first three levels, pretty accurate data on which rooms were currently occupied, and which were free the day they bagged Alret. He was looking at three rooms, all on level three. He gave the map one last look, ripped it up and tossed the pieces into the sewer grates as he walked up the road to the Tower, the entrance to the citadel.

Time to get to work.

Chapter Two

The process of unlocking the door took some time, there were gears and switches and a vial of quicksilver and other things Alret didn't understand. The whole process just gave him time to wind himself up. Sooner or later the door would open and it would be the ragman come for him and that would be it.

He was just about pissing himself when the door finally swung open, revealing…not the ragman, nor the jailor with his food.

"Pinwhistle!" Alret said.

"Right first time," Aimsley Pinwhistle said, congratulating himself. The small blonde polder took a step into Alret's cell, looked around, and said "Come on."

"How did you…," Alret said, looking at the door. "How did you get in here?"

"In was easy," Aimsley said. "Getting out…,"

There were three bodies in the corridor. Guards. They looked….

"Did you…?" Alret stepped gingerly over them.

"Don't be stupid," Aimsley snapped. "Blackout balls and knockout gas," he said.

Alret nodded. Even the infamous polder fixer from the Cold Hearth wasn't going to kill the ragman's watchers.

The long corridor emptied into a square room with three other doors. The polder walked to the door opposite, pulled. Nothing happened. He stopped, pulled again, nothing.

He looked at the door. He looked at the floor. He went to the other two doors. He went to the open door they'd just come through, he looked at the floor, where the door would be if it were closed. Got down on his hands and knees, blew on the floor for some reason.

"They floated the floor," Aimsley stood up, grimacing.

"What?"

"They floated the floor so the door won't…., doesn't matter. Go grab one…grab two of the bodies in the corridor. Come on!"

Alret was thin, wirey, and not well, but he dared not disobey the fixer.

He dragged first one, then another body into the room.

"There," Aimsley pointed at the door opposite the one they were trying to exit. Alret deposited the bodies.

"Ok, let's go," Aimsley said. This time the door opened smoothly. Alret wasn't sure what had just happened.

They passed the stairs up.

"We're not going up?" Alret said.

"Nope," Aimsley said.

"Why not?"

"The stairs know how many people come down and go up."

"They…they *know*?"

"Told you getting out was the hard part, come on."

A random section of the hallway past the stairs, and Aimsley Pinwhistle stopped.

"We're running out of time," he said. "You ready?"

Alret was more scared now than when he thought the ragman was coming to question him. "F-f-for what?"

Aimsley shook his head. "You're not going to like this part," he said, mostly to himself.

"This part?!" Alret squeaked.

"Thought about mirrors," Aimsley said, pulling an egg from his pocket. Alret frowned at it. "Would have worked, but the only imager I know is pissed at me."

He cracked the egg and something green and slimy slithered out and onto the floor.

"Plus there's all sorts of heinous shit comes after you in here if you use arcanism," he said casually as the thing on the ground grew. Alret couldn't make it out, it was like a green worm.

But it wasn't…it wasn't complete, it writhed and pulsed. It seemed *part* of the floor, like it had grown into the floor since the polder had deposited it. And it was much larger now. There were white protuberances….

It was a mouth. They were teeth. It was a rapidly growing, green, snarling, pulsing mouth. Black within, a snaking red tongue sometimes flicked around the edge. Even though it was flush with the floor, it seemed to be seeking, searching. But there was no throat, only blackness.

"So, demonism," Aimsley said, palm held out, offering the writhing, snarling, toothed maw as an example. It was now almost as wide as the corridor.

"Fuck me!" Alret said.

"It's sniffing for me," Aimsley explained. "Won't close and swallow until I jump in. You first," he said.

"What!?"

Aimsley sighed. "They're coming for you, you realize that right?"

"What?!"

"You want to wait for the castellan's men to find you? I get paid either way," this was his mantra, it was not literally true, they both knew.

"You want me to jump in that!?"

"Ah…yeah, basically. Nothing to it, really. You won't feel a thing. I'll be right behind you. Better than a mirror. Don't have to carry around a big, fuck-off silver frame everywhere."

"I can't do it!" Alret said, looking furtively behind him.

"Sure you can," Aimsley said.

"I can't! I can't I can't I can't!" He was getting hysterical.

Aimsley shrugged. "Ok," he said. "The guards are here anyway," he pointed behind Alret.

Alret looked behind him. There was no-one there. Before he could spin back around and stop the fixer, Aimsley had grabbed his belt, kicked his feet out from under him, and pushed the skinny man down and into the huge maw gulping in the ground.

There was a gulp. But this did not satisfy the yearning, biting, tonguing mouth. It snapped back open and, sensing Aimsley nearby, snapped at him. The red demon-tongue whipped toward him. He batted it away like an errant fly.

In their eagerness, two guards practically fell down the stairs. They started off down the corridor the way Aimsley had come. He could not afford to be seen.

He threw down a blackout ball, and black smoke filled the corridor. He looked down at the demonic mouth as he heard the sounds of the castellan's guards running toward him. Braving the smoke.

He leapt gingerly into the waiting maw. It snapped shut behind him.

CHAPTER THREE

Alret climbed from the sewer in the alley first. Aimsley followed. They were covered in sewer water…and worse.

"Wasn't sure that would work," Aimsley said, trying to wipe some black bile off of him.

"It shat me out!" Alret gibbered.

"Uh, yeah," Aimsley said trying to get the stuff out of his hair. "Mouth on one end, where'd you think you'd come out?"

"It fucking shat me out its arsehole!" Alret was shaking with abject terror. Aimsley shook his head. Poor idiot.

"Yeah, well…," Aimsley shrugged. What was there to say to that?

Alret look along the alley and saw the citadel's tower. They had just come from under there.

"They had me in the citadel?" Alret asked, demonic arseholes momentarily forgotten.

"Yeah," Aimsley nodded.

"Didn't think no one ever got out from there."

"Yeah."

"Didn't think no one could get in," the scrawny man looked in awe at Aimsley.

"Fixer, ain't I?" the polder said, with a sniff.

"Ragman hears you can get in and out…," Alret began, his eyes wide.

"He won't hear," Aimsley said.

Realization dawned on Alret's pinched face.

"Aw shit," he said.

"Sorry," Aimsley said, with some authenticity. "You live, ragman comes after Brick. You die," Aimsley shrugged. "Balance sheet is closed."

"I thought…when you didn't kill me inside, I thought…."

"They can bring you back in there," Aimsley said. "They got priests."

Alret nodded absent-mindedly while he shivered in the night in the middle of the alley. No one would find his body for hours out here.

"Tell Brick," he said, his teeth chattering, mostly from terror, "tell him I didn't tell no one nothin'."

Aimsley nodded. "I will."

"They didn't ask me nothin', anyway."

"I tried to get to you before they could."

Aimsley had his dirk out.

Alret saw it and gasped. An instant later and Aimsley was standing on the other side of him, dirk gone.

Alret collapsed in a heap, gurgling, squirming.

Looking at the Dusk Moon, Aimsley saw it was almost midnight. He stood in the alley looking at the cobbles at his feet, blood pooling around them. The alley emptied out on Gore Street to the north, the direction of the Mouse Trap, and Falmouth to the south, the direction of the Hammer & Tongs.

"He wanted it fixed?" he said to himself. "I fucking fixed it."

Brick would want to know what happened, without *knowing* what happened obviously. Brick wanted a lot. Brick got more out of this arrangement than Aimsley did.

Aimsley turned right and walked north toward Falmouth.

CHAPTER FOUR

"I know how this ends," Tam said.

The count smiled what was, he would assure anyone, a genuine smile. But showing his perfect teeth, with his thick blonde moustache and sharp eyebrows, it looked wolfish and sinister.

He aimed his smile at Garth. The two shared a moment.

"Do you?" The count asked, tilting his head.

The alchemist shrunk a little. He felt completely powerless here, and after weeks of that his dreams of getting out, getting free of the count and his tame killer had evaporated. Now he just wanted everything over. "I know Elise is dead," he said. "When you don't need me…," he didn't finish. He looked at the count "I'm not stupid."

"Noo," the count interrupted. "But you are somewhat melodramatic."

Tam slumped a little, exhausted. "Why lie about it?" he asked.

The count chuckled and walked around the worktable. It was one of three in the small room in which the alchemist Roderick Tam had been perfecting his method for creating the Dust and sealing it into small glass marbles. The room was full of inks and metals and flasks and a whole table piled with *codices*, all open to different pages, stacked on top of each other.

With the table between them, the count looked at the alchemist through the maze of glass pipes and metal cylinders. "Mister Tam, do you know why we chose you?"

The alchemist sighed. "Because I owed all that money to the Truncheon."

"That was," the count admonished, "foolish, I will admit. The midnight man is the most brutal, efficient killer in the city.

Far worse than me," he said. "He rules the Darkened Moon through terror, his agents spend more time fighting each other than mine. Were it not for me, he'd have had you beaten to death, slowly, over days." The count grimaced as he said this, as though the thought disgusted him.

"Why in all Orden would you place yourself in that man's debt?" the count asked.

"I was weak," Tam said, and looked about to collapse in sleep.

"Yes, well," the count said, and glanced again at his fixer, "we all have weaknesses, don't beat yourself up over it. We traded you for someone the Truncheon was eager to kill, slowly. The better fate for you, I promise."

The count flicked his fingers, like he was shooing a fly.

"Anyway I've got lots of people in to me, lots of alchemists too. No, we traded for you because you are *smart*," he said, picking up a crystal and looking at it, shrugging and putting it down. "You worked out all this, for one thing," his gesture took in the whole laboratory.

Tam stared at a thin phial of black fluid. The most recent deposit from the count.

The count followed his gaze.

"You want to know what the source is. Where we get it?"

"No. No, I don't." Tam was eager to deny this.

"You do! Of course you do. How could you not? You're an alchemist, aren't you?"

"I was. I retired. If you tell me, I'll never leave here."

"Fear not," the count said, enjoying the alchemist's distress. "The ingredient is here. He is nearby," the count said, letting a little theatricality seep into his voice. "Does that surprise you?"

Tam looked at the count from under a heavy brow. The source was a "he," not an "it." This was dangerous knowledge. Lethal knowledge.

"What happens to me after this?" Tam challenged. "You can't let me go."

"Well, no," the count admitted. "Bad for business, that. We're partners now, Roderick," the alchemist didn't respond. "You don't mind if we call you Roderick, do you?" the count asked, pointing between himself and Garth.

Of the two, the count was the fit, dashing swordsman. His dirty blonde hair curling in a fashionably haphazard heap on his head, his strong jaw and pointed chin adding to the look of angles and muscle which his military uniform, hereditary of course, accentuated. Garth, by comparison, was shorter, slimmer and in most ways unremarkable. He had no interest in standing out, being recognized, no interest in anything except skill.

"You'll kill me when I'm done," Tam repeated. Every time he said it, he died a little more, making the final blow that much more bearable. Why did it have to end like this? He was a good man, once.

The count sighed and shook his head.

"If we were going to kill you, we'd not bring you here hooded. Roderick you are smart, resourceful, and you work like a dwarf. We'd be fools to have you killed or even treated badly. Haven't we treated you well?" The count feigned insult.

Roderick Tam looked at the floor and didn't say anything.

"You have a fine apartment, good food. What about that girl we sent?" He looked at Garth standing in the middle of the small room. "Garth didn't we have Miss Elowen have a girl put on for our friend here?"

Garth nodded. "Said she liked him" Garth said. "Said he was nice."

"There you are," the count turned back to Tam, his argument proven. "We have treated you well and you have performed well. All this suspicion," The count walked back around the table and stood next to the alchemist. "Quite unnecessary."

"So what...."

The count held up a finger. "If you could pick any place in the world to visit, where would you pick?"

18

"Where would I…," Tam looked confused.

"Take your time, think about it. Have you ever dreamed of studying somewhere more…civilized than Corwell? Capital, perhaps? Best universities in Orden. The Commonwealth?"

Roderick couldn't let the truth show. He muttered the first place that came into his head that wasn't Celkirk.

The count frowned at his fixer. "What was that?" he asked the alchemist.

"Khemarna," the man said more loudly.

"Ah! The great desert, certainly. Now, you will finish up your project here for us," the count said, picking up a newly made glass marble with swirling black dust in it, "and then we'll probably keep you on locally for another project just to make sure this wasn't a fluke."

Tam looked at the count with a mix of hope and suspicion. It sounded so reasonable.

"This may take a couple of years, but you're young yet. You'll work here, for yourself as you like and for me as I like. Plenty of time for both and then, once we're sure of you, we'll set you up in in the City of the Everlasting Sun, as you wish, and you'll get to work on whatever research strikes your fancy and all you'll have to do," the count said, "is a few tasks for us now and then. Minor things, nothing big."

The alchemist stood there, not knowing how to react, unable to trust these men.

"You could have a family again, and why not?" The count said. "Not here, of course, once you're out of the city. We get an agent in the Pharaoh's capital city, someone who can interpret what the Eternal Sun's viziers are up to in a way no spy ever could, and you get to live out the rest of your life surrounded by exotic beauties. An arrangement to the benefit of all parties," the count smiled.

The man stared back, jaw slack with incomprehension. He looked like a peasant. Of course, he *was* a peasant, most alchemists and wizards were. It was a known way to power. But the count had a particular distaste for those who seemed to relish their lowly stature. The man could bottle starstuff and cause the dead to walk again in this new age without deathless, and he still looked like a dirt farmer. *I mean, look at his clothes. Really. Have some dignity. You can afford it now, what?*

He sighed at the alchemist, knowing the man would never understand. Good with the potions, terrible at the real world. He clapped the man on the shoulder and said "Alright off with you. Enough for today, back to your apartment. Your hood awaits."

The alchemist lurched around the table, putting lids on powdered who-knows-what and grabbing a *codex* to read at home, before backing his way out of the laboratory, looking once from the count to Garth, bowed and left.

CHAPTER FIVE

The count clucked his tongue and tossed a night dust marble to Garth who snatched it from the air with a grimace.

"Careful," Garth urged, alarmed at his master's casual treatment of the stuff.

"I don't know," the count said, ignoring him and leaning on the granite-topped table, "maybe we should have killed him."

Garth deposited the night dust marble in his vest. "Never too late," he said.

The count pointed at his fixer. "You're supposed to be the voice of reason."

Garth sniffed, but otherwise held himself perfectly still. "You haven't been very receptive to reason lately." Garth chose his words carefully.

The count frowned. "What's that supposed to mean?"

"I'm not comfortable with the alchemist leaving here," Garth said. "Risky."

"That's why I put you in charge of his comings and his goings."

"Messy," Garth said. "Allowing him to leave means my methods have to be perfect. If we keep him here, we don't need methods in the first place."

"If we kept him here," the count explained again, "he'd break under stress. He'd be of no use to us."

"You asked me what I meant," Garth said, "I'm telling you. You let him come and go, you let the trull live…."

The count raised a finger. "Ah! I arranged for her to be *killed*, it's not my fault the church apparently let her live. You can't count on them for anything anymore," he said darkly.

"And you haven't found her yet," Garth said. "She knows where our operation is, she's alive, and you haven't found her yet."

The count smiled. "She knows, but she does not know that she knows. I mentioned it in passing, she had no context for the statement and wherever she is, she's probably foaming at the mouth right now, gripped by another demonic fit." The count pulled his hands up into a rictus and twisted his face into an agonized grimace for a moment, then went back to normal. "I recognized the problem and took steps."

Garth shook his head.

"Garth I find this melancholy afflicting you quite tiresome. It seems to have gripped you as soon as Violet left the Rose. I should be melancholic in her absence, not you. You should relax and let me handle this."

"I'll relax when she's back here, or dead," Garth said.

"Then you'll soon be back to your normal, lovable self," the count said with a bow. "I've sent Cole and some men to fetch her."

Garth nodded. "Cole is good. He'll make red next year."

"We are agreed," the count said. "Cole is good, and I gave him some night dust to make him better."

Garth pushed himself away from the table he leaned against. He stood at attention. "We agreed only the black would handle the dust."

The count sniffed. "Did we? Why, I wonder, would I agree to that?"

"It's dangerous. It can't be controlled…the whole point of the dust is that it can't be controlled."

"*I* control it," the count stressed, "by who I give it to and why. And if the black scarves disapprove…well, soon we will not need them. When all is done and I am in my rightful place, they will come to heel."

Garth said nothing.

"In any event," the count said, "she's alone in an abandoned inn. No danger to Cole in any case."

Garth frowned. For some reason the reference to an inn reminded him of something...but he could not put his finger on what....

Chapter Six

For years afterward, whenever Vanora wrote anything she would stick the tip of her tongue between her lips in concentration.

Bann and the watchman had left only moments before to tell her they were going to find people to take their place guarding the inn. Heden had been gone for several hours and, once night fell, the pair of guards decided they needed help. None of them really knew when Heden would return.

She knew Bann and trusted him when he said they'd be right back. The watchman, tall and lean and filled with easy confidence, she didn't know. He didn't speak while Bann talked, but leaned against the doorframe with a slight smile on his face. Bann said they'd be back in a turn.

As she carefully wrote her name again and again with ink and quill on a piece of parchment, the harlequin danced and spun on the table. It sang to her. It would sing for hours if she let it, occasionally stopping to correct her writing.

Each time it stopped, it would dance over to the paper on its tiptoes and then observe the page by standing on its hands and walking across the letters. It would then correct her by speaking a short rhyme. It drew example letters by dipping its toe in the ink and then spiraling around the page.

Vanora loved it.

She had mastered the 24 letters in both lower and upper case and was now working on making her name look pretty. The capital V was a source of great attention and improvisation. The 'o' was the most boring letter of the whole lot, she decided, though the Harlequin had showed her how to press down on the quill to make the wet, black line fat or thin and that made the 'o' a little more interesting.

Her fingers ached from the undue pressure she put on the quill, and as she shook them she looked at one of her earlier pages with all the letters of the alphabet written on them, wondering at the options denied her.

She loved the V; it was a bold, dramatic letter, affording all manner of curly-queues at the tip of each vane. 'V' was the first letter in 'vine,' she'd learned and she went through a period where the 'V' in her name was like two little vines curling up, complete with tiny leaves.

If she were being honest, she would admit she sometimes went overboard. Looking at the other letters on the page, wiggling her fingers to get the blood back into them, she wished she had an 'i' or a 't' in her name. She liked the letters that had little flourishes like that. She frowned whenever she saw her 'q.' It was a demon letter. She decided it would be quite easy simply to never write a word with a 'q' in it.

The harlequin sang to her. But it was not the singing of any man. It was a riot of sound, sometimes a single voice spinning and tripping through a melody so complex it made Vanora's head spin, sometimes a hundred voices thundering, sometimes a rich layered sound produced by what instruments she could not tell. The harlequin called it Opera. She could not pick out single instruments and would not have known what they were called if she could. She often found herself just staring at the books on shelves in front of her in the common room, listening to the music, not even realizing she was doing it, like now.

Something important was happening in the music. Vanora realized this when, out of the corner of her eye, she saw the harlequin stand stock still and raise its fist to the roof. It shook its fist and beat its breast as it struck a heroic pose and the voice coming from its tiny mouth was a howl of rage. Then it suddenly lashed out with its other arm, miming the action of snapping a bullwhip, and from its mouth came the crack of the whip.

The melody was so perfect, so beautiful and exciting it made her skin go all over in goosebumps. She had to hear it again, she didn't know what it meant, but she was gripped with the desire to leap out of her chair and mimic the harlequin's actions, pretending she was the singer, the performer, the character in the opera.

It was then, looking up, that she noticed it was dark outside. Time had flown by. What time was it? The room was illuminated by a single large lantern she'd fetched from upstairs. It cast flickering golden light and deep shadows around the common room of the inn.

Suddenly the Harlequin stopped, and cocked its small head as though hearing some distant call.

In the silence, she remembered she was alone. How long had Bann and the watchman been gone? A turn? Longer? Much longer? She had written a great deal. Three turns?

Ballisantirax jumped onto her lap, scaring her half to death. The cat's heavy black muscled body tense. Vanora looked down into the cat's face. Balli's eyes were so dilated, there was only a sliver of yellow marking the boundary between black fur and midnight eyes. She growled deeply, staring up at Vanora. Her mouth open a little, baring her fangs. Her thick claws digging into Vanora's legs. Was she going to attack her?

On the table, the harlequin looked sharply behind her, Balli stopped growling, and Vanora heard a frantic scrabbling at the door to the cellar.

She turned slowly in her chair and looked at the forbidden door to the room below. Balli loped off her lap. The scrabbling got louder, frantic, and then stopped. She watched as the latch on the door handle slowly and silently lifted, and the door swung open without a noise.

A large black rectangle of darkness stared at her. Vanora felt a yawning in the pit of her stomach as she gazed into it, eyes wide, mouth open, breath still.

Like a flood, a dozen small figures came boiling out of the basement in a rolling knot of silent violence. Vanora leapt to her feet and ran a few steps to the front door, but stopped halfway, frozen by what she saw.

They were rats. Or…mice? Each was roughly 2 feet tall with thick bushy fur, some grey, some brown. Many different shades. Short noses with long black whiskers and stubby tails. They all stood on their hind legs.

They wore clothes and bristled with weapons. Standing before her in battle poses like the harlequin, the one closest to her held a short silver sword in one hand and a crossbow in the other, a bandolier of bolts slung over his shoulder and around his chest. The others had bows, daggers, two handed swords, some wore conical leather caps. They stood together, some crouching, all tensed, ready for violence, like a metal spring wound tight. They stared at her with black beady eyes.

The lead mouserat's pink nose twitched. She felt something was expected of her. They looked like they'd stepped out of a children's story, but they seethed with murderous anger. Their long, chisel-like teeth bared, they radiated battle like heat and she was afraid. What did they want with her?

An eerie calm washed over her and her skin flashed all with goose bumps as she realized they weren't looking at her. They were looking past her. For a moment she felt fear flood out of her body and, once again, she turned slowly around.

There were five men dressed in black standing behind her. She started and took a step back, toward the mousemen. One of the men in black was braced above her between the top of the front door and the ceiling. One of them crouched on top of a chair.

They also bristled with weapons. This was impossible, there was no way these men could have gotten in without her noticing. But they *had* gotten in, remained invisible, and she hadn't noticed. But the mousemen had. Noticed, and come out of their warren somewhere beneath Heden's inn to protect her. She now knew who the mice warriors were.

With careful deliberation, without looking behind her, she took another step back toward the fighting mousemen Heden had set to defend her. At this signal, they swarmed around her, the only sound their tiny claws digging into the floor as they moved.

They assumed their battle poses around her, pressed against her, she felt their tiny hands pushing her back. She marveled at them. She was afraid, but she felt the presence of Heden in the room, and this calmed her somewhat. She believed the mousemen would protect her. She felt she was in a dream. This could not be real.

The assassins, for assassins they had to be, wore dark brown leather with black silk scarves tied around their waist, or wrist or neck. And wore dark grey leather helms obscuring their faces.

They stood ready to attack, the lead assassin had a long wicked-thin sword in one hand and a silver dagger in the other. His eyes flashed back and forth between Vanora and the mousemen. None of the men moved. None of them made a sound.

The lead assassin slowly raised his left hand and pulled the leather helm off his face. He had short, black hair and a pale white face, a thin red scar ran from his jaw down his neck. He was short. None of the assassins seemed tall, though none were standing perfectly upright.

"All right," the man said carefully. His voice scarred liked his face. "Let's not be hasty. No reason to get our knickers in a twist."

He was afraid of the mousemen. He seemed unsure of what to do or how to proceed.

"If you're bein' paid," he said, looking just past Vanora at the ratman behind her, "our employer can see you're well compensated for looking the other way, while we…"

There was a 'twang!' and a crossbow bolt shot past Vanora's ear. The assassin slashed at it with his sword and successfully stopped it from embedding in his left eye, but at the cost of having it lodge in his sword arm.

"Unh," he grunted, as the mousemen leapt forward and swarmed past Vanora.

"Squee!" one of them shouted, holding his rapier-like weapon up, commanding the other mousemen.

The assassins were alarmed and amazed, but well-trained. They responded in accord with their close-quarters training, fighting back to back, the sword arm of each acting as the shield arm for the other. But the micemen didn't respect their fighting style, and merely swarmed past their defenses.

The battle was short and one-sided for though the assassins were skilled and well-equipped, they were well-equipped for fighting other men, and their skills didn't including fending off attacks from three or four tiny assailants, each equally well-armed and lightning fast with inhuman reflexes.

As knives stabbed and swords clashed, there was a grunt and one of the mouse fighters sailed over Vanora's head, flung into the far wall by one of the men. This one wore heavier, metal armor and a metal headpiece. The man who threw him across the room was strong, given strength by desperation. The mouse warrior struck the wall hard, hitting his head, and slumped to the floor stunned.

Battle raging around him in the common room, the assassin grabbed at the poisoned dagger protruding from his gut and prepared to pull it out, when another mouseman leapt onto him, this one with a tiny eyepatch over one eye. It grabbed the man's leather chestpiece with one tiny hand, grabbed the dagger's cross-guard with the other, looked into the man's eyes and, baring his teeth in a feral smile, pushed the dagger in, twisting it.

The assassin cried out and grabbed at the mouseman, only to receive a vicious bite in the wrist that caused blood to spurt wide from the wound, and the two went down, soon joined by another, then another mouse, the last the recovered mouse warrior, hacking at the downed man with a large-for-a-mouseman two hander. The room began to stink of iron, the smell of blood. The floor was awash in it. It glittered black in the lantern light.

Vanora gasped, putting her hands to her mouth as the assassin was murdered in front of her. She noticed movement at her feet and saw Balli was standing there, observing it all, her fur standing on end, but otherwise unmoving, protecting her.

The lead assassin held his own. He was cut in many places, there were crossbow bolts sticking out of flesh and armor, but he spun and whirled, his sword and dagger a blur. He leapt from chair to table, using each first as a height advantage, then as a weapon as he kicked each at his mouse assailants, retreating around the common room. He thought he'd taken down two of the mousemen, but could not be sure, they grabbed their wounded and disappeared into the fray.

Suddenly there were more mousemen fighting him, and he realized two of his men were down, probably dead, freeing up more of the vicious little fighters to focus on him. He sneered at his assailants, and pulled a small glass orb from under his leather chest piece.

Vanora forgotten, the lead assassin said "fuck this!" and threw the black glass orb at the floor in front of him. The orb was filled with black powder and when it hit the ground, it shattered and the dust swirled out, forming a thick mist that snaked along the ground, searching, striving, yearning. Flowing past the mousemen who were momentarily distracted, watching the black mist to see what it would do.

It found one of the dead assassins' bodies; the one Vanora had watched the mousemen hack apart. It settled onto him, seeped into his wounds, flowed into his nostrils and open mouth.

The corpse began to twitch. Its broken limbs snapped back together, knotting and twisting. Its skin looked like it was boiling. A scream went up from the body, though of man or something possessing the man, none could say.

The dead man jerked itself up, its skin now grey-green, its eyes burning coals. It snarled, then howled, its breath a putrid stink. Its fingernails long black claws. Just a moment before, it had been a man, then a moment later, a corpse. Now it looked like a nightmare.

The ratmen stood, stunned. Vanora was stunned, terrified. Two of the remaining assassins looked at their leader in shock and fear. He returned their expression, as amazed, as afraid as they were.

The ghoul was taller than the man had been, more massive, and faster. It lashed out with inhuman speed and long, spindly arms, and grabbed the nearest mouseman, who barely had time to struggle before the ghoul had pulled it close, ripped its head off with its black teeth and threw the body to the ground, spitting the head away.

Vanora screamed, and kept screaming. She was rooted to the spot. She felt something tugging at her dress and spun around, snatching it away, only to see Ballisantirax, who looked at her with big yellow eyes, howled once, and ran into the cellar through the open door and into the darkness.

Only for a moment, the mousemen looked on with horror at the corpse of their brother, then in an instant they formed a protective wall between the ghoul and Vanora.

But the ghoul did not discriminate, and leaped across the room, wrapping its body around one of the assassins. Though screaming, and being borne down to the ground, he still attacked, stabbing the thing with twin daggers, over and over, to no avail. The ghoul crouched on his chest and tore him apart.

One of the ratmen, dark brown, a little shorter than his brothers and unarmed, pushed to the fore of the knot of defending humanoid mice, grasped a small rodent skull that hung on a chain around his neck, held out one furry hand, his tiny pink finger-pads splayed apart, claws protruding from each, and spoke a prayer.

The ghoul suddenly sprang up in pain. Black eyeballs exploded in their sockets, a burst of light caused everyone on the room to shield their eyes.

The ghoul cried out, a long, ragged howl. Then it snarled and whipped its rotting, eyeless head around, back and forth, drawing in long breaths through the twin holes in its face where a nose once was. Then it would bark out the air and start sniffing again, homing in on the furry defenders. Robbed of its eyes, it could still sense them.

"Sket!" the mousepriest swore, and pushed his brothers ahead of him. He spoke another prayer and Vanora saw something ripple through them, disturbing their fur. Something empowering them. Giving them hope, giving them a chance.

The mouse defenders ran forward as one, and swarmed over the ghoul. Vanora couldn't watch.

She turned to run upstairs to her room and stopped. The staircase seemed tall and narrow. She looked to her right and saw the black rectangle of darkness that led down to Heden's cellar, and made up her mind.

She darted to her left, scooped up the Harlequin and his stand from where they'd fallen on the floor, and then turned and ran as fast as she could for the cellar, and what, she could not know.

CHAPTER SEVEN

Cole looked around the room. It was the first room he'd found upstairs. The ceiling here slanted down. There was a window built into it revealing the night sky above. A chance.

He pushed the window up and open, jumped to grab the edge where the window hinged, pulled and flipped himself up and out of the room, onto the roof, out of the maelstrom of battle below, and to freedom.

He landed in a crouch and surveyed the slanting rooftop. There couldn't be anyone up here, but his training never left him. Covered in blood, panting with exertion, he stood up, trembling. His breath came in loud and ragged rasps.

The night air was cool and moist. The sky was clear and filled with stars. Standing there on the roof, he looked down into the room below, listening to the sound of battle. He was shaken, completely rattled. No idea yet what had happened. He'd have to replay the whole scene several times before he understood it. He sighed, and then turned to leave.

There was a polder behind him. While he jumped back, to his credit he did not shout.

"Hey Cole," the little man said. He was dragging a nail and letting the smoke escape idly into the night air.

"Pinwhistle!" the assassin exclaimed. His heart was hammering in his chest.

"What's going on?" the small thief asked. He wasn't wearing any armor. He didn't need to. He wore a nicely tailored outfit, gold bracelet on one wrist, no shoes. He brushed his mop of curly blonde hair out of his face with the hand that wasn't holding the nail. His small face was open and friendly and like everything else about him, a lie.

He did not look like someone who, a turn before, had been shat out the ass of an extradimensional demon into a sewer.

"Shit," Cole said, shaking with shock. He looked back down the hole of the open window. "You about scared the piss out of me you little…," he caught himself. The small manlike creature betrayed no reaction, but Cole knew better. "Shit, you're not here to…you're not going to kill me are you?"

The polder shrugged and screwed his face up as though the idea surprised him. "Not at the moment. What are you, ah…," he looked up at the night sky and sniffed, then took another drag on his nail. "What are you doing here, Cole?"

Cole glanced down at the open window behind him.

"Nothing to do with the Hearth," Cole said, trying to maintain his footing in the conversation. He was trying not to listen to the battle below, and trying not to think about the polder's reputation.

"Uh-huh," the polder said. He padded forward and shooed the man out of the way.

"Are you here to kill us?" Cole asked, as Pinwhistle stuck his head down into the open window.

"What's going on down there?" the polder's voice was muffled and echoed in the room below.

He pulled his head out.

"Why's it smell like deathless?" Pinwhistle asked.

"Can I, ah," Cole pointed to the nail. "Can I have one of those?"

The polder shrugged, pulled out a nail, fired it off his, and offered it to Cole.

Cole looked at the offered nail, embers in its tip glowing red, and took a deep breath. He was committed to taking the nail, and smoking it, without his hand shaking.

He reached out and took the nail, dragged it. Let the smoke escape from his nostrils. Acted relaxed. Acted like someone who might smoke out here in the night air with the infamous polder fixer from the Cold Hearth.

"Your men are dying down there, you know that right?" the little man said.

Cole said nothing.

"Figure that's why you're up here," the thief continued. "You've got a good sense of self-preservation, I'll give you that."

"There's rats down there."

The polder took another drag on his nail, and waited for Cole to elaborate.

"Uh-huh."

"Radenwights."

"Yeah," the polder said. "Their warren goes right under here."

"There's a girl down there."

The polder nodded. "So?"

Cole shrugged. "He wants her. I think she…she's someone's daughter or something."

Cole took another drag, tried to talk about what happened without thinking about it. Without thinking about why Pinwhistle might be here. "The rats tried to kill us."

"Uh-huh. What'd you think was going to happen?"

"I didn't know. I didn't case the place. I didn't think…."

"Yeah."

"Shit, you're going to kill me aren't you?"

The polder frowned. "You got a one track mind." He took another drag. "So the count sends you here to get the girl and gives you what, four scarves? Five? Blue? Green?"

"Green," Cole said. "Five Greens."

"You try to bust into this place with five green scarves?" Pinwhistle smiled and looked up at the black circle in the sky where the Dusk Moon hid late at night. "Count's getting sloppy. You're lucky it's just ratmen."

"He gave me these…" Cole pulled four of the small marbles from a pocket under his leather chestpiece. He stared at them, thinking he could see the black dust inside swirling, striving, seeking a way out of its glass prison. Probably just a trick of the eye.

The polder took a long drag on his nail and peered at the small black orbs in the mid-level thief's hand.

"Ok," he said. "What are they?"

Cole was staring at the glass spheres in his hand, then he came back to the world and snatched his hand behind his back.

"Nothing," he said.

"Uh-huh," Pinwhistle nodded.

Cole reminded himself he was a blue scarf in the Guild of Blackened Silk. He was important. Men feared him.

"Why are you here, Pinwhistle?" he asked.

The polder shrugged. "Just keeping an eye on things."

"What?" Cole frowned.

"Same thing the rats are doing," the polder said cryptically.

Cole didn't know what to make of that.

"How many of those little black things you got?" the polder asked.

Cole sagged a little.

"Why?"

"Lemme have them," the polder said, as though asking for a nail in return.

"I don't think...the count wouldn't...."

"Come on, don't be dense. Tell him you used them all. Tell him anything, how's he going to know?"

"I don't know," Cole said, shaking his head. He pulled his hand from behind his back and looked at the horrible glass beads again.

"Must have been fun down there," the thief observed. "Rattle you so much."

"Huh?"

The polder shrugged. "I'm just saying, lot of action down there. You're shaken. You've seen some shit and it rattled your braincase."

Cole nodded, a little relieved.

"I can tell," the thief continued smoothly, "because if you

weren't rattled you'd remember I could just steal the fucking things from you and there isn't anything you could do about it."

Cole gave up. Extended his hand, shaking. Aimsley padded forward and examined the black orbs.

"Don't drop them," Cole warned, and placed the marbles in Aimsley's palm.

Aimsley shot him a look and went back to examining the marbles. Cole relaxed, relieved to get rid of them. Relieved to have something the polder wanted.

Pinwhistle looked from the marbles to Cole. Shrugged.

"They make deathless," Cole said.

The polder's expression didn't change.

"What?"

"I swear by the black brothers, they make deathless," the words poured from Cole's mouth. It was like he was testifying. A witness trying to convince a watchman of what he saw. "I didn't know what they did, I just...he gave them to me and said to throw them at the ground. I thought they were blackout balls."

Suddenly the polder's mind was racing. Cole was a pro, experienced. Deathless would explain his current state. He stared at the black orbs, then looked up into the night sky, thinking.

Cole thought maybe he could run for it. But decided the danger was passed. Pinwhistle wouldn't kill him, he realized. There was nothing Cole had that the little thief couldn't take without violence.

"What's the count up to, Cole?" the polder asked idly.

"You know as much as I do, fixer." Cole was desperate to impress. "I just made Blue this year, I mean sometimes I feel like I know what's going on, but the count doesn't tell me shit. I never talk to him. I see the Fixer sometimes. Otherwise...I serve at the pleasure of the Red," he said with some regret.

"And the Red Scarves, the ones who gave you these...did they seem excited?"

"They were pissing themselves, they were so fucking happy."

Aimsley nodded. "How do they work?"

"I don't know."

Aimsley cocked his head at the man.

"I swear by Saint Pallad I don't know. I threw one down, and this smoke came out and went into Tom. Tom was dead. But then...then he wasn't. Then he was something else. A ghoul."

"There are no more Deathless," Aimsley said, almost reflexively, looking at the tiny glass ball in his hand.

"Well it looked like a ghoul! What the fuck do I know!?"

"Does it need a body?"

"I...I don't know!"

"Has to work even without one," the polder reasoned. "Otherwise what would have happened if you'd used it before anyone died?"

"What?"

Cole was smart, but in his highly strung, badly rattled state, he wasn't able to follow Aimsley's logic.

"Ok," the polder said. "Alright, I believe you. Thanks," he said, holding up the glass marbles as though toasting the other thief. He put them in a small pouch on his hip.

Cole just stood there, nail hanging from his fingers, like someone waiting to be dismissed.

"I take back what I said about the count. Don't tell him what happened. Don't tell him anything. He'll feel stupid he sent you and kill you just to make himself feel better."

Cole nodded. He was sweating in the cold air.

"Better report back to the Fixer. He'll know what to do."

"Yeah," Cole said, nodding. "Yeah, Garth will know."

"Good boy," the polder said. "You got a lot of promise, Cole. Things don't work out with the Guild, you come talk to Brackett at the Hearth. We'll find something for you to do. Something that don't involve deathless."

"Really?" Cole asked, he looked disoriented again. This whole evening left him shaking and unsure what was what. "Why would you…why would you do that?"

The polder frowned. "Dunno," he said. "Just feeling generous, I guess."

Cole nodded, though he wasn't really listening.

"Now fuck off," the polder said. "Your men are all dead—no fault of yours—and I might change my mind about letting you live."

Cole turned and ran across the rooftop. The polder smirked. He turned, looked across the rooftops, and fingered the pouch at his hip. He wondered where the priest was.

He looked down into the open window. The ghoul was still down there. He could hear it. Cole had come for the girl, but hadn't got her. Had got the ghoul instead. The ghoul that was now down there with the girl.

He produced a dirk, and bounded lightly down into the inn.

CHAPTER EIGHT

It was dark. Dark and cold and the sound of battle raged above, echoing through the thick wooden door. Vanora stopped, frozen halfway down the stairs. She'd never been down here, had no idea where the stairs led.

As she thought about it, her world spun. Her balance ebbed. The absence of any visual cues made standing upright impossible. The harlequin in one hand, its metal base in the other, she slowly sunk to the ground, spread herself out on the stairs.

"Harlequin," she whispered.

No response. Something wet happened upstairs and a cheer went up from the mousemen, but the battle wasn't over.

Her mind raced. She was amazed to find herself thinking quickly and clearly, even in the shadow of violence.

She placed the harlequin's brass base on the stair in front of her, hoping she wasn't accidentally balancing it on the edge of the stair in the dark. Then she took the harlequin from her other hand and, eyes watering and blinking with the strain of trying to see anything, she placed the harlequin on the stand. Kept her hand on it to stop it falling off. Hoping for some sort of….

There was a *click* and she felt the harlequin stiffen in her hand. She drew her hand away.

"*Harlequin!*" she hissed.

A warm glow rose from the base, as though it were heating up, and the harlequin was surrounded in light. It bowed deeply. Vanora breathed a sigh of relief; she'd hoped the metal tutor could make its own light, but did not know.

"A spotlight, mi'lady! All any performer desires!"

She looked around, saw the door in the light of the harlequin's base, and saw the stairs stretching down into darkness.

Picking up the base in both hands, she lifted it carefully, afraid the harlequin would fall off.

With exaggerated motion, the harlequin lost its balance and tumbled across the small platform, before rolling upright and planting his feet on the round metal disc. He now seemed attached to the platform, unmoving.

"You need not be gentle with me, young mistress," the harlequin laughed. "I am no enamel eggshell! Rough and sturdy I am! A tutor for young boys as well as young girls."

She grasped the brass plate more firmly and, using its light as a lantern, proceeded slowly down the long stairs.

As she neared the cellar, the air cooled and the stone walls bled moisture. Eventually the stairs ended and she stepped off onto flagstones. It was a large room, she couldn't see the far wall, and there were wooden crates everywhere.

She saw a lantern on one of the boxes near her. She crept forward and put the harlequin down. This, she guessed, was the lantern Heden used. There was a box of slaves next to the lamp. She picked one up, struck it, and lit the lamp.

"Go to sleep, Harlequin," she whispered, as she lifted the lamp, and the harlequin bowed before falling into a cross-legged sitting position. The light from the brass base faded.

Vanora lifted the lantern and checked its well of oil. Satisfied, she explored the room.

The sounds of battle above were muted now and, she thought, diminished. Had they stopped? She was not eager to run back up the stairs and see what had happened. Better, she reasoned, to wait down here for the mousemen. If they had prevailed. They must have, she thought. They must have won. She couldn't imagine their brave efforts in vain.

Whatever she expected to find in the cellar, this was not it. It was all barrels of wine and ale, and crates of food. Some fresh, some…not so fresh. The floor was covered in stacks of boxes, the walls were covered in wine racks. She could read chalk markings on the boxes. One said "plates."

It was everything you needed to run an inn. An inn with no customers. An inn Heden never opened. Why did he buy it? Did he inherit it?

Where did the mousemen come from? Where did his armor, his pack come from? Where was....

There was someone behind her. As she stood in the cellar, frozen in place, she suddenly and with great urgency realized she needed to go to the bathroom very badly. Very very badly.

She turned around, and faced a dozen wounded mousemen gathered at the bottom of the stair. Two of them carried wounded or dead comrades. She smelled blood and sweat-matted fur.

As they stared at her with their small, beady eyes, their priest pushed through them, chattering short prayers to their mouse god and healing them. The diminutive mousepriest seemed annoyed that his congregation weren't moving, then he saw Vanora.

"Kettik," he said. Vanora's eyes were wide.

He barked at the warriors, and they darted forward. Filing past her, toward one of the wine racks which, with a discreet pull at a bottle from a tiny mousehand, swung open, leading to another chamber, this one lit.

The rat-warriors darted in. As the mouse cleric moved past, it stopped and sized Vanora up. It sniffed her with a twitching nose, its whiskers projecting forward and tickling her arm. Then it pulled back and regarded her for a moment before shrugging and moving on.

At the last was a dashing mouse warrior with a conical hat, eyepatch, and rapier. It came up short before Vanora, bowed deeply, doffing its cap, and reached out gingerly to take her hand, planting a miniscule kiss on it, before darting away swiftly.

The hidden door remained open behind the mouseman. For some reason, closing the secret door didn't seem important to them.

Vanora walked to the hidden door and looked in at the chamber beyond, expecting to see a mouse warren. Instead there was another chamber, obviously part of Heden's inn, not the mousemen's home.

There were no mice creatures in here, they had disappeared through some other, secret door they *had* closed. Vanora saw no sign of it. But even had it been perfectly obvious, she'd probably not have seen it.

She was distracted by the huge piles of gold and gems. Weapons, suits of armor, chests. It was a dragon's horde, from a fable. It glowed with its own light and projected its own warmth.

Vanora's mouth hung open slack. There was a tall statue of a man made of bronze with tubes running through and in and out of him. Though disused and leaning against the far wall, Vanora's sight was attracted to it. It reminded her of the harlequin.

The sounds of battle continued to rage above. Rose in ferocity. Then suddenly stopped. Silence. The battle was over. Who was fighting, if the ratmen had come down here?

Possessed by the feeling that this horde was something to be protected, kept hidden, she quickly shut the door, lest whoever was in the common room above make it down here.

Leaving the harlequin behind, she took the lantern and climbed the stairs out of the cellar, grabbed the latch that opened the door to the common room. As she was about to open it she heard a noise coming from the room beyond.

There was someone in the common room. Bann, surely. Or the watchman? Teagan? The mousemen wouldn't have come back down here and left her if it wasn't safe. Would they? She thought of Heden. Would she trust him? She would. Does he trust the mice? He does. She took a deep breath, and opened the door.

CHAPTER NINE

The door opened, the man fell, the rope pulled taught. There was a snap, then some kicking.

The count laughed. No one noticed amidst the cheering.

"You pick the most amusing places for our meetings," he said.

"When I ask to meet you," the Truncheon growled, "you can pick whatever the fuck place you want."

The count nodded. "Fair."

They sat at a table on the rear balcony of a tavern overlooking the throng who'd turned out to watch the hangings. By the look of it, it would be a full day's entertainment. The courtyard below was bounded on three sides by walls of the king's castle.

"Am I right?" The count speculated. "Are we always within sight of the castle or the citadel?"

The Truncheon tore at his food, left the utensils on the table. "When I'm out," he said between bites, "I like to watch the people set to watch me." He looked around the courtyard, nodding at people the count couldn't be bothered to pick out. A bit of duck hung from the Truncheon's lips.

"Fuck 'em," he said.

The count looked at his fixer, standing at attention behind the Truncheon. Garth shrugged minutely, then went back to watching the Truncheon's fixer. A tall, slim girl who stood behind the count, as was traditional in these things. The count didn't turn to look at the girl, but he knew she was standing there, relaxed, watching Garth.

"Things have been good, since the ragman took over."

"Ungh," the Truncheon said. He looked like a dockworker. He was short, thick, mostly muscle, and covered in tattoos. His long greasy black hair was tied into a ponytail. It wasn't any kind of style, it was just something easy when the man's hair got too long.

The count thought he looked like a thug. But that was the whole point. He was a thug. His methods were those of a sadistic thug. Worse than sadistic, tasteless. Indulgent.

There it was again: taste. Style. The Truncheon had neither. No manner about him. Brick, on the other hand, for all his size and bulk, there was a man with style. Not fashion, certainly, but he knew how to play the role.

When the count didn't continue, the Truncheon recognized there was something expected of him. He shot the count a look. Wiped his mouth on the back of his hand.

"I don't give a fuck about the ragman, and neither do you," he said, his voice a saw.

"Well," the count said, rubbing the back of his neck, "that's not entirely true."

The Truncheon stared at him. The count tried not to wince at the small piggish eyes that bored into him.

"Our arrangement with the castellan has been beneficial, but limiting," he said. "We've all experienced a lot of, ah, growth? Stability? But it's been almost ten years, and I know for a fact your operation is at the limit of what can be done without overstepping the bounds we all agreed to."

"You don't know shit about my operation, don't act like you do."

The count sighed. Not for the first time he found himself wondering how this barely conscious slab of meat managed to become one of the most powerful men in the city.

"I know you can't get any more from The Pocket without letting them set up shop here."

The Truncheon put down the melon rind he'd been gnawing. Wiped his fingers on his linen shirt. Sat back and stared at the count.

"Who the fuck told you that?"

"You'd be able to get far more out of Capital, giving up nothing," the count said smoothly, "with the ragman out of the way. With *us* running the city."

The Truncheon appeared to ignore this last, he was concentrating on the count's previous statement.

"You come here to tell me what you know? Let's talk about your operation on the *Gambit*. You think because the water protects you from the seer we don't know what goes on there? We got other resources."

"It's immaterial," the count said with a shrug. "We're competitors only by circumstance. We have no reason to be enemies."

"We got lots of reasons to be enemies. Don't give me more."

"It's the castellan's restrictions that force us into conflict; it's what he's been counting on. It took nine years, but we've reached the limit. The three of us run all the crime in the city. Now there's no one to fight but each other."

The Truncheon couldn't deny this. The count saw the Truncheon thinking. Made his offer.

"I think it's time we renegotiated the terms of our contract," he said.

"The fuck are you talking about?" The Truncheon asked.

"The agreement we have with the castellan. It's time to nullify it."

"You want to ace the ragman? The king's man, are you fucking mental?"

"Ah, the king….," the count raised a hand, "I don't think it's accurate to say the castellan works for the king. The king doesn't have anything to do with what happens within the city walls. He has Baed to worry about after all."

The Truncheon waited.

"If we made a move against the castellan," the count clarified, "I don't believe the king could do anything about it."

The Truncheon leaned forward, and spoke clearly. Sounding

less like a thug than usual.

"You want to move against the ragman, you go ahead," he said. "And when he's done with you," he made a snatching motion with his hand, "we take your operation." He leaned back in his chair and gestured at the castle. "Why the fuck would I move against him?"

"I was thinking this would be something of a joint effort," the count said, taking a very tiny drink of wine. It was early in the morning for it.

"You're fucking joking," the Truncheon said.

"I'm not."

"You are, but you don't know it. You're getting old, worried. I don't know what, but it don't matter. If you're thinking like this now, in a year we'll be running your side."

"I now have the means," the count said, "to change the power structure of this city. My grandfather's father was the city's last Shadow King. Those were profitable times."

"You?!" The Truncheon laughed. Bits of food sprayed from his mouth. "You want to set yourself up Underking? You're welcome to try. Hahaha," he seemed to be genuinely enjoying this. "Don't let us stand in your way."

He turned, twisted around in his chair to look at Garth. "You hearing this, Garth? Your master's gone completely fucking mental. You need to look for a new line of work. You come talk to me any time. My door's always open for you Garth."

He turned back to the count. "You," he said, "can go stick your prick in a pigs arse." He laughed again.

The count looked at the Truncheon sadly. He removed a small black marble from his vest. Carefully, delicately, placed it on the table between them.

"Here," he said, and got up. He felt the Moon's fixer behind him tense up. "Play with that."

The Truncheon reached out to pick up the marble full of night dust.

"Careful," the count warned, slightly smug.

The Truncheon sneered and picked up the glass ball. Looked at it.

The count nodded at the crowd watching the hangings. "Throw it into the crowd," he said. "See what they make of it."

He signaled to Garth and the two men walked off the balcony into the tavern.

Emerging from the front of the establishment, the count smoothed his silk shirt over his vest. He felt dirty.

A scream echoed out from the courtyard behind the tavern.

"Should we talk to the Brick?" he asked Garth.

Garth took a breath. There was now more screaming. Frantic, terrified. And more than screaming, dying.

"No need now," he said. "He'll get the message after this."

The count's sigh was drowned out by the shouting. "Brick is shrewd, there's room for him in our new organization. The Truncheon…he'll have to be put down."

Garth shrugged. "Had to happen sooner or later. We'll have to wait until he's desperate. Then he'll make mistakes."

"Yes," the count said. People were now pouring out of the alleys, desperate to get away from what the black marble had created. "Well, that should be soon enough," he said.

Chapter Ten

The bar blocked her view. She slowly walked around it and saw a small man eating at one of the tables, his back to her. He was surrounded by death. Blood and corpses and pieces of…of what, Vanora did not know.

It was a polder. Of the race of small people that could be found throughout the city, mostly as cooks and minstrels. She had seen them before, but only fleetingly. She'd led a sheltered life in the Rose.

She watched him. She'd been as quiet as she could be, certain the polder hadn't heard her. She smelled duck. He'd gotten his own food from the larder behind the bar. There was ale in a mug. He reached out and drank some.

"Cole and his boys," he said, and she nearly jumped out of her skin, "wouldn't have been a problem for those little rat fuckers" he said, between bites of duck. "But that ghoul was… more than they bargained for."

She slowly walked around, keeping a safe distance from him. He was wearing a brown jerkin and brown leather vest and pants. He had bare feet that dangled off the chair. His curly blonde hair hung down in locks over his eyes.

He turned to look at her, his round childlike face expressionless, betraying nothing while his big blue eyes danced. Then he winked at her and went back to his meal.

He saved the mousemen. They would not have left him up here unless they trusted him.

"Are you a friend of Heden's?" she asked, trying not to sound like a 15 year old girl. Something she used to be good at but suddenly couldn't remember how to do.

The polder looked up for a moment at nothing. "Nnno," he said slowly. "Well, probably not. Maybe," he said slowly with a shrug. "I'm here with a message."

She didn't trust him. She took a step back. Spoke slowly.

"A message."

He picked up one of the five black scarves on the table next to him and, with a flourish, shook it out. A great cloud of soot billowed up. Vanora coughed.

The scarf was green underneath.

"He'll know what this means," the polder said. "They black the scarves with soot so you got no idea who you're fighting. You got to kill them to find out." He was still holding the green scarf out.

Vanora edged forward slightly and took it, darted back a step. The scarf was emerald green and had a pattern sewn into it she couldn't make out. Were they letters? Symbols? Art?

"He'll want to know about the ghoul. Wasn't sure if the radenwights would bother to tell him."

"Radenwights?" she looked up.

"The ratmen," the polder explained. She was staring at him, fascinated, while he was by no means giving her his full attention.

"Radenwights," she repeated, whispering. She was in a dream world with mouse-warriors and little men. She relaxed a little, though fear never left her entirely.

His mouth full, the little man looked at her sideways, frowning. "They're not important," he said, swallowing. He saw her reaction to him and turned to face her, fixing her with a look. "Focus," he said.

She breathed deep and her eyes went wide. She was a world away from the count and Miss Elowen and never wanted to leave. She'd thought of the Rose Petal as her home for years and never thought she'd want to be anywhere else. She remembered thinking she loved the count. Was that only a few days ago?

The polder looked at her suspiciously. He wiped his face with a cloth napkin and hopped off the chair. She noticed he was shorter than her.

He looked around the inn, as though for the first time. As though there weren't several dead bodies and black ichorous vitriol spilled all over the floor.

"What did the Black want with this place?" It was a rhetorical question. The idea of the girl knowing the answer didn't occur to him. "What's so important the priest would have the radenwights guarding it?"

"Me," Vanora said, looking down at hands folded in front of her.

Aimsley Pinwhistle turned his attention to the girl.

"You," he said, looking her up and down. His eyes narrowed. He could smell the truth coming, like the faint wafting aroma of a distant building burning in the night.

She nodded. She didn't look at him.

He looked up, as though he could see the inn's guest rooms through the ceiling. "What," he began. "What did you do... where did you live, before you lived here?"

"The Rose," Vanora said plainly.

"The Rose Petal?" Aimsley asked. The girl nodded. "You worked for Miss Elowen?"

She nodded again.

Why send Cole? Why send green scarves to get a trull?

The thief pointed a small finger at the girl.

"You're the count's girl," he said. It sounded like a dare.

She nodded. The thief took a step back like he'd lost his balance.

"What...," he started, looking at the dead men, the blood, all over the floor and the tables. "Fuck," he concluded.

"Heden saved me," Vanora said, looking at the polder.

"I just helped him," the polder said, his hand to his forehead. "I just helped him and saved you, and you're the count's personal whore."

Vanora didn't say anything. What, she thought, was there

to say?

The polder stared at her. "Does the priest know who you are? That you're the count's, I mean."

Vanora nodded slightly.

The polder whistled.

"He's going to dance with the count, huh? He's full of surprises. He lives long enough, he might piss of everyone in the city."

Vanora couldn't stand there anymore, listening to this little man talking about Heden in his absence. She took a step toward the thief.

"Who are you? Why did you come here if not to help Heden? Is he alive?"

"Well," the polder said, idly flicking some sawdust off the top of one bare foot with the other, "if there's a list of the count's professional enemies, I'm on it. As to the priest...," he threw her a look.

"Last I saw, he was at an inn few miles outside the Wode. Don't know if he's alive or not. Seems like he'd be hard to kill. Either way, probably not a good idea for you to sit around here waiting. That never got anybody anything."

Like a dog hearing the distant sound of his owner's boots, the thief looked up at the door suddenly.

"Not a good idea for me to sit around either," he said. He started toward the front door, lightly leaping over the dead bodies in the room.

Halfway to the door he stopped and stared for a moment, then spun around and headed back to the stairway that led to the second floor, the way he came in.

Passing Vanora, he stopped, turned and pointed at her.

"Stay away from the count, little girl," he said. "Grow up to be big girl." He flashed a smile and then frowned at himself. Shook his head, and fled up the stairs.

As soon as he had disappeared into the dark above, Vanora

heard the door behind her open.

"Sorry 'bout that Violet," Bann rumbled as he walked in from the night outside.

"We weren't successful," Teagan, the watchman said from behind the demiurq.

"Bad time of night to be beating the bushes, scaring up help for…." Bann stopped in his tracks. Teagan almost ran into him.

They looked around the room. At the blood in liquid pools, and several dead bodies including a decomposing ghoul corpse.

"Black gods," Teagan said, his hand on his sword.

Bann looked at Vanora, small yellow eyes wide.

"Did you do this?!"

CHAPTER ELEVEN

The old man had ploughed around the stone for years. After waking just before dawn, he decided today was the day to dig it up, though he had no idea how big it was, buried under the earth and all. Not many years left to enjoy a few more straight furrows, he reasoned. No point in putting it off.

He filled a barrow with the tools he needed, ignoring the ox that moved restlessly in the pen, waiting to be yoked. He'd come back for the ox once he'd dug out more of the boulder.

He pushed the barrow out into the field, the pale light of dawn his lifelong friend. By the time he reached the boulder, the sun was peaking over the far distant trees.

The long walk loosened his limbs so that, even at seventy one, unloading the barrow was no chore.

He heard, rather than saw, the horse approach. He surrendered no obvious reaction. This was his farm, his land. He feared no man while on it.

Shooting a glance out of the corner of his eye, he saw a man leading a riding horse. At first, not wanting to stare, he thought it was the Reeve. A second glance dispelled that.

It was the boy.

The old man took a shovel and dug out a very little around the boulder just in front of him. Exposing it beneath the ground just a few inches to try and get a sense of the shape of it in the earth. Decide where to start with the pick.

When the boy had been standing there only a moment or two, and said nothing, the old man spoke first.

"Still carry your grandad's sword," the old man observed.

The boy, now in his forties and one of three brothers but always 'the boy,' shifted slightly. Suddenly conscious of the weight on his belt.

"Always," he said.

The old man straightened and leaned against the shovel. He looked the boy up and down. He was a mess. Looked like he hadn't slept in days, his breastplate had been split through and repaired, but only for wear. He carried a pack looked full to bursting and his linen pants and shirt sleeves poking out from under his armor were covered in what the old man concluded was blood. He looked like a ghost come walking off the Moss. Little life in him. Little life, the old man thought, for one so young.

"Must be better blades," the old man said.

"Better in some ways," the boy replied. "None as sharp." He looked around the farm, taking it all in. Neither man spent much time looking at the other direct. Just stealing glances. Eyes taking in everything but each other.

"Never had much use for a sword," the old man said, with a sniff.

When he was younger, the boy would have taken this as a sort of condemnation. As though his father were somehow superior for leading a life that never required use of a weapon. But now he knew better. Da was just trying to make conversation and in conversations there were times when you said things, and in those times his father said whatever came to mind.

The boy didn't say anything. Felt comfortable in the silence between them. The growing silence was a kind of warmth. Strange to others, but not to them.

"Nice horse," the old man said.

The boy looked behind him. The horse was snuffling the ground looking for grass. He'd find none, but occasionally munched on an upturned root or a vegetable leaf.

"Good horse," the boy said. "Served me well."

"Got a few good years left on it, looks like."

"Looks like," the boy agreed.

The old man stepped closer, and the boy did the same until

they were only a few paces from each other. An unconscious ritual observed.

"What'cha call him?" The old man asked.

"Dunno. Never asked."

"Should name it, gonna keep it. Tell it who it is."

"Figured it knew who it was," the boy said, looking at the horse. Its ears swiveled around, listening to the conversation.

"Nah," the old man said. "Horses don't know shit unless you tell 'em. They're dumb animals, boy. Happy to stay dumb. Not like a dog."

"You never had a dog," the boy said, turning back to his father.

"Had dogs afore you were born. Had a flock of sheep once. Sold 'em. Dogs passed. Never got another." He sniffed the morning air, nodded. "Like cats."

The son nodded. "Me too."

"Clean animals. Smart. Keep to themselves. Keep the rats down."

"That's important," the boy agreed, and began idly inspecting the soil with his boot.

The old man kicked some small rocks out from around the hole he'd been digging, instinctively looking for the path that would bridge the gap of time. Then he found it.

"Your granddad loved you, you know," the old man said, nodding at the sword on his son's belt.

The son looked up sharply.

"Talked about you all the time. Knew you had a fierce conviction in you. Hated to know someone was done wrong. Hated it even when you was small. He saw it afore any of us. "

"He never said that," the boy said, looking past his father at the infinite plain of farmland and hills.

"Not to you. Figured he didn't need to say it to you. Was proud of you," the old man said wistfully.

"Really," the son said. He tried to imagine his father's father feeling or showing pride. It wasn't easy.

"He'd talk to the other men. Tell them about his son," the old man said. "When the abbot took you, he felt he could die happy."

"He followed Adun."

"Well his da came from Aendrim," the old man explained. "Think it gave him pride to know when it came time for one of his boys to follow Cavall, set root in this ground, he became a deacon."

The boy smiled and ducked his head. "I became more than that, da. After many years service, I became a Prelate."

His father's head whipped around at that. "You trying to stuff me, boy?"

"No sir," the son said, smiling. "No sir that is something I would not do."

"No, and I never knew you to lie." His father smiled, beamed. It was something he wasn't sure how many times he'd seen in his life. When his niece was born. 10 years ago. That was maybe the last time.

"You never said nothing about that last time you were out here."

"Didn't want to put on airs," the boy said.

His father barked a laugh. Any doubt or fear of how life might have changed his son was dispelled.

"Well you sure as shit don't look like no Prelate to me. Thought you had to wear fancy clothes and live in the city."

"The city part I do not dispute. Never had no use for fancy clothes," the son said.

"You ah," the old man said, trying to make the question sound casual, failing, "you get you a woman yet? City woman? Your ma would like to hear you got her some more little ones."

"She has enough," the boy said, then realized he hadn't answered his father's question. Was being disrespectful.

"There was someone," he said. "But...I wasn't...she needed

someone else."

The old man nodded. "Church puts a lot of demands on you. Gives you a purpose. Can be a terrible thing, that."

The boy shrugged. The old man was right, but that wasn't why he wasn't wed.

"There's a girl," the boy said, "a child. No parents. No one to look out for her. I helped her but…I don't know what else to do."

"Well you take an oath for the Church," the old man said, "that's a burden for life. But you ask me…family's the only thing that matters. Only thing that lasts."

The boy looked at his father.

"Who needs you more," the old man said, "the Church or the girl?"

The boy didn't answer. Hadn't thought of it in those terms. Some weight was lifted from him. The possibility of a life without revenge, without death. At the end of a long road.

The father looked the son up and down, looked at his dented and tarnished breastplate, his ragged cloak, his unclean face and unkempt hair. Dried mud and maybe worse caked into folds of cloak and wrinkles of skin.

"You look to me like a man whose been chasing a villain seven times seven leagues, there to do fell judgment upon him."

The son found the force of his father's pride combined with his piercing insight hard to bear. "Reckon I am," he said. "Got a ways to go yet and no sure path to follow."

"Well I says," the old man began, taking a deep breath. Being a father again for a son who needed it. "Any man earned your ire is a villain and no dispute. He should fear the judgment coming on him, or more fool him. You'll find your way. Or make it," his father said. "Never knew nothing could stop you, once you put your mind to it."

The son's eyes were watering, as though he'd been looking into the sun for too long. He took a deep breath, felt refreshed.

Felt renewed. The air out here seemed clean, clear. Like the first day of the world.

This was the longest conversation he'd ever had with his father.

"Come on now," his father said. He removed a pick from the barrow and shouldered it. With one huge swing, he stabbed it into the ground next to the boulder and levered a chunk of soil out. "Got this stone to dig out. Big as a house. Might as well be useful, you gonna stand around."

"Got a pick in my bags," the son said as he watched his father dig.

"Good lad. Always prepared. Fetch it then."

His son went back to his horse. He returned with the pick, having stripped off his breastplate, discarded the cloak, the hard leather vest and linen undershirt and stood next to his father, pale skin and wisps of black hair on his hard muscled frame.

His father regarded him out of the corner of his eye.

"Sun's barely hitched up yet. Time we're done, you'll be baked red and your back'll be sore."

The son nodded and dug the pick into the ground next to the top of the stone where his father had broken the sod. The father smiled to watch his son work.

"Sign of good living," the old man said.

CHAPTER TWELVE

Two figures picked their way across the sea of bones, blood, and mud that was the courtyard surrounding the castle's gallows. There was no pattern to their movement.

They prodded bits of corpses with their boots, turned over errant body parts, occasionally stooped to lift of some piece of clothing to see what might be left inside, and wordlessly glanced at each other across the courtyard.

The tall thin one in her early forties was Rayk. The shorter, older, shapeless one in the heavy cloak, was Fandrick. When they were originally partnered together, Rayk was still youthful and energetic. Twenty years under five castellans ground that out of her. Now there was little difference between her and the world-weary, born-cynical Fandrick.

They and their fellow watchmen were known to the city as the specials. The special watchmen. The special police force. Unlike the regulars, they had no district. They had every district. The watch captains petitioned the castellan for aid when things got bad, or weird, and the castellan dispatched some of his special men.

They were meant to be smarter, better trained, and with more authority than the coppers who patrolled the streets. But surrounded by three dozen-odd corpses, or bits of corpses, or whatever these things that used to be people were, neither Fandrick nor Rayk felt very special.

They would note things, grunt. Sometimes the regular watch keeping the throng of people out of the courtyard would look in, see the two specials, wonder at what they were thinking.

Mostly they were thinking this was a mess.

A metal squeal indicated the gates were briefly opened. The two special watchmen looked as a small figure was admitted by the local constables into the courtyard.

Unlike both Fandrick and Rayk, this person didn't wear leather. He wore woolen pants, grey, and linen shirt, light blue. He had dark brown skin and thick, short black hair. Keen black eyes that took in everything.

As he approached, they realized he was very young.

Eventually he stopped, and stood before them. He smiled.

"I'm, uh," he began. "I'm Aiden," he said.

Fandrick and Rayk looked at each other.

"What you want?" Fandrick growled.

"Castellan sent me," the young man said.

"All right then, give over," Fandrick said.

"What?" Aiden asked.

"What's the message?" Rayk asked.

"I get it," the boy said, rubbing his chin in thought. "The message is; I'm running this investigation."

Fandrick stared at the boy for a few seconds, then barked a laugh and turned his back. Went about his business.

"How old are you?!" Rayk asked.

"Ahh...seventeen? I think?" He watched Fandrick root around in the muck with the tip of his boot. "Around there, anyway. They say I was born the last time it snowed in the city, but then you ask people when that was and everything gets stupid and they argue and no one writes this stuff down apparently. Doesn't matter. Seventeen, basically."

Rayk looked at Fandrick who threw her a look back.

"You're about my parents' age," the boy said. "You want to come by for dinner tomorrow, I'll tell them you're coming. They'd love to meet the folks I'm working with."

"I bet they would," Rayk said mysteriously.

She just looked at him. Eventually Aiden shrugged. "Come on," he said. "How old do you have to be?" Neither of them said anything. "How old were you?" he asked Fandrick's back.

"Older'n you," Fandrick grumbled.

"How old were you?" Aiden nodded at Rayk, who frowned at the boy. "Never you mind," she said. "What'd the ragman send you for? I mean why you?"

"Ragman?" Aiden asked.

"The castellan," she said, drawing the word out.

"Oh, right. Because he wears…I get it. Well, he didn't say why. I don't really know what happened here."

"Lotta people killed," Fandrick said as he poked his boot into something.

"How many?" Aiden asked

"Thirty-seven," Fandrick growled.

Aiden looked around the black morass of vitreous bile and mud that was once a crowd. "That's a precise estimate," he said. "How do you…,"

"We count the boots," Rayk said, nodding to a pile of boots by the gate.

Aiden saw and was impressed. "Sensible."

"We know what we're doing," Rayk said.

Aiden looked at her for a moment. "So tell me what happened here," he said.

"Someone calls up a mess of ghouls," she said, "they eat everyone who couldn't get out. Stampede at the gate."

Aiden nodded as though confirming a suspicion. He strolled away, looking at the ground, at the remains of the people, at the black oily mud.

He crouched down and dipped his finger in the mud. Brought it to his nose, smelled it.

"Any corpses?" he asked.

"None," Rayk said.

From his haunches he surveyed the mud field. It was flat and, except for the gallows, there was nowhere a corpse could be hidden.

"You're sure," he asked, even though he knew the answer.

"Come on," Fandrick barked.

"Not ghouls then," Aiden said, standing up. Fandrick and Rayk looked at each other, and walked over to him.

"Ghouls are animated corpses," he said. "When they die they leave a dead body behind. Even if they ripped all the people apart and then ripped each other apart, there'd still be one corpse left."

"There's no corpse," Fandrick said.

"So not ghouls," Aiden said. "Two more reasons. One, ghouls don't leave this black oily whatever," he said rubbing his fingers together and showing it to them. "I don't know what does. Shadows maybe. Shades. We can find out."

"What's the other reason," Rayk asked.

Aiden turned to her, looked from her to Fandrick as though they might guess.

"There are no more deathless," he said, as though it were obvious.

"People who saw it said deathless," Fandrick said.

"They're wrong," Aiden said. "But whatever they were they look like deathless."

"Sound like deathless to me," Fandrick said. Rayk didn't correct him. She just watched Aiden.

"We'll find out," Aiden said. "Maybe we're meant to think they're deathless. Throw us off the track."

"Not throwing 'us' off anything. It's deathless, so we brace the churches, see which cults they're dealing with, follow the trail."

"It'll lead nowhere," Aiden said. "It's a dead-end. We…"

"We!" Fandrick barked a laugh.

Rayk just looked at him.

Aiden stopped and nodded. "Alright, I get it." He looked from Fandrick to Rayk. Rayk seemed more open, but he was willing to believe this was a trick.

"I'm thirteen, and I apprentice at my uncle's scrivner's shop," Aiden spoke this very quickly. "I'm fifteen and the castellan comes in, he needs a copy made, I do it. I ask him questions about who wrote the thing. I've been looking at writing for a while, at people, at what they come in to have done, why. The castellan gives me this weird look, but he doesn't say anything. I don't even know who he is. He comes back a week later, more work. I ask more questions. I notice things. Like this was written under duress, that was written by someone writing down what someone was saying as they were saying it. I say things like 'I don't think this is what the guy said, I think he said something else, and whoever copied this down misheard him.' He's interested, but he never answers any of my questions and after a while he stops coming in, I think he said something to my uncle, I dunno. Too many questions, I thought.

"Couple of weeks ago he comes in, tells me who he is, asks if I want to come work for him. Doing what, I ask. This," Aiden gestured around the trampled mud of the courtyard. "Just look at things, think about what might have happened.

"'Why?' I ask."

Aiden looked from Fandrick to Rayk.

"'Because you don't think like a copper,' he says. Ok? That's the whole story. He hears about what happened here, he sends you two and a little while later, I don't know why, he sends me. He tells me not to put up with any of your shit, I say 'there's not going to be any shit because I'm going to show up and start asking questions and they're going to ignore me,' no offense. I didn't know who you were, I don't know anyone, I just know how people are, and he says 'tell them you're in charge and I said so and if they don't like it, good,' and that was it and here I am, alright?"

Fandrick sneered at him, but said nothing. "Alright," Rayk said, and nodded.

"So it's not deathless, whatever it is," the young special watchman said.

"If you say so," Rayk said.

"But it seems like it to anyone who sees it and that's good enough for now. So why does someone summon ghouls at a hanging in the morning."

"They want to kill a lot of people," Rayk offered.

Fandrick snorted. "Well they take the prize, then."

Aiden pointed at Rayk and squinted.

"Rayk," she said. "Fandrick," she point to her partner.

"Fandrick what do you think?" Aiden asked.

Fandrick didn't say anything for a little while.

"Could have been an accident," Fandrick said. "Ritual goes wrong or…or maybe someone has something, a reliquary, an artifact, they don't know how it works, they come down here and try it out."

Rayk looked to Aiden.

"That seems alarmingly plausible," he said.

"Alarming, why alarming?" Rayk asked.

"You tell the castellan someone in the city can make this happen," he indicated the morass, "and they don't even know how they did it or why. See how he reacts."

"Yeah," Rayk agreed.

"Let's try it another way," Aiden said. "If it weren't an accident, then why? Why would someone do this?"

Rayk sniffed. Pulled out a nail, fired it. "There's someone in the crowd they want to drag," she said, taking one herself, "and they don't want anyone to know."

Aiden nodded. "Yeah," he said. "They have the means to indiscriminately kill a lot of people, so they use it here."

"Indiscrim…what?" Fandrick asked.

"Means they don't care who gets killed. All these people die, fine, long as their man goes down."

"He went down alright," Fandrick said.

"Or she," Aiden said.

Rayk nodded. "Lotta women come to the hangings."

Fandrick looked at her. "Why?"

She shrugged. "It's mostly men getting hung."

"Huh," Fandrick said, as though that explained it.

"Maybe someone getting revenge on the hangman for someone he killed?" Aiden asked. "Kills people all day, that's gotta make a lot of enemies."

Fandrick and Rayk looked at each other. Aiden noticed. "What?" he asked.

"Hatchetman wears a hood," Fandrick said. "So you don't know who he is. There's maybe twelve of them work for the watch. They got shifts, schedules. Just like 'us,'" he sneered. "Wear the hood so no one knows who they are, which is which."

"Oh," Aiden said. "Well, that makes sense."

"This is a lot of people," Rayk said, surveying the area, the pile of boots.

"Most I've seen killed in one place."

Rayk nodded. "Maybe. King hears about this, the Hart'll show up."

"Be long gone by then," Fandrick said.

"Everyone's going to come," Aiden said. "The guilds, the orders, the churches. Us. Three dozen people die in sight of the king," he looked up at the towers of the castle. The pinions of the family Corwell flying high, showing the king is in his castle.

"Right under his nose," Aiden said.

Fandrick peered at the boy. "What're you thinking, boy?"

"Doesn't matter what you're trying to do," Aiden said, and it seemed like he was working something out. "Doing it like this is a statement. You're making a statement. You've got something to say, you want to say it loud," he looked at the black mud. "You want to send a message," he said, almost to himself.

Fandrick and Rayk looked to each other, then the boy.

"A message," Fandrick said. "To who?"

Aiden looked around the courtyard. The regular watch were still working to keep the gates closed, keep the throng of people at bay.

Then he looked at Rayk, then Fandrick. The three of them the only ones in the courtyard.

"Us," he said.

CHAPTER THIRTEEN

The bench in the corner had a special cushion that allowed Aimsley Pinwhistle to sit at the same height as a man. If you only glanced over, you might not realize he was a polder.

He sat there staring at the shere board etched into the slate tabletop; stared at the black and white checkered squares and the simple carved wooden pieces, with one hand on his chin and the other on his hip. At one point, he bared his teeth and tapped them idly with a finger. There was no drink on the table.

The Mouse Trap was dense with smoke and noise and people. Thin rakes and thick bludgeons. It was hard to move around, hard to see. The smoke was so thick, a man only a few feet away looked like a ghost, and the place was so loud, so relentlessly loud, it was impossible to hear anyone talking unless they were looking right at you. Everyone liked it that way.

Aimsley pushed a lock of his curly blonde hair out of his eyes out of habit and shook his head at the board. A shadow fell across it. He glanced up, and then back to the board with a sigh.

He picked up a piece and moved it.

"Don't know why you hem and haw, we both knew you'd make that move a turn ago."

A large, bulbous, man dropped into the chair opposite. He sneered. Aimsley noticed the man looked old, his bald head had a few spots on it. Happened to everyone sooner or later. Probably was still the strongest man in the room, but for how long? Aimsley had personally witnessed him pick up a blacksmith's anvil and crush a man with it. That was a sight you didn't soon forget.

He had a pale, slimy appearance and newly minted apprentices in the guild had a tradition of calling him 'the slug.' But every master of the Cold Hearth held the same title, passed down for years with pride. The Brick.

Brick glanced at the board, picked up a piece, and moved it. Somehow, he made the wooden piece click against the slate board in an annoying manner. As though the act of actually having to move the piece was beneath him. He ran his tongue across his teeth and looked at the polder.

Aimsley looked at the move, his frown deepening, and leaned back. "Whatever," he said.

A moment passed. The board did not reveal its secrets.

"Alret's fixed," Aimsley said.

Brick made some obscure gesture, like flicking something over his shoulder, and within moments a wench was there with two small drinks.

"Why don't you have something to drink?" the Brick asked. The young wench delicately put the two glasses down, careful not to spill any. Expensive stuff. Only the best for the Hearth. Aimsley watched the amber liquid reflecting light in the glass, listened to the unique 'clack' of glass on slate that he'd come to associate with a lifetime of being with friends, being in the Trap, belonging, being respected, being good. Being the best.

Aimsley rubbed his nose and realized he was staring. He waved the drink away.

"Don't need it," he said.

"I know you don't need it," Brick growled. "Didn't ask if you needed it. Who gives a shit what you need, for fuck's sake? Have a drink. For taking care of Alret."

Aimsley reached out, looking like he was sick. But once the glass was in his hand, he relaxed and drank and the warm liquid burned its way down his throat and everything was back to normal. He'd hate himself later.

Brick smiled. "What you got for me?" he asked.

Aimsley lit a nail and took a drag, rested it on his drink, and went back to brooding over the shere board.

"What's the count up to?" he asked.

"Oh you heard about that too? Fast. News travels fast."

Aimsley said nothing, fingered various pieces on the board. Placed a single, short, thick polder finger on one and idly tipped it back as though it might look more promising from a different angle.

"I don't believe it," Brick sniffed, filling in the silence Aimsley left. "Thirty odd people aced by the castle. I don't believe it. Truncheon's man said something about the count and a deal and some kinda little glass reliquary makes deathless. Didn't make no sense. Count's getting wily now that we're all backed up against each other. I reckon he thinks he can get me and the Midnight Man to go at it. Fuck him."

"Hey boss, what the fuck?" a high pitched scratch of a voice interrupted. Dugal. Aimsley ignored him.

The wiry toady who materialized out of the smoke with a drink in each hand was only a little taller than Aimsley. He looked down his sharp nose at the table where two drinks already sat.

"Thought we were going to ah…," the Brick and Aimsley both ignored him. The little thief shrugged and turned, putting the two drinks on a wench's platter as she walked by. He pulled a seat from another table and sat down.

"What're we talking to this one for, boss? What's he done for us lately?"

Aimsley looked up at the Brick, held out a hand, palm up, and gestured in the general direction of Dugal. "Really?" he asked.

"Hey you got something to say to me little man, you say it to my face."

"When I think of anything worth saying to you, I will," Aimsley said, turning his attention back to the shere board. He was going to lose this game. He finished his drink and immediately wanted more.

The Brick saw this and pushed his drink forward. The

bastard. Aimsley pulled it toward him, but didn't take any.

"Hey fuck you, yeah?" Dugal said, without much rancor.

"Shut up, Dugal," the Brick said without looking at him.

"You ever get tired of this one's shit boss, you just let me know," Dugal said. "I'll do it, yeah? I'll drag him like a nail and leave his body for the cats."

The Brick laughed a little at this. The only sign of laughter was his bulk shaking and some teeth showing. You had to know what to look for.

"I don't know why you bring him around," Aimsley lamented to the shere board. "He's everything that's fucking wrong here," he said. They both knew he meant the guild, and not the inn. Dugal was dangerous. He'd use poisons no one else would use, he'd fight like a desperate rat. He'd do anything just to impress Brick, risk his own life, foolish stuff. No discipline, no training.

"I'd say I do it to annoy you, but you know that already," the Brick said.

"You're a piece of shit, Dal. You know that, right?" Aimsley said, giving his master a glance.

"Hey you can't say that to him," Dugal leaned forward, and looked as though he was going to point at Aimsley, then thought better of it and sat back. Looked up at the Master of the Cold Hearth. "He can't talk to you like that boss. And he called you by your name, too. He can't just do that, you got to earn that shit."

"He can call me whatever he wants," Brick said, a curl of his lips and a gleam in his eyes. "He can say whatever he wants and if you don't like it," the big man's thick head turned to look at the little thief, "why don't you make him stop?"

Under the gaze of the mountainous head and its tiny, all-seeing black eyes, Dugal shrunk.

"You'd be top man if you could do it," the Brick said, turning back to the polder. He crossed his huge arms. "Get all the best jobs."

Dugal sulked and started talking to himself. "He ain't top man," he said. He knew they were both listening. "Ain't been top man for years, who gives a shit about him? Fuck him. Ain't even in the guild anymore."

"Why'd you ask about the count?" Brick asked.

Aimsley didn't say anything for a minute. Then he moved a piece on the shere board and sat back.

Brick, without looking, picked up another piece and moved it.

Aimsley let out a defeated gasp, followed by a "fuck you," and went back to looking at the board.

"Whatever happened at the castle," the polder said, concentrating, "was real. Really happened." Aimsley knew nothing about it, but based on his experience the night before at the priest's inn, he knew enough.

"How the fuck you know that?," Brick asked.

Aimsley reached into his pocket and pulled out one of the black marbles. He carefully placed it on the shere board with a tiny 'clack' and held it under his finger for a moment. Then he rolled it forward.

It danced along the shere board, bumping into and bouncing off the wooden pieces until it came to rest on the other side of the board in front of the Brick.

"Black gods," Brick whispered, his eyes wide. He didn't touch the thing. Aimsley made his move. Brick didn't notice.

Brick looked from the marble up to Aimsley and grinned from ear to ear.

"Fucking fixer," he said. "Best fucking fixer in the city. Count pulls this," Brick nodded at the glass marble sitting on the shear board, "scares the Truncheon half to death, has him shitting in his pants, and you only go and fucking *get one* from him."

He looked around the Mouse Trap. No one was really paying attention. That would be rude.

"Best fucking fixer in the city," he said proudly to anyone

who might listen. "Best the guild's ever had," he looked back at the marble. "How'd you get it?" he asked.

Aimsley told him.

Brick blinked. "Last night?"

Aimsley nodded. He glanced up at Brick. "Your move," he said.

Brick grunted and quickly moved a soldier in, blocking Aimsley's white Prelate.

"Yeah," Aimsley said. "I hadn't heard about the thing at the gallows this morning."

"Cyrvis' boiling bollocks," Brick said in wonder. "He's moving fast. Is it safe?" He pointed to the marble.

Aimsley shrugged. "I had it all last night, this morning. Just don't drop it."

Brick picked it up, examined it in wonder. Something occurred to him. He sucked his teeth in thought.

"No one made it out of the courtyard gallows alive," he said.

"Not surprised," Aimsley said.

"And this inn, this closed up in last night…any scarves make it out?"

"One," Aimsley said. "I braced him for that. The rest got torn apart."

"So the count don't control these things. Whatever comes outta here," he said looking again at the swirling black dust, "it kills what it wants."

"I thought about that," Aimsley said. "You might be able to use that. But you need to move fast. Count has enough of those, he's not going to care about you or me or the Midnight Man or the ragman."

Brick nodded. "So where's he get them?"

"No idea," Aimsley said, still looking at the game. "I went to his club this morning, try and see him, talk to his men."

"Count would love to get a visit from you," Brick said smiling.

"Well he weren't there in any case. He's picked up."

"Picked up what?" It was unusual for Brick to be slow, but this was an unusual situation.

"The whole thing. He's not out of the club anymore. He's moved his whole operation."

"What the fuck?" Brick asked, more obviously affected by this news than by the rest. "Where the fuck did he go? What's he playin' at?"

"Hiding, best I can figure," Aimsley said. He picked up a priest and then, obligated to play it, regretted it. "Getting ready to go to war."

"Fuck him," Brick said. He put the marble back on the board, rolled it back to the polder, who picked it up more out of annoyance, to clear the board.

"Work that," Brick said. "Find out what it is, where he gets 'em. Talk to Calvus. How many are there? Did he find them? Make them? Reckon Calvus owes us. We don't got a lotta time."

Aimsley appeared to ignore him, moved the priest finally, and said half to himself, "Calvus works for you, you fucking talk to him. Send Dugal. Send anyone. I don't talk to your employees for you. I'm the fixer."

Aimsley was a tight and didn't mind. Picked up his second glass and drained his drink and when he put it down, the Brick smashed a hand into the table, causing Aimsley to jump. The Brick wiped the two empty glasses and all the shere pieces off the board, leaned into the polder's face and shouted.

"Then fix it!"

CHAPTER FOURTEEN

She sat alone at a table by the fireplace. It was afternoon, so there was no fire and with her cloak on and hood pulled up she was sure no one could see her face. That was important.

She watched for two turns. The Fool was nowhere near the most expensive tavern in the city, but it was known for food that was 'sufficient' in taste and portions, the number of people it could seat, and its friendly atmosphere. No fights, no drunkards, no thieves, no nobs. Artisans and craftsmen ate and talked here. Families.

It approached an hour of her at the table nursing an ale she didn't want. She counted the number of tables again, figured how many patrons they could serve. Watched the barkeep, the maids. Saw how they communicated, how they served the patrons. How they got paid. What people ordered. How long it took. Watched the barkeep, watched how payment worked. She figured it all over and over. She had to rely on her memory. She wished she could write it all down, but that wasn't possible. Not yet, at least. She smiled at that. Soon.

Coming in had been difficult. She was afraid of the confrontation and afraid she didn't know what she was doing. She just assumed she could figure it all out, but standing outside the door she'd gone all clammy with fear that it would never work. That she'd not understand anything. That she wasn't smart enough.

Once seated, that fear evaporated. It wasn't that complex. She laughed to herself. Couldn't be that complex, Lian did it. She started to feel giddy. She could do it. She could really do it. Lots of people did it. It wasn't hard.

She watched Lian serve and take orders. There were three maids working the tables. All girls, all about the same age.

Customers liked being served by pretty girls, that was obvious. She smiled again. Pretty girls could be arranged. Pretty girls were no problem.

The bartender had been watching her not drink for a few moments. She knew he'd do something about her sooner or later and it looked like her time was almost up. She'd planned on going to two or three inns and taverns, but now she was excited to get started.

The bartender barked at Lian and nodded toward the table by the fireplace. Lian, tall, with long brown hair almost down to her ass, frowned and tucked her serving plate under her arm. She walked reluctantly to the table by the fireplace.

"You want anything else?" she said, sighing as she did so.

"How many people work in the kitchen?"

Lian curled one lip up as though she smelled something offensive. "What?" Her voice was nasal and sounded like a whine.

With a flick of her wrist and a shake of her head, the stranger at the table snapped back the hood.

"Vanora!" Lian cried. Then she put her hand over her mouth and looked around to see if anyone heard her. No one seemed to, or if they did, they didn't seem to care.

"Hey Lian," Vanora said, smiling sweetly. "Sit down."

"What are you doing here?!" Lian asked, whispering.

"Sit down," Vanora said again. The smile dropped. "How many people work in the kitchen?"

"You're gonna get me in trouble!" Lian hissed, looking to see if anyone was watching.

Vanora half laughed, half frowned. "How?"

"I don't know," Lian looked at the bartender. He seemed to think a little girl wasn't much threat and maybe they knew each other, and was content with that.

"What if father finds out?" Lian whined, but she sat down.

Vanora looked at her quizzically. It was such an incongruous statement to make. But slowly, light dawned. Lian was not the brightest and their father was...difficult. Even though Lian was 19, a woman by anyone's judgment, she was still instinctively afraid of their father.

Vanora's eyes unfocused for a moment and she stared at nothing. Lian had the life Vanora always wanted. Or thought she wanted. Their father's favorite, a real working life, earning her own keep. And now with one statement Vanora realized that whatever else had happened, she no longer lived in fear. She was afraid of the count, she was afraid she'd have another attack, but these were real. Lots of people were afraid of the count. Her father was just a man. And not much of one at that.

She watched her older sister fret. "How is he going to know? Unless you tell him."

Lian looked confused. She didn't know how their father would find out, but she had a hard time imagining him not finding out. "I don't know," she sulked.

Vanora shook her head. "You're so stupid, Lian, I swear by the black brothers."

Lian flared hotly at this. "I am *not* stupid! Don't you say that to me you *whore*." She gasped and her hands flew to her mouth.

Vanora sighed and rolled her eyes. "Yes, Li. We both know what I...," she stopped. She found it difficult to say. She waved her hand dismissively, the way she'd seen Miss Elowen do. But she'd never found it difficult to say before. "But I'm not here for that right now."

Lian looked at Vanora's blue dress. "Why are you dressed like that?"

Vanora looked at her dress and frowned. She liked the simple blue dress Heden gave her. It reminded her of her mother.

"What's wrong with it?" Vanora asked, fingering the material.

"Normally you're dressed like a nob."

Vanora sighed. Now she understood.

"I thought you were at the Rose Petal."

"I was," Vanora explained patiently. "But I'm not right now. Right now I'm here in the Fool talking to you."

Lian gave up and slumped in her chair, waiting for Vanora to tell her what to do.

"Now," Vanora said, and she smiled wickedly at the thought of what she was about to do. "Do you want the man behind the bar there to know you invited your sister, who is a trull, to visit you at work?" She nodded at the bartender and watched as Lian's face dropped. Lian had no way of knowing it was a bluff. Vanora would never get her sister in trouble and the bar keep wouldn't have any way of knowing what Vanora did anyway.

Lian looked at her hands, folded in her lap. "No."

Vanora sat back in her chair, triumphant. "No you don't. Good girl." Lian sniffed derisively at that.

"I want to know what goes on behind that door," Vanora said, nodding to the kitchen door.

Lian screwed up her face. "Why?"

"Never you mind," Vanora said. She decided something. "Actually, you'll show me." She stood up. Lian followed suit, her pretty face crinkled with worries. Even though Lian was three years older and fully a head taller, and prettier, and her father's favorite, she was always looking for someone to tell her what to do.

"I don't understand," Lian said, avoiding the gaze of the bar keep as they navigated the space around the tables to the kitchen door.

Vanora giggled to herself. "Don't worry, I'm not going to get you in trouble. If anyone asks, tell them I've come for a job."

She pushed open the door to the kitchen, revealing the hot, thick air and noise beyond. "You have to tell me what everyone does," Vanora said, holding the door open for her sister. "It'll be easy. Oh, and something else."

Lian walked into the kitchen and turned around, waiting

for Vanora. Her younger sister was already counting the people in the kitchen, and noting what utensils they used. She couldn't be sure, but it looked like Heden had all the equipment they had here. She came back to the moment and looked with real fondness at her worried sister.

"How do they figure out what to charge for the food?" Vanora asked.

CHAPTER FIFTEEN

"Never been in here before," Fandrick said. "Nice." He looked at the floor. "'cept for the blood and…," he gestured at the corpses, "all this."

The Hammer & Tongs was closed. Given that it was an hour after midday, Aiden guessed the inn never opened. There was no one in the place, for one thing. No owner. No staff. He walked around the bodies. The blood on the floor was tacky and pulled at his boots as he walked.

"Someone going to clean all this up?" he asked of no one in particular.

"Who runs this place?" Rayk asked the regular watchman who brought them here.

Teagan shifted the sword on his belt. "Priest named Heden," he said.

"Don't look like no one's been in here for a while," Fandrick went on, walking around the common room, staying away from the bodies and the blood, keeping his boots clean. He admired the large bookcase that took up the far wall of the room.

"He never opens it up," Teagan said. The tall, lanky watchman leaned against the serving bar, his long legs crossed at the ankles. His half-smile seemed a response to a joke only he understood. Aiden could tell the man considered all this a nuisance, and why not Fandrick and Rayk were unlikely to get anything from him they couldn't get in a dozen other places.

"Why not?" Fandrick asked.

Teagan shrugged. "Dunno," he said. "Don't know the man. He's friends with my boss."

"And your boss is…," Rayk asked.

Teagan looked at the ceiling and sighed. "Domnal. Watch captain over on Salter."

Rayk nodded.

"Priest of who?" Aiden asked.

Teagan shrugged. "I don't know," he said. "Llewellyn." That didn't mean anything, they knew. If you were a priest in Celkirk everyone assumed you were a priest of St. Llewellyn.

"We'll talk to your captain, see what he knows," Rayk said. "You know where this priest is?"

"Nope," Teagan said.

"But you know him," Rayk said, cocking her head as she watched Teagan's reaction. "You know his name, you know he keeps the place closed, but you don't know where he is or when he'll be back."

"Just a simple copper, me," Teagan said.

"Uh-huh," Rayk said. "So what were you doing here?" Rayk asked.

Teagan sighed.

"Coming off shift from number seventeen, off Salter like I said. I live on Rab Lane, come past here every night. I turn the corner, I can see down the street something's happening inside. Someone's causing an…," he couldn't remember. "An affront?"

"An affray," Rayk said. "You sure you're a watchman?"

"I'm new," Teagan said. "I run down, door's open, I come in, I see this. Whatever happened, it was over. I searched the place, no one here. I see all this, I figure this is not someone doing a little snatch and grab, so I come get you lot."

Rayk nodded. "And between the time you see whatever's going on, and run down the street, the whole thing is over."

Teagan shrugged. The girl was safe, whatever happened was over, and he was not inclined to help the castellan's men if they were going to be asses.

"Found something," Fandrick said. He'd gone behind the bar and was rooting around in the cupboards and drawers.

Aiden and Rayk went to him. Tegan remained leaning against the post, showing no real interest in what they did.

Fandrick pulled four pieces of brown-stained cloth out of a drawer, and laid them out on the bar.

Aiden didn't understand what he was looking at. Bloodstained scarves, so what.

Fandrick and Rayk shared a look.

"The Black," Rayk said.

"Boils on Cyrvis' balls," Fandrick said. "The Black."

This got Teagan's attention and he walked over. Inspected one of the scarves. "That's interesting," he said.

"The black what?" Aiden asked.

Fandrick and Rayk continued their silent communion. Teagan spoke up.

"The Guild of Blackened Silk," he said. "Their agents wear these scarves, sign of station. Red, green blue. Black. But they coat them in soot so we can't tell which is which."

"Until it's too late," Rayk sneered.

Aiden nodded. "Bad guys."

"Worse than most," Teagan agreed. "Not as bad as the Darkened Moon, maybe."

"Boy," Fandrick barked.

"Uh huh," Aiden said absently. Not eager to reinforce Fandrick's attitudes.

"You sure it's the same here as the gallows?"

"Yeah," Aiden said. "Same black goop. Mixed in the blood. I'd guess we clean these bodies up, get 'em back to the slab," he said meaning the operating table where the castellan's physicians and priests divined dead bodies, "we'd find they'd be clawed at with man-like fingernails and limbs ripped apart with unnatural strength. Ghouls. Or something very like."

Fandrick nodded.

"This doesn't make any damned sense," Rayk insisted, mostly to Fandrick.

"The fuck are the Black doing here?"

"Are these their corpses?" Rayk asked, walking around to the ripped apart bodies littering the floor.

"And why are they fighting ghouls? Who summoned the ghouls? Why? Why attack the count here?" Fandrick asked. There were so many question, he gave up.

"The count?" Aiden asked Teagan, the most forthcoming of the three. He held his hand out, and Teagan gave him a scarf to inspect.

"Runs the guild. Hereditary title. Mostly the guild does what he wants, but he's sort of…there's an agreement between him and the senior members of the guild. The guild does what the count wants, as long as the count wants to do what the senior thieves want."

"I think I get it," Aiden said, pulling the blood-stained scarf through his hand. "He doesn't have absolute power."

"No one does," Teagan said absently.

"Castellan's going to lose his shit," Fandrick said.

"Completely mental," Rayk agreed.

"And we're the ones have to chase it all down, which means we're the ones the count's gonna string up by their balls."

"So to speak," Rayk said.

"Count goes after the castellan's men," Teagan said, "then it's a war with the ragman." He seemed a little concerned. Why were the specials talking like the regulars?

"Well that's some comfort," Fandrick sneered. "When my wife's crying over my dead body wondering where her next meal's comin' from!"

"Your wife never cried over anything in her life, 'cept maybe a missed meal," Rayk said.

Fandrick pointed at her. "That's a filthy lie and you take it back."

"Shant," Rayk said, and sniffed.

"I've got a question," Aiden said, holding one scarf up, trying to make sense of the runes stained into it.

Everyone looked at him.

"If the priest who owns this place isn't here, hasn't been seen, and never opens this place…," Aiden put the scarf down and looked at the three watchmen.

"Who put these scarves away?"

CHAPTER SIXTEEN

The specials were gone. Teagan waited a moment until their argument outside trailed off down the street.

"You can come down," he said.

Vanora danced down the stairs and took stock of the mess.

"I'll clean this up," she said. "Can you take the bodies out of here?"

"How old are you?" Teagan asked.

She collapsed a little, and frowned at him. "Really?"

Teagan shook his head. "You should be apprenticed to a seamstress or a candlemaker. Or an ostler. I bet you like horses."

"Fuck that," Vanora said. "I'm none of those things and never was going to be. Can you help with the bodies or not? This floor's going to take days to get clean."

Teagan shrugged. "You should go back to Miss Elowen."

"Miss Elowen's not going to clean this floor," Vanora said, and went about looking for a mop.

"It's what you know," Teagan admitted. "I mean what are you going to…"

"I was at Miss Elowen's and she sent me away!" Vanora barked. "I had a fit, and she sent me off to be…*put down*." She bit the words off. "She said I was special, and I believed her, but *in the end*…." She left that alone. "Heden saved me. I'm not going back to the Rose, fuck the Rose."

"And when he doesn't come back?"

"He's coming back," Vanora said. "He promised."

Teagan shook his head. "I thought you were too young," he said. "I was wrong. You're too old to believe in fairy stories. And a trull at that."

"Shows what you know," Vanora said. "Trulls believe in fairy stories their whole lives."

Teagan watched the girl begin mopping up the blood. He wasn't sure what to do or say, he felt grossly out of his depth, but he knew the priest instinctively the way he was sure the girl could not, and felt she deserved the chance to make up her own mind. So he took a chance.

"Let me tell you something about that priest," he said, and his voice seemed bleak, not youthful as it had been. This drew Vanora's attention. "I know about him. Known men like him. No matter what he promises you, no matter how good his intentions, eventually there'll be someone else needs him more and he'll have no choice. Man like that," Teagan said, and shook his head. "The world heaps everything on him until he breaks. And he will break. 'Cause there's no end to the need. It'll eat him up and then he'll be gone."

"Then I go with him," Vanora said instantly. "He saved me. I go where he goes."

"Why go with anyone?" Teagan asked. This brought Vanora up short. The answer was so obvious, he was being so stupid, so why couldn't she articulate why?

Why be with anyone? Stupid question. She shook her head to get it out.

"I've got a plan," she said. "I can do it myself."

Teagan watched her begin scrubbing industriously. It was a simple problem, blood. But it would take a lot of work. And it seemed the girl was committed. The floor would get clean.

"I'll take care of the bodies," Teagan said.

Chapter Seventeen

"Well that's the end for mister scribbler here," Fandrick said.

Aiden said nothing. His grimace and furrowed brow spoke for him.

"How you figure?" Rayk asked. The three of them stood on the wooden stoop in front of the Hammer & Tongs. The thick midday street traffic creating a low roar they had to talk over.

Fandrick spat. "I said it was deathless, I said it was a cult. We shoulda gone to the church, instead we came here. Wasted time."

"It's not wasted," Aiden said quietly. "We can still go to the church, and probably should. But we learned a lot coming here," he said.

"Learned it's something to do with the count," Rayk agreed. "That's useful. Count's in some kind of pissing match with a cult."

"This happened twelve hour ago," Fandrick said. "Gallows happened *after*, which means we're working backwards and we should'a been working forwards and we *would'a* been working forwards if Mr. Scribbler here hadn't come on with his airs about 'it can't be deathless.' Balls," Fandrick pronounced.

"We found evidence of the count's men," Aiden said, looking at his shoes, "but no cultists. No sign of any cultists at either scene."

"Well someone chewed up the count's men," Rayk said.

"The ghouls," Fandrick growled.

"But who summoned the ghouls," Aiden asked, turning to look at the window into the inn. It was too dark inside to see anything.

"The fucking cultists!" Fandrick barked. "Are you daft? Are you mental? Me and the ragman gonna have a word about you."

Aiden took a deep breath. "Maybe," he said. "Someone summoned those ghouls. Maybe it's cultists."

"Count's in a pissing match with a cult, and this is what happens. Dead thieves everywhere. Better them than us."

"You say that like it explains something," Aiden wasn't going to let someone just ride over him. He didn't know why the... the ragman picked him, but he was in it now and he wanted to know. Wanted to know what was happening. "It's been *three years* since the last deathless was seen anywhere, by anyone. Cultists *can't* summon deathless anymore, otherwise they'd all be doing it."

Aiden and Fandrick stared at each other.

"You don't think it's cultists," Aiden said severely. "You just *hope* it's cultists because that's what you know. Well you take what you know, and you go back in there and look at the scene and tell me it makes any sense."

Fandrick fumed, but said nothing.

"Any of this make sense to you?" Aiden threw this at Rayk.

Rayk shook her head. "I don't know what's going on," she said. "I don't know if cultists is a dead end either way, but I know the count's involved, so I say we watch him."

Aiden nodded. "Let's find out. Let's go talk to the count."

"Talk to the count!" Fandrick said. "You are mental! Fuck you think'll happen if we just roll into his club, brace him in front of all the nobs he holds court with? He'll smile and nod and half a turn later our guts'll be spilled all over the street."

"He does that and it's a war with the castellan. Court on the street."

"Who taught you that?" Rayk interrupted the barking match. "Who taught you 'court on the street?'"

"I read a lot," Aiden snapped. "Now someone, the count, I don't know, is going around the city using ghouls to murder people and he's doing it right in front of us, in broad daylight, and he doesn't give a shit if we know. Doesn't cover his tracks.

Like we don't matter."

"We don't matter," Fandrick snarled. "We ain't thieves, we ain't assassins."

"We're the special watch," Aiden said. "The castellan's men."

"That don't mean nothing," Fandrick said.

Aiden was trying to stop the shaking running through his limbs. He wasn't used to confrontation and didn't much like it. But didn't like being ignored more. "We're both going to have a talk with the ragman when we get back," he said, and stood his ground under Fandrick's glower.

When Fandrick didn't replay, Aiden pushed his slim advantage. "Now here's something neither of you asked," he said and walked down the wooden steps into the street. Foot traffic jostled him, but he didn't move.

"What's this inn have to do with it?" Aiden asked, his eyes roaming around the whole building. "What's in here worth fighting over?" Neither Fandrick nor Rayk offered an answer. They didn't know, and they didn't like not knowing.

Aiden looked at the other buildings in the row, and at the people passing by and said, mostly to himself;

"And where's her owner?"

Chapter Eighteen

Days later, and Vanora's plan was working better than she'd ever imagined. A half dozen men ate and drank in the common room, trying the place out.

"It's cold down there," Martlyn said of the cellar, "and it looks like some of the food just arrived, it's still good. But it's mostly wine and ale and stuff anyway."

Vanora nodded.

"What'll we do? We got so much more wine than…."

"We just lower the price on the wine until everyone's coming here to drink it. Take the money, buy ham and mutton and duck."

"That makes sense," Martlyn said, nodding. "You're a natural at this stuff Violet."

Vanora smiled and caught herself wondering if it was a real smile, or one she put on for effect. She wasn't sure.

"It helps having friends," she said, and Martlyn smiled back.

It all seemed ridiculously easy. Half the girls had worked in taverns before coming to Miss Elowen anyway. Vanora hadn't considered that. Word of mouth spread and eight girls were now spending their off time here at the inn, time they'd otherwise use to drum up business on their own or go shopping outside the Rose.

They all seemed to know what to do and none of them, even the older girls questioned Vanora's role in this. That surprised her more than anything. She imagined constant fighting to see who was in charge, but no. The girls all seemed to…to want someone to be in charge. They were happy that Vanora took that role. It was like this huge secret no one had ever told her. The girls, it seemed, wanted to be useful, wanted to get paid, earn a wage. No one argued with her about anything. She thought it would be nothing but arguing and the inn would never open. But they were opening tonight. It was working.

She wasn't sure how she'd work out the hours. Taverns usually opened mid-afternoon and stayed open until a few hours past midnight, but inns in the city were expected to be open and have staff and food ready all the hours of the day.

Unless Vanora started hiring people, which she didn't intend on doing, they'd only be open a few hours a day, and be unable to rent out any rooms. The girls all had jobs already.

Maybe she should hire some people. Couldn't be that hard. She'd need someone to keep people in line. Someone like Bann. She wanted to ask him, but was afraid that he'd go tell Miss Elowen and she'd tell the girls they couldn't come here. But Miss Elowen had to know, didn't she? She knew everything the girls got up to.

She watched Martlyn go down into the cellar, and decided she'd solve that problem when she got to it. A strategy she was discovering worked better than she'd ever imagined. She remembered her mother, cringing before her father, and she got goosebumps thinking about what she was doing here in this inn. Something her mother would never in her life have ever tried or thought of.

There was a cough that turned into a loud hacking wheeze. An old man nursed a drink at one of the tables. He was alone and, Vanora remembered, had been here a few hours.

She walked over to him. "Hungry yet?" He had a red face and a thin wisp of white hair curling haphazardly around his head. He wore a chasuble of St. Llewellyn.

The old man looked around the common room as though seeing it for the first time. "Yes!"

"Duck?" she asked.

"Mutton," the old man said, and lifted his tankard. "And more ale."

Vanora nodded and went to get the man some food.

When she returned another two men had entered the inn and Martlyn was attending to them. Vanora served the old man his mutton and ale.

"When was the last time you left this building," the old man said conversationally. As though they'd known each other forever and this was a perfectly normal thing to ask.

"What?" Vanora asked.

"You are young miss Vanora, yes?" the old man asked.

"How do you know my name?" Vanora frowned.

The old man nodded to the chair. Vanora put a hand on the chair back, but did not sit down.

"How long since you left the inn?" the old man asked again, digging into his sheep meat.

"Who are you?" Vanora demanded.

The abbot looked at her from under thick white bushy eyebrows. His rheumy blue eyes sparkled. "We have a mutual friend in common," he said smiling.

Vanora puzzled this out.

"I used to eat here, you know," the abbot said, "Before he bought it and locked it up."

"Heden," she said. "You're his friend."

"One of them," the abbot nodded. "Sit down."

Vanora sat down.

"Where is he," she said, her voice almost a hiss. She looked around to see if anyone was watching.

"One thing at a time," the abbot said, enjoying his meal. "How long since you...."

"Yesterday," Vanora said, irritated.

"Mm," the abbot said, chewing. He swallowed. "Until he gets back, I would not advise leaving again. Unless you know any secret ways out of here. There are some!" the abbot said. "But I was never privy to their location or their workings."

"What are you talking about?" Vanora asked. "Where's Heden?"

"The place is being watched," the abbot said, leaning forward and holding Vanora's gaze. "By the count's men, I assume."

"Watched," Vanora said, coming over all still.

"Mm," the abbot said. "They may not snatch you the minute you walk outside, they may follow you. See where you go. But not for long, I shouldn't think."

"I'm trapped," Vanora put her hands flat on the table.

"At least until Heden comes back. What's your opinion of him?" the abbot asked, idly.

"He's coming back!" Vanora asked, her concern about being watched, gone.

The abbot nodded. "Of course," he said. "Well, you knew he was. If you thought he wasn't coming back, you wouldn't have done this," he said gesturing to the common room and the people eating inside. "Brilliant idea, I'd like to add. Don't sit around waiting, do something. Healthy. I see you've got friends helping."

Vanora ignored him. "Where is he!? What happened to him?" she demanded, *sotto voce.*

"Well as to where he is; he's on his way back. It may take him a few days more. What happened to him? That's between you and him. And he and I, I suppose, eventually. But you still haven't answered the question. What do you think of him?"

"He saved me," Vanora said. She didn't know what else to say. It seemed like that said it all.

The abbot nodded. "Yes. He does that. Has been known to do it. In your case I'd like to think it was the Gods or one of the Saints at work. I think he took the job from Gwiddon because he had someone waiting here—you—who he didn't want to disappoint. Which only makes sense if you know how his mind works. And after many years I like to think I do. Of course, you had no idea who he was or what he did or what kind of burden the Church puts on him. But you knowing or not knowing doesn't matter to him. He could shrug off the Church and his duties and his life as long as it was just him, but once you entered the picture, once someone depended on him, well that changes things."

Vanora blinked at him, trying to absorb all this.

"Anyway that's just one man's opinion. What's yours?"

"What's mine?"

"Your opinion. Of Heden."

She shrugged. "He saved me," she said again.

"That simply won't do," the abbot said, frowning. "It's no use you saying 'he saved me' anytime someone asks you about him. You're living in his inn, you're waiting for his return, you need to develop a more sophisticated outlook on the man."

Vanora looked around. Was anyone else seeing this? Was anyone else being interrogated by an elderly godbotherer? It seemed unreal. But she took his question seriously and thought.

"I trust him," she said eventually.

The abbot took a deep breath and went back to his meal. He seemed to like the potatoes. "That will have to do, I suppose."

"Should I not trust him?" Vanora asked.

The abbot raised his eyebrows. "Now *that* is a question. A good one. One I am often asked by many people *about* many people and I find myself deploying the same phrasing every time;

"You can trust him to act in accordance with his nature," he said cryptically.

Vanora winced as she tried this idea out. "What does that mean?"

"Well I suppose it means you can't *always* trust him. Not in the sense that you mean. It *is* possible he will let you down. Anyone has that capacity, no matter how good or righteous. The trick lies in knowing what he would let you down *for*."

Vanora considered this. The abbot liked talking and continued.

"Some men will let you down because they get bored with

you, or distracted. Or because *not* letting you down has never been important to them. Some men will let you down and not even realize you were depending on them. Heden is none of them, you'll be happy to know.

"He is a man who will keep his word *if at all possible*, a condition I think he sometimes forgets. You must not."

Vanora blinked.

"For instance," the abbot continued, "I daresay Heden promised to be back before this."

"Yes!" Vanora said, happy to participate in the conversation again.

"And you trusted him when he said this," the abbot said.

This brought Vanora up short. She was skirting around the edges of the abbot's point, beginning to see the shape of it, but it was unfamiliar territory.

"Yes," she hesitated.

"Now," the abbot said, "Heden did *not* come back when he promised you. And you feel wronged. Slighted."

Vanora nodded rapidly but chose not to interrupt.

"He broke his word to you. And yet, only a moment ago, when pressed, you said you trusted him."

Vanora's eyes unfocused. She looked at nothing, thought. The abbot watched, then nodded to himself and drank more ale.

"I…," Vanora started.

"You get it," the abbot said. "I can tell. You trust his *character* and well you should. There are few men you can trust more. But you cannot trust to circumstance. Circumstance conspires against us all. He promises to return in a day or a day and a night, and a week passes. A betrayal? Certainly you feel you are *owed* something for this slight, a dangerous transaction but one I think it early to speak on, but you *immediately* conclude that something must have happened. True. That something more important, more pressing, prevented him from fulfilling his promise to you. True.

"And this is the nature of things. You don't feel the promise broken, you feel you can still trust him. You can. But this is a lesson, young lady, and one you must learn early. The world puts many demands on Heden. He cares about you, you are important to him, but none of us are important to the *world*. And Heden sometimes finds himself burdened by the world."

Vanora looked at him, eyes wide. "I understand," she said, and was surprised to find it true.

The abbot nodded. "I thought you might." He got up, slowly and it seemed painfully. Threw some coins on the table. "Thank you for the service. The mutton may be going off, not an emergency, but look into it."

He walked with his odd gait to the door and opened it, stepped out onto the stoop. Vanora ran after him.

"Wait," Vanora called out. She closed the door behind her. The abbot stood there with his back to her, watching the people in the street.

"Why did you come here?" Vanora asked.

"You didn't want to know that Heden was alive?" The abbot said without turning around.

Vanora stared at his back. It took her a moment to formulate her thoughts.

"That's not an answer," she said, her brow furrowing.

The abbot didn't say anything.

"I'd have found that out anyway," she said, taking a step forward to stand right next to him. She lowered her voice. "You warned me not to leave the inn," she said looking up and down the street. "Is that why you came here? To warn me?" She knew it wasn't.

The abbot turned around and looked down at her. He wasn't smiling.

"No," he said. "That's not why I came here as, I suppose, you've guessed. You guessed the truth *and* confronted me about it. Which is exactly what Heden would have done, why am I not surprised?"

Vanora felt herself grow a little taller at that.

The old man looked at her and shook his head. The kindly old man was gone. In his stead was the man who kept the secrets of men like Heden.

"Watch me when I say this, young lady, and know that I speak the truth. You'll have to develop a sense for truth, and quickly.

"I came to get a look at you. I have some idea the powers arrayed against you and Heden and I wanted to know if you've got any chance. For one thing, I expect to see him soon, he's going to ask me for advice and I needed a sense of you to give it to him. Or help him find it himself, which is my real job.

"To him…well, I'll talk to him soon enough. To you, I say this: Heden cannot be in two places at once."

Vanora shook her head, like a fly was buzzing around her. "What does that mean?"

"The list of his enemies is growing longer. He cannot make sure you are safe, and stop the count at the same time."

Vanora stared at this old man while she processed this. It was a riddle. She hated riddles.

"I hate riddles," she said. "The inn is safe," she said, looking at the building behind her.

It was the abbot's turn to shake his head. "Young lady," she liked that, "the count and his allies stay away from here, now, because they don't know who owns the place. They made a try for you once," Vanora was impressed he knew that, "it didn't work. They have no idea why. They're afraid of acting from ignorance, afraid of discovering this place is more than just a retired godbotherer's inn. But once Heden returns, they'll find out that's exactly what it is. And neither you, nor Heden, nor this place will be safe."

Vanora stared up at the old man. "You told me not to leave! What am I supposed to do?"

"I don't have all the answers." The abbot looked at the door behind her. "You seem a resourceful young woman."

Vanora frowned. "I'll tell him you said this," it was half-threat, half-promise. She felt as though Heden would not agree with this man, teacher though he may be.

"Do not," the abbot said. "As soon as you bring it up, you put him in danger."

"Why?!" she asked, angry at more riddles.

"They have ways of learning what Heden knows," the abbot said. "It would be difficult for the count's men to take Heden. But having done it, it's very easy for them to find out what he knows. And *if* they believe he knows where you are, they *will* take him. They will waste dozens of men doing it. If they believe he has no idea where you are, they won't bother."

Vanora's mind went still. This made sense. Everything the old man had been talking about now fell into place.

"That's why you came to the inn," she said, and was surprised at how calm she felt.

The abbot nodded. "I'm afraid so. He wants to protect you, but you have to protect him. Go somewhere else. Somewhere safe."

She shook her head. It didn't matter how much sense he made, she was going to be her when Heden returned. "I'm not leaving." *Miss Elowen put me in* jail. "Heden saved me." *I opened my eyes and I wasn't in the jail. And he was there.* "I'm going to be here when he gets back."

The abbot just stared at her for a long while, his lips pressed together.

"In any case," he said, and took a deep breath. "I have to go back to the church for vespers. It takes a long time for me to get there and there will be many people there looking for my help."

He turned and stepped into the street, and walked in the direction of the massive granite cathedral that loomed over the city.

Vanora watched him waddle away.

Chapter Nineteen

It was a small library. A few dozen books, one door, no windows. A small table and chair, an unlit lamp. When the door was closed, like now, no light got in. But the room was small enough that if you moved carefully, even in the darkness, you could avoid bumping into anything.

A flash of white light announced the presence of a runic circle activating on the carpeted floor. Trapping someone within.

"Ow," a voice said. Then a sound that might have been a polder pressing his palms into his eyes and rubbing them.

The figure struck a nail. The small fire revealed a polder in hard leather armor, blonde curly locks bobbing as he shook his head and blinked madly. His eyes still hurt but he was able to look down and see the binding circle he was trapped in. Anyone watching closely would see the flame flickering, as though held in a trembling hand being flexed in a vain attempt to stop the tremors.

"Pigfucker," he said as he turned around to examine the circle, about four feet across. "Prick, arse, rancid cunt. Ow!" this last as the flame burned his finger and he shook it out.

Silence for several moments, then; "Shit."

Time passed. With no visual cues and nothing else to do, he counted breaths. He felt his skin crawl. He sweated. He didn't used to sweat when he was caught. He used to be cool as a gravestone.

He lost count of the time, only noticed when he heard a noise, like something heavy landing on a pillow.

He knew someone was in the room with him. The lantern on the table flared to life revealing a young—to his eye, he often found it difficult to tell a human's age between 15 and 50—human female. Unlike most women in Corwell, she didn't wear a dress. She wore black leather pants and a black and red corset vest.

She was short, with dark, arched eyebrows and black hair. There was a streak of color in it, blue or red…it was hard to tell with his eyes still burning. Wide lips painted dark red against pale skin. Her figure reminded Aimsley of the goddess figurines people found among the ancient Gol ruins. She seemed relaxed, but her eyes flashed with danger.

"Got you," the woman said, arching one perfect eyebrow. She seemed relaxed, but poised. Aimsley's instincts told him she was ready for murder.

His eyes darted, looking for an escape, for anything. He was trapped inside the circle. There might be a way out, but he'd need time and some luck to figure it, and he'd run out of both.

He pointed at the woman in black and red.

"You're Hapax Legomenon," Aimsley said. "The Lens' *occultus quaesitor*."

She ignored him and counted on her fingers.

"The Cold Hearth's fixer is a polder," she said, "that's you I figure. The Darkened Moon's is a woman named Noor. The Guild of Blackened Silk's is an assassin named Garth."

"He's not an assassin," Aimsley said, "he's just a prick."

"A guild fixer killed one of our librarians to cover their tracks after stealing a codex," she said.

"You got a lot of librarians," Aimsley sneered.

Hapax Legomenon's eyes narrowed.

"This one was a friend of mine. And the *quaesitor* doesn't have a lot of friends."

"I know the feeling," Aimsley said.

"Whoever did it, I figured they'd be back," she nodded at the circle and relaxed a little. Content to enjoy the upper hand.

He was trapped. The ward was specially configured for him, or someone like him. He'd probably stolen the codex and probably killed the librarian. He seemed to do a lot of killing these days, though his blackouts meant he didn't remember.

For some reason he thought of the priest he met outside the wode. It wasn't the first time the man had intruded into his thoughts. The priest who stole the count's whore and kept her safe in his tavern-fortress. What would he say?

"I'm sorry about your friend," he ventured. He tried to imagine what it would feel like if he really was sorry about her friend. It wasn't easy. But there was maybe a little twinge of feeling in there. Might help his performance.

Using the same pocket-magics he used to hide his dirks, she produced a large red gem, a fire diamond, held it between her middle finger and thumb.

"Won't work," Aimsley said, shaking a little. He wasn't afraid, but he couldn't control the tremors or the sweats. "I know maybe six people in the guild now. Don't know their assignments."

Hapax Legomenon nodded. "Yeah," she said, "but I don't give a shit about the guild." She locked eyes with the polder. "I want to be certain you killed my friend. Then…."

Aimsley realized he was in a half crouch. Undignified. And stupid, there was nowhere for him to go. He had to get her to drop the ward. For this, there was nothing except the old standby; bargaining.

He stood up, straightened his vest. Tried to recover some of his dignity. Put his hands behind his back to hide the shakes. "I might have done it," he said.

"Might?"

"I kill a lot of people," he said.

Her eyes narrowed. "The fire hurts. It *is* pain. Normally I don't enjoy it, doing that to someone, but I really want to put you under all of a sudden."

"Let me out," Aimsley said, trying not to sound panicked. He played his own voice back in his head. *Not bad*, he thought.

"What?" the wizard asked.

"I didn't come here to kill anyone, I came here for

information. I came here to make contact with you. This is your library, isn't it?" He knew it was.

She stared at him. "You…you want to trade. I've got you by the balls, and you want to make an offer."

"The count has a way to make deathless," Aimsley said.

"There are no more deathless," Hapax Legomenon said automatically.

"I've seen it. It's some kind of black smoke. Dust. I think he's trying to use it to take over the city."

Hapax thought, nodded. "If he's the only person in all Orden who can make deathless," she said, "he'll take over more than the city."

"Uh-huh," Aimsley said, smiling. "So maybe I give you some, and you tell me how it's made. Fair trade."

Aimsley saw the opening. Saw the *quaesitor* think. Watched as she searched her mind. This was his opening. She cared about more than just revenge.

"It can't be priestly magic," she said. "The link between the gods and the deathless is broken."

"I don't think it was priestly," Aimsley said. "I think it's sorcery."

Hapax shook her head slowly. "If there was a way for a wizard to make deathless," she looked at him, "I'd know about it."

"What else is there?" Aimsley asked.

"Alchemy," Hapax said.

Aimsley smiled. "Know any good alchemists?" he said.

"All of them," she said, then nothing for a few moments.

"Nah, I'll just kill you," she decided. "Watch the *Aduro Vera* burn your mind out."

Aimsley produced the small glass marble, held it up. This got her attention.

"If I break this," he said, "here, inside the ward, the smoke in the glass will get inside me. It'll kill me. It'll break my bones

102

and turn me inside out and I'm *guessing*," he stressed, "the ghoul that'll be left won't be trapped by your wards. I'm guessing you made this ward to catch me. And the ghoul will tear you apart."

"I can handle a ghoul," she said.

"Let's find out," Aimsley said. Strangely, he found the threat easy to make. He didn't mind the idea of oblivion. Didn't mind it at all. Looked forward to it more and more. He just didn't want to do it himself. Alone. This would be a good way to go, though. Dramatic. Memorable. Better than dying under the fire of truth. Fuck it.

"I let you out and you give me the death smoke," she asked, thinking.

"They call it night dust. Yeah. Fair trade."

"I think," she said slowly, "that if I drop that ward, you'll make a break for it and screw our bargain."

Aimsley considered this. "Sure. But if you don't let me out, even if you can handle a ghoul, then you've got nothing. No polder thief and no night dust."

Hapax Legomenon considered the offer. It was clear she wanted the dust. Of course she wanted the dust. Things like night dust was why the Orders employed the *occultus quaesitoria*.

She stood up. Stood between the ward with the polder in it, and the door. "Just so you know," she said, putting her hands on her hips, "Once I drop that ward, I'm taking the dust from you."

"You think you can?" Aimsley asked, frowning sarcastically.

"Let's find out," she said, and dropped the ward. Her eyes suddenly flared with green fire.

Freed, Aimsley grinned furiously. *Die fighting the Quill's best agent*, he thought as he leapt into the air, a dirk suddenly in each hand.

Not bad way to go.

CHAPTER TWENTY

People came and went from the inn. The Hammer & Tongs. He looked at the symbol over the door. Couldn't remember how old he was the first time he saw it. Couldn't remember his first time inside. Couldn't remember when it became the place he went, the place they always went when they were done.

The people coming and going seemed happy. As though whatever was going on inside were normal for a tavern. He ran his hand over the beard he'd grown in the last week. There was a knife in his pack he kept sharp for shaving, but he hadn't felt like using it. Now he wished he had.

He looked over his right shoulder at the spires of the cathedral that dominated the city. The journey south from the forest had dulled his anger, but proximity to its source sharpened it again. He resisted the urge to go to the church, resisted the urge to hate. There was time enough for that.

He crossed the busy street and climbed the three steps that led to the doors of the inn.

He didn't know what he expected to see when he walked through the doors. He realized he expected to see Ghannt the demi-thyrs barkeep and owner, Parl and Stewart and Zaar and Reginam and everyone else.

Instead what he found was a normal, if somewhat sparse, tavern common room. Nothing like the ratcatchers inn he'd known years ago. A dozen guests in a common room fit to serve five times that number. He noticed they were all being attended by girls. Young girls. He frowned.

A man at a table near the door watched him. He wore light armor, a sword at his side, leaned back on two chair legs, balancing himself. Muscle to protect the girls. The man nodded at him, he didn't react.

He walked up to the man's table and stood there, watching the people eating, drinking, being served. It seemed loud, unnaturally loud, compared to the last time he was here.

He turned to the muscle.

"How's the nose?" he asked.

The man stopped picking at his teeth. "What?" he asked blankly, then his eyes went wide and he momentarily lost his balance.

Ignoring the flailing guard, he crossed the common room floor. Marveled at the business being done within, at the serving girls. There were about half a dozen of them. He did a quick mental calculation of the Rose Petal's staff, wondered how many of them would be on their own time at any given moment.

A serving girl exited the kitchen and glided toward a table with two men waiting.

"What's your name?" he asked the girl, stopping her.

The girl curtseyed, skillfully he thought.

"Martlyn" the girl said. She had long curly red hair, seemed dyed. Large brilliant green eyes and olive skin. A suspicion grew.

"Martlyn" he repeated, "how long as this inn been open?"

"Two days, your lordship," she said, bowing her head deferentially. "Still working the kinks out," she said.

He looked at the ceiling. "Are there…rooms?"

"Wol," she said, and put a hand on her hip. Her posture subtly changed to produce a certain effect in men. "Not officially. Not for the night." She smiled at him. It seemed a genuine smile. "But for some coin, an arrangement can be made for," she surveyed him, "an hour? You seem tired."

"Coin," he nodded, his suspicion confirmed.

"You're not bad-looking, you shave that beard," Martlyn said.

"Thank you," he said, nodding. "How much for an hour?"

"Two crowns," she said without hesitation. The men at the table waiting for her were growing impatient.

"Two…," there were signs of surprise and alarm, but he restrained himself.

"Worth every copper!" she said, feigning insult. He felt as though she should feel embarrassed or ashamed, but the opposite. The longer they talked the more she seemed to be enjoying herself. He considered himself a hard man to fool. This added to his already substantive confusion.

"Where's Vanor…Violet?" he asked.

"Oh you fancy Violet?" Martlyn asked. How old was this girl? She looked nineteen but that didn't mean anything. "She's a bit busy," Martlyn said skeptically. "Got lots to do, running the place. Don't think she's taken a customer since we opened, but if ah, you're someone special to her I can let her know."

He nodded. "Do that," he said, and started toward the stairs.

"Hey!" Martlyn said. "No one's allowed up there without paying!"

"Good," he said, climbing the stairs.

"Wait," Martlyn said, thinking. "You're…," she looked at his back disappearing up the stairs and snapped her fingers.

"Uh-oh," she said.

CHAPTER TWENTY-ONE

She threw the door to his room open. It slammed against the wall with a bang.

He turned to face her. He'd stripped his shirt off. It lay on the bed covered in dried blood. His breastplate lay on the floor.

Something about him, his realness, his presence, seemed increased since he left. Though his face was lined and haggard and his beard made him look like a prophet from a wode, his body was still lean and compact. There was a relaxed, slackness gone. He seemed ready. Poised. Like a cat on the prowl.

She took all this in in an instant, and then ran across the room to him. Threw herself up and into him, wrapped her arms around his neck.

Though it felt like running into a brick wall, he caught her. Wrapped his arms around her and held her.

Something inside her, something she hadn't realized had been clenched for…for years, forever? Relaxed, and she started crying. Though his skin was pale and he looked carved from cold stone, he radiated strength and warmth and he smelled like leather and oil and wet horse-hair.

He was security. He was safety. It was something she wasn't sure she'd ever felt before. She'd die before she gave it up again.

"You didn't leave," he said.

Vanora shook her head, still buried in the nape of his neck, not saying anything.

"I knew you wouldn't," Heden said. She could tell he was smiling.

CHAPTER TWENTY-TWO

Eventually she pushed herself away, violently. Eyes still brimming with tears, she punched him. Hard.

"You said a day!" she hit him again. "You said a day and then you left me here alone!"

He took her abuse.

"I know," Heden said, smile gone. "I'm sorry. It was stupid of me to…." She looked at him, waiting. He didn't know how to begin to explain to her the complex collection of obligations and burdens she had so recently slotted into. Near, but not at, the top.

He decided to deflect.

"I brought you a horse," he said shyly.

Her anger evaporated. She smiled. Her smile grew.

"Really?" she asked, her voice small.

Heden nodded.

"He's in a stable. You'll like him. I'll teach you how to ride him."

She gasped. He pressed his advantage.

"He likes apples," he said.

Her hands clenched with eagerness. Then she frowned.

"Are you going to leave again?" she asked. She had to ask it quick before fear of the answer made her run from it.

Heden took a deep breath. This was going to be difficult.

"Not like that. Not into the forest again. But there are things we need to talk about."

She remembered the abbot. She wanted to tell him what he said, but she couldn't. It was like he put a spell on her. She deflected, sighing and rolling her eyes as she sat down on his bed with a flop.

"Yes, I know," she said. "I opened the inn while you were

108

gone and since then the girls have come and they…," she waved her hand at the door behind him. "They enjoy…practice," she said lamely. "But I needed the help."

"Uh-huh," Heden said.

"I did!" she objected. "I haven't…had any customers. I thought you'd be…proud."

Heden looked at her, head tilted to one side. "I am. I'm…I'm amazed. If you'd asked permission, I'd have said no. But coming back to this…for some reason made me feel…," made him feel like a younger man. Like the Hammer & Tongs was his home again, like it was with the Sunbringers, instead of a prison.

"Feels like home," he said, summing over all his thoughts neatly.

She smiled again.

"You're not angry at me?"

"Well," Heden said. "No. No I guess I'm not, though…the girls."

Vanora shrugged. "Miss Elowen doesn't mind."

Heden frowned at her.

"I bet she does."

"Well, she doesn't mind *much*," Vanora said.

"And you've talked to her about this," Heden said skeptically.

"Well," Vanora said. "Look she obviously knows, right? And she hasn't told any of the girls no. I mean they're only here a few hours a day," she said and it sounded like she was sulking now. "It's been a problem the whole time; our hours are all messed up."

Heden looked at the girl, and marveled. He couldn't say no to her.

"I mean," she continued, "we can afford to hire help but I don't want to hire anyone I don't know," she said. The words came quickly; she enjoyed sharing her problems with Heden. She was eager for his approval.

"Alright listen," he said. "As long as they…," he made a

gesture with his hands like he was holding an invisible orb. "Constrain their activities to serving and cooking and cleaning?"

Vanora looked at him sadly and took a deep breath.

"Ok," she said.

He scratched his head, and looked around the room. Then looked back at her.

"You just lied to me," he said.

"Oh," she said, crestfallen. She kicked her feet and looked at the floor. "I forgot about that."

"You'll get used to it," Heden said.

"Well, I mean I can *tell* them, but I have no way to *make* them...,"

"Sure you do," Heden said. "Tell them if they do it, they're sacked."

Vanora looked at him. "I can't tell them that, they're my friends!"

Heden shrugged. "Then I'll tell them," he said.

"Alright, alright," she said. "I'll tell them. I'll blame you, they'll believe that," she said darkly.

"Good girl," he said.

She looked at him again and smiled. Incredibly happy he was back.

"Well," Heden said raising an eyebrow, "mostly good."

She laughed. Heden enjoyed that. Then for some reason, unbidden, came the thought of Taethan.

He stopped smiling. He looked at the floor. The room grew cold. Vanora noticed something had changed.

Heden scratched his chest and realized he was still shirtless. He went to his dresser. Pulled a clean shirt from it, smelled it.

"You washed my clothes," he said.

Vanora shrugged. She noticed something in his voice.

"What happened in the forest?" she asked.

Heden ignored her. For the moment. He put a clean shirt on.

"That's what you meant when you said we had things to talk about," she said. "You didn't mean the inn."

He tucked the shirt into his breeches. He looked around the room. There wasn't anywhere to sit but the bed.

"You're different," Vanora said.

Heden nodded.

"There are things I have to do," he said.

"What things?" she asked. And it hurt him, the ignorance he heard there. He didn't know how to explain it.

"Before," he started. "Before I met you, a long time ago, I took an oath."

She nodded. "To serve the church," she said.

"Well," he said. "Not really. To serve...I thought I took an oath to serve Cavall," he said. Vanora recognized the name. The patron god of Corwell. Religion was never high on her lists of interests. "But I met someone, an abbot at the church, and the more we talked the more I thought...that what Cavall wanted was for me to do the right thing."

Vanora looked at him blankly.

"That I shouldn't worry about what the gods wanted," Heden explained, "I should just worry about what was right, and the gods would be happy."

Vanora nodded. That made sense.

"That's why I went into the forest," Heden said with some relief. It felt like he'd found a way to explain things. "Not because the church asked me to, but because I thought it was the right thing to do."

Vanora nodded.

"Well," Heden said, "everything went wrong in the forest. I...I failed. I didn't figure out what I was supposed to do until it was too late," he said frowning.

He seemed in pain, he stopped talking. Vanora decided to say something.

"I think I met the abbot," she ventured. How much could

she tell him?

Heden's head jerked up. "What?"

"A man came here," she said, and explained everything except the conversation on the porch.

Heden listened. "That was him," he said. "I'm glad someone was looking out for you."

"He said something," Vanora tried to remember exactly. "He said the list of your enemies was growing longer."

Heden nodded. "That's true. And I have to do something about it. These people, the count, the bishop," he said, "someone has to be punished for what happened in the forest."

"The bishop?" she asked. "The bishop of the church?"

Heden nodded.

"The man who lives in that great stone building with the tall pointy things?"

"Spires," Heden said. "Yeah."

"What about him?"

"He's responsible for what happened. And someone has to confront him. Stop him."

"Who?" she asked, her eyes wide.

"Me," he said.

Vanora stared at him. "How!?"

"I don't know," he said.

"You can't…," she started. "Can't he just," she wasn't clear on the power of the bishop, "can't he just point at you and turn you to stone, or hit you with lightning from the sky or something?!"

Heden cleared his throat, chose not to mention that she was describing things he himself had done, and the bishop was far more powerful. *Or is he?* Heden wondered. He held out hope that the bishop's appointment might be purely political.

"Basically," he said.

"You can't!" Vanora cried out.

Heden's chest tightened.

"I don't understand. Why do you have to do this? We have

the inn. It's real, I made it work. It was dead when you were here, now it's alive. You can't leave again! You can't...." There were worse things than leaving.

"I have to," he said. "Because of what happened in the forest." Things Vanora would never understand. Things Heden wasn't sure he understood. "Because I'm the only one who knows. Because...," *because he manipulated me into doing his dirty work.* "Because someone I cared about died, and it's the bishop's fault."

He looked at her. He was exhausted; he wished he could sit down. She was desperate and confused.

"So it's up to me to do something about it."

"What?"

"I don't know. I'm going to...have a talk with Gwiddon. He sent me there. He picked me to do the bishop's dirty work. On purpose. Because he knew I'd fail."

She didn't understand what he meant, but she recognized the look in his eyes. His voice was casual, but his whole posture framed rage barely contained.

"You're going to kill him, aren't you?"

Heden cast a dark look at her.

"The man who was down here, that first day." When she first woke up in Heden's inn. "Your friend. That's him. You're going to kill him."

"I don't know," he said.

"And then you're going to kill the bishop?!"

Silence. Then, "I don't know." But she heard it in his voice. He didn't know if he could. But he knew he had to try.

She broke the silence between them. "The polder said...,"

"The who?" he snapped. She pulled back.

"The polder who came and...."

"Describe him," Heden said. His voice had changed.

She described the polder he met at the inn in Ollghum Keep.

He took several deep breaths. He was returning to the state

of readiness she'd seen him when she first came into the room.

"When was he here?"

Vanora described the incident with the ratmen and the assassins and the ghoul.

Heden's fist were clenched when she was done.

"How many…," he asked. "How many of the radenwights were killed?" he asked, though she sensed there was something more important on his mind. Something about the polder.

"A few," she said. "Not many. They saved me," she said.

Heden nodded. "That's something else that worked. And now I owe them, too."

"He'll try again," Vanora said, and though she didn't want it to, a little fear crept into her voice.

"The count?" Heden asked.

Vanora nodded.

Heden rubbed his beard, thinking. He was getting a headache, thinking about everyone he suddenly needed to stop or kill.

"I'll take care of him," Heden said. That would be easy. Well, easier than the bishop at least.

Vanora deflated at that. She didn't want to hear more about Heden going out to risk his life.

"What if this never stops?" she asked. She suddenly felt cold, she hugged herself. "What are you going to do? You can't kill every evil pigfucker in the city."

More silence, but it was shrinking. Heden crossed the room and stood before her. She looked away.

"Don't say pigfucker," Heden said quietly.

Vanora shrugged.

"Do you want me to stay?" Heden asked. He couldn't leave without her permission.

She did. She absolutely did. She wanted it more than she'd wanted anything. But she was used to not getting everything she wanted. And she couldn't ask this of him. She couldn't explain why, she just couldn't.

"No," she said. "I just want you to come back."

Heden took a deep breath. "What did the polder say?"

Vanora looked up at him. Her eyes were dark. Guessing at his reaction, she didn't want to tell him.

"He said to tell you…the Ghoul was only the beginning."

Heden pursed his lips.

"I see," he said coldly. "Well," he took a deep breath. "Listen to me…,"

Vanora nodded.

"These people," Heden said, "all these people. They don't know what I can do. I'm tougher than they think," he was trying to reassure her and she knew it. But she also saw something, some truth there. Something that hadn't been there before he went into the forest. Something new.

"It's going to be hard, when I leave but…I've dealt with worse things than the count and the polder and the bishop." That was mostly true. The bishop was the biggest unknown.

"I don't suppose…," Heden began. Vanora looked at him.

"I am *very* hungry," he said, as though ashamed to admit it.

Vanora smiled a little at him.

"I mean this is an inn, right? You have been serving people my food?"

She smiled in spite of herself and got up.

When she tried to walk past him without saying anything, he reached out to her. She instantly grabbed him, and they stood there, each embracing the other. He was only a little taller than her, but he felt like a titan to her, and she felt like a little girl to him.

Eventually they disengaged and she walked to the door.

"I still have some powerful friends in this city," he said, and she stopped. He was still trying to reassure her, but she saw he was clenching his fists. Something about the polder, something about what Vanora had told him, had added to his anger.

"Well, one less in a little while," he said, as she walked out of the room.

Chapter Twenty-three

"Get up," the king snapped. "You only do that here when you're feeling guilty."

"Sorry my liege."

"Stop it," the king scowled.

"Yes my lord. I forget."

"No you don't." The room was small, too small for any furniture. At best only four people could stand comfortably. At the moment, it was just King Richard and his spymaster. The stone walls sweated in the cool air.

The spymaster stood up and straightened his outfit. He was an actor, first and foremost. A man of many parts. For this meeting, he knew to play the deferential servant. He had been careful not to dress more stylishly or more expensively than his king, for once. The table and rack outside held the king's finery and the two men stood as equals, or as nearly so as a king could.

King Richard was somewhat less inspiring without his crown, his rings or his cape. That was the point of this room. He looked smaller in here. Dressed in the plainest clothes he owned, he appeared thoughtful, not regal. His hair was still long, thick, and luxurious, swept back in a natural wave. A deep coppery red that looked almost black in the shadows of the candlelight. His natively black skin, by contrast, looked dusky, like dark earth in the lamplight. No windows in this room.

It was safe to talk in the small chamber because an ancestor of the king's had destroyed a powerful artifact and embedded its fragments in the walls to prevent any spell or prayer from revealing the room within. Protection from spells could be accomplished by more common means, but keeping the eyes of the gods out of the room was far more difficult. For this reason, it was called the Godblind.

"I didn't realize I was that obvious, you're very perceptive…"

"Stop performing. I have to hold court in a turn and a half and it takes half a turn just to get down to this damned place." the king appeared to notice his master of assassins for the first time. His face looked like he'd taken on five men, and lost. It was lumpy and covered in bruises. By the king's estimation, the fight had taken place days ago.

"Black gods man, what happened to you?"

"The Arrogate has returned to the city, my lord."

The king blinked, parsing this statement. "Heden?"

"Yes, my lord."

"He's alive?"

"Yes, sire."

The king took a steady breath. "Good," he said. "You said he was dead."

"I said I *thought* he was dead."

"That's true, you wouldn't commit. What happened?"

"The Green Order has been disbanded."

"That's unfortunate," the king snapped. "Can they be recalled? Restored to duty? They may be the only…."

"They're dead, sire."

The king stopped breathing for a moment. "All of them?" The spymaster remained silent.

King Richard ran a hand over his thick mane of hair. "Did he…do you have any reason to believe that Heden…."

"That he killed them?" His spymaster had not considered this. "There's no way to know. But it would be grossly out of character, my lord."

"For the man we knew. The man who's been holed up in that inn for three years?"

"I stand by my statement, sire."

"Mm. I tend to agree. Has he reported back to the bishop?"

"Not yet, my lord."

"And why has he not?"

The spymaster took a breath and composed himself. "Sir, according to Heden, whatever happened in the wode was ordered by the bishop."

The king frowned, his head darted around as he tried to place his information in line with what he already knew.

"Are you saying…Conmonoc *ordered* Heden to *assassinate* the Green Order?"

"No my lord. I mean to say…rather, it's possible, but that is not my interpretation. I don't have all the facts yet."

"You so rarely do." It wasn't a real complaint, they both knew. Just frustration bubbling over.

The spymaster considered how to respond. "Something happened in the forest, my lord."

"What do you mean?"

"I mean…something happened to him, to Heden. Something…something changed him."

"Is he injured? Is he…."

"No, my lord. It's…I know of no other way to say it sire. The difference is one of character."

"It worries me when you speak of issues so far outside your brief. Like *character*."

"It worries me too, sire."

"Do try to be more specific."

"He has purpose. He…sire do you remember when you chose Cathe?"

"That was years ago, man."

"You asked us what we thought? I said Cathe was a good man, a good priest, and loyal. But if it came to war with King Adric, Cathe would be overwhelmed."

"I remember."

"Do you remember what you said to me, sire?"

The king didn't speak for a few moments, the import of his spymaster's words sinking in.

"I said if it came to that, if it came to war, we had Heden."

"You wouldn't have said that a month ago. You wouldn't have said it three years ago. But this…this is that man. Like he's returned from the dead, from four years dead. We wanted him out of the inn? He's out."

The king ruminated on this, then remembered who he was talking to. "You say this as though it is a cause for concern."

The spymaster hemmed and hawed, seemed to want to duck the question. "Things are at a delicate state, my lord. If the bishop was ready to move against the Green that means his plan in finally ready and I don't think we are. Not without more intelligence. Heden…Heden *angered*…he could destroy everything."

"How is it you know this? You spoke with him?"

"He found me, my lord."

"Indeed? Does that seem as remarkable to you as it does to me?"

"Perhaps not. He was a priest, he has resources."

"What is it you're not telling me?"

The spymaster looked at his shoes. "It was the first thing he did upon returning to the city."

"Find you."

"Yes sire."

"Find you and confront you." The king took a step back in amazed realization and looked his man up and down. "*Heden* did this to you?"

"Yes sire," the spymaster stroked his still-tender jaw absently. "I was in mortal danger, my lord. I don't mind admitting it."

"By Cavall. I'll have him brought to me. I don't know what happened between you, but I'll smooth it over. If you're right—and I'm inclined to trust you on this matter—he might be able to take care of the bishop on his own."

"I…that's what he intended to do, my lord. I dissuaded him."

"Black gods man, why?"

"If Conmonoc is moving now, it may mean he no longer

120

fears what we can do. In which case Heden would waste himself in the attempt."

The king thought about this. "We could be being too cautious. I respect your decision but…" the king peered at his servant. "How did you dissuade him?"

It was going to come out sooner or later.

"I told him who really runs the Darkened Moon. I told him the Truncheon was a front."

"You…!" The king composed himself before he could explode. He paced across the cramped room and then spun and pointed rudely at his spymaster. "The precedent that allows you to speak freely to me here without fear of retribution is not a law, not a tradition. It is little more than a *habit*. I am reminding you of this because right now I am very close to having you arrested for treason."

"I needed to tell him something, to shock him. Otherwise he'd have gone straight for the bishop."

"In which case either he would neatly solve our problem by destroying the bishop, or Conmonoc would destroy him but *no risk to us in either case!*" Just as the spymaster was free to speak, the king was free to get blisteringly angry, something he never did outside this room.

"Yes my lord," the spy had trouble admitting this. "But I judged in that moment that he had value to us."

"Even though it meant exposing your…our…*my* entire network. Years of work. Dozens of men! Their lives now in the hands of a man beholden to no one! A man who nearly went mad with grief!"

The king seethed at his servant who stood unflinching in the face of his master's rage.

"The only reason I let you talk me *into* taking over the Moon was because I thought it was a chance for those poor bastards to redeem themselves! That was *your* idea!"

The spymaster had no answer for this.

"I submit to you," the king said, "that as my master of assassins and the secret head of the Moon it was in your best interests, and mine, and the organization's and the kingdom's to *let* Heden make his run at the bishop and see what happened. You let personal affairs blind you."

"I felt…sire, such a calculation had not escaped me. But I reasoned that should I, acting for you, loose Heden on the bishop unawares, as nothing more than a gambit, then I would be risking the life of a man you've counted on before. A loyal one, if I may say so. And one who counted you as a friend once. I felt…I felt he'd earned it, my lord. And for me to act then as you entreat me to act now would mean we are no different than the men who plot against us."

The king was affected by this. The spymaster pressed the advantage.

"He saved your life, my lord."

The king flinched. "That is a low blow, I must say."

Richard thought. Reached a conclusion.

"I accept your admonishment. I spoke hastily. And we do not yet know that your choice wasn't the right one. Perhaps he can be converted to our cause."

The two men stood, neither speaking.

"Tell me everything that happened between the two of you," the king said. "Starting with how he found you. And quickly, man. I've court in a few moments."

"He found me at my tailor's shop."

Chapter Twenty-four

Gwiddon walked into his tailor's shop and closed the door behind him.

"Well now, Maddoc, I hope you have a week free for I am in dire need of...." He stopped. He looked at Maddoc the tailor. The man was shaking, terrified.

Gwiddon's skin went all over goosebumps and he tensed. In a flash, so quickly the tailor would never be able to accurately recount what he saw, Gwiddon's hand went to his rapier and, anticipating the gesture, a hand from behind him grabbed his wrist and pulled, yanking him around and off balance.

As he turned, he fell forward. By the time he regained his balance, he had already been disarmed by...

"Heden!"

He was dressed in his campaigning outfit, his breastplate grey and badly dented. The lines on his granite face were deeper and his eyes looked dead. His hands were clenched into fists like stone bludgeons. He looked like the end of the world. Like a god of battle fresh off a bloody battlefield.

"The thief," Heden growled. "Who does he work for?"

"I don't..who are you talking..."

"The polder!" Heden barked. "You and the bishop were the only people who knew I was in the forest. One of you sent the polder to make sure the Order was stopped. In case I failed! You sent an assassin to clean up after me!"

"Heden, Llewellyn hears me when I say this; I have *no idea what you're talking about*. Cavall's teeth, you look like something ate you and then shit you out again."

A light exploded behind his eyes and the next thing he knew, he was on his ass. His jaw felt numb, and he was looking up.

Black gods he can hit, Gwiddon thought. He touched his face, felt no sensation from his skin, saw blood on his hand when he pulled it away. He might have blacked out for a few moments.

"Heden," Gwiddon said again, his mouth wasn't working properly. "Does anyone know you're…."

The arrogate reached down and grabbed him, pulled him back up. Gwiddon grabbed Heden's arm but was unable to twist it away. Heden waited until Gwiddon stopped struggling.

"I'm going to ask you some questions." Gwiddon betrayed no reaction at this. "Then I'm going after the bishop." Gwiddon bared his teeth and sucked in his breath in alarm, but said nothing. This was a dangerous play and if Gwiddon didn't do everything exactly right, he and Heden could both end up dead.

"Heden," Gwiddon attempted.

The Arrogate let go of Gwiddon at the same time he punched him again. Harder than the last time, but this time Gwiddon was ready. He fell against the counter his tailor did business on, then slumped to the ground.

"Wait," Gwiddon said, putting up his hands ineffectually. His head swam, his jaw was going numb. Another hit like that, and Heden might break it.

The arrogate stepped forward and grabbed Gwiddon by his expensive ruff once again, pulled the man up again. It was easy. Though a little taller, Gwiddon was nothing like as heavily-built as Heden.

"Why are you doing this?" Gwiddon asked. He needed information.

"You sent me into the Iron Forest, remember?" Heden asked. Gwiddon tried to stand up, but the connection between his mind and his legs wasn't operating. Two hits from Heden and he was already mildly concussed.

"I did," Gwiddon said, breathing heavily. "And I'd do it again. I thought you were our only chance."

Heden hit him again, this time in the stomach. Gwiddon wasn't prepared, and the blow drove the air from his lungs. He gasped, tried to gulp air.

Heden released him and he crumpled to the ground.

"Was it you, or the bishop?"

Gwiddon held up a hand.

"He…gods," Gwiddon's eyes wouldn't focus, his ears rung. "He said he wanted you, but thought you'd say no. I said I could talk you into it."

Heden grabbed him again, lifted him up, and hit him again. There was a crunching sound. Blood erupted. Gwiddon's broken nose was crushed, he couldn't breathe.

"Gods please," Gwiddon said, his mouth having trouble forming the words.

"You were right," Heden said. "He was wrong and you were right. And now a thousand people are dead. That's what you wanted, right?"

Gwiddon stared up at him, his eyes watering from pain. Heden swam in his vision. "What happened in the forest?" he asked.

Heden clucked his tongue. "Ask your master. Ask the bishop."

"I can't!" Gwiddon shouted, his face smashed. "You don't… what happened to the Green Order?"

"They're dead," he said, looking down at his friend.

"They're…*all* of them?" Gwiddon was sprawled on the ground, looking up at Heden, one eye was closing, tears from pain and shock streamed down his face, his nose and mouth were bleeding all over his white ruff. Heden was like a stone statue about to topple over and crush him.

"They're all dead Gwiddon. And you know why."

"I don't."

"I think you do."

"I swear to you, I don't. You're an arrogate damn you, am I lying to you?!"

Heden shrugged. "You're lying about something," he said. "I

guess it doesn't matter what anymore."

Heden knew it wasn't really Gwiddon he was angry with. He'd punished Gwidd enough. He turned to leave.

"Have an acolyte look at your face," Heden said. "Before your eyes swell shut. I'm going to go deal with the bishop now. Avenge some people."

"You can't!" Gwiddon called out. Heden opened the door.

"Maybe not," he admitted. "But he's an old man. I'll give him a few surprises."

Standing in the doorway, fully expecting to die fighting the bishop, or hang for his murder, Heden turned to his friend sprawled on the floor of the tailor's shop.

It had been four years since the two of them were really friends. All the time in the inn, Heden was basically a ghost. Friend to no one. But they'd once liked each other quite a lot.

"Goodbye Gwidd," Heden said, and walked away, leaving an empty doorway and bright light streaming in.

"Heden I'm the king's man!" Gwiddon shouted. His white teeth covered in blood. This was his last gambit. He had to shock Heden out of his murderous rampage.

Moments passed. Then a silhouette in the doorway.

"What?" Heden asked.

"I'm King Richard's spymaster," Gwiddon repeated. He could barely see. The whole center of his face was broken. He looked like four men had worked him over.

Heden walked back into the shop, pulled the door closed behind him. He could tell Gwiddon wasn't lying.

"You're…," Heden said, trying to absorb it.

Gwiddon stood up. Swayed, blood and spit oozing in a long slow drip down his lip to the floor.

"That's impossible," Heden said.

Gwiddon just shook his head. Used a jacket sleeve to wipe the blood from his mouth, then shrugged and pulled his jacket off revealing the expensive white shirt beneath, already stained with blood.

"That's impossible," Heden reiterated, trying to order the facts in his head.

"Alaric is a front," Gwiddon said.

"That's not…," Heden said, and raised both his hands like he were warding something off. "Richard's spymaster is the Truncheon," Heden said.

"How…," now it was Gwiddon's turn to be astonished. "Who told you that?"

"I spent a year in that fucking war of assassins in Capital!" Heden shouted.

Gwiddon went still. "The Wire," he whispered.

"He tried to have me killed!" Heden pointed at Gwiddon. The rest of his hand a clenched fist.

"He told me he feared *no man*," Heden was yelling now, his arm shaking. "*But the Truncheon*."

"I didn't know you knew," Gwiddon said.

"And then he told me who the Truncheon was!"

Gwiddon shook his head. "I'm sorry Heden."

"Why do you seem like you're telling the truth Gwiddon?!" Heden shouted.

"Because I am."

"That's…I've *met* the Truncheon!"

Gwiddon shook his head.

"Another front. A stand-in." He pulled out another handkerchief reflexively. Pressed it to his face for no real reason. "The man I send to meet the men I cannot be seen to meet with."

"You're the bishop's adjutant," Heden said, as though stating it clearly would make it true again. As though reality were slipping away and his words were a prayer that would put it back. "You," he reeled, "you spy on the king for the bishop."

"No," Gwiddon said. He pulled out a handkerchief and pressed it against his face. "I infiltrated the bishop's organization twelve years ago."

"Twelve…." Heden echoed faintly. Was it possible?

"None of us knew how far I'd be able to take it. Becoming his attaché was just…lucky," he finished lamely. The man's fine words now sounded thick and low. He pulled the handkerchief away and looked at the blood. He threw the soiled cloth away.

"You mean…" Heden said, "when we met…."

"I'm sorry. You should know the truth." Gwiddon swayed in the middle of the shop, blood spattered on the floor.

"You can't be," Heden said. "There's no way you can be the king's spymaster and the bishop's and run an entire thieves' guild on the side! It's absurd!"

Gwiddon looked at the floor. "It's easier than you think. And the more power I have, the easier it gets. I don't get a lot of sleep," he said.

"Who else knows?" Heden wondered out loud. "The Truncheon…the man I met, does *he* know? Is he just a fucking actor?"

"'Course he knows. I picked him. He's good. Looks the part, that's all that's important. Says the right things."

Heden just stared at Gwiddon. Gwiddon, exhausted as much from the moral dilemma as the beating he'd taken, slumped back to the ground.

"It's just a name," he said with a shrug. Beaten, bloody, crumpled in a heap, Gwiddon looked pathetic. He was contrite. Ashamed. He was confessing to being one of the most powerful men in the city, and he was ashamed he'd had to lie to his friend. "A reputation. It's not me."

Neither man looked at the other. But there in the small room, Heden was aware of how bloody Gwiddon was, and realized something. If this was the Truncheon, then he could have defended himself.

"I almost beat you to death," Heden said, looking down at his friend. Seeing the damage he'd done to him. He wasn't sure what was happening, he didn't know what he thought. He just said the words that came into his head.

"Why didn't you…if you're the Truncheon, why didn't you try to stop me?"

"I'm telling you, I'm not the man you imagine. I'm not an assassin. It's all…politics and double dealing. I'm just a man."

Heden knelt down and prayed over Gwiddon. The man shivered, and his wounds began to heal. Flesh repaired itself, broken ribs and nose knotted back into place. But he was still wet with blood and sweat. He'd be fine in an hour, but he'd walk through the city looking like he'd been beaten within an inch of his life.

Gwiddon ran his fingers over his newly healed and still tingling face. "Thank you," he said, lamely. Heden stood and offered his friend a hand. Gwiddon took it. Heden pulled him up and they stood there for a moment, hands clasped.

"Heden if anyone ever found out that I run the Moon… even the castellan, if he found out those men are all secretly agents of the king, all those men's lives are at risk. I told you who I am because you deserved to know the truth," Gwiddon said.

"The truth?" Heden repeated, unsure now what that word meant. Gwiddon and Heden had come up together. Both in the church. Both servants of Cavall. Gwiddon had been one of the few who hadn't deserted Heden after Aendrim.

"No one can know I'm the king's man, Heden," Gwiddon repeated. "Men would die, good men."

Heden reeled at the magnitude of the conspiracy. He pressed his palm against his forehead. "No wonder Richard doesn't have any enemies. You've got a third of the thieves in the city spying for him. Do they…do they know they work for the king?"

"They work for *me*," Gwiddon corrected. "None of them know who my master is and if anyone found out…."

Heden nodded. "And me too. Me too. I'm part of that fucking network of yours, aren't I?" He was getting mad now.

For some reason, this comforted Gwiddon.

"Heden, they think they're criminals, but they secretly work for the king. You of all people should…"

"*Aren't I?*" Heden barked. His voice bounced around the small room.

"…yes," Gwiddon admitted. "Richard likes you, Heden. He asks for you."

"You're saying when I…when the bishop sent me…."

"Don't," Gwiddon warned.

"Was I…?" Heden's world was unraveling.

Gwiddon held his hands out as though trying to will Heden to stop this line of thought. "There's no point in…."

"How often was I working for the king, Gwiddon!?"

"There's no answer to that," Gwiddon said, so matter of factly that Heden believed it. "You can't ask and I can't answer. Best not to think about it. bishop or the king. It was my judgment every time."

"Best not to think about it," Heden repeated dully.

"The Moon is my network. I use it how I see fit. Heden," he was pleading with his friend for understanding. "Heden *overwhelmingly* the church and king's interest are the same."

"Like me," Heden said. "I was your tool to use. As you saw fit."

"The king trusts you," Gwiddon repeated. It looked to him as though Heden were being physically crushed under the weight of this revealed truth.

"You *like* the king," Gwiddon pleaded softly. His face still ached, was still swollen, but he felt like he was the one who'd administered the beating, and Heden the victim.

"You don't understand," Heden's face was expressionless. Dead.

"After Aendrim…after everything that happened you were the only one…," he couldn't say it all in one go. Not for the first time, he wished he'd died in the Wode, and Taethan had lived.

He felt like he was living a false life in a false world. The wrong world. He had no meaning, no substance here but the horrible awareness that in the right world, he'd be dead and Taethan would be alive and everything would be right.

"We were friends still," Heden said, dully. "You were my friend after Aendrim, the only one."

Gwiddon's heart went still as he realized the manner in which his lie was destroying his friend, in a way he'd never planned on. For a while, no one spoke. But as he had many times before, Gwiddon put the work first and delayed payment on another debt.

"The Green Order," Gwiddon pressed.

Heden ignored him.

"How did they die Heden?"

Heden hurled a look of fury and blinding rage at Gwiddon.

"Best not to *think* about it!" he lashed out.

Gwiddon flinched and shrunk. Heden remembered the savage beating he'd just given his friend.

"I'm sorry," Heden said.

"Heden. I have to know. The Truncheon needs to know."

Heden shook his head. "I don't know. It's got something to do with an army of urq. A big army. The bishop ordered the Green to stand down. He ordered them to let the urq march." He spoke, but the words had no emotion or humanity in them. "Probably the first order they'd ever received from the bishop. They didn't know what to do with it. But they couldn't disobey. They thought disobeying the hierarch would…it was a kind of madness. An order they had to obey, and couldn't obey. It drove them mad."

Gwiddon appeared to process this.

"Doesn't matter," Heden said.

"It might," Gwiddon corrected. "Where were the urq marching…."

"I'm going to stop him, Gwiddon."

"You can't," Gwiddon shrugged.

"I'm going to avenge the death of those knights, the people at the keep," Heden said, and looked out a window for no reason. He wasn't seeing anything. "He killed them. When he gave the order not to stop those urq, he murdered them just like I'm going to...," he couldn't finish the thought. For some reason, he thought of Vanora.

Gwiddon looked at his friend and saw a man he almost didn't recognize. Gwiddon had known Heden forever, but right now he had no idea what Heden would do, what he could do. The bishop was one of the most powerful men in Vasloria, but Heden seemed capable of anything right now.

"Heden listen to me," it was Gwiddon's turn to grab his friend. "Listen to me! Your way won't work. He'll eat you alive, Heden. He'll *eat you alive*." Gwiddon was desperate to impress this reality onto his friend.

Heden didn't react, but didn't pull away.

"The only way we can bring him down," Gwiddon said, "is to surround him. He needs to see that he has enemies on every side, that there's nowhere he can turn. He's got too much power to...."

Heden pulled his arm away, and turned his dead eyes to Gwiddon. Gwiddon held his gaze. Then he stepped back. He looked at Heden and saw something. A commitment he knew meant Heden would take this as far as it would go, and nothing in twenty years of campaigning had yet stopped him. Heden had sworn to kill the bishop. An oath to himself, and he was about to fulfill his oath, or die trying.

Gwiddon tried to explain, knowing even as he said it, it didn't matter.

"He will deploy his agents. And they will hire men and those men will hire men and soon every hand in the city will be turned against you. And none of them will even know who they're working for."

"He can try," Heden said. "Maybe he'll order you to kill me."

This sparked some realization in Gwiddon.

"Heden you've got to report to him."

"I'm leaving now Gwiddon. I don't know what's going to happen to me, but you get to live with yourself. Punishment enough."

"Heden in Llewellyn's name will you *listen to me*? You *can't* confront him. You have to report to the bishop, tell him what happened in the wode. If you don't, he'll begin to suspect you're against him. He needs to think his plan is working. By Cyrvis' thorny prick, you were a campaigner for twenty years, *think*. How would you take down a man like the bishop? How would you do it if you weren't blinded by rage?!"

This seemed to have some effect.

"You don't see it, do you? Heden I don't know what happened up there, but you've got to start thinking. What does it *mean*? He's been leading the church since before you were born."

Heden turned slowly to look at his friend, afraid of where this was going.

"And he does not. Follow. Cavall."

"He…," Heden couldn't hold the idea in his head. It was too big. "He's chosen by Cavall."

"No! That's just it! Everyone says that, but he's chosen by the rectors *in camerata*. In secret! He's *elected* by the secret rectors. That's why I was…." He stopped.

Heden saw it. "That's why you were put into the church," he said. "That's why the king sent his spy to the church. You were there to find out how the bishop was chosen."

Gwiddon stepped back.

"And you did." A calm washed over Heden. It frightened Gwiddon. "You're a good spy, Gwidd. You always were."

The two men stood there, looking at each other as friends for the last time. Both of them knew it.

"What are you going to do?" Gwiddon asked.

"I'll report in," Heden said, but it was no concession. "You're right. I can't just…kill the bishop. Not right now at least, and not alone. I'll need help."

"I can…."

"Not you," he said. "Not anymore. From now on if the king wants me he can send Cathe or Alaric," the man everyone thought was the king's spymaster. "Because as of right now I don't talk to you. If I ever see you again, if you ever come to the inn…." Heden left it at that.

Gwiddon nodded. He knew it would end like this.

"The polder," Heden demanded. "Who is he?"

"I'm not sure," Gwiddon tried to push his blood-matted hair out of his face. "It could be Aimsley Pinwhistle."

Heden frowned, shook his head. He didn't know this name.

"In rough terms he's your opposite number inside the Hearth. He's the Brick's fixer," Gwiddon said.

"The Brick. The Cold Hearth. I'll deal with him first."

He turned and walked to the door.

"Heden," Gwiddon pleaded. "What happened up there? What happened to the Green Order? What happened to you?"

Heden's mouth was open as though paused in the middle of a word, his eyes looked at something only he could see. Eventually, he blinked and came back to reality. He reached out and grabbed the door latch and opened it. Noise and light and air filled with the smell of the city flooded in. Heden was framed in bright sunlight. He was just a silhouette to Gwiddon.

Heden walked out the door, leaving Gwiddon broken and alone.

CHAPTER TWENTY-FIVE

Calvus peered over his ink formulation at the spectacle before him.

"You look like shit," the alchemist said.

"Enh." Aimsley Pinwhistle lurched off the door frame separating the alchemical laboratory from the rest of the apothecary.

Calvus stoppered the open vials before him, and stood up. The fixer obviously needed help.

"You can't come here, Fixer. I can't help you. I shouldn't even know this has been done to you, you're putting the whole operation in danger."

Aimsley slumped in a chair. Half his face looked like it had been melted and repaired, It had the tell-tale sign of pinkness, newness. Some of his hair was missing, giving him a more roguish, less youthful look than the alchemist was used to.

"I need you to fix this," he said, extending his right arm. It was covered in glittering welts. His leather armor was torn apart all along his right side, Calvus assumed the red welts extended across his chest as well.

"I can't," Calvus said simply. "You can't even be here, you know that. You've got your own network, that's *why* you've got your own…," he stopped. "Get out," he said flatly.

Aimsley's breath was ragged.

"I saw Iordoros," Aimsley grunted. "He fixed me up best he could. I can see out of my left eye again," he said with a sneer. "But this," he continued, nodding at his arm. "This is, ahh..."

Calvus began packing up his things.

"And it's getting worse," the polder said.

"Can't help you," Calvus said. "You know the rules."

"The ragman's rules," Aimsley sneered.

Calvus stabbed a finger at him. "Brick's rules. Your rules. You and Brick *created* the fixer to *subvert* the castellan's agreement and now you've got to pay for it."

Aimsley coughed up blood.

"Your wife," Aimlsey said.

"What about her?" Calvus stopped picking up his equipment.

"You remember last year, when your house burned down?" Aimsley asked.

Calvus didn't say anything. He was breathing faster.

"That was Brick's idea. Punishment for failing him on the…"

"I know what it was for," Calvus said, tightly.

"That was me," Aimsley said. "You didn't know that, did you? Your wife was out of the house when it happened, you ever think about that? You ever wonder why? How often does she leave in the middle of the night Calvus?"

"That was you," Calvus said.

"Of course it fucking was, you think Brick wanted any survivors? What would have been the point of that, he wanted you to *suffer*."

"I always wondered how…," Calvus looked up at the ceiling, his eyes were red. "I thought it was a miracle."

"It was a miracle," Aimlsey said. "It was a fucking miracle I found a way to get her out without anyone knowing, without Brick suspecting."

"Why would you do that?" Calvus challenged, his voice thick. "Why would you save her? Why would you give a shit?"

Aimsley coughed. More blood. He spoke like he was ashamed. "You're the one fucked up. She didn't do nothing."

Calvus stared at him. Shook his head. Put a monocle in one eye and pulled up a stool. Sat down beside the polder. Looked at him with his unmagnified eye. "Then I owe you more than this," he said, bending down an examining Aimsley's arm.

Aimsley relaxed. It was working. He'd banked these little miracles for the day when the arrangement between the guilds failed. He wondered if Garth and Noor had done the same thing. Probably. He watched the alchemist work.

Calvus looked more like an abbot than an alchemist. He was fat, bald, and looked made of lard. But he didn't act like a complete prick all the time, so Aimsley didn't mind his appearance. The polder liked the alchemist as far as that went.

The Cold Hearth's mixer finished his examination, came to a conclusion. He looked up at Aimsley Pinwhistle with some alarm. "You got in a fight with a wizard."

"Heh," Aimsley said.

"Who was it?" Calvus got up and went to his desk. Opened a drawer and started selecting tools.

"Oh, you know," the polder stretched out in the chair. He was sore all over and exhausted. He looked like he wanted to go home and sleep. A well-known side effect of being healed by the priestly arts. "One of those big wizard shits. I don't remember their names."

"Balls," Calvus said into his drawer.

"Yeah," Aimsley admitted. Wasn't sure why he tried to avoid the issue in the first place. "Hapax. Listen, you got anything to drink in this place?"

The alchemist, half a dozen thin metal tools in his hand, stood up from his desk sharply.

"You got in a pissing match with Hapax Legomenon?!"

"Uh," Aimsley scratched his nose. "Yeah. Found out some stuff though. Worth it, probably. Long as, you know, it stops at this," he indicated his own arm and face.

"She know who you work for?"

"Not sure I know who I work for half the time," Aimsley said. "I'll take whatever," he continued with his request. "I'll take mead, you got it."

Calvus tucked the small metal implements into a pocket in his robe, and poured a small glass of ale for his guest. Then remembered who his guest was, and poured the glass back into the bottle.

He carried the bottle over and handed it to the polder, who took it without saying anything and put it to his lips. He downed half the bottle in one long pull. Only stopping to breathe like he'd just surfaced after being underwater for hours.

"You got out of there ok, I see," Calvus said. He angled his head to look at Pinwhistle's face. "Looks like she burned you pretty bad. You been burned enough, think you'd have gotten tired of it by now. So how did this happen?" he asked, tapping the polder's injured arm. The alchemist began the laborious process of carefully picking out the pieces of crystal.

"There was a lot of…you know, fire and stabbing. Got my own in," Aimsley said with another sneer. "Figure she's seeing a priest too. Ow."

Calvus pulled out the first tiny glittering, blood-dappled projectile. It was shaped like a tiny spiked glass ball. He deposited it in a metal bowl, along with an identical one. "Uh-huh," he said, only half paying attention. "Then what?"

"All I know is," Aimsley said, taking another drink, "she pulled out some kind of stick—looked like a chair leg—and gabbled at me some more. Whole place exploded in glass. I mostly got away, but…," he nodded at his arm. "Iordos couldn't do anything about it. Said I should see a farrier. Heheh."

"Good advice," Calvus raised his eyebrows. "Someone with proper tools for pulling stuff out of hooves. But," he said, dropping another piece into the bowl, "this isn't glass."

"What is it?" Aimsley asked.

"Diamond," Calvus said, holding one up and showing it off. "These little things will worm under your skin, cut everything under there up. Your skin will heal, but eventually they'll dig down into the bones in your arm and it'll die from the inside."

"Wonderful," Aimsley said. "Good thing I've got friends in low places."

"Won't have friends anywhere, you pull another stunt

like that." About half the little spiked diamonds were out of Aimsley's arm.

"It's my job," the polder said, taking another pull from the bottle of ale.

Calvus gave him a look before going back to work. "Not your job to shake down the Lens' quester."

"Got work to do," the polder said. "Need to know how the count is making deathless."

Aimsley hoped this statement would prompt curiosity from the alchemist. It did not have the desired effect.

"Oh, the night dust. Yeah that's a pisser."

Aimsley blinked, composed himself. "Word gets around."

"Well, you know," Calvus said. "Word don't have far to go around here."

That reminded Aimsley of something. Something nagged at him, but he couldn't put his finger on it.

"Tam," he remembered.

"Huh?" Calvus asked, prying another diamond orb free.

"Roderick Tam," Aimsley asked.

"I know him," Calvus said absently. "He was good."

"Was?"

"Haven't seen him for a while. Got in some kind of trouble with the Truncheon."

"Heh," Aimsley grunted. "Good to know. I can follow that. See if he's still with the Midnight Man. See if he's been traded. You talk to him?"

Calvus shook his head. "Not in years. He worked with some ratcatchers for a while. Paid him well but…dangerous work."

"Which ones?"

"Which one's what?" Calvus dropped another diamond into the bowl, there were dozens in there now, and a small pool of blood.

"Which ratcatchers?"

"The Fell Stroke. The Sunbringers. The Tapestry."

"Ok, that's something."

"You shaking me down, fixer?" Calvus asked with some amusement.

"Brick's orders," he said. "You're in the clear."

"Brick don't tell you to do shit."

"Well," Aimsley said, "Brick's forcefully worded suggestion. He was a little short with me."

Calvus laughed. Then stopped when he realized who he was talking to. Pulled the last diamond from Aimsley's skin.

"You're done," he said wiping his hands. "Now get out of here before someone…,"

Without warning, Aimsley darted up. Calvus didn't see him reach for anything, but suddenly there was a dirk in one hand, and a silver ball in another. He threw the small silver orb.

"Shit," a voice said from the thin air.

The silver sphere impacted the wall and flashed bright white as Aimsley leaped in front of the alchemist.

Three men in black were crouched against the far wall by the window. They had been invisible before.

"Hey boys," Aimsley said. "Busy night."

CHAPTER TWENTY-SIX

"Why'd you have to come here, Fixer?" one of the thieves in black asked.

Aimsley shrugged. "You were listening, Ulgar, you know why."

"You know we're going to have to kill you now," another thief asked.

"It's your dumb luck," Aimsley said to Ulgar, "that I was so fucked up when I came here, otherwise I'd have noticed you before I spilled everything to Calvus and you might have gotten out of...what did you just say?" Aimsley interrupted himself, turning slowly to the second of the three thieves and pointing at him.

Ulgar shrugged. "Sorry Fixer, we can't let you leave alive."

Aimlsey looked from one thief, to the other, and then the third.

"You didn't come here for me," he said.

None of them spoke.

"Calvus get downstairs," Aimlsey said.

There was no response from behind him, no word from the alchemist.

Aimsley looked at Ulgar and tilted his head. "You dumb son of a bitch," he said.

"It's not my fault!" Ulgar said. The other two, the thieves Aimsley didn't know, looked at the senior cutpurse.

"Did you get promoted to Black in about the last three days?" Aimsley asked. "Because then we're having a discussion, otherwise you're still Red and I have to fucking kill you because you just burned our alchemist," he said, turning and pointing to Calvus who was, in fact, dead from a poison dart in his neck, "*while* I was telling him what I've been doing all day!"

"Why are we talking about this?" one of the thieves asked. "Use the dust."

"Oh, right," Aimsley said. He had forgotten about the night dust. Three red scarves armed with a flotilla of deathless could probably make trouble for him.

Three black marbles hit the ground in front of him. He leaped back, past Calvus' dead body, and then flipped backward through the window, smashing it.

He heard the sounds of bone snapping and something, something that had been Calvus, snarling. He wanted to see what the effect of three of the marbles would be. But he had other fish to fry.

It had been three years since he'd needed to worry about carrying silvered weapons. He favored a silvered garrote in the old days. But if he was fast enough, if he could beat the red, he wouldn't have to fight the deathless.

He lunged in one inhuman leap from the cobbled street outside to the roof of the apothecary. *Lucky Calvus wasn't more successful.* A richer man would have had a two story shop.

He bounded across the starlit rooftop and, without looking, without time to look, he flung himself out and over the alley separating the apothecary from the building behind it.

Ulgar made the mistake Aimsley had counted on. A mistake no black scarf would make, probably no brown scarf would make. He assumed the alley would be clear, even though he could no longer see Aimsley.

Ulgar was the first out of the window, the same window the three thieves had come in through. He landed in a crouch, and had time to stand up before Aimsley fell on him.

He responded quickly, his training good, but he responded to the wrong threat. He went for his weapon, expecting the polder fixer to pull him to the ground and stab him.

But Aimsley Pinwhistle had a different idea. He latched onto Ulgar's neck, and rolled his body into a crouch as he fell past the thief, forcing the red scarf's back to arch in response.

He leveraged his weight and the fall to pull Ulgar up and backwards, throwing him back through the window. His body crashed into the next thief climbing out, knocking them both back inside the apothecary.

A moment later, and Aimsley was on his feet, dirks out, looking unblinking at the open window. But the chaos had already started. One of the other thieves, desperate to get out of the room, was climbing over Ulgar's prone body, trying to pull himself out the window. But he was caught on something, something else was pulling him down, stopping him from leaving.

The Deathless.

"Aahh!" he cried. "No! Nono!" He kicked and fought but black claws pulled him down. His eyes went wide, terrified.

"Fixer! Help!"

The thief was pulled down into the room. There was screaming and a sound Aimsley could only describe as a man being turned inside-out.

Aimsley pulled a water barrel over, upended it, stood on it, and shuttered the window from the outside. As he closed the wooden slats, he saw the body of Calvus, now a ghoul, ripping Ulgar apart. The thief was desperately stabbing at the thing to no avail. Then the ghoul cracked the thief's ribcage open.

The other two thieves were fighting with what Aimsley assumed were shades. Black shadows of twisting gas, too impatient to wait for the supply of dead bodies to increase on its own.

Aimsley wasn't that interested to find out what happened next. He wedged the shutters closed with his dirk, felt stupid for thinking that would make a difference, and ran out of the alley.

He was happy to let the Deathless feast on someone else, and felt no obligation to stop them.

Chapter Twenty-seven

He kicked the door open. It had been a long time since he'd done anything like that and after dealing with Gwiddon, it felt good.

The door to the Mousetrap flew open and one hinge came undone. As soon as he walked into the smoke-filled room, a dagger and a dart flew at him, bouncing harmlessly off his wards.

He strode into the room, spoke a prayer. The smoke became suddenly heavy and fell to the floor, revealing about three dozen thieves of various genders, ethnicity, and species in the common room.

A war-bred Urq stood up and swung a sword around. A prayer and Heden's arm flashed into stone. He deftly deflected the sword and then punched the urq in the chest. The huge demi-man flew back, knocking several waiting thieves down.

Heden pressed on. More thieves came. But Heden dispatched them. Their poisons failed, their blades betrayed them. For one moment, Heden's entire form appeared to flash into that of a cloud, as he avoided a sorcerous arrow, and then returned to his natural form.

He asked, and Cavall gave. Or was it Lynwen? What would happen when her patience finally ran out?

An army of thieves prepared to spend themselves against then. Then a basso voice from the far end of the room.

"Let him come!" The thieves melted away.

The huge, pale, bald man known as Brick, or The Brick, sat at a table against the far wall. He watched Heden neutrally as Heden strode toward him, kicked the table away from him, and grabbed the guildmaster's thick neck with his hand.

"You send a man to my inn again," Heden said, looking down at the man. "He dies."

Brick stood up. Heden was unable to stop him. He was tall and appeared able to ignore Heden's fist around his throat.

He placed a meaty hand on Heden's stone arm.

"You think you're the first priest to come in here?" he asked.

Brick was twisting Heden's stone arm away, slowly, but without any apparent exertion.

"Been in the game a long time," Brick sneered. "Long enough to know how to deal with one such as you."

"Heden," a voice said.

Brick's strength forced Heden to release his grip. His hand flew to the pommel of his sword.

A dozen swords were drawn and he heard the pull of bowstrings.

"You stay away from my inn, do you understand me?" he said, not drawing his sword. Cavall's favor was not endless.

"Well now, I may, or I may not," Brick said. "That's as depends. Because I got no idea who the fuck you are. But see, when I find out, if your inn happens to be of interest to me, then I will fucking take it. Or burn it down. Or kill everyone inside, or everyone you know, or whatever the *fuck* I feel like doing and there won't be anything you can do about it." Spittle was flying from Brick's mouth.

"Heden, come on," the voice at his elbow said. It sounded familiar, but it didn't register.

"I could kill you right here," Heden said to Brick.

"You think so? 'Cause I don't. You're a priest, and I ain't done nothing to you. So you're going to *stew* is what you're going to do. Because one such as you doesn't walk in here and kill anyone. Because one such as you needs a fucking reason. *Unlike* one such as me."

"Brick," the familiar voice said. "He don't mean nothing by it. He's out of his head. Come on," urged the voice down by Heden's elbow, and he felt something tugging at him.

He looked down.

It was the polder. Aimsley. Why was the polder trying to help him, if the Brick sent the polder to threaten him in the first place?

"Come *on*," he said, pulling Heden around to the back door.

"Now Aimsley here," Brick continued, "he's vouching for you at the moment. And I owe him. A *very little*," Brick stabbed a finger into Heden's chest. "But that's all your life is worth to me right now."

Confused, Heden let the polder pull him away a few steps.

"It's alright, Brick," Aimsley said. "I'll take care of it. No one's dead," the polder observed. "Let's keep it that way." At the polder's urging, Heden started walking to the door.

"You think you're getting away?" Brick sneered at Heden. Heden stopped.

"Come on!" Aimsley said, pulling at the arrogate. Two dozen thieves and assassins waited in the common room to see what would happen. The smoke began to rise again.

"Let me tell you how it goes, little priest!"

Heden allowed himself to be led from the room. He did not take his eyes off the huge bulk of the man called Brick. Guildmaster of the Cold Hearth.

"You come in here," Brick raged, "you think you can stand against us, because you're a man, a *righteous* man."

"This is the wrong fight," Aimsley said to Heden.

"But *nothing* stands against us!"

Aimsley pulled the priest to the door.

"First you bend!" Brick was howling now. Snarling. Heden turned and walked out the back door, the polder behind him.

"And then you BREAK!"

CHAPTER TWENTY-EIGHT

"Do you have any clue, I mean even the smallest fucking idea, what kind of shit you just stirred up?"

They stood alone in the long, thin alley that ran behind the back of the Mouse Trap. Aimsley paced. Heden stood and watched.

"I think I…"

"Shut up! I mean what kind of complete fucking hornets' nest of colossal fucking shit you just created?"

"I do."

"You don't! You don't and if you say you do one more time you're on your own, do you get it? I don't give a shit who you think your friends are, you fuck, because they're all gone now!" The polder gestured up into the air like waving at a bird flying away. "You pissed off the count and now you pissed off the Brick and your *own mother* would run the fuck away rather than be caught between them and you," the polder spat.

Heden kept his mouth shut and looked at the cobbles in the road, his brow furrowed. "Just the count," he said. "You'll keep the Brick off me." His eyes darted to the thief, afraid to make eye contact. Afraid to be wrong.

The polder stopped pacing and stared at the priest. Waiting for an explanation.

"I thought," Heden began. "I thought Brick sent you to my inn as a threat. Show you could get to me any time you wanted."

"What!?" the little man squeaked, so absurd was Heden's suggestion to him.

"I was wrong," Heden said. "I realize that now. I'm sorry."

The polder shook his head slowly in disgusted amazement.

"I swear by Saint Pallad you're the stupidest son of a bitch I ever met. No idea how you're still alive. None. Anyone ever say that to you before?"

"Yeah," Heden said, eyes still cast down.

"Well…" the thief paused in his excoriation. "They were right, whoever they were."

"Yeah," Heden said, nodding.

The polder paced across the alley. Heden looked at him. Watched the conflict in the thief. Couldn't put a name to it, but recognized it.

"Why did you help me? Why not let Brick and me go at it?"

Aimsley threw him a look. "Don't be stupid. Then I lose either way."

Heden waited for an answer to his first question.

Aimsley stopped pacing, but didn't look at Heden.

"You were a campaigner."

"A ratcatcher," Heden agreed.

"Who were you with?"

For a moment, Heden didn't want to tell him. If the thief wanted to know, then the information was valuable, could be traded. But it wasn't a secret. Everyone knew. Stupid to try and hide it.

"The Sunbringers."

Aimsley nodded. "I'm looking for an alchemist," he said.

"Tam."

"Ok," the thief said, giving no indication this was the alchemist he was looking for.

"I haven't seen him in five years. No idea where I would even look."

"Shit," Aimsley said, shaking his head. "Really thought I was on to something there."

"Maybe you were."

Now Aimsley looked at him. Studied his face. Unspoken between them, the fact that Heden gave up what he knew for nothing. Aimsley took a chance.

"You know about the Ghoul at your inn?"

"Yeah," Heden said. "But I don't know what you have to do with it."

Aimsley explained what he'd seen.

"The count can do that?" Heden asked, thinking about what it meant.

The small man nodded, his blonde curls bouncing. "And I think this Tam is behind it."

Heden sniffed. "Could be. Tam was good."

"Good enough to make these?" the thief asked. He pulled one of the small black marbles out of his vest and held it out.

Heden stepped forward and looked at it. Then reached out for it.

"Careful," the polder warned.

Heden glanced at him, nodded, and took the black marble. It was as Vanora described.

"I don't know," Heden said. "Was Tam good enough to create Deathless?" Heden was skeptical. "I doubt it."

Aimsley nodded. "So there's another piece of the puzzle."

Heden clenched the ball in his fist. "You're sure Tam's involved?"

"Yeah," he said. "I have a reliable source outside the guild." He absent-mindedly scratched his arm where the tiny glass beads had been imbedded.

Heden thought about what might have happened to Roderick Tam.

"He wouldn't be doing it of his own accord," Heden said.

Aimsley shrugged. "You haven't seen him in five years. A lot can change in five years."

"Not that much," Heden said.

Aimsley was pacing again, he threw Heden a look, disgusted at the priest's faith in his fellow man.

Heden went to give the black marble back.

"Keep it," the polder said. "I've got more. See what your network can make of it."

"I don't really have a network," Heden said lamely. Then thought of something.

"We should work together," he said.

"Ah," the polder said, pointing at Heden as he paced. Now it was the thief who wouldn't look at Heden. "No we should not."

"Seems like we should. We both want the same thing."

"Ah no we don't," the polder stopped and looked at Heden. Pointed at him as though he was dangerous. "I'm only after the night dust, *you* want to kill the count."

Heden shook his head. "I don't."

"You do."

"It's not about killing the count, it's about saving Vanora."

"You just said the same thing twice," Aimsley Pinwhistle said. "Except the second time, you sound like a complete fucking idiot who thinks he can…I don't know, persuade the count to doing something? Anything? He wants the girl, he gets the girl. You have nothing to bargain with."

Heden was looking at the cobbles at his feet. Thinking about what the polder said. He had a similar conversation with Gwiddon ten years ago. When he first learned Gwidd was a spy.

"Nothing to bargain with," he said. Aimsley watched him.

He looked at the polder. "If we knew where the night dust came from, we'd have something to bargain with."

"Stop saying 'we,' ok? Just stop it. I don't work for you, I work for the Brick…."

"You're the fixer. The fixer doesn't work for anyone."

"Don't try to be *clever*," the little man sneered. "You're not good at it."

"The night dust gives us the leverage we need…."

"No it doesn't! You don't get it! I'm not on your side! I'm not one of the good guys, I'm one of the bad guys! I don't give a shit about the night dust or the count! It's just the job. The Dust doesn't matter!"

"The count's going to use it to take over the city, to grind you down, how does it not matter?"

"It's just a tool! The dust upsets the balance between the guilds. It's my job to put things back the way they were. Maybe that means we get our own supply! Maybe we make a deal with the count! Who knows? It's just business. The dust just becomes part of the deal."

Heden frowned at this mercenary reasoning.

"So it's me against the count," Heden said. From the polder's view, the priest was just staring off into space, thinking. He didn't notice Heden was starting at the spire of the cathedral. Wouldn't have thought it was significant if he had noticed.

"The girl's not worth it," the polder said.

Heden took a deep breath. "If you say that again," the words came slowly, deliberately, "then we are enemies."

The polder stared at him for a long time. Then blinked and looked away. Nodded.

Heden took this as confirmation of everything he suspected about the thief.

"You and me," Heden said slowly, like he was sneaking up on a cat, "we can bring the count down." *And then, maybe....* Heden tried not to look at the cathedral again.

"And then what?!" the polder threw his hands up. "Are you really that stupid? The guild doesn't work for the count, *he* works for the guild!"

Heden frowned. "I don't understand."

Aimsley sighed. There were better things he could be doing, why was he here talking to this priest? "There's been a dozen Counts. There'll be a dozen more. When this one goes, there's another six guys I know, I *personally* know who will take his place in a heartbeat and will be just as bad. Worse. You can't just stop his heart and hope the entire organization collapses. It's not a *cult*." Cults, they both knew, typically only thrived as long as their charismatic leader thrived. "And the first item on the next Count's agenda? Guess!"

"You just told me I didn't have a choice. That I had to kill him to stop him coming after Vanora."

"No, I said you *can't* kill him, so what the fuck are we standing here talking about?"

Desperate, Heden tried another tack.

"So you do what the Brick tells you."

"As opposed to what? Do what *you* tell me to?"

"As opposed to doing what you *want*, what you think *should* be done. As opposed to doing what's *right*!"

"I'm the *fixer*!" Aimsley said, his title a shield. "I serve the guild!"

"You're outside the guild! You have to be or the king's Magus puts you under the Eye and turns you inside out until he knows the name of every agent in the Hearth!"

"I fix the problems the Brick can't handle. Right now, that's the dust."

"And what if it were the count?" Heden challenged.

"The Brick doesn't care about the count!" Aimsley threw his hands up. "He's happy with the count in his place! The Brick wants…."

"No, you! What do you want?!" Heden hurled Taethan's words in the forest at the polder. The same words Sir Taethan had used to assault Heden with.

The polder grabbed his head with his hands, trying to drive the echo of Heden's voice from out his head. "I want you to leave me the fuck alone! I want…," he threw his hands down and looked around as though seeing the alley for the first time. "I want a drink is what I fucking want."

Heden didn't press the issue. They stood there, neither knowing what they were in the middle of, or if it could go anywhere. Neither of them looked at the other.

"I'll keep the Brick off you, if I can," Aimsley said.

"Thanks," Heden said.

"No promises."

"I understand. I owe you."

Aimsley Pinwhistle gave no indication how he felt about this. He seemed reluctant to end the conversation.

"How'd things go in the forest?" the little man asked.

Heden found himself taking a deep breath. The reaction, the tightening of his skin, came on involuntarily.

"They're dead," he said. "The knights. All of them."

Aimsley shrugged. Business. "Did you kill them?"

Heden bared his teeth at the idea.

"Sorry," the polder said. "Well I figured something like that happened," Aimsley said. "When no one asked me to follow up, figured the Order was neutralized."

"Was that your instruction? Was that why you were following me?"

Aimsley waved a hand, dismissed Heden's line of questioning.

"Brick was doing a favor for someone, I don't know who. I don't know why. He doesn't tell me everything. Whatever it was, it's over now."

Heden turned finally to leave, took a few steps toward the mouth of the alley, and stopped. Confronted by the spire of the Cathedral looming over everything.

Heden looked at the Church. "Maybe not."

CHAPTER TWENTY-NINE

Heden looked at the stars.

"Gwiddon told me what happened," the bishop said.

Heden said nothing. Watched the constellations he knew wheeling slowly overhead through the open roof of the atrium. The ox and plow, the river and maid. Thought only of what a colossal fool he'd been.

"Or rather, told me as much as he knew, which he admitted was very little."

Heden looked down at his hand, turned it over slowly. Watched the bright, subtle interplay of starlight across the lines on his palm, the hairs on the back of his hand. Saw the sharp shadow his hand cast on the dirt below.

The starlight was bright enough to read by. Even though everything in the atrium was cast in violent white and black, to Heden's eye it seemed vibrant beyond color. He remembered a girl, a squire, and a hunt for urq under these same skies. Seeing Aderyn's face half in light, half in shadow. Wishing himself a younger man.

"Is this atrium enchanted?" he asked.

"You've never been here before?" The bishop asked.

Heden shook his head.

"No," the bishop smiled. "No these sculptures require… special light," he spoke lovingly over his creations, like someone nurturing a delicate flower.

There were something like a dozen glass life-sized sculptures sitting on the dirt of the atrium. Vines growing around their bases.

'Sculpture' was, Heden knew, not accurate. They were smooth columns of glass. Bright silver lines and points in each column glowed and caught the starlight creating powerfully lifelike images within. Unmoving, but seemingly possessed of motion. Men and women caught in an instant of action; talking, breathing, smiling, laughing.

Under normal light, torchlight, sunlight, moonlight, all one saw was transparent glass. Perhaps some smoke inside the glass. But under starlight, the glass disappeared and figures of sliver light sprang forth.

Heden looked up at the stars again. Wondered where the sun was.

It was just past noon by his reckoning.

And he thought he could walk in here and kill this man. This old man. This villain who'd given the order that destroyed the Green. Killed everyone at Ollgham Keep. This old man who'd blotted out the sun at midday just over this spot so he could work on his starlight images. Maybe the sun never shone here. Was he that powerful? To simply maintain such an alteration without any further effort?

The figures looked so real. Heden knew there was careful technique in crafting the starlight images, though he did not understand it. The man was an artist as well.

"Rector Ullwen," Heden said, looking at one sculpture. The only one he knew. Ullwen's sharp jaw and tiny point of a beard instantly recognizable. He'd met the man several times as a Sunbringer.

The bishop glanced over to the sculpture of Ullwen, and went back to his current work. Bent in close to the glass of an unfinished image. "Yes," he said, caressing the glass in some arcane manner. A pinpoint of light flared and moved deep within the crystal. "I'm glad you recognize him." The bishop's voice was quiet and distracted. Heden wasn't important. Only the image in the glass. "I paint them from memory, you see. Quite a tricky medium to work in, memory."

He straightened, stretched his back, and looked at Heden. "One is never sure, once the work is done, whether one remembers the man or the image in the glass."

"Mmm," Heden said, trying to avoid the bishop's gaze, for fear the older man would see something of the difference in Heden.

He'd come into the city determined to kill this man. A man who'd infiltrated the top of the country's largest church. Now, after the fall of Aendrim, the most powerful church in Vasloria. Was it all politics? He'd convinced himself of that on the way back, after leaving the forest. Convinced himself that this was just a normal man, schemed his way to the top, unable to command the power of a god.

"Do you…," he ventured looking again at the stars, looking for the sun, "reveal the stars when you come here or is this…?"

"Oh no," the bishop waved, dismissing the idea. "It's always like this here." He smiled, stepped forward, his tall, thin frame supporting his bishop's robes like a wooden rack.

Gwiddon said it. The man did not serve Cavall. Where did his power come from? There were few options. Cyrvis and Nikros, the Black Brothers were the most likely. Where was Cavall? His greatest saint, Llewellyn whose church this was? Why did they allow this man to….

That way led madness, Heden knew. He'd long ago given up understanding the politics of the gods and saints. Well before he'd met Lynwen.

The bishop approached Heden and removed a small holly sprig from his robes. Extended it to Heden.

Heden knew what it was, even before the bishop removed his hand. Nine milky white berries. Dywel, Cadwyr, Idris, Perren, Nudd, Brys, Isobel…Kavalen. Taethan. All dead. A three thousand year old tradition smashed. Taethan.

Taethan…

He took the holly from the bishop's hand, looked at it under the starlight.

"I'll…understand if you don't want to talk about it," the

bishop said. The bright white of the stars contrasted and conspired with the inky blackness to make the bishop's face seem more angular, more aqualine than it was.

Was he trying to be compassionate? Or did he simply not care. Worse, most frightening, was he actually compassionate? Which would make him the greater villain? Did it matter?

Heden was prepared, in any event.

"There's not much to talk about, your Grace," he deflected. He was good at that.

A practiced liar, Sir Dywel, the weasel, had called him.

That was unfair, Heden thought.

"Many things went unspoken between Gwiddon and I," The bishop said. "I know the man has long been your friend...," Heden laughed inwardly at this. "And I feared asking him questions he would feel compelled to answer, thereby breaking confidence with you."

Heden said nothing.

"If...if you had to...," the bishop started. Heden knew what was trying to say. *Let him say it*, he thought.

"If you had to kill them," the bishop finally ventured. "I understand. I trust you."

Heden only nodded. Looked at a light sculpture of a woman. "Thank you, your Grace," he said.

"He said something about an army of urq."

Heden nodded. "Yes your Grace." He glanced at the bishop. Tried to keep normal eye contact. Not act suspicious.

"Should we be alarmed? Do you have any idea where they went?"

This, Heden knew, had to be a question of some import. For he reasoned the army of urq was part of some plan. Thwarting the Green was part of that plan. Unleashing the dark power of the Wode on the lands of men. The sack of Ollgham Keep was, he suspected, just a test.

"No your Grace. They sacked a small town, and retreated

back into the forest best I can reckon.

The bishop nodded, as though this confirmed a suspicion. He changed subjects. Casually ran his hand down a light sculpture, admiring his work in the starlight.

"Am I right in recalling that you know the Duke of Baed?"

"Yes, your Grace," Heden said, taken somewhat off guard by the bishop's question.

"Personally?" the bishop asked.

"Yes, your Grace," Heden said. This seemed safe territory and so Heden relaxed a little. "He, ah…he counts me a friend, I think. He taught me a lot about…," Heden was going to say 'warfare,' but as it came to him, he realized he knew nothing about war. The Duke had taught him more important things. "A lot about living, your Grace." And how much of that had Heden done, these past 3 years? These past 20? How little accomplished.

"What kind of man is he, would you say?" The bishop's voice took on a pragmatic, straightforward tone. As though asking a servant the weather.

"That's something of a…broad question, your Grace." Heden squirmed, wishing to get out of the atrium now. Being in the presence of this man was difficult for him.

The bishop nodded. "Is he a man of his word?"

Heden shot the bishop a look. Who could ask that of Baed?

Baed was, Heden knew, a touchy subject among the great and good of Corwell. Under his command, the armies of Vasloria held back the Army of Night. Stopped them flooding out of Aendrim after they'd taken it.

But he was a Duke of Graid, not Corwell, and now that same strategic and tactical brilliance was aimed at taking the land of Aendrim back. The king of Graid had, it seemed, promised all Aendrim to him privately. And now Baed intended to take it and install himself King. Tull, Farnham, Rhone, their regents had enough to worry about. But Richard, King of Corwell was cousin to Edward, King of Aendrim. Cousin and close friend. He considered Aendrim his by right.

And the army Baed had commanded, had been Richard's.

"His word is inviolate," Heden said. There were few men in all Orden Heden trusted as much.

"Would you describe him as ambitious?"

This was a strange question, and one that made Heden think in spite of himself.

"I'd not have said so, your Grace," he replied. "Not before the Oracle." The tower of the Oracle at Adsalor was a powerful strategic asset. One the Army of Night controlled for three years. It lay at the border between Corwell, Graid, and Aendrim. Richard assumed it was his once the Army of the Star Elves retreated.

Baed took it. It marked the beginning of his steady march toward Aendrim's ruined capital of Exeder.

"He never seemed to want anything but to do his duty," Heden remembered. "But the man is a Duke." Kings in Vasloria spent much more time managing their powerful, combative, scheming Dukes than they did worrying about rival kingdoms.

"Mmm," the bishop said. He changed the subject.

"Gwiddon predicted you would retire the Arrogacy upon your return."

"I considered it, your Grace," Heden said.

"It is not for me to say, your station granted by Saint Lynwen and nothing to do with me, but I would be sad to lose so effective a tool."

Heden didn't know what he was anymore. He didn't feel like an Arrogate anymore. Felt more like a priest, but he belonged to no church.

"I don't know…," he said, and suddenly felt incredibly weary. Was there any way to know? Any way to fight this man? There was so much Heden didn't know, and he'd never been the best at figuring things out. He wanted to crawl back to his inn and shut the doors and waste away. But there was Vanora, if she were still there.

She would be, Heden knew. He knew it like he knew his own name. She was waiting for him. He wasn't going to let her down.

"I don't know what I'm going to do," he admitted. "It'll be a while before I'm any use to anyone." He wanted to leave this place and have the bishop forget about him. "I should go," he said, and half turned to leave.

"If it's any consolation," the bishop said. "They couldn't have been much use to anyone up there."

What? Heden thought. He stiffened, tried to hide his anger. Turned back to the bishop.

"Nine knights, three thousand years," Bishop Conmonoc explained. "None of us had ever heard of them. I can't imagine them any great loss. I know you don't like knights, perhaps in this case your distaste was justified."

Heden, mouth open slightly, stared at the bishop. The man had just lied to him. *None of us had ever heard of them.* Heden knew this was a lie. Knew he'd given the order. But there was no trace, no hint, not an iota of an inkling in the bishop's bearing that he was lying.

Heden has a preternatural ability to tell when someone was lying to him, honed over years as priest and Arrogate. This man had just lied to him, and he couldn't tell. It struck him dumb. What did it mean? What power did Conmonoc wield and from whence did it come? Heden suddenly knew some degree of fear. Of the unknown. Of the power behind the man before him.

The bishop's expression changed. Something happened behind his eyes, his muscles shifted under his skin, a reptilian adjustment. Heden blinked.

The man had recognized Heden's recognition. The bishop knew what Heden knew.

Heden took a deep breath. Steeled himself. Gave the bishop

a look straight out of the mud and rain outside the Green Priory.

Did a sneer cross the bishop's face?

"Perhaps they deserved to die," he said, testing Heden.

Heden would not be baited. The anger was there, but more, the drive. He would bring this man down. Fight whatever cancer grew in the church he'd once belonged to. Did the bishop have any idea the power Heden could array against him, if he was patient? No. The 80-year old bishop underestimated him, always had. But then, Heden had done the same to him. There was no way to know the bishop's true power.

"Someone thought so," Heden said, eyes locked on the bishop. A flying insect grazed his neck. He brushed it away.

"I hope someday you discover," the bishop said, raising an eyebrow, making some subtle joke only he understood, "why you, and you alone, had to go into the Wode."

Heden pulled his hand back and saw the insect clinging precariously to a finger. Six legs gripped his index finger as though afraid he might casually kill it, or fling it away.

It was a bee. Heden stared at it. A lone bee here in the starlit atrium. It appeared to look at Heden and wave its tiny antennae.

Concealing his reaction, Heden gently blew on the bee, and it flew away.

"I know why," Heden said smoothly. "Now if you'll excuse me," he said, turning his back to the other man. "I have an appointment." He walked out of the atrium, left the starlight and darkness and headed to where he knew the sun was. Confident he knew the way. "Good afternoon, your Grace." His voice echoed against the stone walls.

Unseen to both men, the tiny bee buzzed after Heden.

CHAPTER THIRTY

"We need to talk."

The abbot looked up from his quill and parchment, looked over the rims of his spectacles.

Heden leaned against the stone archway leading into the study. He looked like someone wrung him out and hung him up to dry.

The abbot replaced his quill and pulled the spectacles off his nose and ears, gestured to the backless, upholstered couch against the wall opposite his desk.

Heden shook his head once, sharply. "No," he said. "Not here."

The abbot sat back in his chair. "Your inn?"

"No," Heden said, pushing himself off the arch. "That's being watched too. Come on."

The abbot frowned, but stood up and followed.

The graveyard was older than the citadel, older than the castle, older than the memory of the city. It was huge, covered the entire northern edge of Celkirk, extending out beyond the walls into the rolling hills beyond. In the days of deathless it was a popular destination for cultists when young acolytes were tasked with patrolling it. But that was years ago. Now the only people who came here were people mourning the dead.

"This is ominous," the abbot said, looking at the name on the headstone.

Stewart Antilles.

Heden looked down at the headstone he leaned on, then looked down at the matted, spotty grass as though noticing it for the first time. "Hm," he said.

He stood up straight, cleaned the top of the gravestone off with the sleeve of his shirt. Then appeared to give up, and went back to leaning on it.

"He won't mind," he said with a shrug.

"I'll take your word for it," the abbot said. Then looked deeply at Heden. "How are you?" he asked, frowning.

Heden took a deep breath and shook his head. "You need to know what happened in the forest."

"You can tell me what happened in the forest," the abbot said, "but first I want to know how you are."

Heden shook his head. "I'm not here to tell you how I *am*," he said, biting the word off. "We're here because we have to talk about what happened."

"What's wrong with you?" the abbot said, scowling. "You look…,"

"What?" Heden barked, looking around the graveyard. He didn't see anyone, but put his hand on the hilt of his grandfather's sword just in case. "How do I look? Say it. We don't have time to play games."

The abbot nodded as though Heden's statement confirmed a suspicion. "You look ready for violence. Did you come back to commit murder, because that's what you look like."

"Yes," Heden said. "I did. I almost did. But Gwiddon talked me out of it. For now."

"Who?" the abbot demanded.

"The bishop," Heden spat.

"Conmonoc?" the abbot said, taken aback.

"Do you know what happened in the forest?" Heden asked.

His face clouded with worry as he absorbed Heden's statement, the abbot shook his head. "Only…only what you told me. The last time we spoke."

Heden pushed himself away from the gravestone and closed the distance between them.

"He did it," Heden hissed. "He sent me up there. He sent me because he thought I'd fail."

"You're confused," the abbot said, and it looked to Heden as though the abbot were trying to convince himself as much as anyone. "He sent you there to save those people."

"He damned them," Heden bristled. "He ordered them to stand down. He lied to us, he said he'd never heard of them, but he needed them to let an army of urq march."

"You're wrong," the abbot said. "None of us had heard of the Green Order. Not for hundreds of years. No one had."

"*He* had. They receive their power from Halcyon, Halcyon is a saint of Cavall. Conmonoc is his bishop," Heden spat the word. "That gave him the right. How many times had he tried before? Tried to assemble an army from the Wode? And failed. Because of twelve knights standing between him and who knows what? Years? Decades? Then he finally realizes why nothing happens. The Green. They do their duty, they stop of the urq and his plan fails. Well not anymore. Now there's an army in the north big enough to take the city and no one left to stop it."

"No one…," the abbot couldn't absorb it all. "They're dead? All of them?"

"He ordered them to abandon their duty, just this once. But that's *all they had left!*" Heden's face was red with rage and other emotions. The abbot could see it. "And he took that away. Leaving them *nothing*."

The abbot found himself unable to deny Heden. "Why… what does he gain? Why would he do this?"

"You tell me," Heden asked.

"I have no idea," the abbot said, eyebrows raised. "I'm not even sure I understand the…I don't know what…."

"Let me explain it to you!" Heden barked. "Conomonoc is the Bishop of Cavall. But he is Cavall's enemy."

This brought the abbot up short. "Heden. That's impossible."

"*Is it?*" Heden was going to force the abbot to see the truth. "Tell me something, how is he chosen? Is he chosen by Cavall?"

"Yes!" the abbot said.

"Is he *really?*" Heden took a step forward. The abbot took a pace back, looked alarmed. Would Heden strike him?

"He's…he's chosen by the rectors *in camerata*," the abbot said.

"In *secret*," Heden said.

"But they're…Cavall speaks to them. They choose on his word."

"But in secret! No chance of *politics* is there?"

The abbot's eyes stared off into the distance, past Heden. Through him. He was breathing rapidly. He put a hand to his chest. Overweight, aging, he felt his heart might burst.

"I went to talk to him," Heden continued. He paced over Stewart's grave. "I wanted to give him a chance to…but I could *see it*. The more he talked…I could see it. He's the most powerful man in the city, Corwell, maybe the whole region. And he doesn't belong to us. Maybe never did. What in the worlds below was *I* going to do?" He couldn't save anyone.

Heden found himself staring at his aging hands. He clenched them into fists.

The abbot pressed his hands to his eyes, tried to clear his head. When he took his hands away, opened his eyes, and saw Heden standing there, his whole body clenched for violence, his way was made clear for him.

"Heden," the abbot said. The arrogate ignored him. "Heden!" the abbot said louder.

Heden looked at him dully.

"Heden, forget the bishop for a moment and listen to me." When Heden gave no indication he heard or didn't hear, the abbot continued. "This will consume you. After what happened in Aendrim? The battle at Exeter? This will drive you until there's nothing left."

"You going to tell me not to do anything?" Heden asked, his voice flat.

"No," the abbot said. "You can't do nothing. But I'm not worried about the bishop, I'm worried about you. I know your heart. That's what I'm worried about. If you move from your center," he said, pointing at Heden's chest, "you'll be fine. I don't know what will happen, but it will be the right thing, however it comes out." The implication was clear.

"Go on like this?" The abbot warned. "From hate and anger and fear? It will destroy you, and you'll achieve nothing."

The two men stood in the graveyard, looking at each other. Only one seeing.

"Go back to the inn. Talk to the girl. She needs you."

Heden gave no indication he heard the abbot.

"Heden, please," the abbot reached out, grabbed Heden's arm.

Reflexively, Heden pulled it away, looked at the abbot's hand, at the abbot, with disgust.

"You need someone," the abbot said, delicately.

Heden, his mouth twisted into a sneer, looked once at the abbot, then strode off, back to the heart of the city, out of the graveyard.

"You can't do it alone!" the abbot said, unsure if Heden was listening.

He turned to look at the grave of Stewart Antilles.

"He can't do it alone," he said, to the dirt.

CHAPTER THIRTY-ONE

The next day, feeling almost hung over from the rage and poison he'd felt the day before, Heden woke to a nearly empty inn. He went downstairs.

Vanora was washing up.

"I haven't killed anyone yet," he said.

She smiled at him. "Good," she said. There was a distance between them. Heden was reminded of the abbot's advice about children.

Heden pointed to the wall of books on the far side of the common room. A unique feature in an inn.

"Did you do any reading?"

Vanora shrugged.

"A little," she said. "I…," she started. "I liked the harlequin," she admitted. She dried off a plate and held it to her chest like a shield, looking at Heden.

"Good," Heden said. That worked, at least. "What did you learn?"

"Letters," Vanora said, and then perked up. "I can write my name!"

"I'd like to see that," Heden said. Vanora was beaming, violence forgotten.

They talked about nothing for a while. Vanora noticed Heden looking at the door to the basement.

"I had to go down there," she said. "When the ghoul… happened," she didn't know how else to describe it. "I know you told me not to."

"You did the right thing," he said, and crossed to the door.

"All the wine was down there anyway," she said.

Heden nodded. He sighed, not looking forward to doing something, opened the door, and went downstairs.

This time Vanora didn't press her ear to the door. And this time, Heden didn't close the door behind him. She took a stack of plates into the kitchen, then came back out to collect the used mugs.

When Heden emerged from the basement, he was carrying something egg-shaped, but as large as a lantern, and wrapped in brown cloth, like hide.

"What is that?" Vanora asked.

"A peace offering," Heden said.

CHAPTER THIRTY-TWO

The dwarf ignored him.

He stood there, feeling like an idiot, with Zaar's men all trying to work around him

Heden cleared his throat again. Stood there with the thing wrapped up, held out. It was heavy.

"I remembered when we found this and I, ah…," he looked at the sawdust on the floor. "I took it as my share because I… you know, I thought…I knew how much you wanted it and I thought I could get more than my share by…."

The dwarf turned and stared at Heden, his ember-red eyes glowering from under an earthen brow.

Heden took a deep breath.

"I was a complete shit in other words," he confessed.

The dwarf glanced at the cloth-wrapped orb. Heden unwrapped it. It looked like a massive fire opal. It glowed from within mimicking the red hot eyes of the Elemental in front of him.

Heden held it out. The dwarf looked from the Flame Speaker gem, to Heden, and back.

"I lost the…ah. The sword. I lost it. *Starkiller*."

The dwarf's red stone features grimaced. He started breathing heavily. His eyes flared red. Heat boiled off him. Heden had been sweating from it before, now it was almost unbearable. But he didn't move away. He was going to stand there and take it. All of it.

"I had to give it up. There was a naiad and someone had been murdered and I…."

The dwarf maintained his silence.

"Doesn't matter," Heden finished. "I know it technically belongs to all of us." Everyone left. "But I thought I should…"

Heden looked away from Zaar, looked at the shop full of people watching him. Turned back to the dwarf and shrunk a little.

"I don't know what I thought," he finished lamely. He found himself unable to ask for another weapon. Even though several were his by right.

The dwarf ground his teeth, which Heden could hear. It was like a human pursing his lips in thought.

He turned his back on Heden, and returned to his work. Heden stood there, feeling useless, holding the Flame Speaker gem. Everyone in the smithy tried to go back to work, tried to ignore him.

"I wouldn't do it again, you know," Heden said. Louder, and more clearly than he had said anything else up until this point.

The dwarf stopped working and half turned his head, not looking at Heden. Waiting.

"Make a decision like that." He stared at the dwarf's back. Everyone had gone back to watching him and listening. "I was young and...humans do foolish things when they're...." He looked around; almost everyone working for Zaar was a human.

"Don't judge all of us based on one mistake I made, is all," Heden concluded. He looked down at the Flame Speaker gem. It was beautiful. "Well," he muttered, "maybe not just one mistake."

Staring into the gem, Heden didn't realize the dwarf had turned back around until he saw Zaar's four-fingered stone hands reach out and grasp the thing. For a moment, they were both holding the gem. Heden looked at Zaar. The dwarf would not return his gaze. Heden knew something of the provenance of the crystal. Zaar considered it a holy relic, left over from a race of dwarves now long-gone. A race Zaar's people had considered their elder brothers. Better versions of themselves.

Zaar made a noise, like "angh," and took the gem from Heden. Turned and looked away. Heden stood there for a moment, his breathing coming easy. A burden lifted. He wondered if this was as good as it would get between the two former comrades. Decided, if it was, it was good enough. More that he deserved.

He walked out of Zaar's shop, empty handed.

Chapter Thirty-three

Business in the inn was picking up by the time he got back. The sun was getting low in the sky. There were about a half-dozen girls here, serving. He recognized Martlyn, the red-head. He wondered how many girls Miss Elowen employed. How many of them came here now, when they weren't working?

Ignoring Morten in his chair by the door, Heden took a table near the library. He liked the library. Always wanted to show it off once he opened the place. It was a catalog of every place he'd been, all the places the Sunbringers had plundered. Books were incredibly valuable to his family, any farmers really. Even here in the city a family might own three books? Four? Heden had hundreds.

It was just something he'd started doing. Making sure to take the books they found. Only a fraction of the books on the wall behind him were written in Tevas-gol. Even the ones he couldn't read were fascinating. There was a book in there on dwarven stonemasonry techniques. When Heden saw it, and realized what it was, he thought it was probably worth a thousand crowns. It might be. Might be worthless, he didn't know. He just liked having it.

Martlyn walked over to him. Enjoyed walking over to him, showed herself off to him in what she thought was a subtle manner. Heden tried not to roll his eyes.

"What'll it be, boss?" Martlyn asked, her green eyes dancing, one hand on her hip.

"I'm not the boss," Heden said. "That's Violet," he said.

Martlyn smiled. "Uh-huh," she said. "How about a drink?" she asked. "On me," she added, her smile growing.

"On you, huh?" Heden asked, amused. "You're going to serve me my own drink for free?"

"I could charge you for it," she said, her eyes wide, "if it would make you feel better."

"It would not," Heden said. Another girl saw the two of them interacting and frowned. She cat-footed over and smoothly assumed a stance next to Martlyn. "Something to eat, sir?"

Heden pointed at her and thought. "Caerys, right?"

She smiled like the sun coming up. "That's right, your lordship," she said. She had short dark hair and while shorter and apparently younger than Martlyn, she seemed more developed. It was probably just the way she was dressed, Heden thought.

"And you'd be Heden," Caerys said, dropping a curtsey. She bit her bottom lip and looked at Heden with wide brown eyes. Martlyn made no effort to hide her displeasure.

"Don't you have people to serve?" Martlyn reprimanded. Heden believed she was second-in-command after Vanora.

"Don't you," Caerys said, nodding at a table with two men at it, impatient and leering at the two girls.

"I was here first, now get back to work," Martlyn hissed under her breath.

"I just finished with a man and he's quite satisfied, you'll be happy to know."

Was it…was it *possible* she was just talking about bringing someone food and drink? Heden wondered.

"Girls," Heden said. They both stopped arguing and looked at him, Caerys tried to be attractively demure, Martlyn tried to be attractively assertive. "Ale," he said, pointing to Martlyn, "mutton," he said pointing to Caerys. Whatever else, they couldn't be plying their trade while getting him a meal at the very least.

Martlyn rolled her eyes. "A diplomat," she said exasperated, and turned to leave. Caerys smiled, considering Martlyn's frustration a triumph, and curtseyed again, before following the older girl.

"This is not going to work," Heden said to himself.

Something was going on by the door. Something he hadn't noticed when Martlyn and Caerys were standing in front of him.

Morten was arguing with a man, a customer. There was a girl, one Heden didn't recognize, watching from behind the bar, using the bar as a shield.

The man had the look of a sailor, which Heden found strange. What word had gotten out about his inn, that someone would come all the way here from the docks? He looked at the girl, behind the bar, beautiful and innocent-seeming, and formulated a suspicion about why the Hammer & Tongs might be popular. 'Practice,' Vanora had called it. Were they not charging for their services? Heden had a hard time imagining that.

Well, Heden thought, *they're making money off the food and wine and Vanora has my...*, he stopped himself. Looked at the door to the cellar. Narrowed his eyes.

Morten and the sailor were now having words. Things were escalating. Morten sneered at the man, and stabbed him in the chest with his finger. The sailor grabbed the finger and twisted and Morten fell to his knees.

Heden sighed and prepared to get up when the door opened and Bann walked in.

The massive, war-bred demiurq surveyed the room. Saw Heden, nodded to him, then pulled the two-hander he carried off his back, scabbard and all, and bashed the sailor over the head with it, dropping him to the ground.

Morten got up, favoring his finger, and genuflected before Bann. The two of them talked for a moment, with Morten nodding and trying to impress. Bann made a gesture and Morten nodded. Grabbed the sailor by the collar and dragged his unconscious form out the door.

Bann, holding his scabbard, shook his head and walked over to Heden's table.

He leaned the two-hander against the table. It was huge.

"It's like that with terrans," Bann said, sitting down.

Martlyn came out of the kitchen with his ale, and stopped when she saw Bann. Heden held up two fingers and then pointed to himself and Bann, and she went back through the kitchen door.

"Terrans," Heden prompted, returning his attention to Bann.

"Humans. Morten," he explained. His voice sounded like distant thunder. It was impossible for him to sound otherwise. "He sees me, he thinks he does what I do, he'll get the same reaction. Don't work."

"Because he's not an eight-foot tall urqwight," Heden said.

"Basically," Bann said. "Not bad for him to learn here. Good place for it."

"That why you're here?" Heden asked. "Check in on Morten and the girls?"

Bann cleaned his teeth with his spearhead fingernails. "What do you think?"

"I think Elowen's about fed up with all this," Heden said.

Bann nodded once, slowly.

"It's not the time off that matters," he said. "Got plenty of girls to cover for them, and more to spare. But these girls, working here, for you...you don't give a shit. Makes them feel...," Bann didn't know how to say it.

"Independent," Heden offered.

Bann nodded again. His huge, ink-black face impressive, his needle-thin tusks jutting up out of his jaw a discreet few inches.

"Can't be having that," he said. "That is bad for business. Girls need to know who runs 'em. And Miss Elowen runs 'em."

"And the count runs her."

Bann shrugged. "Runs all the trulls. Miss Elowen gets by better than most."

"So how does this end?" Heden asked.

"You tell me," Bann said. "Your inn, your girls."

Heden shook his head. "They're not my girls," he said.

Bann looked at him. "That's right. They're not yours. They're the count's. How long you think you can keep this up, before it gets back to him?"

Heden shrugged. "How about I kill him?"

Bann howled a short laugh. Everyone in the inn looked at him. He stopped abruptly and looked at Heden.

"Oh, you're serious. Shit."

"He's gotta go down sometime," Heden said.

"Well, his like don't die of old age, I grant you. But they don't die from lovestruck priests trying to save a trull."

Heden didn't say anything. Waited for Bann.

Bann held up his hands. Recanted. "That was mostly pigshit," he admitted. "But the point stands. Takes more than one pissed off old ratcatcher to bring down the count."

Heden had to admit this was a reasonable assumption.

"Vanora's staying here," he said.

Bann shook his head. "That ain't no kinda solution," he said. "None of this matters, you keep Violet."

Heden nodded. "Well, I'll admit, I haven't really thought about what happens next...."

"Ratcatchers," Bann shook his head.

"But I guess I figured," Heden said, leaning back in his chair, "that either the count, or his men, would make a play for Vanora, or me, and then all this would come to a head."

"Piss off enough people," Bann said, "eventually someone goes for you."

"Worked before," Heden said.

"When you were a younger man."

"We're none of us the men we once were," Heden said with some humor.

Heden looked at the man, not a friend, but a friend to his friends. Lots of campaigners went to the Rose Petal. Heden didn't judge. Never seemed to be any of his business.

"I need someone to look after the girls."

"You got someone to look after the girls," Bann said, nodding to Morten.

"You know what I mean."

Bann's smile waned. His eyes slowly took in everyone in the common room.

"Miss Elowen trusts you, for some reason," Bann said, "so she ain't done nothin' except ask me to explain that all this," he said, incidating the inn and its customers, "can't last forever."

"Might not last the week," Heden said.

Bann nodded. "Specially once the count figures out who you are and where Vanora is."

Martlyn and Caerys brought drink and food. Neither of them seemed happy to see Bann. They curtseyed, and left.

Bann bent his head down, began spearing the mutton with his fingernails and bringing it up into the maw he called his mouth. "You want me to look after the girls, but he ain't coming after the girls. You want me to watch Violet…," he shook his head. "He wants her bad enough, he'll send some black scarves and…." He looked at Heden. "I like Violet," he said. "I like you. But this ain't the Rose."

Heden nodded. "I understand," he said.

"I work for Miss Elowen," Bann explained.

Heden nodded.

"If it was her asking me," he said.

Heden understood. He liked Bann because Bann kept his word. If he said he was going to do something, he would do it. No matter what. Part of that meant saying no when you knew you couldn't keep your word.

Heden took a bite of the mutton.

Bann watched Heden eat. "Couple of days," he said. "All be over one way or the other."

Heden nodded. "Yeah."

Bann stood up, put his ale down, picked up his sword.

Heden noticed Morten stand up, like a soldier at attention for a commanding officer.

"Count probably don't know who you are," he said, "you were out of town for a while. He figures it out, this place won't be safe."

"Yeah," Heden said.

"We all like Violet," Bann said. "We'd all rather she be here than with him."

Heden nodded.

Bann looked around the inn. "Nice place," he said, as though seeing it for the first time. Then he shook his head at everything, and left. Morten waited for him to pass, then sat down.

Vanora took the opportunity to come out from the kitchen where she'd been trying to listen to the conversation over the sound in the common room.

She sat down where Bann had been.

"What did Bann want?" she asked.

"Just checking in on you," he said.

Vanora seemed to believe this.

"What happened to Martlyn?" Heden asked. The girls seemed to disappear at random times.

"She had to go back to the Rose," Vanora explained. "They all do sooner or later. They can only help me here on their time off."

Working on their time off, Heden thought. That said a lot.

"You're paying the girls with my money," he said, switching subjects. Vanora looked at the table, fingered Bann's half-full ale. "That's why they can afford to ah...ply their trade without charging, and that's why this place is getting popular."

Vanora rubbed her temples. Heden wondered how much sleep she got. She seemed up all hours.

She looked at him, desperate. "You do have an awful lot of money."

Heden sighed. "That's not the point," he said. "You have to

pay the girls, I don't mind. The problem is now we're going to get all sorts in here, men who think they can get it for free. Morten's not up to that," he said, nodding at the guard Bann had leant them.

"So they should charge for it," Vanora said, nodding. Acting like she wasn't getting away with anything.

"They shouldn't do it at all!" Heden said. Vanora flinched. "It's a dangerous business. Why do think Miss Elowen has Bann?"

"Before," Vanora started. "Before I paid them, the girls all… they volunteered," she said, looking at Heden desperately. "They did it all for free, cleaned the place up with me, helped me with the food, the ordering, everything. They did it for nothing, just to have something outside the Rose. Something of their own. Most of them didn't even like me before."

He sighed. "If you're paying them anyway," he said, "why do they stay on the game?" Vanora didn't answer. "How much would you have to pay them to get them to stop?" he asked.

Vanora shrugged. "I don't know. They do it because they like to," she said. "Why should they stop?"

Heden watched her. She was conflicted. She loved her friends, and with good reason. But she wanted Heden to approve of her.

"But you don't sell yourself anymore," Heden said.

He face crinkled, like she'd tasted something sour, when he said that.

"No," she said.

"Why not?" Heden asked, playing the abbot for a moment.

Vanora shrugged. Heden tried not to smile at the gesture. "I don't know," she said. "Miss Elowen never does it."

That made sense, even though Heden didn't like it. She was casting herself in Elowen's role. But was that the only reason? Heden didn't think so. But he'd grilled her enough.

"Well," he said, "Elowen won't put up with this for long. She knows you're in trouble, so she's indulging me."

"And when I'm not in trouble," Vanora asked, her face unreadable. "All this stops? The girls all go back to the Rose?"

Heden poured himself a drink. Just ale.

"One problem at a time," he said.

Vanora watched him, and said nothing.

CHAPTER THIRTY-FOUR

"I'll go," Vanora said. Heden had gone upstairs to sleep and the girls were cleaning up the common room after closing.

"Do you have money?" Caerys asked, worried.

"Yes," Vanora said, putting on a dark green cloak she found in the basement.

"Do you want me to go with you?" Caerys asked, obviously hoping the answer was no.

"No, you go back to the Rose," Vanora said.

"Why not go in the morning?" Caerys asked.

Vanora looked at her. Why was Caerys acting like this? Did Bann say something? No, there wasn't time.

"Because the monger gives us leavings, we show up in the morning asking for an order. Have to place the order in the first three hours after midnight if you want first choice come morning."

"Oh," Caerys said.

Vanora looked at her. "What's wrong with you?" she asked.

"Nothing," Caerys said, her voice small.

Vanora stared at the girl hard. Caerys wouldn't return Vanora's gaze, just sat there fretting.

"Good," Vanora said, upset at Caerys now for some reason she couldn't articulate. "Will you be here when I get back?"

"Oh," Caerys said, returning to life, "I suppose. Yeah. I'll wait. I'm not in a hurry to get back to the Rose," she managed a weak smile.

Vanora nodded, still unable to make anything out of Caerys' attitude. She flipped the hood of the cloak up over her head. "Be back soon," she said.

"Good luck," Caerys said.

Vanora left the Hammer & Tongs, stopping to look up at

Dusk Moon, now bright red. She marked the facing to tell the time, and headed north up Cassel St.

The fishmonger was a full turn away, down by the docks. The streets were mostly empty near the inn, but closing on the water they became more and more crowded until eventually it was as thick as ever, might as well have been daytime, there were so many people and so much light.

She waited her turn in the line at the fishmonger. She wasn't the only young person, nor the only young girl. Lots of places used serving girls to place their orders. As far as anyone here knew, she was no different from any other.

She walked through the door, leaving the line and the press of bodies behind her, and ordered ten pounds of fresh whitefish from the thin, bearded, grizzled man with the apron covered in blood and fish scales.

"Ten pounds a lotta fish," the old man said with a crooked smile.

Vanora smiled back. "Business picking up."

The old man held up the fist full of her coin, "Good business for both of us then," he said. "I'll get your chitty."

He walked through the door in the back, which suddenly and loudly slammed shut behind him.

Vanora heard a shout, the old man. Then something else behind her. A voice.

"Hey there girlie," a man said behind her, and the icy steel of it made her almost piss her pants.

She turned and there were three men in black cloaks and black leather.

"There's someone been looking for you," one of them said, she wasn't sure which one. They each wore a black leather half-masks covering their mouths.

"My...," Vanora stuttered. "My mum and da are waiting back at the Fool," she tried.

"Heh. Nice try kid," one of them said. "Come on, grab her."

The lead thief reached out, Vanora found herself unable to move. Then, just as she'd heard the thief's voice behind her a moment ago, she heard another voice behind her. A woman's voice.

"*Dracones ossa liquescen*," came the voice, and the lead thief screamed. His hand flared, the bones inside glowing so bright, so quickly, Vanora could see them, inches from her face. Then the flesh of his hand vaporized in a flash of light and ash and Vanora was coughing and the man was screaming, holding the stump that had been his hand.

"Black gods," one of the thieves observed, pulling a small, one-handed crossbow from his belt.

Vanora looked behind her. There was a woman there. Short, not much taller than Vanora. She had brown hair curled tightly behind her head. Brown skin and brown, oval eyes. A heavy red dress with expensive patterning and a cinched waist.

The woman's hands were clenched, her muscles tight. She looked strong, as strong and compact as Heden, her skin was smooth and glowed with health and her eyes were filled with murder.

She was the most beautiful woman Vanora had ever seen.

A twang and a flash of fire burst in front of the woman's face. She didn't blink. It took a moment for Vanora to realize the thief had fired his crossbow bolt and some invisible force turned it to fire in an instant before it could find its target.

"One chance," the woman said, her voice iron.

"This isn't worth it," one of the thieves said.

"My fucking arm!" the first thief said from his knees.

"The girl is worth it," the third thief said. "Use the Dust."

The woman made a sound like 'tch,' as the second thief pulled a black marble from his vest.

"*Comburet cortuum exte*," the woman said, and all three thieves froze in place, their mouths agape. And then, horribly, Vanora could see their hearts begin to glow from inside their bodies.

They howled, but only for a moment. Vanora closed her eyes and felt blasted with heat, her hair blown back with it, she had to hold her hands up to protect herself. She was afraid she'd open her eyes and there'd be only stumps left.

But once opened, her eyes saw only three ashen marks on the floor. Silver, of weapons or coin, bubbling in puddles. The wood floor was scarred but otherwise untouched. The glass marble and the smoke inside, gone.

Vanora spun back around in time to see the wizard behind her relax and straighten up. She looked around the small room as though invisible enemies were possible. She looked like a queen surveying her territory.

Then she looked at Vanora.

"You're safe."

"Who are you?!" Vanora blurted finally. "How did you DO that?"

"I'm not important," the woman said automatically. When she was done sizing up Vanora she made a sound like 'hmph.'

"Show me how to do that!" Vanora pleaded.

"You don't want to know how to do that. Trust me. There's such a thing as terrible knowledge," she said. "Ask Heden."

"You're his friend!" *He has friends!*

The woman signed and grimaced, deflating a little. "Listen, I can't be…there's only a couple of us. And we can't be everywhere. This is maybe all the help I can give. You have to be careful. Next time you won't be so lucky."

"Take me with you!" Vanora said, remembering what the abbot said.

The woman shook her head. "Took me two years to get into the Quill," she said. "Can't just knock on the door."

Vanora didn't know what this meant, but she felt she had to keep talking or this moment, this woman, would slip away.

"How do you know Heden?" She asked quickly, taking a

daring step forward. "Did you…campaign with him?" She wasn't sure this was the right term.

A silent moment as the woman looked, not unkindly, at Vanora.

"Be careful with him," the wizard said, opening the back door.

"He's got a thing about lost girls."

Chapter Thirty-five

Heden left his clothes in a heap on the floor of his room and slipped into bed naked. As he pulled the sheets around his body he felt another body, warm and smooth next to him.

He froze, every instinct cried out to leap from the bed and arm himself, but he knew it was a woman next to him. He thought it was one of the girls, exhausted, asleep, but the body stirred and writhed against him. He could smell her hair, a fragrance he knew. Her hand ran through the hairs on his chest and then slid down. He was like a stone. The woman giggled.

"You're so predictable," a voice purred. He recognized it, should have known her from the fragrance, and relaxed.

"Hello Lynwen."

Heden sighed and gritted his teeth. The woman, his saint, laughed and slid on top of him.

Her face an inch from his, her warm breath across his lips, she started to kiss him, his neck, and he let her. She ran her hands along his body and he held her in his arms, gently. In the best approximation of love he could manage.

It was not enough.

She pushed herself up. "Gods, you're doing it now aren't you?"

"I don't know what you...."

"You are! Gods," tears welled in her eyes. "You...."

He didn't say anything. She was still on top of him.

"You're doing this on purpose. You're letting me do this because you know it's what I want." She was right. "You know it's what I...."

She couldn't say it. She didn't need to. She got angry and pushed herself roughly off him and out of bed and stood there accusing him.

"You're the only man I…and you know it and it's fucking sympathy. From you! From the man I…from a mortal!"

"It's not *just* sympathy," Heden said, staring up at the ceiling, adjusting his body and the sheets to conceal anything he might be embarrassed by.

"Shut up!

Heden clapped his mouth closed and put his hands behind his head.

Lynwen stood there, seething.

"Well?!"

"Ah, you told me to…."

"Shut up!"

"Ok."

"You've got an inn full of trulls, they all look up to you, they all compete for your attention, and you sit there like a fucking knight pining for her in her tower," she said, pointing in a random direction.

It always came back to Elzbeth. Heden wished, not for the first time, to be somewhere else, somewhere where no one knew him, or the things he'd done, or the people he knew.

Lynwen seethed.

"You know she doesn't love you?"

"I know."

"You know you could…."

"I made a promise."

"You were *nineteen!*"

"I knew what I was doing."

"No you didn't," she said. And for some reason seemed out of breath. "No you did not." She shook her head.

Heden was staring at the ceiling.

"Look at me," Lynwen commanded.

"I'd rather not," Heden said.

Lynwen waited.

Heden sat up, trying to make sure the sheets covered him

discreetly without making it look like he was trying to stay covered.

He looked at her.

She was beautiful, of course. She died when she was 29 and thus would look so forever. She was tall and blonde and standing naked before him she looked like a statue from the Commonwealth. Perfect in proportion. A certain curve to the hips and breasts that a tailor would ache to fit. He wondered, looking at her, trying to focus on her face, her red lips, her blue eyes, if this was really how she looked in life, or if it was put on for show. He wasn't sure, and he wasn't going to ask.

When they first met, she and Heden were physically more similar in age. Now he was in his mid-40s. He was aging past her. This didn't bother him so much, but he knew it bothered her.

"I wish...," she said, her voice going soft. "I wish you could see what I see."

He didn't want to ask, but didn't know what else to do.

"What do you see?" he asked, just to be saying something.

"I see a man, noble and strong and good. The best I've ever known. And every time I see you, the best in you is better, and the world is weighing down on you more. And someday...," she said, her voice a warning.

He didn't know what to say to that. She seemed to shrink a little.

"You lead such short lives," she said, reminding him of the difference between them.

"Lynwen," he said, deciding to defend himself. "Do we have to go over this every time we see each other?" He let the weariness show in his voice. "You act like you're a normal girl, you're not. You act like we can be together, we can't."

"We could have some time together," she said, and it looked like she was going to cry.

Heden looked at the floor. Looked at his bare white feet

poking out from under the sheet.

"She's not waiting for you, you know," Lynwen tried again.

"Can we stop talking about her?"

"She moved on a long time ago, why won't you?"

"It's got nothing to do with her," he explained, not for the first time. "It's me. The promises I made...they don't depend on her. It wasn't a bargain. A contract. It was an oath," he threw a meaningful glance at her.

"Don't you dare say that to me!" Lynwen said. "Do you think I don't know? Do you think you can lie to me? About *this?*"

Heden kept his mouth shut.

"I can't read your mind, but I can see inside your heart," Lynwen said. "Everyone has sympathy for you because they think being an Arrogate is so hard, it's such a burden," she said, rolling her eyes. "They have no idea. No idea you took your oath to me to forget your oath to her. They can't see what it does to you. They don't see you thinking about her every night. Thinking about her every time you see another girl, every time you see a happy couple. Every time you see a mother and father with their children, you go back to her. To what might have been."

"Please stop," Heden said, tired more than anything else.

"They don't see your dreams," she said. "I'm sorry, did I say dreams? They're nightmares. You wake up in the middle of the night sweating because you've been seeing her with another man, her with a happy family, *laughing* at you. At how stupid you were to ever think you could be together."

"You're in an exceptionally bitter mood tonight," Heden said.

Lynwen was seething. Her hands balled into fists. But she stopped.

"Don't you have anything better to do than watch my dreams?" Heden asked.

"No," Lynwen said, and wiped the welling tears from her eyes. She already hated herself for what she'd just said. "You're my only follower. My last follower."

This provoked a reaction, finally. "Last?" Heden asked.

"I can't do this again, Heden," Lynwen said, sniffling and shaking her head. "Not after you. I don't have anything left. I've given it all to you and I don't have anything…," she stopped.

Heden let the thought linger before he said the inevitable.

"Now you know how I feel," he said, looking at her with a sad smile.

"Oh gods," she said. "That dumb bitch has fucked up both of us."

"Don't blame her," Heden said.

"Fuck you," Lynwen said mildly. "I'll blame whoever I want. She's the one who left. I'd never have met you otherwise."

"Lucky for both of us then," Heden said, and managed a smile.

"Don't patronize me," Lynwen said without much feeling.

He continued looking at the floor. She walked across the floor until she was standing within arm's reach of him. Until he could smell her again.

"If you came here to distract me, it's working," he said.

"That's not why I'm here you prick. You complete shit. I have a message."

"Um," Heden said, adjusting his position in bed. "From who?"

She stamped a foot. "From who? Who do you think?"

That meant Cavall. He cleared his throat.

"What's the message?"

She sighed, waiting for him to look at her again. He looked up at her, fixing his eyes on hers.

"This is why you were made Arrogate." she said.

He looked down at his naked body half covered in white linen, and then looked at her, also naked.

"This?" he asked.

"I hate you so much right now," her eyes rolled to the ceiling.

"Maybe you could be a little less cryptic."

"I mean *this,*" she said, gesturing with her hands as though to encompass the whole room.

"You mean the bishop," he said.

"We can't...," she started. "We can only aid those...," she stopped. "It's hard to explain."

"Try," he said.

"We knew Conmonoc didn't belong to us before you were born," she said. "But we couldn't do anything about it because *he* wasn't...until *now.*"

"I think I get it. Because he was acting as the bishop would. And now you can do something about it."

"Well, maybe," she said. "We have to sort of...wait until people get an idea, or ask directly, and then nudge them in the right direction."

"Why?" Heden asked. "Who makes these rules?"

"I don't know," she said, sullenly.

"But now you can do something about it," he said.

"You *are* what we're doing about it," she urged.

He shook his head. "It's not enough."

"I know," she said. "It'll have to do."

"What about the rest of the church?" he asked.

"They don't suspect," she said. "And if they did...even if you could convince them...I think most of them would just try and exploit the situation. That's what we're trying to avoid. Politics," she said.

Heden looked down at the floor again. "I don't know what I can do."

"We believe in you," she said sincerely.

"Oh good," he said.

"You need friends," she said.

"I had friends, they're gone."

"You need new ones," she urged gently.

He looked up at her. He'd almost forgotten she was naked.

"They're out there," she said. "I know you think you failed before, but you did everything for the right reasons."

"I wish you hadn't brought that up," he said.

Silence for a moment, then she said, quietly, "You won't fail again."

The room went still. Neither of them spoke.

"When I need you," Heden said quietly. "When I ask for your aid," he looked up at her.

She was staring at him, hungry. She needed him. He wished there was something he could do about that.

"I'll give you everything you ask for," she said, their voices now near a whisper. "Because I know you'll use it. Because I can't say no to you."

After another moment's silence, she backed up. As the distance between them increased, her voice got louder.

"I shouldn't have laughed at you at the river, with the squire," she said. "I should have let her seduce you. It would have been good for you."

Heden sighed. "Later," he said, "you'll regret saying that to me. You'll feel bad you tried to manipulate me."

She looked at him. She grabbed her left elbow with her right hand, which had a certain effect on her breasts that Heden wished he hadn't noticed.

"Maybe," she said.

He took a deep breath and lay back down, pulled the sheets up to his chest. "I'm going to bed now Lynwen," he said.

When there was no response, he closed his eyes. He knew she was already gone.

CHAPTER THIRTY-SIX

When he woke up, his door was open, and Ballisantirax was sitting on his chest, staring at him with her wide, black, yellow-rimmed eyes.

"Mow."

One of the girls must have opened his door to let her in. They'd do that if she was persistently yowling to get in.

He stretched and looked at his cat.

"You hungry?"

"Mow," Balli said, still staring at him. She jumped off the bed and padded to the doorway. She turned in the doorway and looked at him, eyes still wide. Hunting mode.

"Mow."

Heden sat up and watched his cat.

"What's wrong?"

Balli disappeared out the door and, after a moment, stuck her head back in the doorway.

"Mow."

"You want me to follow you?"

"Mow."

"Uh oh," Heden said, and went downstairs. It took him a few moment's searching before he understood why Balli was worried.

Vanora was gone.

Heden stood in the middle of the common room, not panicking. It was morning, and the girls were setting up, and none of them were acting strange. If there was a problem, he was sure they'd show it.

He noticed the shorter of Vanora's two lieutenants, Caerys, watching him expectantly from behind the bar.

He walked over and put his hands on the bar calmly.

"Where is she?"

Caerys shook her head quickly.

"You don't know or you won't say?"

"She wouldn't tell me!"

Heden nodded slowly, just to be encouraging. "Is she alright?"

"I…I think so," Caerys said.

"Tell me everything," Heden said.

Caerys nodded, wound herself up, and let go.

"She went to the fishmongers last night and I asked, I said, 'do you want me to go with you?' And she said 'No,' and I said 'ok,' and she went and came back two turns later and something had happened, I could tell and she said 'I have to go,' and I said 'what else is there to do?' because there's just the fish buying at night and she said 'No, I mean I have to leave', and I said, 'where are you going?' And she said 'I can't tell you,' and I asked 'why not?' And she said 'because if you know, they can get it from you,' and I said 'Violet what are you talking about?' and she said 'I'm not sure.'"

Caerys took a breath finally and Heden blinked at her.

"Ok," he said, with some idea what was happening. He let his suspicion stay unformed in his mind, the way he was taught. "Did she give you the impression she went somewhere safe?"

Caerys nodded.

"Hm," Heden said, frowning.

"You're worried she went back to the count," Caerys guessed.

Heden shook his head. "I would be, but no one knows where the count's operation is."

It was Caerys' turn to stare at Heden blinking.

"Violet knows," she said.

A chill went down Heden's spine. "What?"

"Violet knows where he is."

"You don't…," Heden began. "He has a club. You're thinking of the Lamplighter's club. But he's not there anymore."

Caerys shook her head. "Un-uh. Everybody knows about this club. This is his other place. Violet said he told her all about it once. His hideout. We sort of thought he meant like a second house? Lots of clotpoles have second houses they use to see the girls when they want an overnight."

Heden ran a hand through his head as he looked around, at nothing, stunned. "Black gods," he said.

"But I'm pretty sure that's not where she went!" Caerys offered quickly. "I mean, she talked like she was going somewhere safe, somewhere she'd be ok. I sort of thought she meant the Rose, but that doesn't make sense because she could just tell me and anyway the count would just…."

Heden stepped around the bar, and put his hands firmly

"Caerys," he said. "Are you sure Vanora knows where the count's operation is?"

Frightened, she tried to back away, but Heden held her fast. "I don't know! She said so! Maybe."

Heden realized he was scaring the girl and pulled back. He stood up straight, his mind reeling. "And she never said anything about it? Where it was? What kind of place it was?"

Caerys shook her head. "I didn't…none of us thought…," she shrugged. "It didn't seem important. They all brag about stuff."

Three people walked into the inn. Heden saw them and recognized them as Not Customers. They didn't look like thieves, which left little room for anything else.

"Alright listen to me," Heden said to Caerys quickly and quietly. "Do not tell anyone this. No matter what, never tell anyone that Vanora, or anyone knows where the count's hideout is. And try not to lie, just *don't answer*. Can you do that? Can you just twist the conversation away from the question?"

One of the three customers asked a girl, and she pointed the Heden. The other two, and older man and woman, went and found a table.

Caerys nodded, smiling. Happy that Heden seemed to know what to do now. "Oh sure," she said. "It's easy to change subjects when a man asks you something."

Heden nodded. That was probably true. "Alright," he said. "Back to work, act like nothing happened."

The younger of the three approached Heden.

"You're name's Heden," he said. He was young, maybe a little older than Vanora. He had sandy brown hair and blue eyes. "You own this place."

Heden watched the older two of the three as they ordered. What was going on?

"Yeah," he said to the lad. "Why aren't you eating with your friends?"

"Oh, a lot of reasons," the lad said, seeming more adult than he looked. "We're from the castellan," he said.

Heden looked at the two watchmen sitting waiting for their food. They had the look, absolutely.

He looked back at the lad, skeptical. "I'd recognize the sigil gets you into the citadel."

The boy raised his eyebrows in surprise. He reached a hand in through the top of his jerkin, fished around, and brought out a silver amulet on a chain, showed it to Heden.

Heden held it in his palm and looked at it. Minor magic on it, he could tell. Not impossible to fake, but given the circumstances he was willing to believe the boy.

"You're a little young for a special," he said, letting the amulet drop. The lad stuffed it back in his shirt.

"Look," he said, "I'm not going to do the whole thing I did with them," he nodded to his partners, "with you all over again, ok? I'm young, you're old, I get it. Is there someplace we can sit and talk?"

Heden looked around the inn. It was mostly empty, this early in the morning.

"I mean in private," the lad said, looking at some of the other patrons suspiciously.

"This is my place," Heden said. "It's as private as I get. Pick a table."

Once seated, the boy introduced himself.

"Nice name," Heden said. 'Aiden' was the southern version of his own name.

"You probably haven't heard, but there was a fire last night in the rookery," Aiden opened.

"I was nowhere near the place," Heden offered.

The lad frowned, giving Heden a sharp look, then relaxed. "Oh you're being funny. Somewhere over thirty people died. Maybe more, it's going to be a while before know. If we ever know. And this isn't the first time. Nor will it be the last. The entire city is under attack."

"What's this got to do with me," Heden asked.

"The fire was started by a half dozen ghouls on a murderous rampage," the boy said, watching for a reaction.

He gave the standard reply but, he realized, it took him just a blink of an eye too long, and the lad saw it. "There are no more deathless."

"Uh huh," Aiden said. "And you don't know anything about this," he said.

"Nope," Heden said.

"And you didn't hear anything about a ghoul ripping a half-dozen thieves apart in this room we are now sitting in."

"I wondered what that mess was," Heden nodded.

Aiden ran a hand through his hair.

"You want something to drink," Heden asked.

"I don't drink," Aiden said. "We figured, you being out of town at the time, you had no idea what happened in here….,"

"That's true."

"But then something interesting happened last night," Aiden continued.

"In the rookery?"

"Un-uh," Aiden shook his head. "Down at the docks. Fishmonger says three assassins came into his place, assaulted him, and then tried to kidnap a girl. Customer of his."

Heden went still. The specials knew about Vanora know, and knew the connection between her and the inn. No point in playing anymore.

"Did they get her," he asked, flatly.

Aiden took a deep breath, through his nose. "Well, that's where things get interesting because the fishmonger says a woman, a wizard he thinks, stepped in and there was a fight."

Heden frowned. "Who was the woman?"

Aiden gave him the fishmonger's description.

"Black gods," Heden said. Reginam. Looking out for Vanora. For him.

"You know her?"

Heden stared at the special watchman. The castellan's man. Who'd given up a lot so far without any promise of return.

"Yes," he admitted. "She's a wizard of the Quill. Reginam. Before she joined the Quill, we were campaigners together."

Aiden nodded and gave Heden a strange look. "Thank you," he said. "When was the last time you talked to this wizard?"

Heden shook his head. "Years ago."

"So why is she looking out for this girl?"

"I don't know," Heden said, and wasn't sure if it was a lie or not.

"Interesting," Aiden said, watching Heden. He got the impression the boy could read his mind. "So these three assassins come in to grab a girl, but they're thwarted by a wizard you used to campaign with. Which is doubly interesting to me," he said, "because the fishmonger said the girl was from here too."

"Her name's Vanora," Heden said.

"Fishmonger said Violet," Aiden said

"She was a trull," Heden said. "Went by Violet. Real name Vanora."

Aiden twisted around to see Fandrick and Rayk, eating and talking. Then he turned back to Heden, smug. "They thought coming here was a waste of time," he said.

"What happened to the girl," Heden pressed.

"Well, by the time we got there, the assassins had been melted, so we're pretty sure they didn't get her. But melted or not, they made a play for the girl and at *this point*," the young special said, "I start to feel like I've got all the pieces of a very large puzzle.

"You tell me how this sounds to you. The count wants this girl, we don't know why, doesn't matter. He sends his men here a fortnight ago. You're not here, but the girl is. And someone else. Maybe this Reginam. Someone looking out for your interests while you're away. They try and thwart the Black," Aiden said.

"Thwart?" Heden said.

"I read a lot," Aiden shrugged, and continued. "So the Black conjure up a ghoul. We thought the ghoul was brought up to stop the Black, but I think it's the other way 'round. But the ghoul can't be controlled and it ends up killing everyone while the girl gets away.

"Assaulting this place didn't work so he waits. Eventually the girl goes to get some fish, Count tries again. Again, someone stops them. This time, before they can create more deathless. So the girl gets away, again. And I have it on good authority," he said, looking over at Fandrick and Rayk at the next table eating in silence, "that we're lucky because if the count got her there wouldn't be a damned thing we could do about it."

"Can't arrest the count," Heden said.

"Well, that's not…," the young man said, squirming in his seat, "that's not completely obvious to me," he said in frustration. Heden smiled. He liked this boy.

"So how am I doing?" the boy asked.

Heden nodded. "Pretty good," he said. "You got the connection between the count and the Deathless, between the girl and here. You know just about what I know."

"Why don't you help me fill in the gaps," the boy said.

"I'm not obligated to help the castellan," Heden said.

"I'm not obligated to help you find the girl," Aiden countered.

Heden gave Aiden a skeptical look. "I'm not sure you can help," he said. "I don't know where she is, and if I don't, probably no one does."

"Someone does," Aiden countered. "She's not alone. She needs help, if the count's after her."

Heden shrugged.

"Give me something," the boy said, "so I don't look like an idiot in front of my betters," he indicated the other two watchmen.

Heden didn't count the castellan a friend, but nor was he an enemy. He was someone it paid to stay on the good side of.

"She used to be the count's personal whore," Heden offered. "He tries to keep it to one girl at a time. Limit the number of people who can get close to him."

"And that's it?" Aiden said, disbelieving.

"That's what I know," Heden said, omitting the fact that Vanora also apparently knew where the count's secret operation was, reasoning that he'd only learned it a moment before and therefore wasn't yet obligated to give it over.

"What's the girl to you?" he asked.

Heden shrugged. "Needed someone to work the tables," he lied.

"Ok, well," Aiden said. "That was a lie, but I can't really…I can't force you to help me. I can tell the ragman you didn't tell me everything."

"He won't be surprised," Heden said. "Also won't like it, he finds out you called him that."

"I'm picking up bad habits," Aiden said with half a smile. He sighed and looked around the room, then looked at the table, thinking.

"I'm new at this," he said after a moment. "I don't have the experience my older, more cynical fellows have. But I think the count is after the girl, he's got the kind of power now, he can get what he wants and he wants a lot. He wants the city for one thing, and I think he's going to get it if we don't stop him."

"We?" Heden said, pointing to himself and the young watchman.

Aiden shrugged. "We the rest of the city who can be counted on to do the right thing. Which may or may not include you. Anyway. He wants the girl, he's going to get the girl, unless you stop him. Which I have no idea how you would do, but everyone says you're the type to try."

"Everyone," Heden said.

"We asked about you," Aiden said. "I met several people this morning willing to go on record saying you can upset a lot of people when you want to."

"Sometimes I do more than upset them," Heden said.

"Don't…," Aiden said, holding up a hand, "don't try and show off to me, I don't care. I mean, I find this whole thing… it's absurd. Counts and guilds and deathless, I'm still not sure why you're not all in jail. But I'll figure that out later. *I think*," he continued, "that you knew the girl wouldn't be safe while the count was out there, and so you've decided to go for the count and to do that, you needed to get the girl out of the way. So you get her somewhere safe, now you can make your play."

"That would be smart," Heden said. *I wish I'd thought of it.*

Aiden nodded. "Do not make a move for the count," he said. "I don't know the castellan well, but he does not like it when people take the law into their own hands and he *especially* does not like it when they do so after he's sent his own special watchmen to come talk to them on his behalf and warn them off."

Heden blinked. "Ah," he said.

"Yeah," Aiden said. "He seemed to get very angry when he

learned you were involved in this."

"I have that effect on people," Heden said. Aiden was looking at him expectantly.

"I have no plans to go after the count," Heden said, truthfully. "I wouldn't even know how to go about it," he said.

Aiden took a deep breath and watched Heden's face. "Maybe," he said. "Do you have any idea where he gets these ghouls from?"

Heden shook his head. "I have no idea. I've never even seen it happen."

Aiden looked around the room, dejected. "Dead end," he said. "For the moment. Alright," he said getting up.

He looked at Heden like he was trying to solve a puzzle. "I have no idea what you're doing in all this, but talking to folks, the castellan, if you're in it and the count's in it, sooner or later one of you will make a move for the other. I'd rather that didn't happen. I'd rather you let us deal with it. But on the off chance you do get in a dust-up with the count and live, do me a favor and come tell me what you learned. We've got a whole city about to go up in flames. It's more than just you and a girl."

"What are you going to do?" Heden asked.

The young man shrugged. "Find another thread. Pull at it until something unravels."

Heden nodded. "Always worked for me," he said with a smirk.

"Wonderful," the special watchman said, and went to collect his fellows.

CHAPTER THIRTY-SEVEN

It was three days before the count made his move.

The inn was packed, it was an hour before dusk and there wasn't a spare table in the common room. The count came in, with Garth right behind him.

Garth nodded to the table where Heden sat. The count walked over. Garth followed.

Because he looked royal, dress and manner, and maybe because he was royal, everyone noticed him and no one got in his way as approached Heden's table. No one noticed Garth walking behind him.

The count stopped and stood before Heden, cocked his head, appraised the man sitting down with an untouched mug in front of him. Heden returned the look.

"Probably I should have waited." Heden said, "until I had fewer enemies before I opened this place."

The count smiled and nodded. "If you're planning on making a lot of enemies," he said, "be hard to find."

"Good advice," Heden said. "I don't plan that far ahead, I guess."

The count nodded to the chair. "May I?"

"Sure," Heden said.

The count whipped off his cloak with a flourish and laid it over the back of the chair before sitting down. Garth remained standing.

"We have never met, but we are enemies" the count began.

"Yep," Heden said.

The count grinned. It seemed genuine. Maybe it was.

"We are only enemies of the moment," the count said. "Someday, someday soon I hope, we will no longer be enemies. No reason we can't be cordial until then," the count said, gesturing to a serving girl. It was Caerys. She stared at Heden, eyes wide.

Heden nodded once. Caerys scurried away to get drinks. The count noticed the exchange.

"No reason," Heden said.

"Circumstance aimed us at each other. You had no idea who Violet was when you rescued her from the jail. I had no idea who you were...."

"Her name's Vanora."

The count covered his mouth with his hand as his grin turned into a wide smile. "Of course," he said.

"Now," he went on, "I know the whore is not here." Caerys returned with drinks for the two men. "Well," the count said looking at the girl as she curtseyed, "not the whore I'm looking for at least."

Caerys threw a look at Heden, who shrugged in response.

"You have hidden her somewhere, and why not? You wish to protect her. Completely understandable. But you must know that I will find her. I very nearly control this city and I will enjoy killing many people, many people dear to you, dear to her, until I find her."

"You don't control the city yet," Heden said.

The count's smile evaporated. He snapped his fingers.

Everyone in the inn, every guest, men women, old folks, young, all stopped talking, instantly. All put their food down, their drinks, and stood up. They all stared at Heden.

The serving girls stopped in their tracks, looked confused at each other, and then Heden. When Heden seemed unconcerned, they relaxed, but only a little, as they waited to see what would happen next.

"They're still going to have to pay for their food," Heden said. The count just stared at him. "Oh," Heden said. "Sorry, I'm supposed to be scared. it's just that it's been a long time since anything scared me and I'm a little rusty. Should I piss myself a little?" he asked, frowning. "I'll need some more ale for that."

The count took a measured breath, then flashed a smile.

"Drama," he apologized. Garth made a sharp gesture and the entire common room began filing out silently, leaving the serving girls nothing to do. "I'm making a point. You have power, I have power. But yours comes from one source, mine from many. I have money, for instance. A great deal of money. I know you were a campaigner for thirteen years and came back with sacks of gold, it's not the same. I bought all these people, for instance. Most of them guild members. All of them criminals."

"And you sent them here, take every seat, order, pretend to be guests, to let me know you can get to me any time you want," Heden said.

"Just so," the count said. "My grip on the city becomes tighter by the hour, the number of people keen to be in my employ grows. That will never be you, but there is no reason we must be enemies."

"As long as I'm willing to give you the girl," Heden said.

The count shrugged. "She belongs to me."

"She doesn't belong to anyone. She's hers," Heden said.

The count pursed his lips. "I am here merely as a courtesy to both of us. I came to you because you know where the girl is, and I know where you are. If you knew where my operation was, you would have come to me, warned me to stop looking."

Heden nodded. "I would have."

"We are alike," the count said, taking no pleasure or satisfaction in the statement.

"Like enough," Heden said.

The count leaned forward and pressed his index finger into the table. "So, just as I know it, you must know it; none of this matters. What matters isn't what we say. It's who has the power to enforce their will and you *must know*," the count said, raising his voice, "that my power is now very nearly limitless. I could have the king if I thought there was any benefit to it. If I thought he was a threat. You are nothing."

Heden sniffed. He looked sad. He glanced at Garth.

"How did you end up with this streak of shit?" he asked.

Garth shrugged. "Times are hard."

The count twisted around, looked behind him at Garth, then at Heden, then back to Garth.

"You two know each other?" he said.

Garth's eyes never left Heden. "Sure," he said.

The count suddenly became very calm, stared at Garth.

"You and I should talk later."

"We can talk now," Garth said, not taking his eyes off Heden.

"How is it you know this man?" the count asked.

"I campaigned with him for a while," Garth said. "Years ago."

The count turned back to face Heden. He had an entertained look of renewed interest. "Indeed! You were allies?"

"Not exactly," Garth said. "We agreed to put off being enemies for a while to our mutual benefit."

The count nodded. "And what kind of man is he?"

"He's tough," Garth said.

"But fair," Heden said. Garth ignored him.

"He's not very smart and he knows it. Usually has someone else do his thinking."

"Does he have many friends?" the count asked. Heden had the sense the count already knew the answer.

"Not anymore. He was never easy to get along with."

"Not like you," Heden said, nodding his head deferentially.

"The whores always liked him," Garth said. "Because they couldn't get to him. Because they trusted him. I could never figure out why he gave a shit."

"I think I might know," the count said, one eyebrow raised. "If I asked you to kill him, could you?"

"Sure," Garth said.

"Does he know this?" the count asked.

"Yeah," Garth said.

Heden's eyes rested for a moment on the rapier at Garth's hip. *Apostate*. The weapon Garth chose from a mountain of treasure, on purpose, because he knew someday, someone would tell him to kill this priest.

Heden looked back at Garth. The count noticed all this, but the significance was lost on him. He leaned forward conspiratorially.

"Come," he said as though Garth couldn't hear him. "Let's end this now and go back to that pleasant time when neither of us knew the other existed. Where is Violet?"

It looked, to Heden's eye, as though Garth's head shook once in disapproval.

"Go fuck a pig," Heden said.

The count flashed his charming smile, completely genuine, no hint of artifice. He stood up, swept up his cape as he did so.

"You are alone," he said as he fastened the cape about his neck. "You have no friends, no allies, and many, many enemies. Whereas I am days away from controlling all crime in the city. Already I have more allies than I have use for. Isn't that true, Garth?"

Garth let his gaze flicker away from Heden for a moment. "He knows it's true," Garth said.

"We will find the girl and then…," the count shrugged. "Then you will be of no consequence to me and we will no longer be enemies."

Heden and the count stared at each other for a moment. Then, without taking his eyes off the count, Heden said "See you later Garth."

The count's smile dropped for a moment. Garth turned to leave and, after a moment's hesitation, the count followed.

Chapter Thirty-eight

It was two hours after noon. The inn was empty, except for Heden and the girls. The count's demonstration had left the place with no customers. *No matter*, Heden thought as he stared at his mug. *More will come.*

Caerys approached tentatively. "You can't fight the count," she said. It was almost a whisper.

Heden rolled an idea around in his head, said nothing.

"I don't know," Martlyn said, from behind Caerys. "Maybe he can."

Heden took a deep breath, eyes still fixed on his drink. "It's not the count," he said. "It's Garth."

"You know him," Caerys said. "He said you travelled with him or something?"

"I campaigned with him. A kind of travelling. The dangerous kind."

"You're afraid of him," Martlyn said, and seemed disappointed.

"He's the deadliest man I ever met," Heden said, as though remarking on the time of day.

Caerys looked at Martlyn. "He always treated us nice," she said.

"Garth did," Martlyn said. "Not the count."

"No," Caerys agreed, mostly to be saying something, "not him."

"He wouldn't be cruel to you," Heden said. "Garth has a kind of honor. He'll do what he says he'll do."

Martlyn nodded. Caerys didn't seem to understand why this was worth remarking on.

"Doesn't everyone?"

Heden sniffed and looked at the girls. Caerys and Martlyn

and three others standing behind them listening.

"Nope," he said. "No, most people…most people are like the count. Say one thing, do another. Whatever's convenient. Even normal people. They mean well, but they get scared, they make bad decisions. They regret," he said ambiguously. "No, men like Garth," he said nodding at the door, "when they agree to do something, they will absolutely do it, no matter what."

"Could he kill you?" Martlyn asked, businesslike.

"Sure," Heden said. "Well, probably. It's not certain. We never tested it. He's better with a sword than me but that's not… lots of people are. Mostly it's that he's never valued anything that didn't make him a better killer. He made a study of death the way other men learn to work wood or metal. You sum that over a lifetime…," he didn't finish the sentence.

The girls watched him. Waited to see what he would do.

"You should all go back to the Rose," Heden said.

Martlyn made a 'tch' noise. "Don't think we'll do that."

"Vanora would get angry with us," Caerys explained.

Martlyn frowned at Caerys, as though what Vanora thought wasn't important. Then she cocked her head at Heden. "Someone has to look after you," she said.

Heden's eyebrows raised. "Me? I can look after myself. But I can't do that and look after you at the same time."

"That's why Vanora left," Caerys said, nodding. It was a simple statement, but it's clarity impressed Heden.

"Yeah," he said.

"Well," Caerys continued, "that's no matter then. The count's not after us," she smiled.

"That's true," Heden admitted. Neither the count nor Garth were likely to make a move against him in the inn. In front of people.

"I noticed Morten's not here," Heden said, trying to sound relaxed. Trying to force things back to normal.

"I think Miss Elowen's fed up with all this," Martlyn said.

"Doesn't let Morten come by anymore."

"Mm," Heden said. "So how come you're here?"

Martlyn smiled at him. "It's still our time to do as we want. She won't crack down on that unless things get bad at the Rose."

"I'll talk to her," Heden said. "Explain what's going on here."

"I wouldn't do that," Caerys said.

"Why not?" Heden asked.

"She might say no," the younger, dark-haired girl explained. Heden smiled.

"Better to ask forgiveness, than permission," Martlyn said.

Heden laughed. Every girl in the room jumped a little. None of them had ever heard him do that before.

"Well, you'll need a guard at least," he said. "To look over things while I'm out."

He stood up, made sure his sword belt was tight around his waist. "Need to find someone who won't get," he looked at Caerys and Martlyn. Martlyn put a hand on her hip and smirked. "Distracted. Think I know someone," he said, and walked to the door.

"Customers'll be coming in soon," Heden said. "Real ones, this time. I hope. Tend to their needs," he said and looked from Caerys to Martlyn. "Food, drink…," Caerys dipped a curtsey.

"And nothing else," Heden said.

The girls looked at him sweetly and said nothing.

He sighed, and left the inn.

Chapter Thirty-nine

"Spare him?" Domnal asked. "Spare him for what?"

Heden sat in Dom's office, across the desk from the watch captain. He kicked some of the sawdust from the floor off his boots.

"Just keep an eye on the girls at my inn while I'm gone."

"So hire someone from the docks," Dom said, leaning back in his chair, his fingers laced together over his fat belly. "What d'you need Teagan for?"

"I trust him," Heden said.

"'Course you trust him, he's a watchman. But we can't be lending out coppers to work the inns and taverns. They got jobs already."

"I'm not suggesting you make a habit of it," Heden said, impatient. "It's just me, just for a fortnight or so. Just Teagan. I trust him because he used to be a ratcatcher."

"That ain't no reason to trust someone," Dom observed, and pulled himself up out of his chair.

"Where are you going?" Heden asked.

"See what the man himself thinks." He pulled open the door that led to the rest of the jail and bellowed Teagan's name, then came back and sat down.

Teagan walked in. A little over six feet, and thin. His short, sandy brown hair emphasized his youthful look, though Heden suspected he was in his early 30s.

"Well, close the door," Dom said.

Teagan did as instructed.

"You remember Heden," Dom said.

The lanky watchmen nodded at Heden. The faint smile Heden remembered, like he was enjoying a private joke, never left his face.

"We had some fun together at the Rose," Heden said.

"We killed three yellow scarves," Teagan said. "You have a queer idea of fun," but his smile broadened.

"He wants to sort of, hire you on, keep an eye on his place for him while he runs around the city pissing people off," Dom said.

Heden frowned at his friend's description.

"So hire some muscle. Why do you need me?" Teagan asked.

"Same as the Rose," Heden explained. "Problem with the count."

Now Teagan frowned.

"Count never did anything to me," he said. Heden raised an eyebrow at this.

"I just need someone to look after the girls," Heden said. "No one's going to come after them, but someone might come looking for me."

Teagan looked at Dom. "What do you say, boss?"

Dom shrugged. "I say what you do on your own time is your business, long as you're here when the cock crows. I know Heden. If he's asking, means he needs more than hired muscle. You're good with a sword," Dom said. "Good without one."

Teagan nodded. "There's something I'm better at," he said, and rubbed his chin. "Minding my own business."

This response surprised Dom. "Never knew you to show fear," he said, narrowing his eyes at Teagan. "You afraid of the count?"

Heden could tell Dom was trying to help in his own way. Press the watchman, make sure he was making the right decision for the right reasons. It's what made him a good captain, a good leader.

Teagan shrugged. "'Course I am, man's got an army of trained assassins. You think we hang out inside this stone building out of confidence?"

Heden smiled at the man's logic. "He's right." He stood up

and looked Teagan up and down. "The count isn't his enemy and helping me might change that. It was wrong for me to ask." He looked at Dom. "Thanks for trying to help, though."

"Now how come when he says it," Dom thrust his chin at Teagan, "you all of a sudden listen and when I say it you come over all deaf?"

Heden looked from Dom to Teagan. "He's younger," Heden said. "More handsome. Makes him more persuasive."

"That's true," Teagan nodded.

"Sorry I bothered you," Heden held out his hand. Teagan took it.

"No bother," he said. "I'll stop by your place after work days. On the way home. Stick my head in, make sure everything's ok. No reason not to."

"Thanks," Heden said. "That'll probably be enough." Heden walked to the door.

"Where you off to?" Dom asked.

Heden pulled the door open. "Gotta go talk to a wizard," he said. "Hope I'm more persuasive with her than I was with the watchmen."

CHAPTER FORTY

The wizard came down to see him. No one was allowed beyond the receiving room without undergoing certain checks that Heden was in no mood for.

Watching her quickly descend the spiral staircase, he was reminded of her impressive figure. Something most men she met never forgot. But to Heden, she was always a face in his memory. A perfectly sculpted face with dancing eyes that saw everything Heden tried to conceal.

She was among the most distracting people he had ever met.

"Hey gorgeous," Hapax said once she was in earshot. "Long time no see."

She danced up to him and grabbed his elbow, steering him around and locking arms with him.

"Where are you taking me," she asked, "to celebrate our reunion?"

Heden allowed himself to be steered.

"It's on me," Heden said. "Your choice."

"Of course it is! How about we go to the Ship?" she suggested, and made a motion like she was snuggling up to him. It was a degree of familiarity Heden wouldn't normally put up with, but he knew Hapax. It was just her way. She was like this with all her friends. Heden wasn't special.

"Sure, I like the Ship," he said.

"Me too. And I love the idea of being seen there with you of all people."

It was a turn's walk from the tower of the Lens to the expensive end of the docks, where the Sinking Ship tavern was. It was the kind of place you could only eat at if you were making a lot of money off the trade coming in and out. Heden considered it a waste of money, but liked the food. He found it hard to reconcile his father's frugality with his own taste for good food, expertly prepared.

They talked about nothing as they made their way down the cobbled streets, found a table at the Ship, easy at this time of day, and ordered drinks.

"Why must our love go unconsummated?" Hapax asked, typically theatrically.

"You're not my type," Heden said.

She lowered her head and gave him a very knowing look. "Really."

"I don't go in for women with, ah…," Heden said.

Hapax looked down at her impressive landscape.

"…husbands," Heden finished.

Hapax rolled her eyes. "Whatever," she said. "Everyone knows what that's about."

"Everyone," Heden said.

"I wasn't always married," Hapax said, no longer flirty or theatrical. "But you were always a shit."

Heden liked her better this way.

She let her eyes wander over his face.

"I can't imagine what you'd be like now if she hadn't sunk her claws into you."

"We're not doing this," Heden said. Why did she have to ruin it? "I need some information."

Hapax pursed her dark red lips. "I got all kinds of information, what are we talking about?"

Heden took a deep breath, reached into a vest pocket, and pulled out the black marbles the polder thief gave him.

"What is this?" Heden asked, holding it between his fingers.

Hapax looked at it, and smiled.

"It's night dust," she said. Heden looked from her to the marble in his hand. "Keep it, I've already got some."

"You're fast," Heden said.

"Not always," she said, smiling sweetly.

Their drinks arrived.

"How much do you know?" Heden asked.

"Not much," Hapax said, taking a drink. "A little. What's it worth to you?"

"Depends," Heden said, sitting back in his chair and relaxing. He was happy to have someone like Hapax Legomenon dealing with this. "I guess I was hoping it falls inside your normal brief."

"It does," she said. "Have you heard what the count's up to?"

"Sort of," Heden said. "I've been out of the loop for a few years."

"You were never in the loop," Hapax said, taking a drink. "It was part of your charm."

"If you're already working the night dust," Heden said. "I guess I can relax. Let you take care of it."

"Take care of it?" Hapax asked.

Heden shrugged. "Does that not qualify as a reliquary?"

Hapax held the black marble up. Peered at the smoke swirling inside it, like a living thing trying to escape. "We're working on that," she said. "We're not sure where it comes from. We have some ideas, but that doesn't mean we're going to charge off to war against the count."

"That's between you and your charter," Heden said. "I'm happy to stay out of it."

She put the marble down, used the tip of her finger to stop it from rolling.

"You're thinking about a censure," she said. He could see her mind working. This gave him assurance. Having someone smart dealing with it. Why were all the smartest people he knew women?

"Depends on how many of those the count has. If it's a dozen? No. If it's a hundred? An army of deathless? You tell me."

She looked exasperated, but not at him. "Heden we have to get approval from the castellan to field a Censure in the city, you know that."

"Shouldn't be hard. You'd be doing it to protect the city."

Hapax nursed her drink. "You'd be surprised how different the castellan's idea of protecting the city is from ours."

"You stopped that whatever-it-was that was turning people into those snake things last summer."

"Yeah and like 200 people died," the wizard snapped. "It took 12 of us throwing everything we had at it. We had to get help from the Sundial. You know they had to *slow down time* in order to stop the outbreak?"

"Ah," Heden said, a little taken aback. "No, I didn't know that."

"Well these are the kinds of things we deal with," she said, getting angry. "The kinds of things you idiots keep digging up." She nodded at the black marble.

"I'm not a campaigner anymore," Heden pointed out, defensively.

"And yet here you are with more dug up crap."

"You have no idea where it comes from!" Heden got the sense he'd stepped over some line, was eager to step back.

"You know there's something like 60,000 years of dead civilizations buried around here," she gesticulated, indicating the whole world. "Not including whatever bizarre mindbending shit the elves got up to before the dwarves came along. Lives are at stake whenever someone digs some of this shit up, and no one but us to stop it. So you come to me with this and say 'censure,' and I tend to get upset. I start to think you want me doing your dirty work."

Heden pursed his lips and was properly contrite. He let Hapax cool down.

The food came. Neither of them started on it.

"You said you knew a little," Heden said.

Hapax grabbed a fork and skewered her meat, taking her anger out on the dead duck.

"It's alchemical," she said.

Tam, again. He knew about the alchemy connection but chose to say nothing lest it upset her further. He grabbed some bread and buttered it.

"Covers a lot," he said. She nodded.

"But there's something else," she said. "It's alive."

This was new.

"Alive?" Heden asked. "What does that…how is that possible?"

"We don't know yet," she said. "We're doing research. There's a fungus on the big island of Ix, can have a similar effect. We don't think this is a fungus, but it's a lead."

"You'll let me know more when you find out?"

Hapax waggled her head back and forth, weighing the idea. "Probably," she said. "I'm a sucker for feeling needed."

Heden let her eat in silence.

"I'm shouldn't have tried to dump this on you," he said. "Take advantage of our friendship. I'm sorry."

Hapax said nothing for a moment, slicing off another piece of duck. Then without moving her head she threw Heden a glance. "How sorry?" she asked, smiling a little.

Heden smiled. "Not that sorry," he said.

Hapax shook her head. "Probably for the best," she said. "After all these years the act could never live up to the anticipation."

"Oh yes it could," Heden said, his voice low.

Hapax put her fork down and stared at Heden, suddenly speechless.

Heden snickered. Turnabout was fair play.

CHAPTER FORTY-ONE

Martlyn pulled the door open. She knew there was something wrong immediately, although it took a moment to recognize it. Apart from the girls running down the brightly lit, red carpeted hall in a panic, there was something else. A smell.

Smoke. The building she was in, the Rose Petal, was burning.

"What's going on?" her clotpole asked from the bed behind her.

"Get dressed," she barked, no longer an innocent girl.

"But we haven't…"

She spun, grabbed her robe and shawl.

"The building's on fire idiot," she said.

Throwing her clothes around her, she abandoned her customer to his own devices and went out into the hall.

Girls were running back and forth, milling around, some customers were trying to get out. She saw Bann descend from the third floor, called his name.

"Martlyn" Bann said, his voice tense but not afraid. He pushed his way toward her, annoyed at the mad activity around them. Even though she was taller than most of the girls, Ban loomed over her. "Good. Take this," he said, and pressed a long coil of rope into her uncomprehending hands.

"What's happening?"

"The building's on fire," Bann said. "The entrances are blocked. The count's men are killing anyone who tries to get out."

"Black gods," Martlyn was panicking, her legs felt like jelly.

"But you're going to get everyone out," Bann said, pointing at the rope in her hands.

"Where am I supposed to go?" Martlyn asked, her bowels freezing in fear, far more worried about where to go and what to do than the fire. This was home, she'd been safe here. Would no safety last?

Bann grabbed her by the shoulders. "Stupid," he commented to himself. He spun her around, faced her toward the second story window.

"Where do you think?" he growled, his voice carrying above the screams. Girls were running past them in every direction. He pointed at the window. "The Hammer & Tongs. Find the priest," he said. They both knew who he meant.

She turned back around, the rope hanging limp in her hands.

"I can't!" she said, afraid.

"Yes you can," he rumbled, turning her around again. "Chest of drawers," he pointed to the heavy oak chest at the end of the hall perpendicular to the window.

"Tie this to the leg," he said, taking the rope from her, only to push it back into her chest, make her hold it

"Tie it tight, like I taught you. Pretend it's a clotpole's ankle or wrist," he said, trying to smile. "Then out you go. The other girls will follow, let them. Lead them to the inn. To the priest's inn."

Martlyn stared at the window, blackness outside. Bann squeezed her shoulders.

"You got it?"

She nodded.

Bann drew the huge two-hander from his back. Turned to go back downstairs.

"Where are you going?" Martlyn asking, panicking. Bann couldn't leave her.

"I'm giving you a chance to get out," Bann said. "The fire is a diversion."

Martlyn watched as Bann pushed his way to the stairs down, disappearing into the smoke.

She turned back to the window at the far end of the hallway. She clasped the rope to her chest.

The stairs down were now impassable, whether because of Bann or fire or both she didn't know. The girls were now desperately looking for her to do something.

"I don't fucking believe this," she said, angry and crying at the same time, cursing her fate.

She pushed her way to the end of the hall, the other girls following her blindly.

CHAPTER FORTY-TWO

"Where is Violet?"

The count lit a cigar, sat back in the velvet upholstered chair and crossed his legs. He smoothed his blonde mustache with one hand after taking a drag on the cigar. The flames from the back of the building were not yet visible, but smoke seeped in from under the doors.

Miss Elowen coughed, and spat up blood.

"Heden's got her," she said. She tried to get comfortable, but the leather straps holding her to the chair prevented much movement.

The count raised his eyebrows and looked at Garth.

"The priest," Garth said from his position behind Miss Elowen.

"Right," the count said, nodding.

"She was with Heden," Garth explained. "She's not now."

"Where is Violet?" the count asked again in exactly the same sing-song voice he used the first time.

"I don't know," Miss Elowen said.

The count took a drag on his cigar.

"Where is Violet?" he asked again, this time smiling.

"I did what you asked," Elowen said. "You wanted Violet gone, I took care of it. I waited until she had a fit, I went and got the church, and they took her away. They said the exorcism would kill her. That's what you wanted, right? That's the last I saw of her. She's nothing to do with me now, go ask the church."

Garth looked at the count expectantly. Not only did Elowen do what the count asked, she did what the count wanted, which was harder. Making sure people died when they needed to with no direct connection to the master of the guild was not easy. Garth knew this better than anyone.

As though reciting from a prepared script, which for all Garth knew he was, the count continued as though Elowen hadn't said anything.

"We are currently without a wizard," the count said, "so alas we have no access to the *Aduro Vera*. But!" he said, flourishing his cigar, "I think a more common fire may urge you to tell the truth.

"I am telling the truth," Elowen said. Garth held his tongue. Talking would just make it worse for her.

"Well, that's the benefit of the wizard's fire. It removes all doubt. Forgive me," the count said with a little bow from his seated position. "I don't mean to say I doubt you, I don't really. It's just that I'm not certain and, also, I enjoy the idea of burning down the only thing you've ever cared about," he gestured to the Rose Petal. It was very warm now. They could hear screaming upstairs.

Garth took a deep breath, but held his tongue. Miss Elowen and the Rose Petal had been a useful front, an easy way to scrub their income clean, a font of information. The count was getting reckless thanks to his newfound power, and he knew it, and he didn't care if Garth knew it and bringing it up would just cause this woman more pain.

"I'm in a position now, you understand, to indulge myself," the count continued. "Also, I wanted Garth here to witness the fact that I did not rape you, in spite of the fact that many in the guild assumed I would."

Elowen shrugged. Her years of refusing the count were going to catch up to her someday, she knew, and this was a better end than many she'd imagined. *At least*, she though*, Bann got the girls out*. It never occurred to the count that Elowen might not care about the building, only the girls.

"What is it about her?" Elowen wondered. "I gave you a dozen girls, you don't care about any of them, you never cared about Violet. What is it about her? What does she have over…,"

Elowen's eyes narrowed. "What does she *know*?" Elowen asked, one corner of her mouth curling with a knowing smile.

The count took a drag on his cigar again. Theater. Then repeated, "Where is Violet?"

Elowen sniffed again, blood from her nose flooded into her mouth. She spat it out, one huge bolus of snot and spit colored almost black with blood smacked into the count's right eyebrow, spattering all over his face.

The count surged to his feet with a snarl. Stood over Elowen seething.

Garth suppressed a grin. *She won*, he thought. In the decade-long contest between Elowen and the count to see which could finally provoke the other to anger, Elowen had the last word. Garth regretted she had to die.

The count produced a kerchief to wipe his face. Once used, he threw it to the ground and produced a dagger. Pressed it against her cheek, drew a little blood. Elowen didn't flinch.

"I could ruin your face," the count said, "but what would be the point. It will be a melted pile of boiling fat in a few moments anyway."

He turned, strode to the table next to his chair, picked up his drink, tossed it onto the expensive, imported tapestry, and lit it with his cigar, then dropped the cigar, turned, and walked out.

"Come on," he said to Garth as he walked past.

CHAPTER FORTY-THREE

Garth and the count stood on the street while the Rose Petal burned, lighting up the night sky.

"That felt very good," the count said, smoothing his hair back. "She always thought she'd get the best of me. Stupid bitch."

She did get the best of you, Garth thought. *Wasn't difficult.*

He thought about what Elowen had said. About why the count had his horn up so bad for the girl. There was something there.

She was smarter than the count. Smart enough to have thought ahead.

"Come," the count said. "We must away. It's still early for us to be seen outside."

Garth hesitated. The count frowned.

"I need to check on something," Garth said, and walked back up to the door of the burning Rose.

He opened the door. Miss Elowen was standing, rubbing her wrists. Coughing in the smoke. Next to her, the explanation for how she got free.

Bann. The seven foot tall war breed stood, unflinching, facing Garth. He pressed Miss Elowen behind him, and she ran. Back through the flames. There'd be a window, a door she could exit through.

Garth turned to the count. "You go back," he said, raising his voice above the sound of flames. From the street, the count could not see that Miss Elowen was escaping. "I'm going to make sure the job is done."

The count bowed sharply. "Very well," he said, and walked away crisply, his cloak flowing.

Garth entered the room with Bann. It was like the inside of

an oven. The rear wall was on fire. Soon the whole room would be on fire, like the upstairs, and then the building would collapse on them.

Bann didn't run. He was buying time for Miss Elowen.

"This is stupid," Garth said.

"As stupid as burning the building?" Bann growled. "As stupid as slicing up Miss Elowen, who never did nothin' but what the count asked?"

Garth gritted his teeth, in tacit agreement with the warbreed.

"Why waste your life too?"

Bann grunted. "Not a waste if Miss Elowen gets away."

Garth looked through flames. There was nowhere she could run to that he couldn't follow. But maybe he didn't have to.

"Alright," Garth nodded, "your life for hers."

Bann relaxed a little. His death would not be in vain.

He drew his massive two-hander. Garth drew *Apostate*.

The contest was short. Bann took one roundhouse swing. Garth stepped neatly back. Bann swung overhand, Garth stepped to the side. The massive broadsword slammed into the floorboard, buckling them. A blow that would have split Garth in two, if it had landed.

Bann feinted, swinging his broadsword in one hand. When Garth leaned out of the way, Bann grabbed him with the other hand.

Bann sneered. His yellow eyes sparking in the fire. His white teeth and tusks practically glowing against his black skin. He'd been able to give Garth a surprise.

But Garth didn't mind surprises. Once grabbed, he let Bann pull him closer and while the war breed opened his mouth to tear at Garth's head and shoulders with teeth and needle-sharp fangs, Garth simply stabbed him. Once. Through the heart. With *Apostate*.

Bann froze, sucked a final breath in. Dropped his sword, put a hand on the blade in his heart. He looked down in confusion at Garth.

His legs buckled. Garth didn't have the strength to hold him up on the sword, and so let him drop, pulling *Apostate* from the war breed's chest.

"Sorry, Bann," Garth said to the gurgling, gasping figure at his feet. "This wasn't your fault."

He finished the job, wiped off his blade, and turned his back on Miss Elowen, and the Rose.

CHAPTER FORTY-FOUR

When Heden returned from dinner with Hapax Legomenon, he found a packed inn. Standing room only. Something was happening. Something he wasn't in the mood for.

There were something like 30 girls, all sitting and standing around. In and amidst another 20 customers. There was a low roar as they all talked and frittered. They were shaken. Something had happened. None of them seemed to notice Heden.

He pushed his way through them and noticed they were all young, and all dressed...dressed very nicely. Dressed like Martlyn and Caerys.

"Oh no," he said out loud.

One of the girls turned around. Caerys. He hadn't noticed her.

"Your lordship!" she called out, putting one hand on Heden's chest as the other flew to her mouth.

"What in the horny hells is going on in here?" Heden asked.

"Uh, well," Caerys said, looking around, her pretty face pinched in a worried frown, "there was a ...something happened," she said, trying to answer him without saying anything.

"The count burned down the Rose Petal," a voice said. Heden turned to see Martlyn, looking older.

Heden slumped a little more and put one hand to his forehead. "Gods," he said. "Cavall."

He looked around the inn at all the girls. Now he knew why they were here and so desperately afraid.

"'It's not safe to be your friend,'" he quoted under his breath.

"What?" Caerys asked, it was hard to hear with the noise in the inn.

He looked at her. She looked back at him. Without saying it, he read the expression on her face. 'What are we going to do?' it said.

"Is everyone alright?" Heden asked.

Caerys looked around. "No!" she said. "They're terrified. Bann...no one knows what happened to him."

"He stayed behind," Martlyn said flatly. "To give us time to get out. I don't think he made it."

"Now they're afraid the count's coming for all of us," Caerys said.

Heden shook his head. He gestured and the girls stepped closer.

"That's not going to happen. He won't come in here. He won't attack this place. He tried and it cost him three men. Everyone's safe here, do you understand?"

The girls listened, looked at the others milling around in the common room. Many had stopped talking and were watching Heden, aware the man was someone important.

"Can they stay?" Caerys asked.

"I don't know," Heden said straightening up. "I don't...,"

"We want to tell them they can stay the night," Martlyn said. There was something in her voice.

Heden looked at her. She was going to leave. If Heden didn't agree to this, Martlyn would leave and then Caerys would leave. What would Vanora do, he wondered. Stupid question.

"Alright," he said. "They can stay. For now."

Caerys clapped her hands together. Martlyn just nodded.

"Where's Vanora?" Caerys asked. "We need her."

"No we don't," Martlyn said.

"She's safe," Heden said. "For now. I have to work fast. I need to find an alchemist named Tam. You'll be safe here while I look. The count wants Vanora, not you."

"We can help!" Caerys said, but Heden wasn't paying attention. Something had distracted him. Someone in the inn.

The press of bodies randomly parted and closed, revealing a woman sitting at a table by the fire. She was alone. She held a small glass of uske beet as if the glass itself gave her warmth and sustenance.

She was pretty, but plain. Her hair was long and brown, she was Heden's age, and wore no makeup. Her eyebrows looked thin and her lips almost non-existent. She was wearing a plain brown cloak.

Heden looked around. None of the girls recognized her. Without her magically enhanced hair coloring, her makeup, her finery, they didn't realize Elowen was sitting right there with them. The woman under whose roof they had worked and lived for years. Now as anonymous as any other patron.

"Take care of the girls," Heden said. "Keep the place open, serving customers. Give them something to do." Caerys and Martlyn nodded as Heden walked away.

He approached Elowen's table, pushing his way past the girls and occasional patron.

He stood in front of her. She looked up at him. Her eyes were red from crying and, seeing Heden, it seemed all about to start again.

Heden's hands balled into fists as his restrained his anger at the count.

"Meet me at the bridge," he said.

Elowen looked up at him, and then back down at her drink. She nodded.

He retreated and went to the door to the cellar.

CHAPTER FORTY-FIVE

"What do we do?"

Martlyn pressed her palms into her eyes, tried to clear her head. Think. She and Caerys stood in Vanora's room trying to determine their fate against the low roar of activity from the common room below.

"What are we going to do?" Caerys asked again.

Martlyn pulled her hands from his eyes, and grabbed a drink. Threw back a shot of uske. "I'm going back to the Rookery," she decided, and planted her empty glass on the table.

"You…," Caerys fretted. "You shouldn't do that!"

Martlyn shrugged. "What choice do I have?" She still smelled of smoke even though she'd changed her cloths at the inn. It was in her hair.

Caerys, her whole face knotted up with worry, pleaded wordlessly with Martlyn.

"I'm not going to work for him," Martlyn said, "he's going to get us all killed."

"So we help him," Caerys said. "He can stop the count."

"Not alone he can't!"

"He's not alone. We can help," Caerys stressed.

Caerys looked at Martlyn hopefully. Martlyn sneered and shook her head once. Her red curls looked black in the moonlight.

"Help," she spat.

"We help him," Caerys repeated, "he kills the count, and we can do whatever we want."

Caerys suddenly realized that Martlyn could not really be as skeptical, as hard, as she wanted everyone to think, otherwise she would have already left. She wanted to be convinced.

"We help him," Caerys repeated, "and we run this place like

Miss Elowen ran the Rose."

Martlyn was obviously intrigued by this idea "What can we do?" she asked.

Caerys took a breath, tried to calm down. "He needs to find an alchemist named Tam. Us? The girls? How many clotpoles do we see? Some of the girls work here, they work at the Wheel, the Purse. How long do you think it would take to find this alchemist? To find anyone we need?"

Martlyn nodded. The idea appealed to her.

"We don't do anything," Caerys said. "The priest has his horn up for the count, he'll go after him on all his own. All we have to do is find the alchemist."

Martlyn fired a nail. Took a drag.

She blew the smoke out, held her right elbow in her left hand the way she'd seen Miss Elowen do when she smoked.

She looked down at the younger girl. "Tam?" she asked.

Caerys smiled.

CHAPTER FORTY-SIX

Wellbridge was a small stone bridge, running over a canal used to divert water from the Wehl river for use in the city's sewage system. The water, as it ran under the arch of stone, was clean and the smell and sound were pleasant. Lovers often came here. At times, the Dusk Moon spun overhead lighting the river with a dull red color that made the water look like wine. Now it sparkled in starlight. The same starlight under which Heden had only two hours before, killed four black scarves.

He heard, rather than saw, Elowen take a position next to him on the bridge. He turned to look at her.

She stood there, a cloak around her for warmth, leaning on the stone, looking out at the river. She wasn't wearing heels. She looked like a normal girl. For some reason, to Heden, this made her more attractive.

"I'm sorry," he said.

She nodded.

"This is...it's probably my fault," he said.

"I know," she said flatly, not looking at him.

She sighed and shook her head.

"Here," Heden said, handing a collection of papers rolled up with twine to Elowen. "Take these."

Elowen took them gingerly, and gave Heden a look. "Parchment?" she asked.

Heden shook his head. "Paper. Money. Few thousand crowns. Capital currency."

She gripped the rolled papers tighter. "Capital," she said in a whisper.

"There's a deed in there to an apartment, mine. I've signed it over to you."

"You have an apartment in Capital?"

"Yeah," Heden said. "It's not much, a few rooms. Some servants. Been years since I've been there. Doubt I'll ever go back."

"Servants?" Elowen's voice squeaked a little.

Heden shrugged. "Comes with the territory. I've given you right and title to all my holdings in Capital," he said. "There's a few tens of thousands of crowns in an account in one of their banks. I never needed it. And there's this," he said, handing her something else.

She took what looked like a sliver of wood, a few inches long. White bark on one side, like someone had peeled the bark off a birch tree and some wood had come off with it.

"Wood?" She asked.

"Ok," Heden said, pressing his hand to his forehead. He hated explaining things like this. "We did a favor," he said meaning the Sunbrighters, "a big favor, for one of the Lords of Capital." Elowen looked at him, her eyes wide, reflecting the stars above them.

She nodded.

"Her name is Lliara," he said. "Well, that's not her full name; I could never remember the whole thing. Take this to her. She'll help you. She'll give you all the help you need. More. She owes me a lot. A lot more than a brothel."

Elowen looked at the pale wood. It was hard to tell in the starlight but it looked bluish.

"What is this?" she asked.

"It's some of her skin," Heden said.

Elowen snapped a look at him. "*What?*"

Heden shrugged. "She's one of the Lunar Celestials. There are a few still left in Orden. She can't leave Capital for some reason, she never explained it to me. I did her a favor and there was some kind of ritual and afterward she took a knife and…," he gestured to the wood. "It's like…you know, when men are being stupid and cut their palms to make an agreement? Same thing," he said.

"She's made of wood?" Elowen asked.

"She doesn't look like a tree or anything, she looks like a normal woman. Well, 'normal.' You'll see."

Elowen took the wood and bundled it with the parchment. "I'll see?" she said dully.

Heden shook his head. "I'm sorry about all this."

"You're giving me something like half a million crowns in coin and property and you're apologizing to me?"

"Which would you rather have," Heden asked. "The Rose and the girls, or that," he nodded to the parchment.

Elowen smiled that smile she used when Heden was being stupid. "This," she said, holding the papers up. "Don't be stupid." She laughed a little. "You get my place burned down and I end up a rich woman. Typical. And you want to apologize."

"You were happy in the Rose," Heden said, not accepting her answer. "You don't like change."

"No," she corrected, "*you* don't like change. I've been dreaming of Capital all my life," she said. "You're so naïve sometimes. Especially with women."

"I guess," Heden said.

She gave him a look.

"What?" he asked.

She stepped closer to him.

"Come with me."

Heden took a deep breath. Not this again.

"Someone has to look after the girls," he said.

"Heden the girls will be fine," Elowen said, smiling, shaking her head. "They don't need looking…*you* need looking after," she said. "You need a woman like a boat needs water. Everyone knows it."

"Everyone."

"Most everyone," she said. She turned and leaned on the stone railing of the bridge, looked out at the water under starlight.

"I know you've never…," she shook her head. "You've never thought of me like that," she began.

"What are we talking about?" Heden asked, leaning on the stone, watching her watch the water.

She looked at him for a moment and looked like she was going to cry again. Then the softness disappeared.

"I was never stupid enough to let myself fall far you," she gripped the roll of parchment. Heden raised his eyebrows.

"But we could be happy in Capital," she said. "It would be a lot of fun," she urged. "You could use some fun," she said. "You deserve to be happy," she said.

Heden tried not to let his distaste at her use of the word 'deserve' show.

"It's tempting," he said.

She spun on him. "No it's not," she snapped. "You'd never consider it a million years. I'm not enough. You want to know why I never…because I'm not enough. You've got such a twisted sense of…Negra wasn't enough. Rhiaan wasn't enough. She wasn't enough, apparently," she held up the bark. "None of us can compete with," she threw a hand in the direction of the Tower of the Quill, "which is stupid, because we're not competing with Reginam," she said, and tapped her forehead. "We're competing with the completely horseshit version of her you created in your head when you were kids. No one can compete with that, not even the real thing."

Heden felt helpless again, as he often did around women who wanted more than he could give. Why was this all his fault?

"You're like a fucking knight, except even the Hart comes to the Rose," she said. "It was stupid of me to ask. They burned down the Rose because of you and I should be furious, but all I feel is stupid because I asked you to come with me."

Heden didn't say anything. Silence grew.

Eventually she held up the papers. "Thanks," she said.

"Careful with them," Heden said. "It's all paper. They do everything with paper there. You'll get used to it."

"Probably," she said.

"I'm going to take care of the girls," he said, and realized he was swearing another oath.

"Find them nice homes?" she asked, looking down at the water. She wouldn't look at him.

"Maybe," he said. "I don't know, I'm trying to take this one day at a time. Some of them have already been…doing business there for days. Nothing horrible seems to have happened. They seem like nice normal girls."

"Of course they do, what did you expect?"

"I don't know," he said. "I guess I thought…,"

"Trulls are just like anyone else," she said with a sigh. "I don't imagine any of them are as fucked up as you."

"Ok," Heden said, letting her know he'd gotten her point.

She let go of something inside, relaxed. Turned to him.

"I know how your mind works," she said. "How long will you be able to ignore what they're doing? Act like nothing's going on? This isn't a problem to solve, Heden," she said.

"Well," he said thinking. "I don't like what they're doing."

"Do they like it?"

"Yeah," Heden said. He wasn't answering the question; he was confirming its legitimacy. "Don't think it matters what they like."

"Doesn't matter a little?"

"You think if they'd had different lives they'd be on the game?"

She couldn't argue with this.

"But they didn't have that life," she said. "This is what they know, it's what they're good at and most of them enjoy it."

Heden thought about this.

"No," he concluded. "No, you're wrong." She gave him a look. "I think," he added diplomatically.

"They enjoy the sense of family," he explained. "They enjoy belonging. They enjoy having a place where they feel safe. Feel like someone's watching over them. They enjoy feeling like they're earning a living, feeling like they're independent, have some control over their lives. And they maybe enjoy having this sense of power over men. But it's horseshit. It's the men who have the power, the men who pay."

"Is that why you never opened the inn?" she said.

It was like someone had slapped him. "What?" he shot back.

"You serve a customer. He pays you," she said. "You have to do what he came in for. You're obligated. He has the power."

It was Heden's turn to stare at the river, his eyes unblinking.

"You'd never accept any man having that power over you, except maybe Richard."

For a moment, Heden felt like he was going to topple over and fall into the water.

"You're right," he said.

She raised her eyebrows, surprised at what Heden was willing to admit.

"Most people don't have that problem," she went on. "Most people earn a living offering a service, think nothing of it. Not you. You're so…you. You won't compromise, you won't ever give anyone any speck of control over any part of you."

"This isn't about me," Heden attempted.

"Uh-huh," she said.

Heden kept thinking.

"I'm going to give them the choice."

She nodded.

"That's it. No pressure. Every girl there gets the chance to earn a living, fair wage, for running the inn. Might have to open my own butchers shop. Maybe start buying stuff direct from the pier. Doesn't matter. The girls will have the chance. They can make the choice; I won't make it for them."

"Some of them won't make the right choice."

"Nothing I can do about that."

"Some of them, you'll never know what the right choice was."

"Now you're just stating the obvious," he said. "I never know what the right choice is."

"Just making sure," she said with a smile.

Heden stared out over the river. Elowen watched him.

She stood up on her toes, and kissed his cheek. He let her.

"Goodbye Heden," she said. "Treat the girls well. They're nice. They'll take good care of you. Maybe they're just what you need."

He didn't say anything.

"When you kill the count," she said, taking a step back. "Do it slowly."

He turned to her and smiled. She smiled back. Then her smile turned into a wry smirk, she sighed, and turned, and walked across the bridge.

Heden stood on the bridge alone. For some reason, relieving himself of all his Capital holdings felt good. Liberating. He wished he could wait a few years, and visit Elowen there. She was going to love it.

He looked across the bridge, the direction she'd left, and wondered at what his money had bought him. Her happiness? Maybe. Worth the burning of the Rose Petal if.... A thought struck him.

He realized he'd just bought a brothel. Complete with experienced staff.

Chapter Forty-seven

Daryn opened the door, dressed in a frilly black lace skirt little more than a belt, heels, and nothing else. Her great smile muted when she saw there was no one on the bed.

She looked around. Her clotpole was supposed to be here. The chair was empty, the bed was undisturbed. This was her usual room.

"Hello?" she called out tentatively.

"Hello," a sarcastic voice announced right behind her. She jumped.

There was a girl hiding behind her door. Tall, red curly hair. But not one of Mr. Padgham's girls.

The redhead closed the door behind Daryn.

"Who are you?" Daryn asked, a little alarmed, mostly confused.

The redhead opened a velvet purse. She was older than Daryn. Nineteen maybe? That seemed old to her. She didn't look like a nice person.

"What's your rate?" the redhead asked.

"What?" Daryn asked, as she walked backwards to her bureau and started getting dressed. She wondered if she should call someone.

"How much do you charge?" the redhead asked, raising her eyebrows and speaking slowly.

"Oh, um…," it didn't occur to Daryn to lie. She still hadn't worked out what was going on, but she didn't feel like this was a dangerous situation. "Ten silver."

"There," the girl said, tossing a tensilver on the bed. "That's your hour and this won't take five minutes."

Daryn kicked off the hated heels and walked barefoot to the bed. Scooped up the tensilver piece and sat down.

"Look," she said, looking up at the taller girl, "you have to tell me your name or something."

Martlyn put one hand on her hip and looked at the younger girl.

"Martlyn," she said, one corner of her lips twisting in a half-smile.

"What's this for?" Daryn asked holding up the coin. "You want to spend an hour with a girl you don't have to...."

"What's your name?" Martlyn asked.

"What?" Daryn frowned.

"Your name sweetheart," Martlyn asked with no affection. "That's what the tensilver is for."

"Daryn," the girl said.

"Uh huh," Martlyn said, pulling a plush chair over and sitting across from Daryn. Sitting made them almost the same height.

"Now," she said, taking Daryn's hand and trying to act like a nice person. "What's your *real* name?"

"My real..."

"...name, yes. The coin is real, I want your real name."

Daryn shook her head as though trying to dislodge a thought. She was trying to remember her real name.

"Lisbeth," she said finally, relieved. It felt very strange, that moment where she knew Daryn wasn't her name, but couldn't summon the real thing.

"Good," Martlyn asked, smiling. Now she seemed happy. Nice. Daryn smiled.

"And your last name?" Martlyn asked.

Daryn frowned. Why did she want to know that?

"Tam," she said. "Lisbeth Tam."

Martlyn, now smiling hugely like she'd just met her best friend, leaned back in the chair and crossed her legs.

"Your da's name is Roderick, right?"

Daryn nodded.

"The girls say you visit him every fortnight," Martlyn said. "Is that right?" Martlyn was surprised at how accurate the information she and Caerys had been getting from the other girls was. It looked like the network of trulls was a very efficient way to learn almost anyone about almost anyone. Anyone male, at least.

Daryn nodded again.

Martlyn sighed. "Not a lot of girls have fathers they'd like to see again."

Daryn shrugged. "I do," she said simply.

Normally talking about any of this would make her very uncomfortable. Talking about relatives at all was something no one ever did with outsiders. But this was another girl asking, and obviously another working girl. It didn't occur to Daryn to lie.

"You're going to see him again this Disdane, right?"

Daryn shrugged. "Yeah," she said. "Is that alright?"

"Sure," Martlyn said. "Where do you normally meet?"

Daryn told her. Unaware she was giving away a secret.

Martlyn shook her head, astonished. She was done. It hadn't even been five minutes.

"She said it'd be easy," Martlyn said as she stood up.

Daryn had no idea who she meant.

CHAPTER FORTY-EIGHT

The shop was permanently closed now, had been for over a year. Even in the dark, in the middle of the night, a layer of dust was visible in the starlight pouring in through the windows.

Glass shone dully. Tubes and flasks, sitting dry for months.

The air and silence were both disturbed by a door opening. Fresh air and bright starlight poured in.

A silhouette entered the room, disappeared once the door was closed again.

Nothing in the room moved, no sound. Then the rough noise of a table being moved out of the way. The tinkle of one piece of glass hitting another.

"Lisbeth?" a voice called out hesitantly.

A lantern flared to life, illuminating Roderick Tam standing just inside the door. He covered his eyes and looked into the light, at the figure who lit the lantern, looking like a shade haunting the room.

"Hello Roderick," the pale shade said.

"Who are you?" the alchemist said, pointing and backing up.

"Give it some time," the voice said. "It'll come back to you. I know you were expecting your daughter. Sorry to have to surprise you like this."

Roderick stopped retreating. Stood up.

"Heden?!"

Heden picked up the lantern and walked forward.

"Do you know where Lisbeth is right now?" he asked.

"What are you doing here?" Tam asked, looking furtively around the room. For what? For his daughter, or for agents of the count? Heden couldn't tell.

"She's at the Spinning Wheel," Heden continued. He set the lantern down now that he was standing only a few paces from Tam. Now that there was nowhere for Roderick Tam to go.

"I...she's supposed to...," Tam started.

"Why is Lisbeth on the game, Tam?" Heden pressed, his voice louder, threatening violence.

"I was trying to protect her!"

"Protect her?"

"I sent her to the Wheel so the count wouldn't find her," Tam explained.

Heden stared at him. He looked back, pleading.

"She's all I have," he said.

Heden was not interested in Tam's contrition.

"You belong to the count now," he said.

Roderick Tam nodded.

"You make the night dust for him."

Tam kept nodding. He was crying now.

"You used to be a good man, Roderick. Someone we could trust."

"I know," he said, sobbing. He was curled up on the floor, one hand held up trying to ward Heden away. "I know."

"Where does he get it, Tam?" Heden asked.

"I don't...," he didn't try to lie, or avoid the question. He looked at Heden. He was still smart, as far as that went. "I don't know. He never showed me the source. But I can...," he was desperate. "I can take you to where it's made. His new headquarters."

"You're going to do more than that," Heden said.

"I'll do whatever you want, just please don't tell Lisbeth what's happened to me."

Heden was momentarily taken aback by a father's desperate desire that his daughter not know the truth, about what a failure her father was. But those thoughts just made Heden more angry at the man he once knew and trusted.

He reached down and picked Tam up. Slammed him against

the door.

"You're done Tam," Heden growled. "I am going to drag you to the ragman and he's going to wring it all out of you and then I'm going to the count and I'm going to pull his entire operation down around him."

"You can't!" Tam cried out. He'd stopped crying. Heden watched the warm lantern light reflecting off the tears running down Roderick Tam's cheeks. "Garth is with him now," Tam warned. "Garth can take you!"

"I know," Heden said.

"He could take on your whole team!"

"I know!" Heden shouted at the man. "You were afraid of the wrong men, Tam. You were worried about them, you should have been afraid of me!"

Tam shrunk. "I'm not afraid of them," he said, exhausted. "They don't need me anymore."

Tam's words brought Heden back to the moment. "Why not?" he asked, pressing the issue. There was a sense of urgency here he couldn't identify.

"He's got so much," Tam said, shaking his head. "I've already given him all he needs."

"How much," Heden urged. "How many Deathless can the count create because of you, Tam?" Heden's hands were balled into fists. He wanted very badly to hit this man, but held his temper.

Tam looked at Heden, tears in his eyes. "Thousands," he said. "Thousands. And now he'll kill me," he said.

Heden thought about what this meant. Thousands of deathless in the city. An army. Enough to take over.

"You son of a bitch," Heden said mildly. "Do you have any idea? Any idea how many people are going to die because of you?"

He released Tam. The alchemist slumped against the door.

"You'll see Lisbeth again, Tam," Heden assured him coldly.

"I'll make sure she visits you in the citadel."

Roderick frowned, looked around, confused. "How did you...," he started. Then his eyes went wide with surprise.

Heden watched as two hands appeared from behind Tam, through the door. Two black clad hands grabbed the alchemist and yanked him backward. Tam reached out, tried to grab Heden, but it was too late. He was pulled through the door. As though the door were not there. As though the door were an illusion, he just disappeared into it.

Heden's was just as surprised as Tam. It took him only a second to realize what had happened. He bolted to the door, pushed it open, and ran outside, into the night.

It was too late.

CHAPTER FORTY-NINE

Roderick Tam lay dead on the street. Heden had moments to get to him, to bring him back.

But there was an obstacle. A man in black leather stood over Tam, wiping a rapier clean. Though illuminated by starlight, Heden didn't need to look to know who it was.

Garth.

He saluted Heden with his rapier, and then stepped into the shadows cast by the buildings on the far side of the street.

"No you don't," Heden said, and prayed to Lynwen, placing one hand over her talisman where it hung over his heart.

The other hand he raised, and sunlight poured out of it, illuminating the entire street like broad daylight.

Garth was gone. In his place were five other men in leather armor.

It was the Black. Five scarves from the Guild of Blackened Silk. Probably black scarves. Maybe brown, but the difference wasn't meaningful.

Heden wasn't ready. He had come to Tam's old shop wearing only his leather chestpiece over wool, no other armor. He took a step back, but the battle had already begun.

The five scarves flooded toward him like advancing fog. He tried to get back into the alchemist's shop, but one step was all he had time for. Then they were on him.

A short sword cut his throat. Poison. A dagger in his ribs, another in his back. He went down on his knees. He was already poisoned and wounded, but he needed room to maneuver. He spoke a prayer.

His skin flashed from a man's to a dwarf's. The thieves' blades struck and sparked against it.

With the strength of earth and stone, he lunged to his feet, managed to surprise one of the scarves, grabbing him by the throat.

They don't know, he thought. They had come for Tam, they hadn't known Heden would be there. Didn't know they were fighting a priest.

One thief gripped by his supernatural strength, he spoke another prayer. A gust of wind exploded outward from him, knocking the other thieves away, throwing them in the air and on their ass, while Heden lifted the one he'd caught off his feet.

The thief couldn't escape Heden's grasp by force, so he wrapped his body around Heden's arm and torso, used his legs to try and crush Heden's chest.

Heden bent the thief backward, down. Until he had to grasp Heden's arm to stop from falling. He didn't cry out, he tried to pry Heden's fingers away with one hand, while stabbing Heden with his dagger. Heden's leather armor offered no resistance, but his skin was like stone.

"Didn't Garth tell you I was a priest?" he sneered at the thief. "You're going to need more than poisons and blades...."

At that last, Heden heard something metallic hit the ground. He looked out of the corner of his eye and saw the thief's dagger. The thief had dropped it to reach into his vest.

Time seemed to slow. Heden was well-familiar with the tactics of thieves. And now that they understood what they were fighting, if not exactly who, they would change tactics too.

Heden released his grip on the thief just as he heard something snap. A twig, an eggshell, it didn't matter. The thief's body flashed into shadow before it could hit the ground.

He could appear anywhere. But he would *not* appear anywhere, he would press the attack. He was not trying to escape, merely reposition himself for advantage.

Heden's instincts had already taken over. He spun and drew his sword, flinging it out behind him. A blind attack.

The thief's body materialized directly behind Heden. The

nameless assassin was fast enough to produce a snaking whip-line of cord that glittered in the starlight. *Diamond*, Heden thought. The cord snapped tight between the thief's hands. A diamond garrote. Possibly sorcerous. Possibly powerful enough to cut through his wards and his skin, even with his prayer.

But the thief would never find out. Heden's entirely mundane blade sliced through the air, anticipating the thief's reappearance and location, and chopped through his neck, cutting the man's arteries and windpipe. The thief dropped the garrote and clutched his throat with one hand, desperately trying to stem the flow of blood and air.

As he collapsed, he pulled a hilt-less throwing knife out with his free hand. Crystal. And made a feeble attempt to throw it before he fell to the ground, dead.

That was a black scarf, Heden thought. Incredibly well-trained. Relentless. They knew no fear, thought of nothing but the objective, cloak and vest stuffed with enough weapons to take down an army, and lightning fast reflexes.

One thief dead, Heden turned to face the other four. They had recovered from his attempt to separate them, and watched as he dispatched one of them. Judging his strength, seeking weakness.

Heden saw the one on the far left's eyes shift to look at his nearest teammate before looking back at Heden. *A brown scarf*, Heden thought. No black scarf would waste time worrying about the disposition of his teammates.

"This is going to be a long night," Heden said to them.

One of them, one of the two on his right, he couldn't tell which, said, "Not for us," and there was a *pok* sound, like a tiny piece of glass being broken. Then another. Then another. Heden couldn't count them all.

Each thief was hurling black glass marbles at the ground. Each marble hit, broke, and released its deadly, grasping, shadow.

Heden spoke another prayer, and starlight immediately

reflected off him. He was coated in golden plate mail, the same mail he once warded Squire Aderyn with.

The thieves were done summoning death, and retreated into the shadow to watch the results. A dozen shadows rose from the street and drifted toward him.

A shade poured into Tam's corpse, through his open mouth, through his nostrils. And Heden despaired at ever bringing him back. It was probably already too late. Spirits forgot their bodies quickly, in Heden's experience.

He watched, he didn't want to, but he needed to see it happen. Tam's body jerked and twisted. A sound, not Roderick Tam's voice, came out of his throat. It was despair and hate, and the sound had traveled a long way by the time it escaped Tam's body.

It jerked to life, it seemed to grow larger. It rose from the ground, stood there slavering, its teeth and fingernails, long and black and rotting. Its eyes now burning red with hate.

Vanora hadn't lied. This was one of the deathless, a ghoul. Its strength could match Heden's, even with his prayer for the strength and skin of a dwarf.

The ghoul lunged forward. Heden hacked at it with his sword. Tam's ghoul-corpse ignored Heden's sword, the blade of his father's father, and grabbed the collar of his armor.

The ghoul sneered and bit deep into Heden's flesh. His prayer, his stone-hard skin had no effect.

Heden cried out. The ghoul snarled, something like a laugh, as it ripped some of Heden's shoulder out. His entire body felt like it was on fire. Though wounded, the pain galvanized him.

The shades or shadows or whatever was contained within the black marbles swarmed over him, as the ghoul held him fast. They were strong, inhumanly strong, and possessed of immortal will. And there were enough of them to overwhelm him, tear his holy armor off, pull his limbs from their sockets if he gave them the chance.

Thinking desperately of what prayer would grant him the strength to defeat these creatures, he wondered if Cavall would grant him a dominion. Then, thinking of the winged servitors of his god, he remembered his own purpose.

It had been four years since anyone, Heden least of all, had fought any deathless. He had forgotten how. *Stupid*, he thought.

As one of Tam's black-fingered hands grasped Heden's jaw, threatening to rip it out of his skull, Heden spoke a prayer.

Tam's ghoul, all the shades, shadows, and spectres froze, locked in place.

Heden spoke another prayer, and a brilliant light exploded out from him, like the wave from a rock dropped into a pool of sunlight.

As the wave reached each deathless, they were vaporized, eliminated, evaporated.

A moment later, the street was clear, Tam's corpse was gone, and four black-clad thieves stood there in the starlight looking around in confusion.

"Well that still works," Heden said to himself. He looked at the thieves. "Next time you try and kill a priest," he said, "bring more than deathless."

"We did," one of the thieves said. As usual, Heden couldn't tell which one spoke.

He shot at Heden with something from his cloak, a crossbow, a small single-handed crossbow. Heden wasn't a thief or an assassin, he wasn't fast enough to get out of the way. Wouldn't have been fast enough even if he'd seen the weapon pointed at him.

A bolt lodged in his right side, just under his ribs. It was sorcerous, it penetrated his golden armor, his stone-hardened skin, and more, it sapped his strength.

"Ungh," he grunted, reaching down to grab the bolt, but something tugged on it. There was a thin cord attached to the bolt, leading to the thief who'd shot him. The thief had dropped the crossbow and was grasping the cord in his hand. As he yanked, Heden felt something, some part of him, his strength, his will, wrenched out of him, enervating him.

Another bolt slammed into his left side with the same effect. He went down on one knee but, as he fell, he slashed at one of the cords with his sword, breaking it.

"Black gods," one of the thieves said. They had never fought a prelate before, never faced someone capable of resisting them, and more: capable of fighting back.

Heden grabbed the remaining cord, and pulled, causing the thief on the other end to stumble forward.

He prayed and pointed at the thief. All the air was sucked from the black-clad assassin's lungs and he grasped and clawed at his throat, trying to get any air. He fell to one knee; he and Heden in the same pose, on opposite sides of the street.

Heden stood and closed the distance. If this was a black scarf, he'd be able to fight off the effects of the prayer if Heden gave him the chance. He was not inclined to do so.

He sliced at the thief's shoulder, hacking into his collarbone with his ordinary blade. The thief fell over. The twin attacks took the life from him, and Heden stood over another dead thief.

Two of the three remaining thieves lunged at him simultaneously.

Heden blinded one, and turned the cobbled street below the other to mud. The blinded thief shook his head, but continued advancing, trained to fight in complete darkness. Meanwhile, opposite him, the other thief took one step into the mud, sank, and then disappeared.

Heden again guessed where the shadow-walking thief would reappear. He prayed and gestured with a hand, and a gust of wind lifted the blind thief off the ground. He twisted harmlessly in the air.

With another gesture, the wind hurled the thief toward the street, just as the other thief reappeared. The blind thief smashed into his conspirator and, making a mistake fatal to both of them, attacked with his poison blade, mistaking his teammate for Heden in his blindness.

As the poisoned thief clutched at his back with one hand, fumbling in his vest for the antidote with the other, Heden stepped forward and ran the blinded thief through. When the blind thief cried out, clutching the blade protruding from his chest, he realized he'd killed the wrong man, and the mistake cost him his life.

These were battle tactics; the kind of fighting Heden was used to. Had done for years. Though expertly trained, the thieves had nothing like the experience Heden did.

He walked forward casually and grasped the hair of the poisoned thief from behind. The man gave up searching to the antidote to the poison, and attempted to stab Heden. Again the blade glanced harmlessly off Heden's golden armor.

Heden drew his blade across the man's exposed throat, and kicked him in the back, causing him to tumble forward onto his face. Another dead thief.

His body pulsing with battle fury, Heden felt no remorse. These men were trained killers.

One thief was left, he stood there, watching, apparently terrified. This would be the brown scarf. A brown scarf was nearly a match for a black, but whatever the difference was, it meant this one was scared. Watching men he considered unbeatable, invincible, be eviscerated on the cobbles in the middle of the night had scared the piss out of him.

Heden walked toward him. His golden armor glinting in the starlight. The thief pulled three throwing daggers, and threw them at Heden. They were well-aimed, but Heden batted them away.

Then he was on the thief, grabbed him by the throat, as he had the first of the group he'd killed.

"Tell your master," Heden said, his body shaking from the

fight, his breath coming fast and hard, "you tell Garth, I'm coming. I'm coming for him and the man who holds his leash."

The thief nodded frantically, and Heden released him. He fell to the ground, then scrabbled away before getting up and running into the night.

Heden stood there alone with four corpses in the middle of the starlit street, trying to master his breathing. He walked over to Tam's old shop. Stood on the stoop and pulled the door closed. Then he turned and slumped against it.

He slid down until he was sitting on Tam's stoop. He dropped his sword. His golden armor vanished and his skin returned to normal.

Then he put his head between his legs, and threw up.

CHAPTER FIFTY

Breathing heavily from climbing up the granite stairs, the abbot waddled around to his desk, but did not sit down. He looked at the bookshelf behind him, searching for a tome.

"Ooh," he sang to himself. "Why can't you organize yourselves?" He fingered one book, and then another. Then found the tome he was looking for. "Ah-hah!" he said, and turned to sit down.

An assassin stood in front of his desk.

Seeing this apparition materialize caused the abbot's knees to buckle. He fell, drooped the book he was holding. Tried to catch himself on the desk, failed. Crumpled to the ground in a heap.

"Get up," the assassin sneered.

He wrested himself to his knees, looked over the desk.

"Where's the girl," the killer asked.

The abbot's face was pained, reflected pain. "You don't have to do this," he said.

"No, I don't. I enjoy it."

"You'll never find her," the abbot said, shaking his head. "This place is a maze, on purpose."

"Doesn't matter," the assassin said. "I just needed to know she was here. Now I can find her myself."

The abbot deflated a little. He should have kept his mouth shut.

"Sit in the chair," the assassin said.

The abbot agonized over pushing himself up. Dropped down into his chair with a sigh.

"Is this because of the girl?" the abbot asked curiously. "Or because I'm Heden's friend?"

"Yes," the assassin said, removing a garrote from his belt.

"What's that for?" the abbot said, staring at the black cord in terror.

The assassin looked at the garrote. "Stops you calling out."

"Can't there be another way?" the abbot asked. "I abhor violence."

The nameless assassin shrugged. "There's lot of ways," he said. "How about poison?"

The abbot nodded.

"You got any wine?" the assassin asked.

The abbot bent down, fumbled under his desk for the bottle.

When he sat up again, bottle in hand, the assassin plunged a dagger into his heart.

The abbot gasped, grabbed the dagger, looked at his murderer in shock.

"You don't get out that easily old man. This is about causing *pain*."

The abbot's corpse slid out of its chair.

The assassin's eyes instinctively went to the wall where the only hidden door could logically be. The girl, beyond.

"And I'm only just getting started."

CHAPTER FIFTY-ONE

The three specials picked their way through the abbot's office. Dead animals stuffed and posed, suspended orreries, and phials of unguents balanced on towers of tomes made this difficult.

"Black gods," Fandrick growled. "Don't they got closets in churches?"

Aiden, having just arrived, surveyed what appeared to be a wreckage but was probably just an old man's office.

"What do we know?" he asked.

"Come in through the door," Rayk said, pointing to the doorway. There was no door, just an arch. "Kills our man here, probably in a moment. Then he leaves through this passage," she indicated the narrow, open hallway and the door leading to it, pulled open, creating a hemispherical clean space on the floor where it swept the debris of the abbot's life away.

"Left it open, didn't bother to cover his tracks. Didn't care if anyone came after."

"He got whatever he came for," Fandrick growled.

"Which was what, exactly?" Aiden asked. "What's down there?" he stepped over the piles of books and peered down the dark hallway. A cool breeze blew on his face. Air made cold by granite walls far from the sun.

"I checked that," Rayk said. "It's a maze. I found libraries, more secret doors. There was an apartment, a cot, a pot for cooking. No idea who stayed there. Food around the place, fresh, more or less. Could have been whoever was in there our man was after."

Aiden turned his back on the secret corridor, looped his thumbs into his belt.

Heden was standing in the doorway.

"The girl from the fishmongers," Aiden said, no surprise at

seeing Heden. "Isn't it?"

Heden walked into the room. Fandrick and Rayk looked at him, then to Aiden. Aiden seemed prepared to handle the questioning.

Heden said nothing. Just walked over to look at the body of his dead friend.

"Our man wasn't very careful," Aiden said. "Kills a rector in the middle of the church. Someone comes by in time, they could have brought him back. Saved his life. Gotten a description of the murderer."

"He weren't being careful," Fandrick said, picking up the bottle of wine and smelling it to see if it had been opened recently. "'Cause he don't give a shit."

Aiden sighed. He walked up to the priest, staring at the dead man on the floor. No expression on his face.

"You don't happen to have any idea why the count would want to murder a random rector in the middle of the church?" Aiden asked.

"abbot," Heden corrected, his voice rough. "He was an abbot. He was a friend of mine. That's why he's dead."

"And that's the only reason," Aiden said. "Piss you off."

Heden said nothing.

"Some friend you turned out to be," Aiden said, his voice clipped.

Rayk threw the young man a look, letting him know his comment was in poor taste. Fandrick betrayed no reaction. Fandrick had no taste. If Aiden was trying to provoke Heden, it didn't work.

"Yeah," the priest said.

Aiden let his disgust show. "You know, I'm trying to figure this out. Rose Petal burns down, turns out you know the proprietor. She was a friend of yours too. Now probably dead." Heden didn't bother correcting him. There was no benefit to doing so at the moment. "The count is trying to take over the city, everything's exploding, and somehow," the young man stressed, "the bigger it gets, the more it all comes back to you. How is that?"

Heden shrugged.

"Yeah," Aiden said. "Ignore me. Good idea. See what happens once I'm pissed off enough."

"I'm not ignoring you," Heden said. "I'm just thinking. If there was something I could do to help, I would."

"Why don't I believe that?" Aiden asked. Fandrick and Rayk watched the back and forth.

"I dunno," Heden said. "It doesn't sound very believable, I guess."

"We go to the castellan," Aiden said, indicating his two partners, "and we tell him all this," he pointed to the dead abbot, "and your name comes up, *again*, how do you think he's going to react?"

"He'll want to talk to me."

"No, he *wants* to talk to *us*," Aiden said. "You he's going to lock up until this all blows over in case more people end up dead because of you."

"That's reasonable," Heden said.

"Cavall's balls," Aiden exclaimed, "you're a stubborn prick."

"Yeah," Heden said.

"You got nothing you want to tell us," Aiden said. "Any other friends about to get stabbed, burned alive?"

"Not at the moment," Heden said. What, after all, did he know? "I think of anything, I'll come to the citadel."

"Won't that be a surprise," Aiden said. He spoke over his shoulder to his partners. "We got everything?"

"Dead body," Rayk said. "Missing girl…"

"What else is there?" Fandrick asked.

"Come on," Aiden said. "Let's leave the man with his *friend*."

The specials exited through the stone doorway. After a moment, Heden walked over to the divan and dropped himself onto it.

The books, the room, the divan, all smelled the same. Nothing had changed. Except now the abbot was dead. Would always be dead, now.

Why did the abbot try and help him? Why get involved, why the girl?

What a stupid question. He rolled his head back until it hit the granite wall behind him, and stared up at the ceiling.

"Fuck," he said.

Chapter Fifty-two

The count stood before his table. The same table he always sat at. He liked being easy to find.

Heden stared at the count, saying nothing. He was alone this time.

The count indicated the packed room. "Real customers this time," he said with a grin. "Not in my employ."

Heden said nothing. The count blinked, waiting for a response.

"I'm going to sit down," he said, and hesitated, waiting for Heden to object. When Heden did not, he pulled out a chair, sat down.

"I trust we are now clear," the count opened.

"This is a strange way to commit suicide," Heden said finally. "Come in here, alone, without Garth."

"Please," the count said, affronted. "You're not going to kill anyone in cold blood. If you were a watchmen, maybe you'd try and arrest me," he admitted. "But you're not and never should be so. I told you I'd get her, and I have her."

"And you murdered my friend in the bargain," Heden said.

The count raised his eyebrows. "I did? I'm sure I didn't."

Heden shrugged. "Did it, or had it done. Doesn't matter. The last time you came here, you said we were enemies. You have no idea."

The count held up a finger. "We are no longer enemies. I have the girl, I no longer care about you, or this place, or your friends, alive or dead. No one in my organization had anything to do with delivering the girl to me. That's the point you persistently mistake. Power attracts friends. People who want to please me, get in my good graces. I didn't have to lift a finger. No order given, I assure you."

"You should enjoy running the city while it lasts," Heden said, attempting to be genial, failing. "Because once I find your operation I will take it apart, brick by brick, and then you. Piece by piece."

"Don't be ridiculous," the count sniffed. "Why would I want to run the city? Bureaucracy. No, I intend to run all the *crime* in the city. All the profit, none of the overhead," he smiled, making a joke.

He looked at Heden and his face fell in disappointed. "Ah well," he said. "Waste of time, I suppose."

He stood and fastened his cloak.

"If you come after me," the count warned. "If you make an enemy of me, I will kill everyone you've ever known, ever loved, everyone who's ever cared about you."

Heden locked eyes with him, his face betrayed no emotion.

"Too late," he said.

CHAPTER FIFTY-THREE

"Everyone's saying Garth killed a rector," Brick said, moving a piece. "Broad daylight, middle of the church, just walks in and drags him like a nail. Fucking rector."

"Abbot," Aimsley corrected, staring at the board.

"Turns out this godbotherer was hiding the girl," the Brick smiled. "Friend of the priest. Soon as he's dead, the count comes over all friendly like with me."

Aimsley fingered a prelate, tilting it back and forth on the board.

"Everyone says 'look what the count has brung us to,'" the Brick was hugely happy. "'All this violence!'" Brick laughed. It sounded like an old man wheezing to death.

"Yeah," Aimsley said. He moved the prelate, blocking Brick's castle.

"Man's gotta lotta balls, walk into the church, ace a priest." Brick was proud. "Figure, with all this shit going on, the dust, the deathless, who's gonna notice? One more priest dead. Who's gonna notice?"

Aimsley ignored him. Brick, eyes on the polder, moved a peasant to threaten Aimsley's prelate.

Aimsley looked at the new situation in disgust. "How's it now between you and the count?" he asked.

"Fine, fine," Brick said, looking around the Mouse Trap. "He's got his little chickie, whatever good that does him. Never seen a man had his horn up for someone so bad."

"She knew something," Aimsley explained. "She's probably dead by now."

Brick shrugged. "No one notices a dead priest," he said, "who gives a shit about another dead whore?"

Aimsley nodded. "Who gives a shit," he echoed. He sounded

hollow inside.

"Speaking of dead priests," Brick said, "count says if I'da killed that one come in here, things'd be a lot better for everyone."

"He means better for him," Aimsley said.

"Right now, that's good for us," Brick said.

Aimsley said nothing.

"Then I thought, I thought 'why'd I let that streak of shit live, anyway? He come in here and try and brace me?' Then I remembered. You vouched for him."

Aimsley picked up a piece, moved it. Thought he had Brick on the defensive for once.

"I let him live, 'cause you said," Brick explained.

"Your move," Aimsley said.

Brick picked up a piece and moved it, staring at the polder all the while. He had not moved the piece Aimsley was attacking, but rather put the fixer's king in danger.

Aimsley moved his king out of the way.

"So way I figure it," Brick said, "he's your problem."

"You take care of him. You're working for the count now, you don't need me," Aimsley said.

"Don't work for the count," Brick said. "Do some business with him. More, now. Good business. Acing this priest, that's good business."

"Whatever," Aimsley said. "You say it however sounds good to you. Either way, you don't need me no more. You got no deal with the ragman, you don't need no fixer."

"What's this?" Brick asked, suddenly taken aback by Aimsley's assertion.

"I'm done fixing for you," Aimsley said, looking up from the board at the huge man.

"You're done when I say you're done," Brick said levelly.

"So say. What's it gonna take?" Aimsley said.

Brick just stared at him.

"What's it gonna take," Aimsley stared back. "You tell me,

Brick. You show me the piper, I'll pay him. Free and clear and I am quit. You name your price."

Brick, without looking at the board, picked up Aimsley's last prelate, and snapped the wooden piece in half. Tossed the pieces on the board.

Aimsley looked at the broken prelate. This would buy Brick a lot. Enough to weather the storm. Enough to ride out the war.

Aimsley picked up the pieces of the shattered priest, secreted them away in his vest, and left the table and the Mouse Trap.

CHAPTER FIFTY-FOUR

The inn was open, nearly full. Martlyn and Caerys ran the place and without Heden needing to do anything, the inn was ticking over. It was busy, and more; it was alive. Heden liked it. He didn't like what the girls did upstairs, but he'd work on that after Vanora was safe. Whatever else happened, he wasn't going to close the inn, go back to the way things were before the forest, the way they'd been for three years. That would be death now.

He looked at his ale, and thought about the abbot. "It isn't safe, being your friend," someone had said. He couldn't remember who. Why would Garth kill an old man? There was no way the abbot stood between anyone and Vanora. *Just take the girl*, Heden thought, *leave the old man alone*.

Another account that needed to be settled. Him and the count, him and the bishop…him and Garth.

He tried to put it out of his mind. He leaned back in his chair, focused on the success that was the Hammer & Tongs, and took a drink of ale.

When he pulled the mug away from his lips, Hapax Legomenon was standing before him.

One of the serving girls dropped her tray, and several guests spit out their food and drink.

Heden frowned. "Gonna be that kind of inn, I guess," he said with a shrug. "People teleporting in and out.'

"Sorry," she apologized, "but this is important." Her normally flamboyantly fashionable, wizard-typical dress was enhanced in this case by a stylish black half-cloak with red trim. She grabbed the cloak at his shoulders and snapped it up when she sat down, so when it lay flat it lay over the chair.

"Have a seat," Heden said to the seated wizard.

When it was obvious Heden wasn't worried, the serving

girls returned to their business and cleaned the mess made by reactions to Hapax Legomenon. More than one man in the inn was watching her speculatively.

"You owe me," she said, incredibly pleased with herself. Heden raised his eyebrows.

She made a gesture with one hand, and there was a black marble between her fingers. She carefully placed it on the table between them.

"You know what it is," Heden said.

The short, impossibly-built wizard nodded, unable to contain her smug joy. "What's it worth to you?"

"Name it," Heden said, seriously.

Hapax canted her head at Heden, a wry smile curled at her lips. She looked him up and down. "Nah," she said. "Wouldn't be fair. How about that Brass Man you came back with?"

"He's downstairs. You want him, he's yours."

Hapax nodded. "That'll do."

"I could never make him work," Heden pointed out.

Hapax shrugged. "I'm more persuasive than you," she said.

Heden waited. Hapax leaned forward.

"It's the blood of a star elf," she said, "treated by alchemy."

Heden was stunned. He looked at the ceiling. "Tam, you idiot."

"Somewhere in this city," Hapax said, "there's a major power, and no one knows it."

Heden shook his head. "There's no way," he said. "There's no way the count is in league with an Astral Celestial."

Hapax shrugged, and sat back. "Someone's hiding a star elf," she said. "If you can do that, you can make night dust. How the count did it, we have no idea. We're not having a lot of luck tracking him down. He might be on water," she added, frowning. "It messes with our divinations."

Heden put a hand to his forehead. "Garth you dumb son of a bitch," he said. "You of all people."

"If I were you," Hapax said, "I'd sit this one out. We'll find him sooner or later. You wanted a censure," she said, "you may get one."

Heden was no longer listening. Someone else had entered the inn. Heden didn't notice at first, and for good reason. The guest was only a few feet tall. And people were coming and going all the time now. But the heavy tread of footsteps spoke loudly enough.

The guests near the bar, standing between the common room and the door, parted, and Heden saw the dwarf. He was carrying something. Something wrapped in a cloth bundle. All eyes in the inn were on the dwarf. No one commented when the assassin in red silk came in, but everyone shut up when they saw the dwarf.

Zaar looked around the room, saw Heden, and approached him. He tossed the bundle on the table.

The stout creature, half flesh, half stone, gazed at Heden with glowing coal eyes, then looked at Vanora—her mouth open, her eyes unblinking—then back to Heden.

"Enh," he said, and turned and left.

Heden watched him leave, then started breathing again. He felt…less alone than he had in years.

'You need friends,' Lynwen had said. 'They're out there.' Maybe he and Zaar weren't through.

He picked up the bundle.

"Probably a good idea to hang on to this one," he said, thinking of *starkiller*.

"Is that who I think it was?" Hapax asked, looking where Zaar had gone.

"Probably," Heden said.

"Heden," Hapax warned, "if you're thinking of getting the old troupe back together for this…,"

Heden started to unwrap the bundle.

"Most of them are dead," he said. "And the rest won't talk

to me."

He exposed the gift within. Revealed a dull metal scabbard. Seeing the hilt, Heden was already in awe. He drew the sword. His face, the table, Hapax, illuminated by warm sunlight from the blade.

Solaris. The blade of Pentalion Sunbringer, Saint of Adun. The sword they recovered twenty years ago. The sword they became famous for.

Heden smiled. Widely, openly. He whistled low.

"I thought Stewart took this with him," he said to himself.

"It's beautiful," Hapax said, also noticing Heden genuinely smiling.

It was long and thin, on edge almost a rapier. The blade was made of a metal like steel, but with a yellow tint. As though the steel were transparent, covering a layer of gold shining under it.

The hilt looked like someone had poured molten gold over a flower, then taken the flower away. Jewels glittered on the pommel.

"That's a celestial blade," Hapax said.

"Yep," Heden said. "And not just a blade."

Hapax leaned in to look at the weapon. "*Iallir*, the sun-metal."

"It is," Heden agreed.

"Heden, you need to be careful with that."

He slipped his hand inside the twisted fluid-seeming metal of the hilt and grasped the grip. His hand was too large, thick and meaty compared to the hands intended to wield it.

You need me, a voice in his head echoed. It was neither male nor female.

Yes, Heden thought, trying to calm himself.

I cannot be commanded, the voice said.

I know, Heden thought.

But I can be…persuaded.

Don't worry, Heden said, *you'll get no argument from me.*

Heden put the sword back in its sheath. He was suddenly reminded of how they acquired *Solaris*.

He smiled at Hapax.

"Heden" she warned. "Do not."

"I'm going to find the star elf," Heden said. "And stop the count."

Hapax's mouth fell open. She closed it.

"You…Heden…."

She looked around the room.

"Heden, do you have any idea…you of all people!"

Heden stood up.

"This is no joke, you dumb son of a bitch…," Hapax opened.

"Hey," Heden said in defense as he affixed the scabbard to his belt.

"It's a *star elf*," Hapax said. "It's alive and it's here! That means every person in the city is at risk!"

"And I think I know how to find it," Heden said.

"Tell me," Hapax said.

Heden thought. If he did, Hapax would be obligated to act. This was, in a general sense, why each wizard order was granted a charter.

"No," Heden said.

"Heden you *have* to tell me," Hapax urged.

In a sense, she was right. Heden was, had been, might still be technically, an agent of the king. He took the king's crown once upon a time and that was probably something that didn't expire. Even if you fucked up and an entire nation was murdered as a result.

"I can't," he said. "If I did, you'd be obligated to act. As it stands, you're just upset at me and it ends at that."

Hapax stood up, almost lunged out of her chair.

"Do you have any idea what kind of risk you're taking? You *have* to leave this to us!"

"You're going to have to trust me," Heden said, looking

down at the younger woman.

"I don't," Hapax said. "Not with this. I'm going to go to Cordatus," she said, naming the head of her order, "and he's going to tell Ignam. And Ignam will tell the king, and then it'll be all three orders, and probably the Hart, and probably the Mirror Circle."

"The Circle is a week away," Heden said.

"You'll be dragged down to the castle and put under the fire," Hapax said. "Heden don't you understand what this means? Do you have any idea how many enemies you're making? How many bridges you're burning?"

Heden looked around the inn, then smiled at Hapax. "Only if I fail," he said.

He walked out of the Hammer & Tongs with *Solaris* at his side. Renewed by the visit from Zaar.

Chapter Fifty-five

It felt like he was a mile under the city. He imagined he could feel every ton of rock above, pressing down on him. His chest tightened, like he couldn't take a deep breath, and he feared he was having another attack. He realized he was gritting his teeth, his jaw ached. He tried talking to his escort to distract himself.

"He get a lot of visitors?" No echo down here. The damp walls of the limestone tunnel took the sound of Heden's voice and whisked it away, absorbed it, reflected it, so that it sounded like it was coming from inside his head. That didn't help his mood.

The guard escorting him sniffed. "Some," the guard said. "A few. Maybe a lot for all I know. The ragman doesn't like us working regular shifts, stops our guests from getting to know us too well."

Heden didn't say anything. "He hears you call him 'the ragman,'" he said, "you won't have a problem with shifts, regular or otherwise, 'cause you'll be looking for another line of work."

His escort, tall and blonde, looking more like a knight than a watchman, glanced down at him, the threat appearing to have no effect.

"You're in a bad mood," the watchman said. Heden frowned at the familiarity.

They came to an iron door.

"You know the drill?" the guard said. "You go in; you hear this door lock behind you. Then the next door unlock. Then you're on your own."

Heden nodded.

The guard hesitated.

"Someone said you were the one put him away."

"Eight of us."

"But you were there."

"Yeah."

"You know what he can do," the guard seemed concerned.

"Just let me in," Heden said.

The guard shook his head once. He took a vial of red liquid from his belt. Unstoppered the cork sealing it, and poured the fluid into a small hole at the top of the door. It was almost certainly blood, Heden knew, but the blood of what, he couldn't guess.

There were channels carved into the iron Heden hadn't noticed. As the blood flowed through them, splitting as the channels divided, it burned and sputtered, bright red and orange.

The symbol the flowing blood burned as it raced down through the channels was elaborate and unrecognizable to Heden. He tried not to stare at it. There was probably nothing to fear, but he wasn't taking any chances.

When the blood finished burning its way down the door, the guard grabbed the round metal hoop affixed to the center of the door.

He held up another vial with silver liquid in it. "This goes in once you go in," he said, nodding to the top of the door. "Pull the cord on the inside when you want out."

It was the elixir that would seal the door against its occupant. Heden nodded.

"Good luck," the guard said without much enthusiasm.

CHAPTER FIFTY-SIX

It appeared to Heden that there was no-one in the room. The cell was divided in half by a set of iron bars, but unlike normal bars these bent and twisted. No straight lines.

There was a cot on the far side of the cell, but no one was in it.

He heard a rustling like a pile of dead leaves. He looked up and saw what appeared to be a mound of dirt and leaves sticking to the ceiling above the cot.

"The guard was afraid I might overpower you," a hollow voice whispered languorously from the mound on the ceiling.

Heden looked for a place to sit. There was none. Visitors to Saint Alithiad, the Dark Veil, the Saint of Worms, were not encouraged to stay long.

"Is that likely?" Heden asked.

"Not immediately," the voice hissed. "I like having someone to talk to. Even a human."

"Do you get many visitors down here?" Heden asked, trying to sound casual.

The lump on the ceiling twisted, a sound of crinkling paper.

"I'm not sure. A few," came the voice.

The rustling continued and the shape moved. Suddenly it fell to the floor with a wet thump and the smell of moss and compost. Heden watched as the mound sat up. Assumed the form of a man, hunched over. He couldn't make out its face.

"Wizards mostly, I think," the figure said. It was smooth, soft. Educated. "Scribes? Loremasters? Not many priests I don't think."

"You don't think?" Heden asked, just to be saying something.

The lump shrugged. A very human gesture. "I have a hard time telling humans apart. I would make an analogy about you and insects," the voice said, "but you would know I was just being dramatic."

Heden walked forward. He tapped one of the bars.

"Iron?" he asked.

The creature stood. The vampire saint was only about five feet tall. Supernaturally diminished. When Heden had first met him, he was almost seven feet tall.

"Mundane but effective," the creature said. "Iron under these conditions is an acid for my people."

Saint Alithiad walked forward. Closer to Heden and now in the light, Heden could make out his form. He looked like a withered man in rags, but his skin was brown and peeling. It looked exactly like dead leaves. Black eyes stared out at Heden. When the creature blinked, the eyes flashed a sickening green color, like mucus. Some kind of membrane retreating slower than the eyelid.

He looked at Heden.

"You're older," he said.

"Sure," Heden said.

"I can see it," the vampire said. "You're losing elasticity in your skin and your hair is losing its pigment."

"Uh-huh," Heden said.

"Doesn't happen to the elves or dwarves," the vampire saint said.

"Or the deathless," Heden said, raising one eyebrow.

"I am not deathless," Saint Alithiad said with a smirk. Bits of dead skin or leaf or whatever flaked off his face and spiraled gently to the ground.

"No," Heden said, biting a lip, thinking. "I thought you were once, but I know better now. That's why you're still here after Aendrim. You're not a Man are you? You never were."

"I am from another world," the vampire said, and stretched his arms. Long sticks like poorly carved wood covered in moss and then desiccated.

"The World Below?" Heden asked.

A sigh slowly slipped from the thing before him. The room seemed to get colder.

"You have the blade," Alithiad whispered.

"Not a good idea to come down here without it," Heden said. *Solaris* had been key in defeating the Saint of Worms, all those years ago.

"How long have I been in here?" the saint asked. Heden concluded this creature was not from the World Below, might not even know what it was.

"Seven years," Heden said.

"Mmmm," the saint said. "That figure doesn't mean much to me."

"I need to know something," Heden said.

The old man made of dead leaves tilted his head

"Why should I help you?" he asked.

"Because we didn't kill you when we had the chance," Heden said.

"Mmm," the saint said. "That's true. Still, not much motivation."

"Because you're bored and have nothing else to do," Heden offered.

"Also true. Time doesn't pass for me the way it does for you, though. Ask your question."

"Is there a new power in the city?"

The vampire made a hollow noise Heden chose to interpret as a laugh. "In the *city?*" he said. "The city. Heh. How can you be so blind? How can you walk around with that thing," it said, nodding at *Solaris,* "and not feel it? How did you find me, if you can't sense it?"

"Hard work," Heden said. "And I had help. You weren't making it hard to follow you."

"Mmm no. I got careless. You found my temple. Did you marvel at what you saw? At what I had done to the young boys, the animals? What I turned them in to?"

"No, I think I threw up then." The feeling of nausea wasn't far away at the moment, either.

"Strange reaction. Regurgitating a meal. Body reacting to the perception of poisons, toxins. The perception," the black saint said, "not the reality. How fragile the mirror of the world you build in your mind, that an image can have the effect of a poison on you."

"It's because we're fragile that we're so tough," Heden said.

The saint nodded.

"The elves call that *loiil*," he said. "Truth arising from a logical contradiction."

"I like that," Heden said.

"I thought you would." A moment passed. Heden waited. "Why should I answer you?" Saint Alithiad asked.

"You already answered me," Heden said. "You forgot, you said, that I'm mortal and can't sense it myself. That means there's something there to sense."

The saint smiled.

"I wondered if you were paying attention. Lynwen chose well."

"That's a compliment," Heden said.

"And why not? We are not enemies," the vampire seemed affronted.

"No," Heden said. "I know that, now, too. You're something else. You wore the skin of a Man because you were bored. You gave yourself to Nikros because it helped you hide. But this, all this," Heden said gesturing to the cell, but meaning the city, "it really is beneath you. You don't hate us, you're just curious. I don't think it occurred to you that we could feel pain. Dread. Fear."

"You are more than I'd guessed," the Saint said. "But only a little more. I never guess you could master me, even with that," he said, indicating *Solaris*.

"So what happens to you now that you know what we can do?"

The vampire shrugged. "I'll forget. I'll wait this out. A few hundred cycles, a few thousand. It doesn't matter. Maybe I'll be trapped down here, it won't be the first time. Eventually another civilization will dig me out and I'll be free again. Hopefully I'll remember what you can do next time. Probably I'll be a feral mindless thing and have to start all over."

"How long has this new power been here?" Heden asked. "How close is it?"

"Time is difficult for me," the Saint of Worms said. "Distance, too. This hive of yours, it's large for creatures like you?"

"The city, you mean. Celkirk."

Saint Alithiad sighed. He hated when Heden couldn't keep up.

"There are many powers here, especially after the other hive collapsed."

"Exeder." The capital city of Aendrim.

"The new power, a celestial perhaps." Heden congratulated himself at getting the information out of the Black Saint without giving anything up. But the Saint of Worms wasn't done. "And at least one power greater than me, but slumbering. I tried to wake it but reconsidered when I heard a whisper of its name."

"A dragon," Heden concluded. "Here? You're trying to distract me."

"Is it working?" An eyebrow arched in curiosity.

"A little," Heden admitted. There was a dragon in the city?

The saint appeared to be breathing quickly. Heden frowned.

"You should leave," Alithiad said, turning and shuffling to his cot.

"Why?" Heden asked, worried.

"I can get through the bars," the vampire said casually, almost like he was exhausted. "They don't know it, but I can. It's easy. I don't have to keep this form. Please leave. I can smell it in you." Saint Alithiad sat down.

"What are you talking about?" Heden's curiosity for such things was getting the better of him. But you never knew when you were going to learn something critical to fighting whatever this creature was. Such curiosity was useless for a priest, but necessary for a ratcatcher.

"It's a...," Saint Alithiad chose his words carefully, "substance your body produces. I can smell it. In your brain. It gives my people life. Leave. Please leave. I'd like to be alone for another hundred cycles at least."

Heden backed up, turned and strode to the inner door.

Closing it behind him, he pulled on the cord in the antechamber, thinking on what Saint Alithiad had said, what had just happened. Why would the Dark Veil spare Heden, if he could kill him? His motivations were opaque.

After a few moments, the guard let him out. Stifling the urge to panic, the danger over but not forgotten, Heden raced out of the citadel. Neglecting to inform the guard of what the Saint of Worms had told him.

CHAPTER FIFTY-SEVEN

It was late and the girls asleep. There were only a few hours of night between their closing up and the start of business the next morning. It felt strange, to have the entire common room, the ground floor to himself.

He put *Solaris* on the bar and began arranging the chairs for the next day's business. He enjoyed helping the girls. Feeling useful doing something simple.

He lost track of time. Then he realized the room around him, behind him, was unnaturally quiet. He turned around.

Aimsley Pinwhistle stood on the other side of the room. Several tables between them. *Solaris* on the bar behind him.

"You're going after the girl," the polder said. He was braced like he had a weapon in both hands, but they were empty. Heden knew this didn't matter. When he needed then, the twin dirks would be there.

The polder's face was red with controlled fury. He was coiled like a spring and in Heden's eyes he seemed infused by drink. It was part of who he was. Whatever it did for him, he needed it. Whatever he needed to forget, whoever he needed to be, someone who did things that needed forgetting, the drink gave it to him. Let him be that person. Freed him from the pain and guilt while allowing him to accumulate more of it.

It was killing him. With Vanora in jeopardy, Heden's moral sense was heightened and he saw inside the master-thief. Didn't know why he hadn't seen it before. The drink was killing him and at the same time it was the only way he ever felt alive. There was no in-between here. There was no line to walk for the thief. No choice. Only a certain spiral of destruction.

Heden needed him. Needed him and needed to help him. Needed him to stop the count and needed to help him to banish the vision of Sir Taethan that lay behind his eyelids.

A month ago, a year ago, Heden wouldn't have known what to do. It would have been an unanswerable riddle. But that man died in the mud outside a distant priory. The man who stood in the inn, the man who was going to save Vanora, knew exactly what he had to do. What he should have done for Taethan. What he *could* have done for Taethan.

"Yeah," Heden said, answering the thief's question.

The polder gritted his teeth and shook his head once. "Don't."

"You could stop me," Heden said. He looked down at the floor and with his boot, kicked idly at a bit of food ground into the floor. He wasn't going to stare down the polder.

"Yes," the thief said.

"But you'd have to kill me."

"I know that!" the polder was furious. At who? Heden didn't know, but he knew. He was furious at the Brick for sending him here. Furious at Heden for being someone who had to be killed, and furious at himself for coming.

Heden looked at the little man. It wasn't pity he gave the polder, it was understanding. Not only an understanding of the creature before him, but of the future and what was about to happen.

"Brick sent you here to stop me."

"Brick sent me here to kill you, you shit."

Heden nodded. In this state, like this, the polder was unpredictable.

"If you have to do it," Heden said with a shrug, "you have to do it. Nice of you to talk to me first though."

The thief looked like Heden had slapped him. Heden's acceptance just wound everything inside the polder up.

"You piece of shit," the thief accused. "You don't get it, do you? You think you've got everyone figured out."

Heden stared at him blankly. What was he talking about?

The thief took a deep breath.

"*I killed the abbot*," Aimsley said.

CHAPTER FIFTY-EIGHT

Heden stood there, uncomprehending. The thief had done what five black scarves could not, he had stopped Heden dead in his tracks.

"You…," he said, blinking. Trying to absorb the information.

"You didn't know that, did you?" the thief barked. "You think you've got everyone figured out, but you couldn't see it."

"*You* killed him," Heden repeated.

"What did you think the Brick would do?!" Aimsley shouted, his face red, the veins and tendons on his neck standing out.

"You killed the abbot. You killed…and then you took Vanora to the count."

"You know the count has him over a barrel and you know he's got his horn up for her and you knew they'd send me to find her!"

"You killed him," Heden repeated, and a bowel-freezing calm came over him. "And now you've killed Vanora. You took her to the count, and now he has her. And if she's not dead already…."

"I *told* you the girl wasn't worth it. I *told* you this would happen!" The polder was raging, furious, barely able to control himself.

"And now you've come to kill me." Heden felt detached from his body. As though he were watching a scene play out from the audience.

"I told him I wanted out!" Aimsley said. He was sick of the killing, Heden could see it in him, but it was all there was inside. He was made of it. "He said this is the price! The priest who fucked everything up in the first place."

Heden's mind spun. He made a moral leap.

"You could get her back," he said.

"What!?" the thief squeaked.

"You could do it," Heden urged. "You could find her where I can't. You could find her, get her out and no one would know it was you!" He spoke the ideas as they came to his mind.

"Why the *fuck* would I do that?"

Heden pointed at him. "Because it's the right thing to do!" he leveled this at the thief like a prayer of commanding. He was trying to will the thief into action through sheer weight of moral authority. The thief reeled in response. It almost worked.

Breathing fast for no reason, the thief steadied himself. "You're living in a fucking fairy story!" he said.

Heden realized he was also breathing rapidly. Senses heightened. It would be difficult, beating the polder without killing him…or dying in the process. But the prospect of saving someone, anyone, this thief who needed saving more than anyone he'd met, made the attempt worthwhile.

"I won't kill you," Heden said calmly. Anger had fled. Only readiness now.

"You'll wish you had," the polder said.

"I doubt it," Heden said, deliberately provoking the little man. "There's nothing left inside you but the drink."

That was enough. The thief ignited with rage. From Heden's point of view, it looked like the drink took him over in that moment.

The shadow-magics master thieves practiced produced only short bursts of advantage, and took their toll, draining those who used them. Aimsley disappeared, and in a blink was six feet closer, on a table, as though he had leapt there through empty space. Another blink and he was above Heden, in the air, the two long, thin razor-tipped dirks in his hands ready to plunge down into Heden's shoulder and neck, severing vital arteries.

Heden buckled his left leg, allowing gravity to pull him down, roll away out and under the polder's attack. As the polder sailed over him, inches from where he had been standing, he felt one of the dirks sink into his back.

Heden's right side clenched with pain, but he couldn't allow himself to panic. Only then did he lose.

The polder landed and rolled away, knowing that even without *Solaris* or his breastplate, if Heden got his hands on him, things could be over quickly.

That first cut was deep. He forced himself to straighten and turn to face the thief. One of his legs buckled and he tried to brace himself on a table, which upended at the imbalance.

Aimsley leaped forward and everything moved in slow motion. A dozen prayers flew into Heden's mind. It was getting easier to sort them all out now, purely a tactical exercise. But he forbid himself. He was going to save the thief. Either he was going to save him, or they would both die here on the floor of the inn.

As the thief danced past him, a dirk slipped between his ribs, and he let it. The prayer that would turn his skin to stone, unspoken.

Dull aches in his gut and back told him something important, some organs, had been damaged badly. He spun and feinted and the thief leaped to stab thinking Heden was stumbling. Heden took the advantage and put everything he had into the punch he knew he could land.

Heden was not a big man, but he was all muscle and he knew how to hit. The punch cracked the thief's jaw and sent him spinning.

Before the thief had even hit the floor, there was poison on his blades. Where it had come from, Heden couldn't see. Some secret pocket. That the thief could find and apply the poison while in the air, in the same instant his jaw was dislocated, meant he was better than any thief Heden had ever fought or campaigned with.

Aimsley Pinwhistle landed on his feet, catching himself before almost falling over, and threw a red-eyed baleful look at the priest. *This is it*, Heden thought.

The thief sprang into the air, his twin dirks poised to plunge into Heden's heart and there was no way Heden could move fast enough.

"*Noxa*," Heden said. Not a prayer, a curse. One of the most powerful he knew, and Cavall gave it to him.

Three feet in the air and halfway to Heden, the thief suddenly plunged straight to the ground. Like a rock dropping from the sky. He smashed into the wood as though he were heavier than a cask of ale. His dirks scattered across the floor.

Pinned there under some incredible weight, the polder managed to push himself up, the muscles in his arms and shoulder straining to the breaking point. All he managed to do, however, was flip himself onto his back before collapsing again. Gasping like the inn was resting on top of him.

Heden walked over to him. The pain forgotten. He was bleeding all down his trousers from where the thief had stabbed him. It didn't matter.

The thief's eyes spun wildly. He could barely move his head. He strained for any advantage, any clue of what was going on. He couldn't breathe.

"Is a curse the weight of every evil deed you've ever done?" Heden asked, his voice coming from somewhere Aimsley couldn't see, couldn't move his head to look. The air was being crushed from his lungs, his face was bright red, his teeth bared with effort and hatred. He would kill this priest. If only he could find him, get close enough. Where was he?

"Or is it guilt? I don't know. I've never known. Cavall knows."

Heden stepped into his field of view and looked down at him.

"You know."

As Aimsley struggled just to breathe, gasps exploding out of him, Heden walked over to the upturned table, righted it, and began taking off his shirt.

"You have no idea what I can do," he said. Aimsley fought again to push himself up, but couldn't move his arms. He couldn't get any air. He was going to die like this.

"You killed a man I loved. I betrayed everyone I cared about and everything we worked for," Heden said without feeling. He pulled the buttons from their loops at the neck of his linen shirt, and pulled it over his head, exposing his chest and arms, pale and scarred. Whips of black hair covered his chest. There wasn't an ounce of fat on him.

He folded the bloody shirt and placed it on the table. "And the entire country of Aendrim died." He looked at the shirt and the blood.

"A whole country," he said, looking out the window at the empty street outside.

He turned and walked back to Aimsley, stood over the thief and looked down, loomed into the polder's field of view again. The veins on the little man's head and neck throbbed, his eyeballs bulged. He grimaced back with hate, about to die.

"Did you think I wouldn't kill you?" Heden asked, his head cocked. "Or were you counting on me killing you? Putting you out of your misery?"

The priest began to fade, to swim in Aimsley's vision. All he could think about was how badly he wanted to slip his dirk into the man's heart.

Denied that satisfaction, without any breath, he tried to spit one sneering, last hate-fueled rebuke at the man. All he managed was some spittle that dripped down his cheek. He closed his eyes as the life ebbed from him.

Heden watched the polder dying. He looked across the floor and saw one of the thief's dirks lying on the wooden floor. Then looked back at the thief.

He spoke a word, and the curse was released. Aimsley's eyes flew open and he gasped, heaving air into his lungs.

Heden stepped over him and walked across the floor. Bent

down, and picked up the dirk.

Aimsley rolled himself over, pushed his chest off the floor, but was too weak to get up.

"Gwiddon asked me what happened in the wode," Heden said, looking at the weapon. "So did Vanora. I couldn't tell them." He turned around and faced the polder struggling just to keep his head up, drool dropping into a pool on the wooden floor. "Let me tell you."

He walked back across the room, chest bare, dirk held in his hands like a wounded bird.

"There was a man," Heden said, looking at the weapon in his hands, seeing something else. "A good man. A man I loved. I would have done anything to save him. I felt like…like that was the only reason I was here, the only way anything in my life made sense. If I could save him." If he could save anyone.

He looked up from the polder's weapon and saw the room, his inn. A dream he had. Dead. He saw Taethan, and wondered again at what he could have done different to save him, and sacrifice himself.

"When he died," he managed to continue. "It was like…like it was happening to me. I was dying then. I didn't have a choice, I was either going to give up and die…or find a new way to live."

He went down on one knee in front of the thief, grabbing the polder's hand, pressing the dirk into it. Gave him the weapon he needed to kill Heden. The polder looked up at him, eyes red swollen with tears and rimmed with hate. Heden locked gazes with the thief.

"And now I'm going to do the same thing to you."

Aimsley reeled. The curse was gone, but it had nearly crushed the life out of the little man. He braced himself unwillingly with one hand on Heden's shoulder. Heden grasped the hand the polder held the dagger with, and pulled it up until the tip was pressing into Heden's flesh. It was sharp enough to draw blood, even as feeble as Aimsley was. Heden ignored it.

"Brick sent you here to kill me," Heden said. "You failed. But now I'm giving you the chance."

Aimsley leaned forward, seeming desperately to want to push the dirk into Heden's bare chest, but did not. He grit his teeth with effort.

"If my death buys your freedom," Heden said, and the thief lifted his head to look at the priest through bloodshot eyes. "If killing me means you're free. Free from the guild. Free to do what you want. What you think is *right*...." Now he had the thief's attention. Aimsley's mouth hung slack as he absorbed the import of Heden's words.

Eyes locked with Aimsley's, hand wrapped around the polder's, Heden pulled the dirk further into his chest. "Then you *have* to do it," Heden said. Aimsley stared at him, wide-eyed. "I'll help you," Heden said, and pulled on the dirk, scraping his breastbone.

The thief looked down, saw what he was doing and yanked himself away. Fell over with a shout. A grunt. Tears were streaming from his eyes and he was still propelled by hate. But not for Heden.

Strength flowing back into his limbs, he got up, dirk forgotten and staggered to the bar. Heden watched him disappear behind it. He couldn't see him, but he heard the sound of glass. The uske. Choking, coughing. The thief was pouring it down his throat.

Heden got up and went behind the bar. The thief was covered in alcohol, poured the last of a bottle into his mouth, coughing and spitting most of it up, weeping openly as he did so.

With one bottle empty he smashed it into the others and glass and amber liquid went flying. He grabbed another bottle and wrenched it open, sobbing as he did, gritting his teeth with concentration on the task at hand. He would kill himself like this. Deliberately. Heden saw it. He would consider it a fitting and just end to die finally at the hand of the demon who taken everything else away.

"No!" Heden said, and lunged forward knocking the bottle out of Aimsley's hand. "Not like this!" He pulled the thief up by his jerkin and shouted into his red, wet, weeping face, inches from Heden's. "You don't get out that easy!" Heden slapped the dirk back into the thief's hand and grabbed his wrist, brought it to his neck this time. The polder didn't have the strength to fight him.

Heden produced the second dirk, and pressed it into the polder's neck.

"You want out!?" Heden shouted. "We go together! But *you have to do it!*"

The thief let his hand fall open, and the dirk fell from it. Heden was holding him up by his wrist now. The little man just dangled. Heden let him go, and he fell onto the floor of the bar unresisting. Heden tossed the second dirk on the floor.

Aimsley lay there, covered in drink, cut by the glass that had shattered all around him. His chest heaved with sobs.

"Help me," he gurgled as he wept. "Please. Please help me. Help me."

The words came from some other place, some place beneath his conscious mind. He wasn't even aware he was saying them. But the tears came from him. The powerlessness, the complete inability to control himself, stop himself. The things he did, the horrible things he'd done to distract himself from what he'd become.

The thief begged for help until, with a gurgle and a quiet snort, he passed out.

Heden took a deep breath and said a prayer over both of them. Then another, and another. His wounds, the ache in his back, tingled away and the thief started to snore. Heden looked around the bar, the inn. Saw the path of blood and destruction they've left, and relaxed. It had worked. He didn't know how it would end, but when the polder asked for help, he knew it was over. Knew there was hope, and that was enough. A beginning.

Heden reached down, grabbed the collar of the polder's jerkin, behind his neck, and lifted the little man until only his boots touched the floor.

He turned and began dragging the polder by the collar toward the door.

"Dangerous way to start a friendship," he said to himself.

Chapter Fifty-nine

Domnal hefted his bulk around the chair, sat down, and pulled the mug of ale across the table.

"What the fuck was all that about?" he asked, cocking a thumb backwards to the stone cell where Aimsley Pinwhistle lay, unconscious.

Heden took a deep breath. "He killed the abbot," he said.

"Shut the fuck up!" Dom said. "That little streak of shit?!"

"He'll need to go to the citadel eventually," Heden said. "Once he comes to, he'll figure a way out of the jail."

"Black gods," Dom said, "why do you bring this stuff to me?"

"Sorry," Heden said. "It's been a long week."

Dom twisted around to look at the door beyond which lay the cells and the polder, then turned back to Heden.

"He killed the abbot and you bring him to me? You didn't kill him yourself?" Dom asked, amazed.

"I'm not in the murder business," Heden said.

Dom gave him a look. "A passel of thieves killed on Moorfield the other night," he said.

"Oh?" Heden tried to look innocent.

"Someone chewed up and spat out a bunch of thieves and an alchemist went missing a few months ago."

Heden sighed. "No shortage of alchemists about," he said. "Or thieves. Easy to replace."

"Alchemist named Tam, turns out."

Heden said nothing.

"You used to know an alchemist named Roderick Tam," Dom continued. "Used to be friends with you lot," Dom said, meaning the Sunbringers.

"Name sounds familiar," Heden said.

"You knew those thieves were going after this Tam? You'd

stop 'em, if you could. You'd kill 'em if you couldn't. I know you. 'Not in the murder business' my arse."

Heden said nothing.

"You're going after the count," Dom guessed.

Heden looked around the room. Then back at his friend.

"Yeah," he said.

"Shit," Dom said, disappointed and angry.

"You think the count can take me?" Heden asked.

Dom spit on the sawdust covered floor of his office in the jail. "The count is a little streak of shit, I could take him. You got to worry about Garth."

"I know Garth," Heden said.

"Yeah you do. No love lost there, I reckon. Both of you happy to keep it that way."

Heden didn't say anything.

"Ragman finds out you were here, probably ask me why I didn't arrest you."

"For the murder of Roderick Tam?" Heden asked.

Dom made a noise like 'psh.' "Ain't no one think it's you going around killing alchemists. But those thieves didn't drag each other and everyone knows you're after the count now…and Tam was your friend. Ain't hard to put two and two together."

Heden didn't say anything.

"Plus…you coming in here…telling me you're about to go murder a man…even the count…Ragman sorta considers that his territory."

"You know he doesn't like it when people call him that," Heden said.

Dom barked a laugh. "Then he should get a woman, find someone to do his washing for him, knit him some new clothes."

Heden couldn't argue with that.

"I could arrest you," Dom said, admitting the possibility.

Heden said nothing.

"I should arrest you, I guess," he offered, both of them

knowing he wasn't going to.

"For what? For the ragman?" Heden asked.

"For you," Dom said, putting his elbows on the table and looking at Heden. "Garth will chew you up," he said. "You realize what that makes me, right? Makes me the last person to see the victim alive. Which is also, just sos you know, how we figure out who to press around here."

He looked down at his mug. "Means if I let you leave, knowing what I know, I'm responsible. A little at least. Which is enough."

Heden looked at his friend. Thought of the real bind he'd put him in. But the count had Vanora.

"I know," Heden said. "I'd feel the same way, if it were me."

Dom looked up from his drink, a sad smirk on his face.

"But you're not going to lock me up," Heden said.

"No," Dom said.

"Not a long term solution," Heden said.

"No," Dom said. "Best I could do would be throw you in with the polder. Wait for you lot to get yourselves out, get yourselves killed."

Heden stood up.

"I'm going to go now, Dom."

Domnal nodded without looking at Heden.

Heden went for the door.

"You're a good man, you know," Dom said.

Heden turned around. Dom was still looking at his mug.

"Many is the time I wondered what you would do, when things were thick down here."

He looked at his friend.

"I'm better for having you as a friend," Dom said.

Heden just stared at Dom.

"Me too," he said, and turned back to leave.

"Maybe that'll make the difference," Dom said.

Heden tried to remember to breathe as he grasped the door

handle. Noticed he wasn't shaking. Hadn't had a fit of terror since he left the Wode. Since he got back in. That was one problem solved.

"Maybe," he said.

CHAPTER SIXTY

The alley connecting Rile St. and the Broad Road allowed Heden to get from the jail to the castle quickly. It was just after noon, the sun was bright, the sky was blue and he was in no mood to appreciate either.

He was going to find Gwiddon. Going to confront the king, and demand to see Gwiddon. Gwiddon would know how to find the count. And Heden would force him to tell.

As his mind played out the upcoming scenario, he noticed there was no one in the alley. Was that unusual?

He looked behind him. No one. He turned back around and saw him.

Garth.

He stood at the end of the ally, in his black leather, casually standing with his weight one his right leg and one hand resting on the pommel of his rapier. *Apostate.* The prayerbreaker.

Heden put a hand on *Solaris*.

"You knew sooner or later I'd have to…," Garth shrugged. "I mean, how did you think this would end?" Garth asked. He seemed sad, disappointed.

"I guess it ends when one of us kills the other," Heden said.

"No point wondering who'll come out on top," Garth concluded.

"Nope," Heden said.

"We'll find out, and then we'll know," Garth said.

"One of us will," Heden said.

Garth nodded. "Don't imagine you'll have any regrets if it me who goes down."

"Just one," Heden said.

Garth raised an eyebrow.

"Sorry I didn't do it sooner."

Garth smiled and walked forward. Heden walked to the right, forcing Garth to the left. Garth had the initiative, but Heden the defensive advantage.

With his left hand, Garth reached behind him and pulled out a dagger. Heden prayed, and his skin flashed to stone. The strength of Cavall.

Garth threw the dagger, Heden deflected it with his forearm, but in the same instant Garth produced a hand crossbow, and fired a bolt at Heden.

The bolt struck Heden full in the chest, and he gasped as the flood of power given him by the granite prayer fled his body. It was an experience completely new to him. Like vomiting with your whole body.

This was no poison. It was some kind of curse. That bolt was cursed, cursed by a dark god. Nikros or Cyrvis. One of the black brothers or their saints. But the power of the god must be great to strip away Heden's defenses. The stone skin, the strength. All gone. He felt naked. Felt like someone had punched him in the diaphragm and forced all the air out of his lungs.

"Did you think the dust was our only trick?" Garth sneered. "Never show your whole hand."

Heden was out of breath and the fight hadn't even begun. He wrested the bolt from his chest, staggered once, but mastered himself.

"I'll remember that," he said, and gripped *Solaris. I need you,* he thought.

Together, the voice of the sword echoed in Heden's head, *we shall cast light into darkness. Cast shadows out.*

There was an eagerness. *Solaris* had been waiting for this moment. Garth was the shadow. *Solaris* yearned to destroy him.

Garth saw Heden's play, and drew his unholy rapier.

Unbidden, with swordsmanship Heden never possessed, *Solaris* willed Heden's arm to draw itself from its sheath, and counter Apostate.

As their swords clashed, Heden's entire body erupted in flame.

Garth leapt back, his hand burned, but did not cry out. He assumed a dueling pose, relaxed, as he tried to understand what happened.

Heden felt healed, renewed. *Solaris* was drawn. Something like lava, liquid sunlight, dripped from the blade. When it hit the street, it splashed in rainbow crystals like prisms, bouncing and disintegrating on the stone cobbles.

Heden looked like a summoned creature of elemental fire. His entire body blazed.

Garth's eyes went wide as he saw the relic Heden wielded. A blade of immense power. More than a match for *Apostate*. He looked back at Heden and his eyes went cold. Dead. He'd made one mistake, one missing element in his research. He hadn't considered Zaar might forgive him, hadn't known the dwarf had come with a sword. *The* sword.

Garth would not make a mistake like that again.

Armed with the black steel blade, Garth catfooted forward, back on the attack.

Now, aided by *Solaris* the blade of Saint Pentalion Sunbringer, Heden began to fight for his life.

Shadow and sunlight, the assassin and the priest danced across the cobbled street. Heden relaxed that part of his mind that controlled his body, and let *Solaris* take over.

Heden lunged forward, a memory of skill, experience, suddenly present in his mind. All he had to do was let it happen. Easy.

Garth betrayed no surprise at Heden's blazing form, his newfound swordsmanship. He parried and feinted, his acrobatics more than a match for Heden's but *Solaris* was a match for Garth.

Solaris cast a spell. A wall of fire erupted behind Garth, blocking his retreat.

Instead of retreating, Garth flipped over Heden, an inhuman leap deftly clearing the priest's reach.

Heden spoke a prayer, a shaft of sunlight stabbed down at Garth, who effortlessly danced out of the way, recognizing the spoken prayer.

Garth produced three crystal throwing daggers, threw them at Heden. Each unerringly struck Heden in the chest, but melted upon contact with his blazing form.

They crossed blades again. They danced out of the alley where it emptied onto a bridge that crossed the Kirk river, the river that snaked through the city, and circled the king's castle.

Solaris cast a spell. Heden spoke a prayer. The street around Garth turned to mud, but *apostate* prevented the stone Garth stood on from liquefying. A crystal cube formed on the spot Garth had been standing, it would have permanently trapped Garth within it, but Garth was not there.

Heden whirled around.

Garth was behind him. He produced a garrote with glinting diamond powder embedded into it. The same kind of weapon one of the black scarves tried on him. But this cord had a weight at one end. He twirled it and flicked the weight at Heden.

Heden misjudged the attack and deflected in the wrong direction. The diamond cord snaked around his neck, Garth pulled, and Heden felt the cord bite into his neck, draw blood, cut deep, ignoring the blazing form granted by *Solaris*.

He was surprised and for a moment did not react. But *Solaris* was not surprised. The sword, unbidden, slashed into the cord cutting it.

His body still made of living sunfire, Heden retreated out onto the bridge, skirting the pool of mud, the crystal cube.

Garth followed. Neither man spoke. This was a fight to the death. Garth had previously been cocky, conversational, because he believed the fight was over before it began. Now he made no commentary. He was focused on nothing except the fight. The same campaigners' instincts that keep Heden alive now gave Garth the advantage he needed. *Kill the Arrogate*, would be the command from the count. Nothing less.

There was no space in Heden's mind for the future. He possessed no awareness of what might happen next, of who was winning, of which of them would yield, which would die. There was only the moment. Ratcatchers who thought of anything else in the heat of battle died quickly.

Garth grimaced, and spoke his own spell.

His body flashed into a shadow. A living shade, like the ones summoned by the night dust. But unlike those, this form was thick and solid, not a wisp of twisting ethereal dust.

Heden recognized the spell, had seen Garth use it. The *vile form*. The shadow magic expert thieves and assassins learned. It sapped Garths' life as he maintained it, but he wouldn't have to maintain it long.

Apostate's black steel darted out like the tongue of a snake. *Solaris* burned white hot and met the enemy blade.

Sunlight and shadow, flame and darkness clashed and danced further onto the bridge. People were watching now. Gathered at the far end of the bridge.

The living shadow whirled, tried to find an opening. *Solaris* permitted none. Garth summoned darkness, *Solaris* banished it.

More! The blade called in Heden's mind. It relished the fight, drank in the power arrayed against it. Ached to be tested further.

Heden wondered which of them was in control. Would *Solaris* deliberately prolong the fight just to get a chance to manifest its long-slumbering might? As long as the sword kept him alive, it didn't matter.

As fire-sword and shadow-blade clashed, *Solaris* found an opening. Stabbed into the black mist.

Garth retreated out of the shadow, resumed his normal flesh and blood form. The spell had drained him, sapped him of needed will, and now he was wounded. He grasped his left breast where *Solaris* had pierced his armor.

Apostate fell to the ground, clattered on the stone bridge. Heden took a moment to get his breath, thinking *Solaris* had created an advantage. Thinking he had won.

Then he saw the small crossbow in Garth's sword hand. He hadn't dropped his weapon because he was injured. He'd merely traded one useless weapon for one proven to be effective.

Garth shot Heden again with an unholy arrow. *Solaris* darted out, attempting to deflect it. But the sword was not fast enough. The bolt hit Heden and again he felt his body wrench.

The form of living sun blinked out, leaving Heden a flesh and blood man.

Garth recovered *Apostate*.

Heden could hear the voice of *Solaris* but it sounded far away, indistinct. Somehow, the connection between him and the sword had been broken. He had not known that power existed.

Where did he get that power? Heden wondered. Even as he asked the question, he knew the answer.

Unable to match Garth, come anywhere near matching him, in swordsmanship, Heden retreated across the bridge.

Garth pressed the advantage, stopping Heden's retreat just as he reached the middle of the bridge. Heden tried to defend, but his sword training was practical. Garth was a master.

Both of them wounded, neither of them able to muster their full strength, flanked by crowds at either end of the bridge, the priest and the assassin fought desperately, each knowing this was the end.

Heden managed to deflect one lunge, then another, retreating all the while. But Garth had set him up. The two attacks were feints designed to get Heden's sword into position.

Garth's black steel blade ran and danced along the edge of *Solaris*, twisting and spinning the blade in Heden's hand until he had to let go of it, or break his wrist.

The sword flew out, over the side of the bridge, into the river.

"Shit," Heden said. The dwarf was going to kill him.

Out of options, Heden remembered his battle with the thief in his inn.

'*Noxa,*' Heden said, and Garth shuddered. His whole body clenched...then slowly released, and he resumed his fighting pose.

Garth had warded himself against curses. This meant the aid of a powerful enemy priest, a servant of one of the Black Brothers.

Heden began to speak a name. The name of a dominion. But Garth proved faster.

He threw a trio of darts, needle-thin, at Heden. Heden held up his right hand, managed to save one eye. A needle dug into his left eye and the whole left side of his face blossomed with pain like fire.

Heden pulled the dart his left eye. He'd lost it. That eye was gone now. A feeling like panic washed over him. He tried to master it, but in the process forgot the name he'd been searching for.

Apostate slipped into Heden's ribs under his left arm.

"Angh!" Heden cried out.

Garth was there, next to him, had followed up the blade thrust, and now with one deft motion grabbed Heden's left arm as he held it to his dead eye, and in a fluid jerk, snapped Heden's arm back, dislocating his shoulder.

Heden expelled his breath in one last prayer, a ball of light exploded in front of Garth's eyes, blinding him. This bought Heden one instant.

Bracing himself on the stone railing behind him, he kicked Garth full in the chest, sending the man sprawling backward.

Blind, Garth hadn't seen the kick, wasn't ready for it. By the time he landed on his ass, he could see again.

Heden wasted no time. Knew the battle was lost. There was no way to win. But he didn't know how to give up. Twenty years of instincts took over. *Get away!* they said.

Heden turned and leaned his body on the rail of the stone bridge. One eye burning, one arm useless, up onto the stone railing, he levered his body onto the railing. The exertion almost made him pass out. He'd lost a lot of blood. He heard Garth leap from a prone position to standing, guessed what he would do next.

In wool clothes, a steel breastplate over leather armor, a heavy cloak, Heden pushed himself off the bridge, and let himself fall into the Kirk.

The cold water shocked him for a moment, gave him some life. He saw the sun through his good eye, its light dappled and scintillating through the waters. The waters that grew darker, that blotted out the light as he sank.

He wondered if he would drown. He lost consciousness before he could find out.

Chapter Sixty-one

He was aware of someone in the room with him, sometimes more than one person, but as he swam in and out of consciousness he couldn't tell who it was, or where he was, or how much time had passed. He spent much of the time assuming he was dead.

Eventually he realized he was awake, though he couldn't remember waking up, or what had come before. The light streaming through the stained glass told him it was early morning, but the glass itself left no impression on him. He thought, for a moment, he was back at the priory. Back in the wode.

He blinked. There was something wrong with his vision. He lifted a hand to his eyes and felt something alien clinging to his face where he expected his left eye to be. He panicked at the foreign object and then realized it was cloth. Bandages. That's right. He'd forgotten.

He'd lost his eye.

Just then he noticed someone standing in the room, watching him. Leaning against the open doorway into the convalescent chamber.

The castellan.

Heden stared at him for a moment, unsure at what rate time was passing. The castellan looked like a wastrel. He was a big man, but he stooped and had a limp and his clothes hung off him like he'd walked under someone's window when they threw out their old, soiled rags. He had a tangled beard and bad teeth.

Heden had never seen him clean, never seen him in new clothes, and had never seen him off-work. He was Heden's age. Of that same generation that now mostly ran the city. The castellan was, as far as Heden could tell, perpetually on the job. He always had a nail hanging from his lip or from his thick fingers. His long, craggy face made him look like he was a bit thick, the way his jaw jutted out and his mouth often hung open slack. He was not thick.

"How you feel?" he asked. The ragman's voice was rough from decades sucking smoke.

"What day is it?" Heden croaked.

"Cetain," the castellan said.

Three days. Three days since the fight on the bridge.

"Groggy," Heden said. "Not much pain."

The castellan nodded. "Give it some time. You'll start feeling something alright."

"Oh good," Heden said. It was hard to talk.

"You'll get to keep the eye," the castellan gestured at the bandages. "The priests here saved it. Called in some favors, I guess. I told them it was a waste, but they seemed to feel obligated."

Heden relaxed. He still didn't remember all of the fight, the loss of the eye didn't seem real yet, and now it wasn't. How many times had he been torn apart and put back together? He couldn't remember. There was a limit, he knew, but he'd not yet reached it apparently.

"The abbess says you can go home tomorrow if you're feeling up to it."

"I'm in the church," he'd been staring at the stained glass, not realizing what he was seeing. The bishop was somewhere in the building. And the abbot was not. Would never be again.

The castellan nodded.

"I'll go home today," Heden said, and tried to sit up. He started to feel it. His ribs were bruised like they'd been broken and healed again, which they had been, and his right leg was swollen and was starting to throb. His face was numb as though his jaw had been broken and he couldn't feel his left arm. He was exhausted after only a moment's exertion, and collapsed back in the bed.

"Uh-huh," the castellan said. He let the butt of his spent nail drop to the floor and stamped it out with his boot.

Heden looked at the castellan as though seeing him for the first time. "What are you doing here?" he asked the ragman.

The castellan gave him a weary look.

"You come to arrest me?" Heden asked, and he cleared the sleep from his new eye. Mostly just testing to make sure it was real. He blinked. The pain from the assassin's darts still a vivid memory.

Pushing himself away from the door, the castellan stood and fired another nail.

"Could," he said. He took a deep breath. Held it. "Lot of people be happy right now if I locked you up and threw away the key." He blew the smoke through his nose.

Heden had killed four men on a city street and almost murdered another on the bridge over the Kirk. These were things the castellan would not ignore.

He came around from the end of the bed, pulled up a large oak chair and sat down in it next to Heden.

"You want to tell me about it?"

"Ah," Heden appeared to think. He took a deep breath, but it hurt too much and he gave up. "No."

The castellan nodded.

"Five men dead last week on Moorfield."

Heden shrugged. That didn't hurt.

"Three of them dead from sword wounds. Could have been anybody." He looked around the room. There were other beds, currently unoccupied. "One of them ripped apart, another spread all over the road like I don't know what. Not a lot of people in the city can do that."

"Sure there are," Heden said.

"Someone, probably Garth, kills your friend, the abbot, right here in the middle of the church and the next day the two of you are dancing on the High Bridge. Lotta people asking me what the fuck is going on. Say it's all about the night dust, say you know something about it."

"I don't know anything about the night dust," Heden said. This was probably not true, but it certainly *felt* like he didn't know anything.

"You've got stab wounds all over you like a fucking pin cushion," the castellan continued. "And enough poison in you to kill a dwarf. If I bring the king's Magus in here, he'll be able to show me what happened. We can go back a week if we have to. You wouldn't enjoy it."

Heden grunted and sunk back in the thick bedding.

"The men you killed, all members of the Guild." There were three guilds, but they both knew who he meant. Only one of the thieves' guilds actually called themselves a guild. "Except the alchemist. We sort of know they were after him, that's probably not your fault."

Heden maintained his silence; let the castellan fill up the space between them. He hadn't asked a question yet.

"Your victims all appear to be known criminals and wanted men," he continued. "Except for the one you turned into soup, but we can make some conclusions based on the company he kept."

Heden nodded. That didn't hurt either.

"You're going to run around my city butchering people, you could have done worse."

There were very few people in Celkirk who could legitimately say 'my city' without hubris or exaggeration.

He was waiting for Heden to chime in. After a moment's silence, when it was obvious Heden was going to keep his mouth shut, the castellan got on with it.

"You need to understand something," he said, and got Heden's attention with his tone of voice. He leaned forward, putting his elbows on his knees. "I serve the king, and the law, and not in that order. I can help you, I *will* help you, but only as long as I think you're on the same side of this I'd be on if I knew what was going down. That means you got to *tell me* what's going down, because I don't trust you. You making a move against the Guild?"

"They attacked me," Heden said.

"I bet they did," the castellan said. "And you have no idea why?"

"'The pure heart is the constant target of evil men?'" Heden quoted.

"Uh huh," the castellan said. "Listen," he reached down, under Heden's bed, and pulled out the empty chamber pot, knocked some ashes into it. "I don't want to get involved with this," he continued.

"I don't *want* you to get involved with it," Heden said.

"If I get involved with it," the castellan said, ignoring him, "then you'll probably end up in the citadel and whatever you're working on, I won't be able to get as far with."

"Nice of you to say that."

The castellan shook his head. "You been holed up in that inn for three years," he said. "You come out and all of a sudden people start dying."

"People didn't die while I was at the Inn?"

"You know what I mean." Heden knew what he meant. "You're not as young as you were. You're not as smart as you think you are. But you might be as tough."

"Better to be lucky than good," Heden said, letting his eyes close.

"And you're probably the most moral person any of us know."

"Present company excluded," Heden offered.

The castellan shrugged. "If you're dancing with the count," he said, "I won't be able to save you. But I want to know about it so I can go after him once you're dead."

"That's comforting," Heden said.

"It is the count ain't it?"

Heden waited just a moment, and nodded.

"Alright," the castellan said. "Give it to me."

Heden told him everything, leaving out the bishop for now. One problem at a time.

"You know as much about the Dust as we do," the castellan said. "Where's he get it?"

"I don't know," Heden said, shifting in his bed. He was starting to feel like he could eat something. A horse maybe, or a couple of cows. Maybe get out of bed in a few years. "Maybe I can find out."

"This isn't a race," the castellan said, pointing to Heden. "You find out where the Dust is coming from, you tell me before you make a move."

"Maybe," Heden said. "Haven't decided what I'm going to do."

The castellan reached out and tugged on a sheet, straightening it, making a point.

"Good place to do your thinking."

"You're saying I'm in over my head and was lucky to get out of there alive."

"They sent five black scarves and Garth after you. The scarves are dead and you're here talking. Not sure luck has anything to do with it, but they won't make that mistake again. You got lucky with the sword from the dwarf."

"Oh you know about that?" Heden asked, surprised the castellan had learned about Solaris.

"Garth won't make that mistake again. We both know Garth could take you. Garth could take you in his sleep."

"Show's how stupid he is then," Heden said resting his eyes. "Coming after me in his sleep."

The castellan stared at Heden.

"You're going after the Guild," he concluded.

"I'm going after the count," Heden corrected.

"Because of the abbot? The girl?"

Heden didn't say anything.

"I was you," the castellan said, finally, "I'd do the same thing."

Heden smiled weakly, thought of what he'd say to the abbot about all this. Then remembered.

"Garth didn't kill the abbot," he said.

The ragman raised an eyebrow. "Eh?" he said.

"The Hearth's fixer, Pinwhistle, did."

"That cock-high thief?"

"Yeah," Heden said.

"You know he's been hanging around here?" the castellan asked, incredulously. "The fuck is he doing hovering around you after he kills the man who brought you up?"

"I dunno," Heden said, and realized that was a lie. "Probably he wants someone to forgive him."

"Hah!" the castellan barked. Then he realized who he was talking to. His eyes narrowed. "You and the polder," he said, making a leap. He took a long, slow, measured breath.

"There are things I can't do," he said. "Because of who I am." Heden nodded. He knew what he meant.

"Last three castellans," Heden said, "city might as well have been run by a donkey."

The castellan shrugged. "I like to think I've earned the king's trust." Heden knew he'd earned more than that. "That gets me a lot. The king trusts me because he knows I will do what I say I'm going to do."

"That and you're a grand master hard-ass," Heden observed.

"But there are many things I cannot do." He looked meaningfully at Heden. "Things you can do."

He stood up. Made a feeble effort to smooth out his clothes.

"I can turn a blind eye for a little while, but only a little while. Richard doesn't want to see this place turn into Capital." He looked at Heden's recumbent form and shook his head with pity. "And you definitely need help."

He walked to the door and opened it, then turned back to

Heden.

"You're thinking about asking that little thief," the castellan said, "might think again. I'm sure he saw me coming in. If he's who I think he is, his docket's thick as a codex. If he knows what's good for him, he's left the city by now, which means you're on your own."

He gave Heden a sympathetic look and walked out the doorway, pulling the heavy door closed behind him.

The polder was standing behind the door, smiling broadly.

CHAPTER SIXTY-TWO

"If you knew what was good for you," Heden said. "You'd be outside the city."

The Polder shook his head sharply. "I hate the country," he said and ambled over to the chair the castellan had just vacated. "Everyone's dirty and poor. No fun."

He tossed something on Heden's bed. Something heavy. Heden looked down.

Solaris.

"Might want to hang on to that," Aimsley said. "Seems useful."

Heden put his hand on *Solaris*. "Thanks," he said. He gave the polder a look. "Guess you didn't come here to kill me," he said.

The polder shrugged. Like what happened at the inn was just an argument. "Tried that, didn't work. Figured I try something else."

"What?" Heden asked.

"Help you out, maybe," the polder said, nodding to *Solaris*.

Heden put a hand on the sword. "This doesn't make us even," he said.

The polder shrugged. "Whatever I've done to you," he said, "you're not in any position to do anything about it."

This was true. *Whatever I've done to you*. Heden wondered what this meant.

"Shame about the eye," he said, nodding to the huge bandage on Heden's left eye. "Figure you got away lucky."

"They say I get to keep the eye," Heden said. "Agent of the church, even a former agent, has its benefits."

Aimsley nodded.

"You got out of jail," Heden ventured, watching the thief.

Waiting to see what would happen. How, if at all, the incident at the inn, his time in the jail, had affected him.

"Sure," Aimsley said. "Well, you knew I would. Wasn't hard. They brought me food, drink. Nice of them. Mostly I just sobered up. That was fun," he said sarcastically.

Neither of them said anything.

"You clean now?" Heden asked.

The polder shrugged. "Haven't had a drink in a while. Couple of days. Longer than...well, longer than I can remember. Sort of...I dunno, sad, upset, that I missed the party on High Bridge."

"Not sure I need your kind of help," Heden said.

"Well," the polder said. "I did say I'd have been on your side, but...," he smiled a little. "Helping you would have meant I didn't have to fish that thing out of the river," he indicated *Solaris* resting on Heden's bed.

Heden understood. "You come just to bring me this?" he asked.

The blonde polder scratched the back of his neck.

"Count's got the girl," Aimsley said. "Sorta feel...feel a little...," he bobbed his head back and forth, weighing a thought.

"Responsible? Guilty?"

The little man frowned at him, as though the comment were in bad taste. "Feel like I need a drink."

Heden didn't say anything. Looked at the sword.

"How's that going?" he asked, as though it wasn't important.

"It's going fucking bad is how it's going," the thief said, but without rancor. "I can't go in a tavern. Can't even have an ale. Can't...," he was wrestling with the idea. One hand shook as he talked. He didn't bother trying to hide it. "I feel like my skin is three sizes too small, only way I get to sleep is in a pool of sweat, exhausted. Which is like no sleep. Any time I see someone with a drink, which seems like it's all the fucking time now, I have to get out. I just can't...."

Heden kept his mouth shut.

"As long as I'm not in a tavern," the thief continued, "I'm ok. I can deal with it. It's tough, but...I just...I need to make sure I'm not in a place where I can make bad decisions." He took a moment to survey the hospice.

"Ale?" Heden asked. "Take the edge off."

The polder shook his head. Heden noticed he had one of his custom-made dirks in his hand. He didn't see the polder produce it, it was just there one moment.

"Only one thing takes the edge off," Aimsley said, and gave Heden a dark look from under his blonde eyebrows. It wasn't a threat, but the way he held the dirk, Heden knew what he meant. When Heden was working, he didn't have his fits either.

That's why the polder was here. He needed the work, needed the purpose. Needed something to replace the drink, and couldn't wait for Heden to recover. He needed Heden. Needed someone who wasn't a criminal to give him something to do. It was a burden Heden hadn't considered but every time he blinked he saw Taethan dying in the darkness behind his eyelids. He'd assume any burden now.

"What did you do to me?" the polder asked. "Back at the inn?"

"A curse."

"I thought only priests of the Black Brothers could curse," Aimsley muttered, looking at the floor, unhappy to discover ignorance.

"Nope. Anyone can do it. As long as your god...ah, approves of your intent and judgment. Which is rare. Helps if you know your god," Heden added, omitting *or your saint*, "pretty well. It only works on people who deserve it."

"Well," the polder said, looking at his feet. "I've done enough bad things."

Heden watched him. "You killed the man who raised me," he said flatly.

Aimsley looked up at him, his face slack, without expression.

"I did?" he said. "When was this?"

Heden sat up more, tried to get a better look at the thief before him.

"Five days ago," he said. "He was hiding Vanora. You killed him and took the girl."

"Huh," the polder said, looking around the church. "I thought I remembered being here before."

Heden tried to master his emotions, watched the thief staring at him, clouded brow under blonde curls.

"There's something I need to say to you," the thief said.

He looked down again, taking a deep breath. Heden waited.

The thief looked back at the priest.

"Okay," he said. It was a piece of slang only campaigners used. Part of a unique pattern of speech. It was, Heden realized, like the cant of the Green Order. Didn't matter where you were from. Once you'd been a ratcatcher, it became your nation. Your language. Separated you from everyone else. You all started talking alike, more in common with each other than your own countrymen, your own family.

"I don't…," the thief began. He was having trouble forming the words. Or maybe the ideas themselves. "I don't remember what happened at the inn," he confessed. He looked to Heden, his blue eyes filled with fear, confusion, and a desire for someone, anyone, to tell him it was alright.

"I know I was there. I know we went at it. But I don't…I can't remember anything specific. I get flashes. I know you helped me. I can sorta guess you could have killed me, but didn't. I know it was you who locked me up. Told the jailor to leave me in there until it was out of my system. I know you took a risk for me…."

Heden remembered the little man covered in cuts and drink, begging for help and wondered: if this man in front of him couldn't remember that, who was it who asked for help? What part of him?

314

The thief took another deep breath. His body shook, struggling with the words.

"It's not just the drink," Aimsley said. "I mean, I know it's the drink, but it's not only when I'm tight. It used to be. I'd have these times when I knew I was up and moving about and talking and being myself, but I couldn't remember it afterwards. And no one seemed to notice." He shook his head. "Couldn't figure that out." He looked at Heden.

Heden waited. The polder was not done.

"Then it happened on a job. I don't even remember which one. I was talking to Brick and I realized we were talking about a job I'd just done and I couldn't remember it. That scared the shit out of me." He looked at the stained glass. It seemed, to Heden, as though it was getting easier. His tone was steadier.

"Then I realized it had probably happened before, forgetting a whole job, and I couldn't even remember there was anything to forget. I was basically tight all the time by then. Then it would happen for days. Two, three days at a time.

"It felt like I was better on the drink, but that don't make sense. I couldn't figure out why it didn't seem to affect my ability. My skill."

"Probably it did," Heden said.

Aimsley remembered Dugal saying he hadn't been top man in years, and sighed.

"Yeah. Probably. Gets to a point where you can mostly get by on reputation."

He didn't say anything for a long time. Watching him, Heden no longer experienced the strange sense of talking to a man in a child's body. He just saw the person, Aimsley Pinwhistle. Polder. Thief. They didn't really look like children anyway. It was just his youthful face.

They sat there together for a while, Heden in the bed, Aimsley in the chair, no one saying anything.

"I lost a whole year," the thief said, his voice flat.

He waited until he was sure the polder was done. "That wasn't easy to say."

The thief poked a finger in his ear and wiggled it about. "Talking helps," he said. "Got no one to talk to besides you."

Heden knew this was also not easy to say.

"Let me tell you something," Heden said, and pushed himself up to be more sitting and less lying down.

The thief waited expectantly. Heden told him about his episodes. About the paralyzing, unreasoning fear that gripped him, triggered by any hint of his old life. About how it started. About the inn, hating to go out, white knuckling through even the most mundane tasks if they meant leaving the inn.

Aimsley listened like it was a revelation. Like a saint had come to speak to him.

"Shit," the thief said, when Heden was done.

"Yeah," Heden said.

"You think maybe…," Aimsley looked at the door, heard an abbess tending to someone outside. "You think maybe everyone's fucked up like this and no one ever talks about it?"

Heden shook his head. "No."

Aimsley smiled. "Nah, me neither. Well, good for us. We're special."

"Helps to talk about it."

The thief nodded. "Yeah."

Neither of them spoke for a few moments.

"I killed your friend and you could have killed me, but you just locked me up," the polder said, unbelieving.

"Yes," Heden said.

"Why'd you do that?"

Heden shrugged. "I saw it in you," he said. "Saw what the drink was doing. Didn't think what happened to the abbot was you. Not really."

The polder looked like he was going to throw up. "What if it was?" he asked, worried.

"A man is better than the worst thing he's ever done," Heden said.

Aimsley barked a fateful laugh. "You sure about that?" he said.

"Yes," Heden said.

"That mean you forgive me?" the polder asked, looking at the stained glass. Furtive glances at Heden, never keeping his eyes on him long.

"That what you want?" Heden said, and realized it was the abbot speaking through him. The abbot gave Heden what he needed to forgive the man who killed him.

"Maybe I don't deserve it."

"Deserve is a tricky word," Heden said.

"I mean…maybe I gotta…earn it," the polder said.

Heden nodded. He liked this line of reasoning. "And how do you plan on doing that?"

This, the polder was ready for. "I stole the girl from you," he said. "Delivered her to the count. Made everything worse."

"No one knows where the count is," Heden said. "What can you do?"

"Thief, ain't I?" the polder said, letting a smile play across his lips, waiting to see the priest's reaction.

Heden smiled. The polder let his smile grow. Friends?

"Let's steal her back," Aimsley Pinwhistle said, grinning madly.

CHAPTER SIXTY-THREE

Heden pulled his boots on. He'd been desperate to leave the day before, desperate to try and help the Polder, but he was too weak and the abbess tending him wouldn't allow it.

"Don't think it's right for you to be gettin' up like this," the woman said. Talking to her, Heden had learned they were the same age, but she seemed older to him. She probably thought the same of him.

"I know," Heden said.

"You need more rest," she said, folding the sheets from his bed.

"That's true," Heden said.

"Here, stand still," she said. He obeyed and she gingerly picked at the gum holding his eye bandage on. Then she ripped it off in one smooth tug.

"Ow," Heden said. His left eye watered from the light, he had to keep it closed for the moment. Squint.

The abbess appraised him.

"Maybe I ort to send someone with you," she said. "Look after you."

"You could do that," Heden said mildly. He was going to agree with everything, but leave of his own accord. She couldn't keep him here. Somewhere, the count still had Vanora.

"Why don't I fetch...," the abbess began, and stopped when a young boy entered the room.

He was dressed in red and gold, the king's colors. He was clean, well-dressed. The abbess stared at him. Heden did too, but with resignation rather than surprise.

"I'm here for him," the page boy nodded.

The abbess raised her eyebrows and looked at Heden.

"I've got a message for you, sir," the boy said, promoting

Heden to knight.

Heden deflated in his bed. There was only one person who would send a page dressed like this to deliver a message.

"How do you know who I…," Heden tried deflecting.

"For the Arrogate," the boy clarified, interrupting him.

"Oh," Heden said. "Yeah that's me."

"His majesty politely requests your presence at court."

Heden nodded.

"Politely," he said.

"That's the message, sir," the boy said.

Heden sat there, feeling incredibly old.

"Is there a knight standing outside right now?" he asked.

"No sir. His majesty said," the boy cleared his throat, "'The knight would just piss him off,' he said sir. 'And he'd not come just to spite me for sending one,' he said."

"He said that," Heden's voice was flat.

"Yes sir."

"'Politely,'" Heden repeated.

"He stressed that, sir."

Heden looked at the abbess watching the whole thing with wonder. A messenger from the king!

"Means 'now, dammit,'" Heden explained to her.

"Well you best be off!" she bustled, helping Heden up.

"You don't think I should stay?" he asked weakly. "Man in my condition?"

"Go, go, go!" the abbess said, shooing him out.

"Ugh," Heden said. "Alright young master," he put a hand on the page's shoulder, as though he were an old man.

"Let's try and make it to the castle without either of us being assassinated," he said.

The boy looked up at him and smiled bravely. "You're in the company of the king when you're with me!" he said proudly.

Still weak, Heden tried to stand up straight, took his hand off the boy's shoulder. Started walking to the door.

"Uh-huh," he said.

Chapter Sixty-four

A trumpet blared.

The sound meant his father was about to appear. Would always mean that. Mean the theater was beginning, and his da was about to enter the great hall, with his crown and sword, his long ermine-rimmed red robe, take his seat on the throne, hear the grievances of the guildmasters, and the occasional petitions from his citizens.

Because his father taught him what it meant to be a man before teaching him what it meant to be a king, he always saw the king holding court as a performance. That man up there had little to do with his father. It was an act. His privy council knew it. Probably the civil authorities knew it. The people watching, however, the citizens, had no idea. This was the king, they thought.

Now, at 38 years of age, his father long dead, he knew it would always be thus. The trumpet would never be his sound. He had no children...yet. Probably would have none, he thought. And he would never hear the trumpet and think of it has anything other than the opening of his father's court. Ah well. Did da ever hear it as his own? Hard to imagine. Surely he heard grandad's trumpet.

But then Richard never adopted the performance. Maybe his da really did hear his trumpet. He certainly acted like it was his. Gave no indication it ever belonged to anyone else, heralded the opening of twenty generations of the kings of Corwell.

The trumpet blared again. Richard shook off his reverie and strode through the door.

"All stand," the herald said. The room was already standing of course, had been for a few minutes. "For the king, Richard, Sword of Cavall." There were other titles, but Richard eschewed them except when he needed to make a point to visiting dignitaries. Here, in his own hall, Sword of Cavall was enough.

Richard strode purposefully but, he knew, much less magisterially than his father, to the throne. He wore the crown and sword, but no cloak. He wasn't a man interested in theater. He was interested in justice. And for some reason, as king, found the theater of state distasteful in its pursuit.

He sat down, and the great hall sat. Except for the guards lining the walls and his knights. To his left and right, stood two of the White Hart.

Before him, on a lower platform, sat his privy council. Four men representing his best advisors. Because they were on his side of this whole affair, they faced away from him.

Facing him, in two rows of chairs placed on the floor, were the heads of all the guilds, and orders, the churches, civic leaders from every section of the city. They were the official reason for this meeting. Behind them, a row of guards in chain with pike, and behind them about two-hundred citizens. Agitated, fearful, hopeful. Hoping the king could do something, fearing he couldn't, or fearing it would be too late, or just fearing because they had so little power in the whole thing.

Absent was the one man who could actually do anything about the count and the deathless plaguing the city. The castellan. The ragman, they called him, and for good reason.

The king took a deep breath. Nodded at the herald. The young man said, in a clear, masculine voice that echoed through the hall, "Having charged the members of the city council with bringing order over the city, the king will hear their reports."

The hall exploded in shouting from the people.

"Order!" Sir Anduiros, one of the knights standing by the throne shouted.

The king nodded to a man in long black robes.

"The king will hear the report from the Archmaster of the Quill!" Sir Anduiros said, his voice echoing in the hall.

Laqueus, the Archmaster of the Quill and first among the three equals of the wizard orders, stood up.

"Master Laqueus," the king said. "Half my city is currently under the control of the count, and the other half become ungovernable with fear. He has mastery over an army of deathless. I asked you to look into this. Now what have you found?"

"Your majesty, we know much about the night dust now," he said. "But we cannot find its source, or discern the means by which it is manufactured."

The crowd agitated at this.

"And why have you not?" the king asked. He knew the answer, had already gotten all the answers he needed, but the people needed to see the process.

"He has taken precautions my lord. But he's not invulnerable. He has a network, weaknesses. We'll find him."

"Someone knows where he is!!" a woman shouted.

"Indeed," the king said as the guards policed the crowd. He nodded at another councilmember.

"The king will hear the report from Bishop Conmonoc of the Church of Llewellyn the Valiant!" Sir Anduiros bellowed.

But the bishop was nowhere to be seen.

"Where is the representative from the church?" the king asked, as if he didn't know.

"Ah," a handsome, well-dressed man stood up. It was Gwiddon. "His grace Conmonoc, Hand of Cavall, Bishop of the Church of St. Llewellyn the Valiant, is old and could not make the journey," he said. There was a rumbling among the people. "As his personal attaché, he sent me to speak on his behalf and assure the king, his council, and the people, that the church remains well-disposed to handle this threat, and has already dispatched many of the deathless the count's agents have summoned."

"You can't be everywhere!" someone in the crowd shouted,

causing the crowd to further erupt in chaos.

Gwiddon pursed his lips and sat down.

"The wisdom of the people again shows itself," the king said. "The church has power over deathless, but priests are few and the count's agents are many. The church is not sufficient to the task."

This went on, with other council members either complaining about the situation, or apologizing for being unable to do anything about it. After a turn, the king stopped the whole thing.

"Alright," he said wearily, then raised his voice to be heard. "Our thanks go out to the Quill and her allies, and the Church and her efforts," he said. "But as the will of the people cannot be denied or subverted, it is incumbent on me to act on their behalf."

The crowd was silent. Everyone waited for the pronouncement they all demanded.

He took a deep breath. "As Count Irlicht of Haas presents a clear and immediate threat to the well-being of the city, as he has taken up arms against us, committed murder, treason and…," the king waved his hand. "And as he has furthermore refused to produce himself and answer these charges as is required by the noble charter that grants him his title, I hereby charge the knights of the White Hart to seek out the count, to capture him, and bring him here before this court where judgment will be done upon him."

The knight to the king's right shouted; "So sayeth the king!"

"The king!" the people shouted. "The king! The king!" This was what they wanted. The Hart on the case. How could the count stand against the finest knights on life?

King Richard stood up, nodded to the knights of the Hart to his left and right, threw a wary glance at the assembled city council, and strode off the stage where his throne sat.

323

CHAPTER SIXTY-FIVE

"The Hart's never going to find the count," Heden said.

The king removed his crown, threw it on a large divan, and closed the door behind him.

He appraised Heden for a moment. The arrogate was leaning, arms crossed, against an ancient bookshelf.

"Don't you think I know that?" the king snapped.

"So…," Heden offered.

Richard removed his gloves and poured himself a drink. He glanced at Heden.

Heden watched the brown liquor splash into crystal and shook his head. Drinking now would be a kind of betrayal, he felt. Though he couldn't articulate why. He was used to being unable to explain his moral sense.

"I have to do something, dammit," the king said.

"Have to be *seen* doing something," Heden said.

The king took a drink, put his glass down.

"Don't quote me back at me," he said. "I'm the one taught you the difference between the perception and the reality. As I recall you hated it, and made sure I knew you thought less of me because of it."

"I was a young man then," Heden said.

"You were an insufferable prick."

Heden nodded, "You were an entitled, arrogant wastrel."

Richard nodded. "That's true. Probably why you were the only ratcatcher I trusted."

"You didn't trust Stewart?"

The king took another drink. Quickly, mechanically. It was powerful stuff, from Rhone, and Heden knew Richard was trying to drink it no more quickly than propriety allowed.

"Stewart was a good man. But motivated by piety, you by

morality. I invite you to think on the difference, and consider why you are still here while he is not."

"I don't want to talk about Stewart," Heden said darkly.

The king shrugged. "You brought him up," he said.

They both sat down. The king on one couch, Heden on another in the small receiving room. A huge portrait of the king's father hung on the wall to Heden's right. The old king had the same dark, dusky black skin all the kings of Corwell had for generations, but all had jet black, tightly curled hair while Richard's was coppery red.

"Did your granddad have red hair?" Heden wondered. The old king, his black hair grey in the painting, radiated health and power. His skin looked earthy. Like dried sod that might soon blow away. He reminded Heden of his own father.

"Nope," the king said.

"Where do you get it?" Heden asked.

The king shrugged. "Somewhere in the frenzied fucking of my heritage one of the menfolk rutted with a young lady with some Gol blood. Comes up every few generations they say."

"Caelians have a lot to answer for," Heden said. It was the Caelian Empire that last conquered the world, destroying as much of the distinct cultures that came before them as possible through an aggressive program of expatriation. The best way to make Caelians of all the world's people was to drag many thousands of children away from their parents and resettle them in distant lands.

It was painful, bloody, but it worked. Even four hundred years after the fall of the empire, everyone in Orden spoke Tevas and wrote in the Delian script.

"They liked order," the king said. "When I was a boy, I thought they were brutal dictatorial thugs. Now that I'm king, I appreciate their position better."

Heden smiled. The king didn't smile back. He'd brought Heden here for a reason.

"The count is going to rip this city apart," he said. "And he doesn't even know it yet. If he becomes Underking, his subjects will be rats and fleas because that's all that'll be left within the city walls."

"How does it happen?" Heden asked. "How does one become the Underking, or the shadow king, or whatever?"

"It's a negotiation, like anything else," the king explained. "The count goes to the castellan and says 'it's time we worked out a new arrangement,' meaning he gets free run of all the crime in the city. One guild, under the count. He'll say he wants his men to get special treatment from the citadel. The castellan says it'll be up to the count and his guild to keep all the thieves and murders and rapists in line. There'll be concessions and threats and everything you'd expect."

"And the castellan will have to deal."

"Of course he will, that's not the point. The point is it'll be a *bad* deal. He'll have no leverage. With three guilds, he can play one off the other. If the count can eliminate his rivals, then he gets to call the tune."

"How long have we got?" Heden asked.

"Brick already folded," the king said. "He had no choice."

"What about the Truncheon?" Heden asked.

"I don't know," the king said. "He's a meat-brained thug it's hard to guess what…."

Heden coughed discreetly. Reminding the king what he knew.

"Oh, right," the king said. "Gwiddon will *never* fold. The Darkened Moon is a pit of murderous, sadistic, evil men and Gwiddon thinks working for me is their chance at redemption. And *someone*," he said, sneering at Heden, "gave him that idea."

"I never said anything like that," Heden said.

"No, but you wouldn't, would you? You lead by example. Did you know it was four months after you became Arrogate that Gwiddon proposed he take over the Moon? Turn them into our tool? Give them a chance at salvation through murder and theft? Where do you think he got *that* idea?"

"Don't pin this on me," Heden said.

"Someone has to stop the count," the king demanded.

"Because Gwiddon won't relent."

"I may have created a monster," the king said. "Gwiddon has the power, as my secret minister of operational affairs to keep the Moon running long after any other thieves' guild would have to relent. It'll be war. A war of thieves in my city. And no one has any idea how it will end."

"What do you want me to do about it?" Heden asked.

"I want you to forgive him," the king said.

Heden stared blankly at his king. This was not what he expected.

"You need each other," the king said.

When Heden recovered from being stunned he said, methodically;

"You said the Moon's thieves were 'Murderous, sadistic, and evil?' Gwiddon can *have* them. They deserve him."

"You hate him," the king said.

"A little," Heden nodded.

"Do you know who else hates him?" the king asked. Before Heden could answer, the king pressed on. "My enemies."

Heden had no answer for this.

"You think he manipulated you, lied to you, and that your friendship these last 12 years was a deliberate fabrication."

"It's a little more complicated than that."

"Heden if I asked you to undertake a mission, in secret, and I told you that for the good of Corwell you couldn't tell anyone why, would you accept?"

"You've done that before."

"And did you tell anyone? Your brothers, your father? The abbot?"

"No, my lord."

"Do you think they shouldn't trust you because of that? Because you were keeping my secrets?"

Heden bit his lip. "No, my lord."

The king let the reality of this seep in.

"Do you know what Gwiddon did before I placed him under the bishop?"

"He told me he was a solicitor in the…"

"He was a squire for a knight of the White Hart."

"What?" Heden was unable to process this. It was a day for revelations.

"The year before you met him," the king began smoothly, enjoying telling the tale, "he was about to become a knight, getting his spurs in the traditional ceremony. It's a fortnight of fasting and there's something about throwing the spurs into a soup tureen that I've never understood. The purpose of the fasting is to cause the supplicant to enter into a delirium wherein he sees visions, presumably of his god, but after a week's fasting I think mostly he sees fish and fowl with carrots and sauce. Normally the knights sneak in and bring him little bits of food in secret, it is a fraternal brotherhood after all, but in this case it's the White Hart and so no one," he said, emphasizing the point, "brought him anything."

Heden was fixated. The king's speech flowed on.

"Twelve days into this and seeing who knows what, the rectory was attacked by the High Necromancer deliberately targeting the building because he knew all the knights would be there for the ceremony and there was fire and a dozen ghouls, the real thing you understand, not the kind the acolytes used to bring up in graveyards.

"Naked, armed only with a sword, Gwiddon put down eight of them while the other knights spent a whole turn getting their armor on. When they found him they thought he was dead because he was unconscious and covered in blood and his back had been broken.

"He'd saved the rectory and almost single-handedly saved the Hart. The priests healed him, of course, but when they did some of the bones in his back fused together and that couldn't be cured. He couldn't walk for six months, could never become a knight, and has to spend the rest of his life sleeping on a special bed that keeps him upright.

"Now then," the king straightened up. "I am your king, sanctified by Cavall and I could order you to allow Gwiddon to place his prick into your bunghole, and you would have to do it but I have plans for you and they don't involve either you or Gwiddon getting ass-fucked by the other."

The king let this sink in. His voice more gentle when he continued.

"So. I leave it to you. Do what you want. But you might want to consider just this once, forgiving Gwiddon because I asked you to, and he was only lying to you under my explicit command."

There was silence for a few moments. The king smiled.

"I would have forgiven him on your command without the history lesson," Heden said.

"Not the same. I'm not ordering you to forgive him, I'm asking you to."

Heden took a deep breath.

"I need his help."

The king nodded. "I could order him to help you, and he would have to."

"Yes."

"But I won't."

"For the same reason you're *asking* me to forgive him, not *telling* me to?"

"Correct."

"You can be a real piece of shit sometimes, you know that my lord?"

The king suddenly smiled as broadly as Heden had ever

seen. "We are brothers in this."

Heden frowned.

"Alright," he said. "I probably wouldn't have been able to stay angry at Gwiddon anyway but…," he stopped. King Richard raised his eyebrows in anticipation.

"I would have liked trying for a little while longer at least."

The king nodded and stood, Heden followed suit.

"What an insufferable prick he is," the king said, and then put his arm around Heden. "Not like us, huh?"

CHAPTER SIXTY-SIX

Smoke drifted across the board. Three spectators had gathered. Already people sensed something was happening.

Brick moved a piece, stared at Aimsley. Never looked at the board.

Aimsley dragged a nail, and moved a piece. Never took his eyes off the board.

Brick moved a piece. Aimsley exhaled smoke from his nostrils and furrowed his brow as he thought.

The crowd gathered. Someone had said something was up. It was thirty moves into the game. This was the longest Aimsley had ever held off the Brick.

Aimsley watched the board like a cat waiting for a mouse to exit its hole. He took his time, his emotions played across his face. His eyes darted, he searched for weakness, openings. Sometimes his lips moved.

Brick never hesitated.

Aimsley moved a piece.

Brick moved a piece, the wood making a sharp 'clack' on the slate shere board.

"Priest almost dead," Brick said. "Figure that should suit the count for now. Nice to have you back where you belong."

Aimsley ignored him. Picked up a soldier, held it for a moment. Tapped it against his teeth, then placed it down.

"Ambush," he said. A murmur went through the crowd.

Brick smiled a thin, wry smile, and took Aimsley's soldier with his own.

Aimsley nodded, and moved again. Offering up one of his prelates.

Brick's eyes narrowed at Aimsley's gambit, but he couldn't see it, so he took Aimsley's prelate with his soldier.

Aimsley took Brick's soldier.

"Ambush," he said again.

Now there was no room around the table. A dozen people watched the game. Half were narrating the action to the other half.

Brick moved his king out of position, exposing his prelate for the attack.

Aimsley retreated in response. But he'd forced Brick's king back. This was a major event in the history of their games. But Aimsley was just getting started. It looked as though he'd stopped blinking, so fiercely was he concentrating on the board.

Three moves later and Aimsley had not managed to lure Brick's king out.

Brick moved a serf into Aimsley's second row.

Aimsley captured the serf, picked up the piece with two fingers and tossed it away like a spent nail.

The gesture caused Brick to clench his teeth, the tendons on his neck stood out.

No one in the Mouse Trap made any noise.

Brick gave up his right flank and pushed with his left. Four moves later and he took Aimsley's Tower.

He picked it up and, never taking his eyes off the polder, he crushed the piece in his fist, until only powder remained. He let the powder run through his fingers onto the floor.

Aimsley had no plans for the captured Tower, but he'd also not planned on Brick's last soldier being in his rear row. He looked ahead, he saw what the Brick was doing. Three moves from now, there'd be an opening, and Brick would use his tower to force an ambush. Aimsley countered with an attack of his own.

He had to sacrifice two serfs to do it, but there was no opening for Brick's tower. Aimsley had cut off his line of attack.

Brick took a breath. Then he looked at the board. Some of the spectators knew this was significant.

He brought his queen out. Took two of Aimsley's serfs. Aimsley countered with his prelate.

"Ambush," he said, and the piece clacked into place.

"Ambush," Brick said, and blocked Aimsley's prelate with his tower, putting the polder's king in jeopardy.

"Shit," Aimsley said, and took Brick's tower.

Brick took Aimsley's prelate.

Brick snapped his fingers and a tray with drinks appeared. He downed his in one go and placed the other on at Aimsley's right hand.

Aimsley dashed the glass away with the back of his hand, spilling uske on several spectators. They pulled away, but didn't complain.

Aimsley smacked a piece down.

"Ambush," he said.

The Brick blocked the attack with his queen. Several of the spectators gasped.

Aimsley wasted no time. He exposed his king, placing himself in ambush, but ambushing Brick's king at the same time, forcing Brick to use his queen to defend. "Counter-ambush," he said.

Brick pursed his lips, he could see where this was going. There were only a few moves left.

He moved his queen. Aimsley took it.

"Ambush," Aimsley said.

Brick made one last gamble, pushed his last serf one row away from a promotion, forcing Aimsley to choose between losing his queen or granting Brick a new queen.

But Brick hadn't noticed the manner in which the board had changed since he set up that gambit several moves ago.

Aimsley took the serf, with the same piece that now threatened the Brick's king. There was nowhere for the king to move.

Brick looked at the board. Took a breath. No one spoke.

He tipped over his king.

"The king is dead," Aimsley said, and hopped off his chair. The crowd parted for him. Brick was still looking at the board.

"I quit," the polder said, and left the Mouse Trap.

CHAPTER SIXTY-SEVEN

"What the fuck is a star elf?" Aimsley asked.

They were alone in Heden's room. A table and chairs and a large meal provided by the girls. The meal cooled between them. The girls were eager to please, but neither of them was hungry. They needed to think.

"Demigods," Heden said. "Banished to the World Below when they betrayed their brothers, the Sun elves, the Moon elves, and the Sky elves."

"That's a lotta elves," Aimsley said.

"Not as powerful as dragons," Heden said, "but close enough."

"And the count has one of them all bound up."

"Presumably. I have a hard time imagining an astral celestial cooperating with the count."

"We can assume is that he's in the city somewhere," Aimsley had a full glass of cider in front of him, but wasn't drinking it. It was mostly to have something in his hand.

"Hapax Legomenon said she thought the count's operation was on water. A boat or a barge. Said that could foil their oracles."

Aimsley looked at Heden, unaware the priest knew the same wizard he had braced a fortnight ago. "She said that, huh?"

"Yeah but that was a while ago and since then, nothing. If he's over water, they'll get to him before we can. So assume he's not."

"I think we can rule out the castle," Aimsley continued. "Probably if he were sleeping with the king we'd know about it. Probably."

"There was an order of knights," Heden said, "in capital. Their guildhouse was a floating keep."

"A what?" Aimsley said flatly.

"An *invisible* floating keep," Heden elaborated.

"You're fucking kidding me."

"Un-uh," Heden said. "If the count can get his hands on a star elf and make the night dust, maybe he's floating over the city somewhere."

"Well that's no fucking good either," Aimsley dismissed this. "If he's got that kind of power we're fucked. Never find him anyway. Gotta focus on places we can get to. The city proper."

Heden nodded. "The city," he said absently. Something bothered him. "Somewhere in the city."

There was something about the way Aimsley said it that reminded him of something. Not exactly the way he said it. But something close.

"The *city*," Heden said out loud. That was it. Emphasis on the city. He could hear it in his mind, he could hear the voice, but he couldn't place it.

"What?" Aimsley said, his voice flat.

"The…," Heden remembered. "I asked him."

"You asked who? You asked the count?"

"I said," Heden was thinking too hard to listen to the thief now, "I said 'is there a new power in the city,' and he said, 'in the *city?*' exactly like that. He was expecting me to ask something else."

Heden looked at Aimsley.

"He was expecting me to ask something else."

Aimsley fished in his vest pocket for a slave, produced a nail from somewhere Heden couldn't see, fired the slave and lit the nail. He took a long drag on it. "Take your time," he said with a shrug. The priest would get around to explaining himself eventually.

Heden's face was blank. "I know where the count is," he explained.

Aimsley looked at him, smoke curled from the polder's

nostrils.

"Good," Aimsley said, eventually. Then added, when he realized it meant they were going to go and try to kill him. "I guess."

"Do you know where I was yesterday?" Heden asked.

"I wasn't following you," the little man said. And then, because it served to keep up appearances, added, "in that instance."

"I was at the citadel."

Aimsley frowned. "Ok," he said. "Why?"

"We captured…," Heden began.

"The Sunfuckers," Aimsley interrupted. "Your old team."

"Y-yes," Heden said, not letting Aimsley succeed in goading him. "We stopped a cult of Cyrvis from summoning the Black Brothers. The cult was led by a saint."

"A…," Aimsley recovered himself. "Really?"

"Well, sort of. Alithiad is complex."

"I don't know that one," Aimsley said.

"Saint of Worms," Heden added.

"Him I know," Aimsley recovered smoothly, nodding his head in long slow loops. He took another drag on his nail.

"He's in the citadel."

"Figures," Aimsley said. Then he sussed it.

"You went to see him?" Aimsley said, his eyebrows raised. "This undead saint?"

"He knows things. He's not really deathless, and he was never a human. He can sense…he knows when there are new actors on the stage."

"Oh shit," the polder said.

"Yeah."

"You wanted to know about the night dust. You asked this saint if there's a star elf in the city. And he said yes."

"Yeah."

"And this evil demon saint friends of yours, he's *in* the

citadel."

"Yeah."

"And *you* were in the citadel when you asked him. And he was surprised you asked about what was going on…*outside* the citadel."

"You've got it."

Aimsley's eyes went blank. He was looking past and through Heden, at nothing. "Ah hah," he said without humor.

"'Ah hah?'" Heden asked.

"The citadel," the polder chuckled. "Right under the ragman's fucking nose. And every kind of ward, priest wards, wizard wards locking that place down so tight no one can see in," he said. "Always wondered why he chose Garth. Now I know. Black gods."

"If we're right…," Heden began.

"Oh we're right. The count is running his operation from inside the citadel. It's fucking brilliant. No oracle can find him, he's untraceable. As long as they can keep their operation secret inside that fortress we can't touch him."

Heden sighed. "Well now I can relax. We tell the castellan," he said. "Let him do what he…,"

"Hah!" Aimsley said. "That's why…you don't get it?"

Heden sniffed, looked affronted. "I thought I got it."

"The count's in the citadel *because* it's the castellan's fortress. The castellan is *protecting him.*"

Heden was confused. Happy, though, to have someone who could figure these things. He'd never had a reputation for being the clever one. That was Elzpeth.

"Why would he…," he flailed. Aimsley put him out of his misery.

"I don't mean literally! What would the ragman do, if we tell him the count's operating under his nose?"

Heden saw it. "He'd arrest him."

"Yep!" Aimsley declared. "I mean, castellan might be able to

338

maneuver the count so he'd have to be put down, but he doesn't impress me as that kind of Man."

"He's not," Heden agreed.

"Yeah. He plays it straight. Arrests him. Then what happens?" Aimsley didn't wait for Heden. "He goes from being *secretly* locked up in the citadel to *publicly* locked up in the citadel. And that buys him, what, another three months of protection? Magistrates and solicitors? No way he stays in the hole three months, he'll be out in three days. And all the while the castellan and his men and his fortress and his whole operation is stopping all the people who *would* kill him from getting in there."

"Including us?"

"Including…," Aimsley's eyes narrowed.

"Garth got in. Set up a whole front in there. Could you do it?"

Aimsley took a long even breath and held the priest's gaze. He didn't answer Heden's question.

"*You* got in," Aimsley said. "You can get in whenever you want. Brick, the Truncheon, they couldn't get anyone within a hundred feet of that place, but you're the ragman's friend. You can come and go as you please."

Heden nodded. "And I'm betting you can too," he said.

Aimsley did not confirm or deny.

"Castellan won't kill him," the polder said.

Heden shook his head. "Nope."

"Guilds can't get in."

"Nope."

"So *we* go in. We go in, and we ace the count, and maybe Garth."

"And maybe Garth," Heden nodded.

"You up for that? And you a holy man? Strolling in there, murder a man in cold blood."

"You remember what you said to me outside the Mouse

Trap? You said if I went after the count, if I got him, that whoever took over would come after me. They'd keep coming after me until they got me."

Aimsley understood. "But you ace him inside the citadel, no one ever knows. Hell they'll think the castellan did it."

"Improve his reputation," Heden grinned.

"But someone still has to *do* it. That you?" Aimsley challenged.

"I've done worse," Heden said without feeling or expression. "I'm the Arrogate. And it won't be cold blood. Comes down to it, it's easy to provoke the count. Force his hand. It'll be self-defense."

Aimsley swirled the cider around in his glass, a smile growing on his face. He nodded slowly to Heden. "It surely would."

"So," Heden said. "Does this mean you can get into the citadel too?"

Aimsley down the cider. Placed the glass on the table with a little more force, a little more theatricality than normal.

He smiled broadly. "'Course I fucking can," he said.

Chapter Sixty-eight

There was a knock at the door to Heden's room.

Aimsley looked sharply at Heden. "You expecting company?" he asked.

Heden frowned. "No," he said and got up.

He walked to the door, grabbed the doorknob, and looked back at the table.

The polder had disappeared. In spite of there being no obvious place to hide.

Heden nodded and opened the door.

A bottle of wine was thrust under Heden's nose. He looked at it, looked at the man offering it, and frowned.

"It was going to be flowers," Gwiddon said, "but I thought people might talk."

Heden held the door open and stared at his former friend.

"Are you going to let me in?" Gwiddon oiled, "or shall we do our business in the common room?"

"Ugh," Heden said, and retreated inside, leaving the door open. Gwiddon followed, closing the door behind him.

He took Aimsley's seat and watched Heden put the bottle away.

"What was your polder doing," Gwiddon asked, "visiting you in the church?"

"He's not my polder," Heden said.

"Uh-huh. Are the two of you moving against the count?"

"Are you asking on behalf on the king, or the bishop?" Heden asked.

"The king," Gwiddon answered plainly, as though Heden's question hadn't been filled with venom. "I seem to be doing a lot of work for him these last few days," he added casually. "Are you moving against the count?" Gwiddon asked again, less casually.

"Last week," Heden said, cleaning up the uneaten meal, "I was almost killed on High Bridge."

"I know," Gwiddon said. "We weren't having you followed then, I apologize. We are now."

"'We' being The king's spy network, or the Darkened Moon?"

Gwiddon yawned and stretched his legs out, leaning back in the chair. "The Moon doesn't have any interest in following priests. Though it would have been nice if you'd taken care of Garth for us."

Again, Heden reeled at the mind of a man able to keep all this in his head at once.

"Useful to be the head of a spy network and a thieves' guild," Heden said.

"And I double for the church," Gwiddon pointed out, a little challenge in his voice.

"I hadn't forgotten," Heden sneered.

"I've noticed. Why'd you let me in, if you're just going to be peevish at me?"

"I need a favor," Heden said.

"I thought as much."

Heden explained his plan to Gwiddon. Gwiddon's eyebrows slowly climbed up his forehead as he listened.

"Somewhere in this city there's a plan of the citadel," Heden finished. "I need it."

Gwiddon blinked.

"Are you joking? No, are you *mad?*"

"You owe me, Gwidd."

"Not that much I don't."

"Yes you do. Because the polder and I are going to do your dirty work. We're about to go into the ragman's fortress, ferret out the count, kill him, arrest Garth, and bring their whole operation down, and you walk away clean. Everyone gets what they want. You got a better plan?"

"By Cavall," Gwiddon said. "You're serious."

"Don't say that," Heden snapped. "Say what you're thinking. I'm right. It will work."

Gwiddon's eyes were unfocused.

"It might."

"Can you get me that plan?"

"I don't…I'm not sure…," Gwiddon was, for once, at a loss for words.

"Gwiddon," Heden said, and the master spy looked up at his friend. "Vanora is in there. You remember her, right? The little girl you sent me to kill before sending me into the wode to slaughter those knights?" His fists were clenched.

"*Get* me that plan," he barked.

A moment of silence. Gwiddon stood, looked down at Heden.

"Get more friends," he said, and walked out, sweeping his cape along after him like a dancer.

Chapter Sixty-nine

"You've gone fucking mental," Teagan said, crossing his arms and leaning against the wall of the jail.

"You, me, the polder," Heden said. He was sitting on a cot in an empty jail cell. "We get in, a priest and a watchman, no problem, we find the count, we down him, we get out. Problem solved."

"Mental," Teagan said shaking his head.

"We save the city."

"City can take care of itself," the watchman said. "Count'll be underking soon, everything goes back to normal."

"Not if the Moon holds out," Heden said.

"Which it won't. How can it? Army of deathless. Come on," he said, asking Heden to be reasonable.

"How many people die between now and then? How many innocent people?"

Teagan took a deep breath, made an "ugh" sound and shook his head.

"You sure about this polder?" he asked.

Heden frowned. "Sort of. We'll see."

"We'll see? You got some balls. The count and Garth against you, me, and 'we'll see.'"

Heden looked at the ground. "There's more," he said.

"Oh of course there is," Teagan said.

"There's a star elf somewhere inside the citadel."

"A what now?"

Heden explained.

"Cyrvis' thorny prick. You got a flattering idea of fair odds, I'll give you that."

"You're the best swordsman I've ever seen," Heden said.

Teagan looked down at the priest sitting on the cot. "Garth," he said.

"Garth's good, but he has tricks. He relies on tricks. Shadow magic. Not you. You took out three yellow scarves in the Rose in the time it takes to blink, and me blinded and poisoned."

"You're not doing a good job convincing me of your own abilities here."

Heden leaned his elbows on his knees, looked at the floor.

"If you're telling me no," Heden said, and then looked up at the man, "I understand. But I need an answer."

Teagan thought for a moment. Sighed.

"We need to ask Domnal," Teagan said.

"No we don't."

"You think I'm going with you into the ragman's fortress without my boss knowing?" Teagan asked incredulously.

"You don't want to do it, I can't make you, but either way bringing this to Dom is a mistake."

Teagan pushed himself away from the wall of the jail cell. "We don't know each other well enough for you to call me a coward."

"You're not a coward, you just need to exercise your judgment," Heden said. "Think about what happens if you ask Dom…,"

"I'm thinking about what happens to me if I don't. I'll be looking for another job, and there's not a lot of steady work for people with *our* background," he said, looking Heden up and down.

"It's a mistake," Heden stressed.

"This whole thing is a mistake," Teagan said. "I'm hoping Dom will talk some sense into you."

CHAPTER SEVENTY

Gwiddon looked at the two maps, compared them.

"You're sure about this?" he asked.

The young man who'd brought him the maps of the citadel nodded. "There isn't a master map," he said. "You know what the castellans' like."

"He's more paranoid than I am," Gwiddon said, looking closely at the diagrams.

"But this is close enough," the novice spy said. He explained the workings of the citadel.

"You bring the keys?" Gwiddon asked.

The young man produced two of the sigils that permitted unrestricted movement with the castellan's fortress.

Gwiddon thanked him. "Any danger this will get you in trouble?"

"Long as you get those back to me in the next…48 hours? Everyone's busy dealing with the count. No one's going to notice two keys missing."

Gwiddon took a deep breath, rolled the maps up.

"When I told you about this, you volunteered. Before I could ask you. Why?"

"I'm the only man you've got inside the citadel," the young spy said, and then shrugged. "And I want to see the priest succeed," he admitted. "The wode, the knights, the girl, the abbot? He needs some luck. I want to give it to him."

Gwiddon smiled. "Takes a rare man to spy for the king," he said. "And a first-rate watchmen to boot."

"Yeah well," Aiden half-smiled back. "Tell that to Fandrick and Rayk."

CHAPTER SEVENTY-ONE

"Tell him," Teagan said.

Heden threw the watchman a look, then turned to his friend, the captain.

"I need someone to help me infiltrate the citadel," he said.

"Infil…what?" Domnal said. Sitting at his desk in his office, he looked from one man to the other, priest to watchman, for an explanation.

"Sneak in without anyone knowing."

"You want to break *in* to the ragman's fortress? Are you mental?"

"See?" Teagan said.

"Heden what the fuck are you on about?"

Heden explained his plan again.

"Cavall's warty nutsack," Dom said, dragging his fingers through his hair. "You want to get killed that's your own business, but you're not taking mine. Anyone gets caught with you, they're through."

"I can't do it alone," Heden said.

"You can't do it at all!" Domnal said. "What happened to you out on High Bridge? You go funny in the head? They let you out of hospital too quick, you need to get back right away."

"Dom," Heden said, and the watch captain calmed down a little, tried to listen. "Dom, the count is in there. The citadel protects him. If the castellan finds out, he'll arrest him and by the time it's before the magistrate the count's agents will be running the city."

Domnal's brow was furrowed.

"Now, I can get in there, Teagan can get in there. We can take care of the count. You got another idea, I'd like to hear it."

Domnal didn't say anything, just stared at his desk, his palms flat on them as though he were trying to stop the desk from flying away.

"The moons are turning, Dom," Heden said. "If you're saying no, I have to find someone else...."

"I'm not sayin' no," Dom said shaking his head, not looking at either of them. "I'm saying I can't send my man when I should go."

"You?" Heden asked.

"Well why you got to say it like that?" Domnal looked at him, his face pained. "I'm captain ain't I?"

Teagan shook his head, once. "Dangerous," he said.

"Of course it's fucking dangerous!" Domnal said. "It's fucking mental is what it is! But what do you think happens to you, ragman comes in and finds you leading this one," he said, waving a hand at Heden, "skulking around in his fortress, murdering people."

Neither Heden nor Teagan had any answer for this.

"Has to be me, for fuck's sake. If it's me, it's the law. If it's you lot, it's a bunch of Ratcatchers going to war with the ragman."

"It's not about him," Heden started.

"Fuck you it's not," Dom said. "You don't get to say how he's gonna see it. He puts everyone in two buckets. Good, evil. That's it. You break into his palace under his nose murder his prisoner, you're in the evil bucket. And this one too," he said, nodding to Teagan.

"You, stay," he ordered Teagan

"I have to go," Teagan said.

"Balls you do," Dom said. "You're the only one in all this gonna have a job when this is over. You fucking stay here."

"I'm sorry," Heden said. "I shouldn't have said anything."

"No you should not have!"

"Let's forget it," Heden said. "I'll figure something else."

"Well I got no choice now," Dom said. "Either I go with you to the citadel or I go straight to the ragman. I'm a fucking copper, ain't I? I can't let you go off and murder people. Only chance we got now is your plan works and maybe ragman lets me keep my job after. Fuck."

No one in Dom's office spoke. Dom got up, grabbed his keys.

"Alright, come on," he said. "Let's get this over with."

He stuck his face out at Teagan as he walked by. "And YOU, stay HERE. Fuck."

Heden gave Teagan a foul look. The tall, lanky watchman frowned, but said nothing.

CHAPTER SEVENTY-TWO

"Twelve more dead on Warren Road," Gwiddon said. "Everyone at the docks, the city gates, all the stables, farriers, ostlers, Count's running them all now."

"All the transport," Heden said. "Smart."

"No one ever said he was stupid."

Gwiddon held up the maps. "Time for you to get to work," the spymaster said.

They were in Heden's basement. They unrolled the maps.

"It's like a warren down there. All twisting stone, darkness. Designed to get lost in." Gwiddon put the two maps next to each other. "This is level nine, and level ten," Gwiddon said. "We did some measuring, compared this with a duplicate set of plans. There's a whole section here," he pointed to the level nine map. "Six cells, extending down a level, completely isolated from the other two floors. There's one way in, a triple-hinged baffled door set back into this wall. No one can see who goes in or out."

"I feel like a campaigner again," Heden said, listening to the elaborate defenses of the dungeon.

"But that's not the interesting part," Gwiddon said.

"I'm listening."

"There's a special guard on that entrance. castellan selects him by lottery. The guard who gets the prize is told anonymously, double-blind. No one knows who it is except the guard himself."

"So you can't bribe your way to him. No one knows who he is."

"Correct. It also means, if you figure out who it is, and replace him, no one knows. We figure Garth ferreted out which one the guard was. It's his style."

"Count's using the castellan's own plan against him," Heden said.

Gwiddon looked at the maps and nodded. "You've got to admire the count's ingenuity," he said. "It's about as good a plan as I'd have devised."

Heden looked at him and smirked. Then his smile dropped. "Gwidd," he said.

"Yes," Gwiddon said rolling the maps up. There was a note of anticipation in his voice.

"You didn't figure all this out in the last six hours."

"No," he agreed, and handed Heden the maps.

"You've got a man inside the citadel."

"Yes," Gwiddon said sharply. "And I'd like to keep him there, so if you would be so kind as to not get found out, I'd be grateful. castellan has access to the *Aduro Vera* I'd hate to see the wreckage from this if you get put under."

"Is this man spying for the king, the church, or the Moon?" Heden asked.

"You'll need these," Gwiddon said, ignoring him while he extracted two of the silver amulets that allowed the special watchmen to come and go from the citadel. It wasn't the only security, but it was among the hardest to forge.

"The two of you wear these, you'll be able to get down to level nine without anyone stopping you."

Heden stared at Gwiddon waiting for a reply. When there was none, he scowled and snatched the amulets from him.

"There's three of us," Heden said. "The polder and a watch captain."

Gwiddon looked at the amulets. "I can get another one, but it'll take a day."

Heden shook his head. "No need. The polder's not coming out."

Gwiddon stared at Heden.

"I thought you were working together," Gwiddon said.

"We are."

"I thought you trusted him."

"I do, for the moment."

"So how come…," Gwiddon started. Heden gave him a look.

"He killed the abbot," Heden said. Gwiddon took a sharp breath.

"I thought Garth…,"

Heden shook his head, once. "Nope. The polder did it. Killed the abbot and got the girl and gave them to the count. That's why Brick is still in business. The polder fixed it."

"And now you're working with him. How is that?" Gwiddon was baffled.

"I forgave him."

"Black gods. Heden that man was a father to you."

"He didn't know what he was doing," Heden explained. "He was out of his head with drink and killing. He doesn't even remember it."

Gwiddon was clearly confused. "So if you forgave him, if he's helping you…."

"The one's got nothing to do with the other," Heden said without inflection. "He killed the abbot, he's going down for that. Me forgiving him is beside the point."

Gwiddon said nothing for a few moments.

"You might be the hardest man I know," Gwiddon said. Heden said nothing.

Gwiddon held out his hand. "Maybe that's why I think this ridiculous plan is going to work."

Heden took his hand, and they shook. Friends again? Neither could be sure.

"Good luck Heden."

"Thanks, Gwidd."

CHAPTER SEVENTY-THREE

She sat at the desk he provided and read one of the books. It kept her sane. The harlequin taught her all the letters and enough words she could make her way. And the challenge helped keep her mind off things.

The room was small, just the desk, a bed and a small bookcase, full. She'd grabbed a selection of knightly romances and discovered one of them was about an all-female order of knights. She'd already read it twice.

The door opened. She didn't bother looking, she wasn't interested. Was never going to show any interest, no matter what happened. She pretended to keep reading as two pairs of boots trod on the stone floor.

"If you like it," a voice said, and she froze, "you can take it back with us. Plenty of room in the library for more."

Heden.

She stood up. Heden noticed the dress. It was beautiful. She noticed him noticing and looked down at herself in disgust.

She pulled and clawed at the thing until it hung off her in tatters. It was too well-made to destroy completely without more work.

She ran to him, grabbed him like she wanted to crush him.

"I knew you'd come," she muttered into Heden's jerkhin, the steel breastplate underneath bruising her cheek. "Knew it. Knew it."

"Sorry it took so long," he said.

She disentangled herself. "You're forgiven," she said. "Let's get out of here."

Heden indicated Domnal. "You remember Dom," Heden ventured.

Dom looked weakly at the girl. The last time they'd met, she was in the grip of one of her fits.

Vanora frowned. "No?" she asked.

"Good," Heden said and Dom sighed with relief. "Now... this is the hard part."

Vanora saw it on Heden's face.

"You have to stay here," Heden said.

"What?!" she barked. "No! Fuck no!"

"Dom, wait outside," Heden said.

"Fine with me," the large man said, and turned around. "I'll keep watch. Hurry."

Once he was gone, Heden said, quietly. "I'm going to stop the count and Garth."

"Good," she said. "I'm going with you."

"You can't. People will die. You're getting out of here."

"*People* will die? Or *you* will die?"

Heden ignored this. "You're safe here," he said.

"I don't care," she said.

"I'll come back when this is over."

She shrugged. "I'll follow you."

Heden shrugged back. "I'll find a guard. Turn you over to him."

She glared at him. Stalemate. She collapsed a little.

"I hate this," she said, he hands balled into fists, her eyes darting around as though a solution might be found.

"Please stay here," Heden urged.

She nodded.

"I need to know you're safe," he said.

"I know. I hate it. I should be there."

"It's dangerous."

"Of course it's fucking dangerous," she said. "You're going to kill the count and Garth and who knows what else. I should be there."

"It won't take long," Heden said.

Vanora thought of something she'd been wondering since

she got here. Something she might not get a chance to ask again. "What happened to the abbot?" she asked.

Heden's mouth went dry. Sometimes he went as long as a whole turn without thinking about his dead friend.

"He's dead."

She pressed her lips together. Her eyes went red. "I liked him," she said quietly.

"Me too," Heden said. Had he mourned his friend yet? Time enough for that later. If they lived.

"It was the polder, wasn't it?" she asked.

Heden nodded.

"Why did he do that?" Vanora asked. "He helped me, back at the inn. While you were gone."

"I think he was punishing himself," Heden said.

Vanora scowled. "What?"

"He knew the abbot was my friend and he hoped, he guessed, that if he killed the abbot I'd kill him."

"He wanted to die?" Vanora said.

"I think so. But I didn't do it."

"Good. I guess." She thought. "I don't think he's bad," she said.

"Me neither," Heden said.

Silence between them.

"Go," she said eventually. "Hurry. I hate this."

Heden left.

She stared at the doorway he left open behind him. The torchlight from the room failed to illuminate the hallway outside the door.

Chapter Seventy-four

Teagan threw his sword down on the kitchen table.

"Hey watch it, watch it!" Gowan called out. He bustled into the kitchen and snatched the sword up. "I'm setting the table," he chastised

He looked at Teagan and saw immediately something was wrong.

Leaning the sword carefully against the wall, he walked up to the man he thought of as his husband and put a hand around his waist. Tried to look into his eyes. Teagan was lost in worry.

Gowan kissed Teagan lightly on the cheek.

"What?" he asked the younger man.

Teagan took a deep breath, glanced at Gowan, flashed a smile. But his heart wasn't in it.

"I think I just did something awful."

Gowan wasn't used to seeing Teagan look anything other than bemused, relaxed.

"You have to kill someone again?" he asked.

Teagan shook his head and sat down lifelessly at the kitchen table. Definitely a bad sign. They only sat at the table when they were eating or arguing.

"I'll get you some bread," Gowan said. "That's ready."

The bread was good. Gowan was a professional cook and not a cheap one, but in this rare instance it gave little comfort.

"Hm," Gowan said, watching Teagan munch the bread mechanically.

Teagan noticed the man he loved was worried. He made a show at enjoying the bread. "It's good," he said.

Gowan threw another roll at him. "Don't patronize me," he said. Teagan snatched the bread roll out of the air.

"I took something to Dom I should have done myself," he

said. "I think I was a coward."

"Took what to Dom?" Gowan asked.

Teagan explained.

"That's madness," Gowan said. "He can't ask you to go up against the count. That's the castellan's job. You're just a watchman."

Gowan was smarter, older, and better bred. Normally Teagan would feign offense at a comment like 'just a watchman,' but this was different. Neither of them was joking.

"But I'm *not* just a watchman," Teagan said. "That's why the priest asked me. He wouldn't have asked anyone else, but he knows I used to be a ratcatcher."

"Well what does that have to do with anything?"

"Means I'm not a normal watchman. I'm better with the sword than any of them."

"You're one of the best," Gowan said tentatively. He was trying to cheer Teagan up.

It didn't work.

"I did the wrong thing," Teagan said. "Someone needed my help, the kind only I can give, and I dropped it on Dom."

Gowan knew better than to argue. "And now you're worried something's going to happen to him."

"No," Teagan said. "Now I'm certain something's going to happen to him."

He slumped in his chair and looked at Gowan watching helplessly. Which was how Teagan felt right now. He threw the roll back at Gowan.

"Shit," he said.

Chapter Seventy-five

"Can we not just kill the man?" the count asked.

"He's gone into hiding too," Garth said. "All the better to hold out against us."

They were alone in the room with the bound star elf. The figure was manacled to the wall, with special silver bindings. It looked like the eight foot tall being's hands and feet had been dipped in metal. Its head was covered in a similarly smooth metal mask leaving no room for its mouth or nose. It didn't need to breath. It was otherwise naked. Night, stars, shifted on its skin.

Thin glass tubes twisted around him, leading into veins and arteries. The glass caked black with dried blood, leading to vials and beakers on a nearby table. There was so much dust now, there'd be no need to bleed him again for weeks.

Neither Garth not the count thought much of the living demigod in the room with them.

"Damn him for being so stubborn. Who'd have thought it?"

"He's the Truncheon," Garth said. "It's his job. He's not the smart one."

"No, that was supposed to be me. But I don't feel very smart at the moment. Does he have *no* family we could torture? Friends we could boil? Send him a ball of matted hair and teeth."

"Wouldn't know where to send it. Maybe we should make a deal," Garth said.

"Would he accept a deal, do you think?" the count wondered.

"Only one way to find out. Are you keen to keep throwing our men at his?"

"No," the count said. "But neither am I keen to make an offer when we have the advantage."

Garth admitted this was not traditional. "Strange time to

bargain," he said, "but we didn't count on the Midnight Man putting up this kind of fight."

"Damn him," the count said. "This would all have been over weeks ago were it not for that slug."

"Maybe we offer a deal and use the opportunity to flush him out."

"He'd see through that," the count said.

"*You'd* see through that," Garth corrected. "He'd fall for it."

"I'm not convinced. He's been acting uncharacteristically intelligent lately."

"I think he's counting on the Hart finding us first."

"Hah! I take back what I said, he's uncharacteristically stupid." The count leaned against a workbench and admired the captive star elf. "The Hart will die of old age before they come within a mile of this place."

Garth suddenly went quiet. Put his hand on *Apostate*.

"What kind of deal…," the count began.

"Shut up," Garth said sharply. The count complied, deferring to Garth's instincts.

"Come on in," Garth said.

Heden and Domnal walked into the room from the dark hallway beyond.

"Garth," the count warned.

Garth's mind raced. "He's told no one," Garth reasoned. "Otherwise the ragman would be here instead."

The count looked at Domnal. "And who in all Orden is this?"

"By all the gods," Domnal whispered, looking at the bound Star Elf. His gaze went from the shackled demigod, to the glass tubes, and then the alchemical worktable. "The night dust," Dom said, eyes wide.

"He's a watch captain," Garth explained. "Not even a special."

"Hah!" the count laughed on seeing Domnal with Heden. "Hahah! What is this?" He looked at Heden. "Why in all Orden would you bring…is this some kind of insurance? You brought the weakest, most feeble defense possible? Afraid I'd hesitate? I'd sooner spare a rabbit."

"You're not in a position to spare anyone," Heden said.

"You're ah," Dom said, tearing his gaze from the celestial in the room with them. "You're under arrest."

"Idiots," the count shook his head. Garth looked from Heden to Dom with suspicion. He could tell something was up.

"Garth, kill them both. Well, the priest at least. The watchmen I leave to your discretion."

Garth appeared to be ignoring the count. "You fought well," he said. "You surprised me with Zaar's little present. Won't happen again."

"I know," Heden said.

Aimsley stepped out from behind Domnal. "Hey Garth," he said.

Garth took a step back, not out of surprise, but caution. His internal arithmetic factoring the situation upward.

"Welcome aboard," Heden said out of the corner of his mouth.

"I didn't have a fucking key," the polder hissed back, nodding at the silver medallions around Heden's and Dom's necks.

The count looked back and forth between them.

"Does this present a problem, Garth?"

"Nno," Garth said, but there was hesitation.

"Kill them both then," the count said, seemingly bored. If it was an act, it was a good one. "Leave the watchman alive, he may be useful."

"I'm not sure that's a good idea," Garth said, peering at Aimsley. Aimsley smiled back at him.

"Why not?" the count asked, suddenly appearing interested.

"This is Brick's fixer," Garth nodded to Aimsley.

"Brick…," the count said, and stopped. "This is his counter-move?" He looked from priest, to thief, to watchman. "This is the best he could do?"

"You didn't think of this," Garth said, taking his eyes off Aimsley to glance at Heden.

Heden raised his eyebrows.

"Take care of them," the count said, "and then we'll take care of the Truncheon."

"Mmm," Garth said, unconvinced. He looked at Dom. "We kill these two and we'll have to kill the watchmen too." Domnal swallowed, but stood his ground.

"You willing to take that risk?" Domnal said. Heden and Aimsley looked at him, watched him stand his ground against one of the deadliest men alive. "You kill me, a Watch Captain, inside the ragman's fortress? You think you'll get to make *any* deal with him after? You got enough of your little black dust for that?"

Domnal standing up to Garth, doubling down on the count's threat, was the bravest thing Heden had ever seen. He looked back to Garth.

Garth's eyes flitted between the two men and the polder before him. Weighing options.

"He has a point," Garth said.

The count shrugged, bored. "Kill them all, and we leave here. Let the ragman stew," he said calmly. He still believed he was master here. Everyone else in the room was ignoring him.

Garth pursed his lips, unsure of the wisdom of this order, but prepared to carry it out.

"This isn't how I thought your story would end," Garth said, resting his hand on the pommel of *Apostate*.

Aimsley saw the move to violence, and played his trump card.

"I don't work for Brick anymore," the polder said.

"There, you see Garth?" the count said. "Neither of them work for anyone, please get rid of them."

Heden was watching Garth. But Garth was watching Aimsley. The assassin looked confused.

"You're with…," Garth said to the polder, nodding at Heden.

Aimsley shrugged. The gesture expressed the possibility that the thief and the priest were working together, but that this could be a temporary state of affairs and in any event, it wasn't important to the little man.

"Garth," the count insisted, staring at his fixer.

Garth sniffed. Looked around the laboratory. Considered how much the night dust had cost them. He ignored the count and turned back to the polder.

"Not the Brick," he said.

Aimsley shook his head. "Nope. Not with anyone anymore. Fuck 'em. They're not worth it."

Garth nodded. Whatever was happening, it was between the two master thieves. Heden and the count were both bystanders.

"Garth will you please kill this pious sack of shit for me?" the count said, pointing at Heden, his voice raised.

Heden watched and waited.

"Brick ever keep his word?" Garth asked the polder.

"Only if it suited him," Aimsley said.

"This one's the same," Garth said, crooking his head to the count.

"What?" the count squeaked. Heden noticed he was breaking.

"Never had to work for it," the polder observed.

"Garth what the fuck is going on?!" the count demanded.

"Everything handed to them. Easy," Garth said.

"Not like us," Aimsley said.

"No. We have to work for it," Garth said.

"Every fucking day," the polder nodded. Heden noticed Aimsley wasn't shaking, wasn't sweating.

Garth nodded, satisfied, as though a code word had been given. He looked at Heden.

"This *was* your idea," he admitted. "I underestimated you."

"Garth what do I pay you for?" The count hissed. A nearly

invisible tension rippled across the master thief's body. Heden almost missed it. He was sure the count didn't see the reaction. "I'm *ordering* you to...." The count demanded.

"No," Garth said, and took a step back, leaned against the wall. His frame long and lean, in that pose, he reminded Heden of Teagan, the watchman. Easy confidence.

"What!?" the count howled. His voice now a nervous screech. "What did you say to me?"

Garth smiled, widely, sincerely, and looked at Aimsley like they were friends. To Heden, such a human expression looked unnatural on the master thief's face.

Aimsley glanced up at Heden, flashed him a half-smile, as though to say 'see? I told you.' When the polder looked back at Garth, he nodded. Aimsley took a couple of steps back and tugged on Domnal's vest, pulling the watch captain back.

Aimsley and Domnal stood against the wall.

"I said no," Garth said, his grin widening. He looked like a wolf. "Kill him yourself."

"This should be fun to watch," Domnal said.

"Garth," the count said, clenching his fists. "I'm telling you...."

"You're not telling me a fucking thing," Garth said, and the words sounded strange, unrefined, coming out of his mouth. "You want the priest dead, you kill him. I want to see you do it."

The count was breathing rapidly. He was nervous. Something was happening inside him, something was breaking.

"I'll get Ladros," the count said, and made a move to the door.

There was a blade at his throat. *Apostate.* Heden remembered Garth had been trained in Capital, where the world's best swordsmen gathered. *Well*, Heden added, *except Teagan.* Teagan was maybe the best Heden had ever seen and apparently derived his technique from years of campaigning. He wondered what would happen when Teagan's long sword and Garth's rapier met, who would win?

The count leapt back from the blade into a kind of half crouch, afraid of the blade and what it could do.

"What are you doing?" he asked Garth desperately.

"I want to see you do it," Garth said, and his voice dripped with oil. He savored this moment. "I want to see you kill him. I want to see you try," he sneered.

The count tried his best to master himself. He drew his rapier, and turned to face Heden.

"I'll deal with you after this," he said to Garth, his voice calm now, but his body shaking. "I studied at the blade when I was six," he said, trying to assure himself more than anything. "I can handle a priest."

"So what are you waiting for?" Heden asked.

The count lunged toward Heden with nothing but fear propelling him. How long had it been since the count had needed to use any weapon?

Heden batted the sword away with his left hand, and delivered a right cross to the count, smashing down into the man's jaw, sending him sprawling across the floor.

"Uuunnghh," the count wheezed, and whimpered. "Ahhngh," he moaned. His jaw was broken.

"Get up," Heden said.

"I surrender," the count said, the words mush.

"That was quick," Domnal said, relaxing. Everything now appeared over.

"Get the castellan," Heden said.

All three of the other men in the room, Garth, Aimsley, and Dom, at the same moment, said "What?"

"The ragman can do what he wants with him," Heden said.

"Have you gone spare," Aimsley hissed. "What was the point of all this?"

"He hasn't killed anyone," Heden said. "If he hangs, it's at the king's bidding."

"Heden think about what you're doing," Garth said. "You'll be a wanted man. The entire guild will turn against you, and he'll be free tomorrow."

"I don't have to live with your conscience," Heden snapped, "I have to live with mine."

"Is he serious?" Garth asked Aimsley.

Aimsley looked at Domnal. "Yeah, he's serious," the watch captain said.

Aimsley sighed, and stood next to Heden. "I'm with him. It's stupid, but the count goes to the magistrate."

Garth grabbed a marble of night dust. Showed it to Heden. "We lost thirty men, brown, blue, green, yellow, black. Because of this. He murdered half the guild with these…."

Garth stopped talking, he was looking at Heden, but not paying attention to him. The count lay gasping on the floor at his feet.

"Fuck it," Garth said, and dropped the marble, letting it fall into the count's mouth.

The count gagged on it. Before he could spit it out, Garth stood over him.

"For the Black," he said, and kicked the count in the jaw.

The marble exploded in the count's shattered mouth.

The count squealed in pain, the sound a high-pitched whine coming from his closed lips.

"Black gods," Aimsley said, looking from Heden to the count. Witness to one of the most ruthless executions he'd ever seen.

The count breathed in, and the night dust went into him.

His body thrashed. He gibbered, as the night dust began ripping him apart. Aware of what was happening. Unable to stop it.

"Cavall's nutsack!" Dom said.

The count lurched to his feet, pulled by unseen strength.

Everyone in the room was trying to stay as far away from

365

him as possible. Domnal stood in the doorway, ready for instant flight, but unwilling to leave Heden behind.

With a supreme act of will, his last, the count plunged toward a crate stuffed with straw, dug his hands into it, and pulled out two fistfuls of night dust marbles. Lifted them up over his head.

"Fuck," Heden said, too late.

The count crushed the marbles in what was left of his hands, and let the dust run down his face.

The night dust, two dozen doses of it, pulled the count's body apart. Bones cracked, skin went black, cracked, and then boiled. The thing he was becoming was unlike any deathless Heden had ever seen.

"Nikros and Cyrvis preserve us," Garth whispered. The revenant was between him and the exit.

"Heden!" Aimsley said. "Should we run?!"

Heden spoke a prayer, a layer of black smoke burned off the thing that was the count, but no more. It would take ten priests to stop this thing.

Garth drew *Apostate* and stabbed at the revenant. The blade did nothing, but the thing that had been the count reacted. It reached out a long-fingered, black-clawed hand and grasped Garth by his leather armor, lifted him effortlessly and slammed him into the ground with such force the assassin was momentarily stunned.

The count, or his corpse, distracted by Garth, Heden dashed forward to the star elf. He put his hands on the creature and prayed to Cavall.

Nothing happened.

Aimsley stabbed the revenant in the back with his twin dirks. The creature ignored him.

Heden turned his eyes to the heavens and called out.

"Lynwen!" Heden shouted, and prayed again. The manacles dissolved.

The eight-foot tall elf fell to the floor. A moment passed while the battle raged behind Heden. Garth and Aimsley both trying to hold back the count long enough to give Heden a chance.

The elf rose from the floor. It didn't stand, using arms and legs to push itself upright, it needed no such mundane instruments. It merely floated upwards, until it was standing, naked, but magisterial. Its violet hair moving in an invisible breeze.

It's skin was utterly black, a void. Looking at it, you saw stars burning. Heden recognized constellations. They moved and shifted as the figure moved, as Heden's head moved. It was like looking through a window.

The elf turned its black-on-black eyes to Heden.

"That is the man that bound you!" Heden shouted, as the revenant attacked Aimsley. The polder danced back but the ghoul was faster and stronger. It grasped the polder by the throat.

The celestial's eyes scanned the room. Its mouth opened and the sound of wet glass being rubbed by a finger came out.

The revenant went rigid. Its eyes swollen and filled with black blood. Ash-grey bone ripped through tattered skin. It dropped Aimlsey, who quickly bound backward out of reach.

The star elf drew his hand calmly into a fist, and the night dust was pulled from the count. His body was restored, flesh and bone knitted back together. When the star elf released his grip, the body fell to the floor in a heap, dead.

More glass-sounds from the star elf.

"What's he saying?" Aimsley said, rubbing at his throat.

"He said the count does not deserve so neat a death," Heden translated.

"Neat!?" Aimsley said, unbelieving.

The celestial reached out a hand, and Aimsley watched as the priest was lifted from the ground by an unseen force.

Twin dirks appeared in the thief's hands and he lunged at

the astral celestial.

"Don't!" Heden gasped to the thief. The polder skidded across the floor, his motion stopped, as his head darted back and forth between the nine foot tall celestial, and the man suspended and strangling before him.

The polder watched as Heden's voice made a noise that sounded like singing without words, just pure tones modulated by the shifting shape of his jaw and mouth.

The celestial frowned. Opened his hand. Heden gasped for breath normally again, but was still suspended three feet in the air.

<You sing our thoughts,> the celestial said in his own tongue. Aimsley only heard the high pitched sound, almost a melody, as of a wet finger rubbed along the edge of a wine glass.

<I have known your kind,> Heden said, turning and stretching his neck, unable to move his arms. <I have been a guest in your world. I was counted a friend of the Last Star Fading With Morning.>

The celestial's eyes went wide. He released Heden. The priest stumbled as he hit the floor, quickly righting himself.

"Heden what the fuck is going on?" Garth asked.

<This is sufficient to stay my hand,> the elf said, and Heden noted he did them the favor of using normal terran grammar even as he spoke celestial. <But only for a moment.>

The elf turned, a fluid motion, as he regarded Garth, Domnal, and the polder. His gaze lingered on Aimsley.

<This one is false,> the celestial said, in its bell-chime language. <It is a made thing.>

Heden glanced at Aimsley. "That's probably true," he said in tevas-gol. Heden wasn't sure where Polder came from and was willing to take the demi-god's word for it.

<I could unmake him with a thought,> the celestial continued in his own language.

<What would that gain you?> Heden asked, turning back

to the demigod.

"Heden," Dom said from the doorway, his voice shaking, "can we please get the fuck out of here?"

‹I will unleash my wrath and bring this hive of yours back to the dirt from which you sprouted.›

"What's he saying?" Aimsley asked.

"He's saying he could kill everyone in this city," Heden answered.

"Could he?"

"Maybe," Heden said to Aimsley. The polder, Dom, and Garth all watched Heden negotiate with the Celestial.

"We would be easy," Heden indicated himself and the others. "But there are powers in the city who would stop you. Our knights and wizards, our saints. And there is a dwarf in the city," Heden saved the best for last.

‹I yearn to kill an adamantine elemental. Bring this one to me and I shall spare you.›

"This isn't getting us anywhere," Heden said, allowing himself to seem impatient. "We knew what you could do once freed, and we did it anyway. That should count for something."

The elf stared at him with silver eyes.

"You could start by speaking our language," Heden said. "I know it's easy for you."

"Why did you release me and invite my wrath?" the elf asked, this time in heavily accented tevas-gol.

"Cyrvis' thorny prick," Garth hissed at the sound of the Celestial's voice.

"Because it was the right thing to do," Heden said. This, in the end, was his only armor against the astral celestial. Aimsley held his breath.

"Morality," the dark elf sneered. "A terran thing."

"It's a good thing. It's the reason you're still alive."

"You bound me out of fear, and released me out of fear, thou insect."

"I do fear you," Heden admitted. "I released you anyway. Knowing it was very likely you would kill the first Man you saw."

The elf seethed.

"I have not taken your life yet," he pointed out.

"I know," Heden said. "I'll be honest with you, I didn't really have a plan after this part, I just knew it was wrong to leave you like that."

Aimlsey made a squeaking noise in his throat. It sounded like: "eep."

One corner of the astral celestial's mouth curled in a sneer.

"I require satisfaction," it said, and looked at the body of the count.

The count's body heaved, his eyes flew open, and he gasped in a breath, alive again.

"Black gods," Aimsley said, taking a step back. He was tensed, ready for battle. He looked at Heden, judging how worried he should be by the priest's demeanor.

"They're made of godstuff," Heden muttered to the thief. "What they think becomes real." He could hear Aimsley breathing heavily now.

The celestial looked at its hands as though seeing them for the first time.

"Val," the elf swore, looking at his hands in marvel. "It is accomplished. The great endeavor."

This was not the first time Heden had heard that term.

"What?" he asked. "What is accomplished?"

The celestial ignored him, marveled at the resurrected count. "I willed it, and it happened."

"Gods please," the count said. "Please let me die. Not again, gods, not again."

"What was the great endeavor?" Heden pressed, fear replaced by a burning need to know.

"Heden," Aimsley warned.

370

Garth looked at Aimsley. "We need to get the fuck out of here," he said. Behind them, Domnal nodded furiously.

"I bestride the boundary between life and death," the elf looked down at his body in awe.

His gaze snapped back to the count, and he sneered. The count's body went rigid again. He howled.

His body was being turned inside out again. The effect of the night dust, but in an instant.

When the screams ended, a ghoul stood before them again.

"Hhhuuurr," the body of the count moaned. It seemed different from the deathless Heden had encountered before. There was something in there. Some spark of spirit that radiated despair.

"I command the forces of the undying," the celestial said, and gestured again at the undead count.

The count's body twisted and writhed in pain, it screamed and Heden was certain something of the count was still in there. This was no normal deathless. Heden couldn't stand by and watch.

"I will rack you back and forth from life to death," the elf said, "until your mind is broken. Then I shall rebuild you and begin again."

"No," Heden said, and drew *Solaris*.

I need you, Heden thought.

A betrayer, the voice of the sword echoed in Heden's head. *For countless cycles I have yearned for such a one. Leave him to me.*

A light glowed from the blade, sunlight. Warm, reviving. But like a detonation, the count's body exploded into dust, destroyed by *Solaris*

The celestial spun on Heden.

"You dare!" it said, and a cloud of inky darkness oozed from its skin like smoking, searching tendrils. "You doom is inevitable! Always you turn back to sin! Only thus could you have bound me!"

Solaris thrust itself into the air. A beam of pure white light struck the dark elf.

Instantly the star elf leapt back, placed a hand over his eyes. The dark cloud vanished.

<I know thee!> the dark elf cried out. <We are kin!>

"*I serve only the light,*" the sword said, its voice heard not by ears, but inside their heads. *"I care not for blood, only will. And the will of the Astrals was always twisted to darkness."*

"Heden!" Aimsley gasped, holding his head in his hands, trying to shut the voice out.

The sword aimed itself at the elf. Heden was not entirely happy with this, but unsure of his options.

"Long have you evaded punishment for Kalas Mithral," the sword said. *"Justice must be satisfied!"*

The celestial fell back in fear.

<Morning!> the dark elf cried, now on his knees. <Spare me!>

Fate spared you, but I shall not! came the booming reply in their minds.

A searing light shot from the sword and smoke rose from the dark elf's skin as his form was boiled by molten sunlight.

The elf screamed as smoke burned everyone's lungs.

"Stop!" Heden said, and dropped the sword.

The light stopped. The voice was silenced. The sword lay on the ground inert.

"You can't act on your own," Heden said to the blade as it lay on the ground. He knew it could hear him. "Someone has to give their consent, that's the pact, that's the check against your power and I do *not* consent!"

The dark elf huddled on the floor like a wounded animal, curled into a fetal position, whimpered.

Heden closed the distance between them, kneeled. Placed a hand on the still smoking flesh, and said a prayer.

The star elf's skin healed, renewed. The whimpering

subsided. Heden took a step back, picked up the sword gingerly. Put it back in his scabbard. *Solaris* raised no objection.

The star elf stood, this time using his arms and legs, like a mortal creature.

"Leave it to him" Aimsley said, shaking his head in disbelief.

"You know not the power contained in that weapon," the elf said, still afraid.

"That's true," Heden said, letting his hand rest lightly on the pommel. "But you do and right now that's all that matters."

"It is the Thousand Rays of Morning," the celestial explained. "A legendary solar who stayed behind to continue his personal war against darkness."

A Solar Celestial, Heden thought, his hand gripping the sword tighter. Still on this plane after his brothers joined their god in Arcadia.

What I was before is of no consequence, the voice spoke in Heden's mind. *Now I am* Solaris *and I will not permit this one to cause more harm.*

"He's not going to cause more harm," Heden said. "He knows that path leads only to pain for all. And it's time to stop the cycle of death."

The elf straightened himself. His gaze shifted from Heden's sword, to Heden. It ignored everyone else in the room.

"I am taught wisdom by a mortal," the elf said, chastised.

"We've all learned something today." Heden said. "It's not too late to do the right thing."

"Verily. I see now why the Last Star counted you as a friend. In my anger I lashed out at those who had not wronged me, indeed those who liberated me from my bondage."

"It was a mistake," Heden said. "We all make them. Let's not make it worse."

The star elf bowed.

"Who bound you?" Heden asked. "Originally. How did you come to be here?"

"A servant of Ket," the elf said. "I know not his name, he wore a skullcap made of adamantine and served a terran dressed all in metal."

A servant of Ket, Heden wondered. Then an image of a man he knew who wore a silver skullcap flashed in his mind.

"Novacula," Garth said. "Duke Baede's wizard. He delivered the elf to us."

The elf looked around the room, at no one. "I know not. You are ephemeral. I was bound, brought somewhere else, and then here."

"You've answered my question," Heden said, trying not to think of what the answer implied. "You're free to go. Let us part in weal and not woe."

The celestial nodded.

"I have already forgotten my rage for vengeance. I no longer wish to destroy you all."

"Good," Aimsley said.

"I have forgotten my fear," Heden said. "And consider myself fortunate to have met you." He knew this to be the proper thing to say.

"The Ray of Morning," the elf said, nodding to Heden's sword, "was wise and I did not heed him. Only one of equal wisdom could wield his power." The elf stuck out his hand.

"I am fortunate to have met such a one."

Heden looked at the extended hand, much larger than his. Inky black and covered with twinkling stars and swirling galaxies.

"This is the custom, yes?" The elf asked. "I cannot say how much time has passed since last I treated with the Terrans, we do not reckon such things," he said.

Heden extended his hand, reaching up to account for the difference in their height.

"This is the custom," he said, and gripped the celestial's hand. It was thin and delicate, but strong.

"Farewell," the celestial said. "This world of yours likes me not."

Heden blinked, and the star elf was gone.

Heden and Aimsley were left alone in the room. Both were shaking now that the crisis was over. Heden wanted to throw up.

"'The Star Emerging?'" Aimsley said.

"What?" Heden asked, still recovering.

"You know a fucking star elf? You've been to the World Below?"

"No," Heden said, shaking his head. "I mean, yes I know a…I knew a star elf." Heden took a deep breath. "He was an ambassador. He asked Richard for help against the Army of Night. But he's dead now. I've never been to their realm."

"You could fucking tell me this shit before we…," he waved his hands around. "I almost shit myself. And you making bell noises and shit."

Heden ignored Aimsley. Looked for Garth.

"Where's Garth?" he asked.

"Domnal," Aimsley said, noticing the watchman was also gone.

They were alone in the room.

"Shit," Heden said, and ran for the doorway. Aimsley followed.

CHAPTER SEVENTY-SIX

"You're here early," Willem said.

Tomas shrugged. "Where else am I going to go?" The younger man fitted his helmet on.

Willem smiled. "Well you're young yet," he said. "You get you a missus, you'll find better things to do with your time than stand watch." Willem didn't bother with a helmet, Tomas noticed.

"Dannec don't seem too eager to stay home with his missus." Tom said.

"Wol," Willem began, all sage-like, "that's because he's old. But you got many years between."

The two men stood before the stairs to the fourth level.

"Been three days since I seen the sun," Tomas said.

"No excuse for that," Willem said. "Plenty of time off. You live and work down here, you don't go out, to the taverns, you go funny in the head. Need some sunlight. Fresh air."

"Which tavern you lot go to?" Tom asked.

"Black Frog," Willem said. "Lotta the castellan's men go there."

"And where is that?" Tom asked.

Before Willem could answer, they heard a growing patter. A strange sound down here.

Skidding around the corner came a young lady in a torn dress. She stopped when she saw the two guards

Willem and Tomas looked at each other, each confirming that what they saw was real, then looked back at the girl at the far end of the corridor. They each put their hands on the hilts of their weapons.

"Shit." Vanora said.

CHAPTER SEVENTY-SEVEN

"Shit," Heden said.

Vanora was not in the room where Heden had left her.

In her place was Domnal's corpse.

"He took the girl and left the watchman," Aimsley said.

"Garth you fuck," Heden said, standing up. His prayers hadn't worked. Was it too late? Did *Apostate* kill a man in such a way as to prevent resurrection? It was possible, given the sword's purpose.

What was the point having Cavall's power if he couldn't use it to save the people he loved?

"Can we find him, before he gets out of here?" Aimsley asked.

"I doubt it," Heden said, exhausted. Unwilling to try. He stared at Dom's corpse. "He planned all this. Planned his escape. Ah, Dom," he said.

The heavy watchman's leather breastplate has been neatly punctured. Run through. His eyes stared, unseeing, pupils fully dilated. Heden hated to see that. Hated to see lifeless eyes.

Aimsley looked at the corpse again. "Quick death," he said. "Clean. Not much pain. Garth was doing you a favor."

Heden shot a look at the little man, but the polder didn't appear to notice. It was purely a neutral observation on the thief's part.

"Let's get out of here," Aimsley said. "Garth didn't kill the girl, let's find her."

"You're not going anywhere," a rough voice said.

The castellan.

He leaned against the doorway, gestured to someone in the hall beyond.

Two young watchmen in uniform dragged Vanora in and

tossed her into the middle of the room. She fell to her knees and immediately sprang back up, seething.

The watchmen looked to their master. He jerked his head toward the hallway, dismissing them.

"Someone want to explain to me what the fuck is going on?" he asked.

Heden ignored him. Put his hands on Vanora's shoulders. "Are you alright?"

She scowled at the man dressed all in rags sucking smoke before them. "I'm fine," she said.

Heden was relieved. Garth was not involved. He straightened up. "What did you tell him?" he tilted his head toward the castellan.

Vanora shrugged. "What I knew."

Heden nodded. "That's fine," he said, immensely relieved she was alive. He put a hand around her.

"I'm sorry I ran," she said, clinging to his arm.

Heden nodded. "I'm sorry I asked you to stay." Expecting her to stay, the same girl who opened his inn to pass the time while she waited for him, was—he realized—absurd.

"She can go," the castellan said. "Don't reckon she's got anything to do with this. But you two may spend the rest of your lives here."

"This man just saved your ass," Aimsley said to the castellan. "Count and Garth doing their dirty work right here, and you too stupid to see it.

The castellan didn't ignore him, but directed his response to Heden. "You should have come to me," he said. "You come to me, your man here," he nudged Domnal's body with the toe of his boot, "would still be alive."

Heden frowned, released Vanora who took a step back. "He's *your* man," he scowled. "Your watch captain. And he came down here with us knowing he might not make it out alive. Stood up to Garth. To *Garth*." Heden put his hand on *Solaris*. "You will give him the respect he earned," and the castellan took a step away from Dom's corpse, "or I will run you through. King's man or not."

The castellan respected Heden's anger, but did not acknowledge it. Took a drag from his nail, sending smoke curling to the ceiling.

"Count's dead," he said. "Garth free. You think all this," he glanced at Dom's corpse, "would have happened, you come and talk to me?"

"You want to pin this on me?" Heden growled. "You think that's a good idea? I lost the abbot. Dom. All because you couldn't see what was happening under your own nose!"

The ragman considered this.

"What happens when I go to the king and tell him?" Heden demanded. "What happens when Richard finds out all those people died, a war of thieves, all because you couldn't keep your house in order? What happens to you?"

The castellan looked from Heden to the thief.

"We're on the same side," the castellan said to Heden.

"That's debatable," Heden spat. "I stand with the king. With Cavall. Whose council do you keep?"

The ragman thought some more. He blew smoke out from his nose. Sniffed.

"Someone goes down for what happened," he said, but it was tentative. An offer.

"Might as well be you, from where I stand," Heden challenged. "The count *made* the dust here! His whole campaign! It only worked because *you* were protecting him!"

"You know how many men I lost to the dust?" the castellan said, getting angry. "You want to trade corpses, see who comes out ahead?"

"Because *you* gave Garth the opening!"

"And you come down here and do my job for me? That's not justice. That's you goin' back to being a ratcatcher. Someone gets sent up for this!" the castellan said.

"Me," the polder said.

Heden turned sharply to look at the polder.

Aimsley looked up at him. "You said it. I killed the abbot." The little man shrugged, remembering something Hapax Legomenon told him. "Killed a lot of people. I'll pay for what I did."

Heden considered this. He could not see any other way. Could see no good reason to argue for Aimsley Pinwhistle to walk out of here.

"You'll never leave here alive," Heden said. "You might hang."

"I don't mind," Aimsley said. He walked over to the cot Vanora had slept on for days. "I'll sleep at night at least. Be able to live with myself maybe."

Heden was impressed at the polder's decision. Freed of the drink, at least for now, he seemed a different person.

Heden turned to the castellan. "Justice," he said.

"Says you," the ragman said, peering at the polder, but talking to Heden.

Heden extended his arm. Vanora ducked under it.

"We're leaving," he said.

"This ain't over," the castellan said as Heden walked out. "Figure I know where you live. But you got a lot to answer for, breaking in here. You had help."

Heden and Vanora were already gone.

"You had help!" the ragman shouted after them.

Aimsley lay back on the cot, looked at the stone ceiling, and said nothing.

Chapter Seventy-eight

Customers waited, most of them patient, when the entire staff flooded around Vanora, surrounded her. The low roar rose and fell as she described what happened and they described what she missed. Heden could tell when they got to the point where the count burned down the Rose, stranding them all here, when Vanora's hands flew to her face.

The sound of the girls nattering, relating to each other, being together, was soothing. Heden didn't mind it.

Until it stopped.

The girls were all looking behind Heden. *What now?* He thought and turned to look.

Teagan.

"You got a lot of balls coming in here," Heden said, no desire to restrain himself.

The watchman's face looked red and raw. "I heard what happened," he said, no inflection in his voice.

"Did you?" Heden asked. "Did you hear that Dom went down there with us, stood by us, even though he was pissing himself with fear?"

Teagan said nothing.

"Bravest man there," Heden said. "Surrounded by killers and thieves and him the only law. And he didn't run. Stood up to Garth. *Garth.* Did you hear *that?*" Heden barked.

"I heard," Teagan said.

"Would Garth have gotten past you?"

"I don't...."

"*Would Garth have gotten past YOU?!*" Heden bellowed. The muscles and tendons in his neck and arms, straining. Everyone in the inn, the girls, the customers were silent. Enjoying the show. Better than a bard.

Teagan looked down. "No."

"No he would not! You shit," he spat. "I asked you for help, you said no."

Teagan decided to defend himself. "I thought I should ask... he's my captain!"

"He *was* your captain, now he's *dead*. Another one of my friends *dead*. I was trying to stop that from happening! That's why I asked *you!*"

"What?" Teagan looked at Heden sharply.

"How long have you been a watchman? An hour? Two? Because if it's longer than that you're the stupidest fucking copper I ever met. If you go to your master, he *has* to deal with it!"

"He could have given it to..."

"It's his fucking job!!" Heden shouted. "He can't give it to you! It was too important and you should have known that!"

Teagan stood there, saying nothing, swaying a little.

"You're no kind of watchman," Heden cursed. "You're a hired thug who hangs around the jail waiting for someone to tell him what to do."

Teagan looked back at Heden, hands held loosely at his sides, a worried, pleading look on his face.

"Get the fuck out of here," Heden said.

Without waiting to see what Teagan did, Heden went to the cellar door, opened it, stamped down the stairs, and slammed it behind him

CHAPTER SEVENTY-NINE

Vanora came down a few moments later with a lantern. She'd noticed Heden had gone down without any light. Was just sitting down here in the dark.

"I'm sorry about your friend," she said.

"Which one?" Heden asked, so flatly Vanora couldn't tell if he was being sorry for himself, or genuinely asking.

"All of them," she said.

"Well you're alive," Heden said. "Safe. That worked."

"He's your friend, too," she said.

Heden looked at her. "What, the watchman? He's an idiot."

"And he's your friend," she said. "You don't think he knew what you'd do, when he came to see you? But he came anyway."

How long was she with the abbot? Heden wondered.

"You're angry," she said. "So you're taking it out on him." On the other hand, the abbot would never have been that direct.

"No harder on him than I'd have been on me. Dom is dead because of him."

"How can you say that?" Vanora asked. "Everything that happened? Garth, the count, the…the elf? You can't just pick up one piece and replace him with another. Who knows what would have happened if you'd taken the watchman?"

Heden thought about what she was saying. Probably the same things he'd be saying if the roles were reversed.

"How'd you get so smart?" Heden asked.

Vanora looked at the glass dome under which her tutor lay in a pile, awaiting the need. "Mostly it's the harlequin," she said.

Heden nodded. "That worked at least."

Vanora walked up to him.

"Everything worked," she said quietly. "You saved me, you stopped the count. You saved the polder. Can't that be enough?"

She hugged him and put the lantern down so he'd have light. "It has to be enough," she said, and then went back upstairs.

CHAPTER EIGHTY

Heden closed the place early, nursed a drink in the middle of the common room while the fire burned in the hearth. The girls were upstairs. He could hear them playing around. Reverting to being youngsters again at the end of the day. He had no idea how they did it.

The door opened and in the dark outside, it wasn't clear to Heden who was standing in it. It could have been Garth. He tensed, but without need.

Teagan walked in.

"Get out," Heden said automatically.

The watchman ignored him. Walked up to the fire. Stood there in profile while they both watched the flame dance.

Heden took a drink.

The tall, thin watchmen pulled something out of a vest pocket, looked at it in his hand. It glinted in the firelight.

It was the king's coin. The copper coin all watchmen carried. The copper that gave them their nickname.

"Ratcatcher for seven years," the watchmen said. "Never gave a shit. Was easy. Then I met someone and…and found out I wanted more than just crawling around underground. Trying to get rich."

Heden once found quite a lot of meaning as an itinerant campaigner, but said nothing.

"Became a copper. I liked that," he said nodding. "Felt useful. Some of the boys…they talk like…like we don't matter. Always be more thieves, more murderers. That's *why* I liked it. A never ending supply of meaning, every man locked up."

He stopped looking at the coin, and gazed into the fire. After a few silent moments, he threw the king's coin onto the fire.

"You come back here, asking for forgiveness," Heden said. "I've got none to give. Not now. Not for a while. Too many dead friends."

"Time to make new friends," the watchman said, without much feeling. Watched the coin as the fire heated it.

"My friend wouldn't have dropped the job on Dom," Heden said. "A job he knew Dom couldn't do. You're not my friend. I don't know what you are."

"I'm a thug," Teagan said dully. "Waiting for someone to tell me what to do."

Heden stared at him as the former watchman looked at the fire. Heden looked at the fire. Thought about what throwing away the king's coin meant.

"You want to stay angry, that's fine." Teagan said. "Stay angry. At Garth. And let's find him."

"You and me?" Heden said, his voice dripping with disgust.

"What, the polder's good enough for you, but I'm not?" Teagan asked.

He thought about what Vanora said. About what the abbot would have said.

Heden stood up and looked at the watchman. Thought about what it took to come back here a second time, knowing the mood Heden was in.

"You remember what I said to you, back at the Rose? When the count's men first took Vanora back?"

Teagan nodded. "In for a copper," he said, staring at his badge of station melting in the fire.

"In for a crown," Heden said. Maybe there was some forgiveness left in him. Maybe a man really was better than the worst thing he'd ever done.

"First thing, we go back to the citadel," Heden said.

"Alright," Teagan said dully. "Why?"

"We need help against Garth. Garth has friends, we need friends. We're going to spring the thief."

"You just put him away," Teagan said.

"Well," Heden said, "maybe I'll talk to the castellan first. Borrow him for a while, instead of steal him."

"Alright," Teagan said

"Then we find Garth," Heden said.

"And then what?" Teagan asked. "Bring him back to the ragman? Stick him in the citadel? Stand him before the magistrate?"

"No," Heden said. "No we're not going to arrest him. You're not a copper anymore."

"Good," Teagan said. He could no longer see the coin. It had melted away.

"I'm sorry about Dom," Heden said. "He was your captain, but he was my friend."

Teagan shook his head. "You don't understand," he said. "I went to Dom because I wanted him to approve. Of me. He was my friend, too. He didn't care about…," he shook his head, "anything. Just wanted to look out for us. Make sure everyone got home at the end of the day, after running down murderers and thieves and spending all day locked up with them.

"He was my friend," he said. "He looked out for me. Only thing I wanted was to impress him. And now he's dead."

"And Garth killed him," Heden said. "Garth may be the greatest swordsman alive."

"Tricks," Teagan said, looking at Heden from the corners of his eyes. "Not the same as skill."

"That can't be all there is," Heden warned. "It can't just be skill against skill."

"There is something more," Teagan said, and turned away from the fire.

"What?"

Teagan drew his sword and looked at Heden, silhouetted by the fire behind him.

"Revenge," he said.

Ratcatchers continues in Volume Three:

Fighter

EPILOGUE

"He what?"

"He freed a star elf from the citadel."

"He freed a…," the king was having a hard time putting these facts in order. He stopped pacing around the Godblind. Focused on first principles, like his father taught him.

"Why was there a star elf in the castellan's fortress?"

"The count bound it there. Its blood provided the source of the night dust. The count found a way to operate inside the citadel without anyone detecting him. Heden cracked it."

Gwiddon felt it important to give credit where it was due, but the king's mind had already leapt ahead. Past the castellan's failing to the real issue.

"How did the count get a hold of a star elf? How did he… there's no way," the king sped to the proper conclusion. Once again, Gwiddon felt relief that his master's intellect matched his character. "There's no *possible* way the count has access to that kind of power. Someone got it for him. Someone set him up."

Gwiddon remained silent.

"So this whole operation, the count, the night dust, his attempt to become the Shadow King, all that was orchestrated by someone else."

Gwiddon's silence stretched on. The king didn't need his input anyway.

King Richard looked at his Spymaster and Master of Assassins. "We pulled the Circle away from Ansalon."

Gwiddon nodded. "With the Hart looking for the count, recalling the Knights of the Mirror Circle was the right thing to do. Everyone agreed, your highness."

"By Cavall," The king said. His breath was taken away by the scope of the operation. "How long would it take to send them back?"

"Ignis could contact them within the hour. It would take longer to compose the message than send it. But...three days for them to return to the tower on horse."

"Three days out, three days back." The king took a deep breath.

"We've lost the tower, haven't we?" he asked.

Gwiddon cut to the chase. It was difficult watching his king, the man he admired most in the world, deal with this series of blows. Better to get to the end.

"My lord it's possible this is all coincidence, but I consider it unlikely. I think Cathe and Ignis would agree. We must assume Baed was waiting for the Circle to be withdrawn. We must assume the Tower at Ansalon is fallen to Duke Baed, and Baed now controls the Oracle."

"He's going to take Aendrim."

"Forgive me, my lord, but I feel compelled to tell you; your obsession with Aendrim is blinding you to the larger point."

"My *obsession?*" The king challenged. "Edmund was my cousin! We went to school together! Aendrim is mine by *right.*"

"My lord it's time we face the reality that Duke Baed is not acting alone. It could not have been he who gave the count a star elf, or the power to bind it. In my opinion there is only one man in all Orden with that power, now that the Church of Adun has fallen."

This brought the king up short. His spymaster was right. He had missed the larger point.

"Conmonoc," he said.

"My lord, I don't believe Duke Baed intends to install himself as King of Aendrim."

"No," the king said, shaking his head but agreeing.

"The duke was never an ambitious man."

"No," the king agreed.

"But pious," Gwiddon said.

"Yes." The king locked eyes with Gwiddon.

"Richard," Gwiddon dared, "I believe Bishop Conmonoc gave Duke Baed the power to bind a star elf. He had the duke deliver the captured being into the count's hands. I believe he did it to disrupt the balance of power in the city and force you to recall the Knights of the Mirror Circle, which you did, thereby affecting transfer of the Tower and the Oracle to Duke Baed, whom I now believe to be acting on the bishop's behalf."

"But…," the king worked the permutations through. "Even the Tower, even the Oracle. It's not enough. We held the Oracle for three years, it gave us an advantage, it didn't give us the war. And Baed needed my army just to hold back the Night."

"But the Army of Night is now leaderless and in disarray," Gwiddon said. "And there's something else."

The king feared more bad news.

Gwiddon took a deep breath. "My Lord, you'll recall my report on the Green Order."

The king frowned. "Yes?" It seemed a nonsequitur.

"It seems clear to me now that the bishop ordered the Green to stand down, so the urq could take Aendrim from the remnants of the Army of Night."

The king put his hand to his head. This was straining even his ability to keep all the pieces in focus.

"Baed and his army and an army of urq?" The king asked. "They would never work together."

Gwiddon shrugged. "Each army promised something different. Neither aware of the other. What other explanation for the events in the Wode?"

"Heden was right," the king groaned. "We should have used the oracle."

"In his defense; we all thought Cathe's advice well-reasoned."

"But Heden had actually talked to her."

"You'll recall I agreed with Heden, my lord."

The king shot him a dark look.

"The bishop wants to be king of Aendrim," the king said, unable to avoid the conclusion any longer.

"Such is my conclusion, my lord."

"I don't...he's already the Bishop of Cavall. Even mastered by the Black Brothers, he's one of the most powerful men in Vasloria. There's nothing *left* of Aendrim!"

"We have more work to do, my lord," Gwiddon agreed. "I think we can take it as read that we don't yet understand the full scope of Conmonoc's plan."

"Maybe we should get out of his way," the king considered. "Give Aendrim to him. Save a lot of bloodshed."

Gwiddon was struck by this. That the king would so quickly give up Aendrim spoke to his ambition, or lack thereof.

"My lord, you've asked a political question, but granting Conmonoc Aendrim only furthers his plan. A plan we do not understand. Duke Baed is one thing. He may live long enough to see Aendrim rebuilt, resettled. Conmonic is an old man. He must have another goal."

"How do we stop him?"

"We have many tools, my lord. The Hart, the Circle, the Darkened Moon."

"None of them appropriate to the task."

"I'm glad we agree," Gwiddon said, bowing. The king was well-prepared to hear Gwiddon's suggestion. "Because I believe we have access to such a tool, nascent though it is."

The king thought. "Are you...talking about reactivating the Shadowkillers?

"My lord, we're looking for an organization with extraordinary experience."

"You obviously have someone in mind," the king said.

"As of now," Gwiddon continued, "this organization is newly formed and has only three members."

The king was confused. "What are you suggesting?"

"He failed us once, my lord. Through no fault of his own. If we give him the second chance he deserves, aid him in public and in secret?"

The king caught on. Gwiddon smiled, a wolfish, feral grin.

"Heden will not fail a second time."

SINE QUA NON

Most of *Thief* was written on a Sony Vaio T Series 15 Touch Ultrabook, for which I thank James Conrad for the discount.

Com Truise and Oneohtrix Point Never supplied the soundtrack.

Chris Ashton and Phil Robb kept me busy and well-paid during the day, allowing my nocturnal scribblings to flourish.

PRIEST

12751160R00233

Printed in Great Britain
by Amazon